Delores Fossen, a *USA T[...]* [...] written over 150 novels, w[...] books in print worldwide. She's received a Booksellers Best Award and an *RT* Reviewers' Choice Best Book Award. She was also a finalist for a prestigious *RITA®* Award. You can contact the author through her website at deloresfossen.com

Debra Webb is the award-winning, *USA Today* bestselling author of more than 100 novels, including those in reader-favorite series Faces of Evil, the Colby Agency and Shades of Death. With more than four million books sold in numerous languages and countries, Debra has a love of storytelling that goes back to her childhood on a farm in Alabama. Visit Debra at debrawebb.com

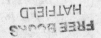

Discover more at millsandboon.co.uk

PROTECTING THE NEWBORN

DELORES FOSSEN

A COLBY CHRISTMAS RESCUE

DEBRA WEBB

MILLS & BOON

First Published in Great Britain 2024
by Mills & Boon, an imprint of HarperCollins*Publishers* Ltd
1 London Bridge Street, London, SE1 9GF

www.harpercollins.co.uk

HarperCollins*Publishers*
Macken House, 39/40 Mayor Street Upper,
Dublin 1, D01 C9W8, Ireland

Protecting the Newborn © 2024 Delores Fossen
A Colby Christmas Rescue © 2024 Debra Webb

ISBN: 978-0-263-32252-1

1124

This book contains FSC™ certified paper and other controlled
sources to ensure responsible forest management.

For more information visit: www.harpercollins.co.uk/green

Printed and Bound in the UK using 100% Renewable Electricity at
CPI Group (UK) Ltd, Croydon, CR0 4YY

PROTECTING THE NEWBORN

DELORES FOSSEN

Chapter One

Staying behind the cover of some sprawling oak trees, Detective Ruston McCullough pressed the night-vision binoculars to his eyes and got his first look of the place.

His target's house.

It was one story with a white stone exterior and was positioned dead smack in the middle of about three acres. Woods and old ranch trails formed a horseshoe around the house and the pasture.

Lots of places for someone to lie in wait.

Lots of places for a kidnapper or killer to hide.

Once, the house had belonged to a rancher and his wife, both now deceased, and their heirs rented out the place. The current renter, Lizzy Martin, had been living there for a little less than a month.

And she was Ruston's target.

Well, she would have been the target if he truly was a scumbag thug hired to kidnap the woman and her baby. He wasn't. He was an undercover San Antonio PD detective posing as a scumbag thug, but the slime who'd hired him didn't know that.

The slime, aka Marty Bennett, believed that Ruston was a dishonorably discharged army combat specialist with a rap sheet for assault who would do the job that Marty had hired him to do. That Ruston would kidnap the woman and baby and then bring them to Marty, so the baby could probably be sold on the black market and the woman could likely become a human-trafficking victim.

Ruston wouldn't be doing that.

No way.

Once he had the kid and woman secure and out of any harm's way, Ruston's fellow officers would move in to take Marty into custody at his San Antonio residence. Then Ruston would start creating another undercover persona while other detectives figured out for certain why Marty wanted this particular woman. Trafficking and the black market were always good guesses in situations like this.

But something about that theory didn't feel right.

If those were indeed Marty's motives, then Ruston wondered how the heck Marty had even seen her and the baby. This place in rural Texas wasn't on any beaten path, and judging from the gossip Ruston had picked up from his moles and snitches about this Lizzy Martin, no one had seen her in any of the nearby towns.

All three of those towns, including his own hometown of Saddle Ridge, were plenty small enough that folks would have recalled a stranger, especially one with a newborn baby. Added to that, he had siblings in law enforcement in Saddle Ridge, and neither of them had seen anyone resembling the description he had of Lizzy Martin.

Marty hadn't given Ruston a photo of the woman. Only her name, address and a few skimpy details. She was supposedly around five and a half feet tall, average build, brown hair and brown eyes. Considering that could apply to many women, Ruston had decided to run a background check on her—a skill set his undercover persona wouldn't have had, so Ruston had had to cover his tracks there in case Marty was monitoring him.

It had taken a while for Ruston to weed through all the possibilities with the name variations for Lizzy Martin, but he thought the one who had rented this place was a website designer who worked from home. Her driver's license photo showed a woman who was indeed as average as Marty's description of her. It seemed to Ruston that Lizzy was actually trying to fade into the background of that DMV photo. That was a lot to assume from a picture, but it had put him on further alert.

People who tried to hide usually had a reason for doing so.

That was why he'd come to the house earlier than planned. Ruston had told Marty that he would take the target at midnight, but he'd arrived four hours before that with the hopes that he'd catch a glimpse of her.

So far, he hadn't.

But someone was definitely inside the house, because he'd seen lights go on and off.

The breeze rustled through the trees around him, and he welcomed the somewhat cooler night air. It was late June, but in central Texas, it could still be scalding hot even at this time of night. Proof of that was the line of sweat already trickling down his back.

Ruston shifted the binoculars when he caught some movement in the front window. It was indeed a woman, and while he couldn't see her face, since she had her back to him, her height and hair color fit Marty's description. He watched as she picked up something.

A baby monitor.

She peered down at a little screen that he saw light up. The binoculars weren't clear enough for him to see the baby she was watching, but he could make out the outline of a crib on the screen.

Ruston continued to watch until she moved out of sight. A few seconds later, he saw the light go on in the front right window. Probably a bedroom or an office. Since he had verification she was indeed there, it was showtime.

Putting away his binoculars, Ruston eased out from the cover of the trees, and he crouched down to make his way closer to the house. He kept watch, looking and listening for anything or anybody, but the only sounds were an owl, some cicadas and the soft drumming of his own heartbeat in his ears.

He stayed low, not going toward that window with the light since he didn't want Lizzy to see him and then call the cops. Because there was a child on the premises, the locals would likely respond fast, and word of that could get back to Marty if he had his own moles and snitches in law enforcement. Ruston didn't want Marty to have a clue this was a sting operation until he had the woman and baby someplace safe.

Keeping up his slow and steady pace, Ruston went toward the back of the house, figuring he would first scope out all sides to see if there was an easy point of entry. He didn't like breaking in, but that was his best bet. Then he could sneak up on her, and before she could make that call to the locals, he could convince her that he was a cop and was there to help.

He stopped at the back corner of the house, peered around it. And because of the dim light coming from the porch, he saw the gun.

It was pointed right at his face.

He automatically drew his own gun. His body jolted, flooding with adrenaline, and he was ready to fight, to get that gun, but then he saw the face of the woman holding it. Not Lizzy and damn sure not the face of the woman in the driver's license. However, it was someone he instantly recognized.

"Gracelyn Wallace," he snapped.

His former partner at SAPD, and a woman he hadn't seen in nearly a year. Correction—a woman he'd been trying to find for ten and a half months. He sure as heck hadn't expected to find her here.

But she had obviously expected to see him.

There wasn't any surprise in her expression, just a steely anger. And some fear. Yeah, she couldn't mask that completely.

Her looks had changed plenty since he'd last laid eyes on her. No short, choppy blond hair but rather the shoulder-length brown that fit the description Marty had given him. Her face was thinner, as if she'd lost weight. And while she sort of resembled the photo on her driver's license, it was obvious that was a fake.

"What are you doing here?" Ruston demanded, though he was pretty sure that was a question she'd been about to ask him.

Her crystal green eyes narrowed even more. "I'm trying to stay alive," she snarled.

He hadn't been sure how she would answer, but Ruston hadn't expected that. "Alive?" he repeated. "Who's trying to kill you?"

Gracelyn huffed, lowered her gun. "Well, I guess it's not you." She tipped her head to the eaves of the house. "I didn't see anyone else with you. Are you alone?"

He glanced up at the eaves, and while it was too dark to spot a camera, one was obviously there. Hell. Whatever was going on, this was not the easy snatch and grab that Marty had said it would be.

"I'm alone," he assured her, "and you're in danger. But I'm guessing you already know that if you have cameras."

"I have cameras and perimeter security. You tripped one of the sensors, and my phone immediately gave me an alert." She made an uneasy glance around them. "Tell me why you're here and then leave. I don't have time for a long explanation."

Ruston mentally replayed each word. That was a lot of security for someone who was no longer a cop. It was more of a setup that a criminal would have. Or someone scared to the bone.

He was going with door number two on this.

And he thought he knew why.

Over ten months ago, Gracelyn and he had had the undercover mission from hell. Deep-cover infiltration of what was basically a baby farm. A place where pregnant women had been held and then their babies had been sold. Some of the women hadn't been there voluntarily either. Many were runaways who'd been scooped up by the SOBs who'd set up the operation. Others were illegal immigrants. Some were victims of human trafficking.

The operation hadn't been sloppy or easy to break into, but Gracelyn and he had managed it by being hired as security guards. They'd been in the facility for less than twenty-four hours and had managed to get absolutely nothing on the person or persons running the place when they realized their covers had been blown. That had become crystal clear when thugs had come into their quarters to murder them. They'd managed to escape, barely, but had then ended up in a seedy motel together, waiting for some fellow undercover cops to come and get them.

Ruston had a lot of nightmarish memories of that night.

And some memories that weren't of the nightmare variety.

Before that night, there had always been an attraction between Gracelyn and him. Always the heat.

Which they'd resisted because they were partners.

But they hadn't resisted enough after nearly being killed. They'd landed in bed, and a couple of hours later, when they'd been safely taken back to headquarters in San Antonio, Gracelyn had put in her resignation papers and had disappeared.

Ruston had not only looked for her, but he'd also continued to hunt for the person who'd run the baby farm. He'd ended up needing to hunt for the farm itself, too, since they'd moved locations. Of course they had. If the powers that be had figured out Gracelyn and he were cops, they would have known the place was no longer safe for their operation.

"I haven't been able to find the baby farm," he admitted. "You're worried about them coming after you?"

"And you're not?" she countered.

"I look over my shoulder a lot," he muttered, doing that now. He didn't like being out in the open like this. Even with all her security, that didn't mean someone couldn't gun them down.

"I have a new undercover identity," Ruston explained. "One that has no connections to the assignment we had together. But I've closely monitored the old identities we used, and there aren't any red flags." In other words, no one was searching for them under those names.

"Then why are you here?" Gracelyn's tone was nowhere close to being friendly.

Since Ruston didn't want to stand around outside any

longer, he just spilled it. "Someone hired me to kidnap you. You and the baby who's living here with you."

But then he paused. And did some thinking. Or rather some calculating.

"The baby who's living here with you," he repeated. "How old is he or she?" Because that was a detail that Marty hadn't given him. And it could be critical information, since Gracelyn and he had had sex ten and a half months ago.

Hell.

Was the child his?

"She's a newborn," Gracelyn muttered, her words rushing out as if to put a stop to the shock that must have been on his face. "She's only two weeks old."

Two weeks. So, the timing didn't fit. "She's your baby?" He had to ask because something else occurred to him.

That maybe Gracelyn had gotten the child from someone. Maybe from a baby farm or someone needing to put the baby in a safe place. That wouldn't explain why Marty had wanted the child kidnapped, though. But there were a lot of things that needed explaining right now.

"She's mine," Gracelyn finally said, but she didn't elaborate. However, she did take out something from the pocket of her jogging pants. The baby monitor he'd seen her looking at when she'd been by the window.

"Let's go inside and talk," he insisted. "Because something's wrong. I'm not sure what, but we need to figure out why someone hired me to kidnap you and the newborn."

She didn't jump at his request, but after another glance at the monitor, she motioned for him to follow her. Gracelyn still had her gun gripped in her hand, and even though it was no longer pointed at him, she didn't put it away.

Gracelyn led him into a small kitchen that at first glance seemed ordinary, with its outdated appliances and flowery wallpaper. Then he saw a tablet-sized device on the counter, and there were four images on the split screen that showed camera feed from all four sides of the house.

"Yeah," he remarked, "you would have seen me coming on that."

She made a sound of agreement and finally slipped her gun into what he realized was a slide holster in the back of her pants. She then triple locked the back door, took out her phone and showed him the same footage that was on the laptop.

"I get an alert if a camera or perimeter sensor is triggered," she explained.

"That's a lot of security," Ruston muttered, holstering his own gun. "Want to tell me why you need it?"

Gracelyn glanced away, murmuring something under her breath that Ruston didn't catch. "You might not have been tracked by anyone from our last mission, but I believe I have been. If not someone from the mission, then someone else."

Everything inside him went still. "What do you mean?"

She dragged in a long breath and kept her attention pinned to the baby monitor. "About a month after I resigned from SAPD, I was renting a place in Dallas, and I wasn't using my real name. It wasn't the same identity I'd used in the undercover op either, and I was being careful. *Very.* Anyway, I realized someone was following me. I set up cameras and got proof of it. I couldn't see his face, but he was definitely tracking me."

Ruston cursed. "Was it a tall, lanky guy about six feet, sandy-blond hair and chin scruff?" he asked.

That got her gaze shifting back to him. "No. Dark hair, about six foot three, muscular build. Why? Who's the guy you just described?"

"Marty Bennett, the lowlife who hired me to kidnap you

and your baby." Now Ruston needed a long, deep breath. "I figured it was for trafficking or a black-market adoption. But maybe not," he added in a grumble.

Maybe Marty had a much bigger part in this.

One that had involved following Gracelyn long before he'd hired Ruston. But if Marty had known where she was all this time, why hadn't he taken her before now?

"Tell me about this Marty Bennett," Gracelyn insisted. "Is he connected in any way to the baby farm?"

Ruston shook his head. "Nothing in his background indicates that, and I dug hard and deep on him. Everything points to him being a somewhat successful money launderer and embezzler. He's got gambling debts, so I figured he somehow found out about you and the baby and thought he could earn some quick cash."

She didn't say anything, but he saw the muscles tighten in her face. Heard the shudder of breath she released. Gracelyn was worried and scared.

"Has anyone else followed you since you moved here?" he asked.

"Not that I know of, but I've moved twice since leaving that apartment in Dallas. I was within a week of leaving here because it doesn't feel safe to stay in one place for long."

Ruston wanted to curse again. And pull her into his arms. Not because of the heat, though that was still there. No, he wanted to try to ease some of that fear. But after what had happened between them, he seriously doubted a hug from him would give her much comfort.

"What about your sister, Allie?" he asked. "Does she know where you are?"

Allie was the only family Gracelyn had. Well, other than the baby. And while Allie and Gracelyn hadn't been especially close, just the opposite actually, anyone wanting to get to Gracelyn could use Allie to do it. Allie had been pretty much a screwup most of her life, and Gracelyn had had to pull strings and call in favors several times to get her kid sister out of a jam.

"Allie doesn't know," Gracelyn answered, and then she swallowed hard. "And I don't know where she is either." She paused. "I'm not sure if she's safe or not."

Hell. Of course, she'd be worried about Allie. Worried about someone using her sister to get to her.

"You should have gotten in touch with me," he said. "You should have told me. I could have helped."

She laughed, but there was no humor in it. It was dry as West Texas dust. "Right. The man with one of the most dangerous jobs on the planet. The last person I wanted to contact was you."

Ruston's stomach twisted. But he couldn't deny what she'd just said. That last op they'd been on together, the one that had nearly gotten them killed, had obviously sent them in opposite directions. He'd kept up the deep-cover work, and she'd chosen to make her world as safe as possible. The pregnancy and the baby had no doubt factored into her lifestyle decisions.

And that brought him back to her newborn.

Two weeks old, which meant Gracelyn had hooked up with her baby's father six or seven weeks after she'd resigned from the force. Since they'd been partners, Ruston knew plenty about Gracelyn's personal life. And vice versa. She hadn't been involved with anyone when they'd had their one-off, and even though that night had been the culmination of the worst of circumstances, he'd thought it would be the beginning of a relationship since there'd always been an intense attraction between them.

Clearly, he'd been wrong about the relationship.

But not wrong about the attraction. It was still there, even now. Or maybe he was reading way too much into it. After all, Gracelyn had been with her baby's father roughly nine and a half months ago, which meant that was a month after Ruston and she had had that one night together.

"Is your baby's father in the picture?" he asked. Ruston watched her face to see if that was playing into this. Relationships went south all the time, and this man could be the threat to Gracelyn and her daughter.

It seemed to him that she tensed even more. Something he hadn't thought possible. After a long pause, Gracelyn opened her mouth but didn't get a chance to answer.

Because of the soft beeping sound.

Her gaze flew from his and went to the laptop monitor. "Someone or something just triggered the security alarm."

Chapter Two

Every nerve in Gracelyn's body was already on high alert, but that little beep of her security system gave her a fresh surge of adrenaline. She cursed herself for not having already moved. If she had, then the nightmare wouldn't have found her.

Maybe Ruston wouldn't have found her either.

She'd have to deal with him. But first, she had to handle this threat that could put the baby, Abigail, in danger.

While she hurried through a mental checklist of her security, Gracelyn went closer to the laptop monitor. She already knew all the windows and the doors were locked, and that every possible point of entry was equipped with sensors.

It hadn't been any of those that'd gone off, though.

That would have been a much louder beep. This softer sound had been because someone or something had moved past one of the sensors set up around the entire perimeter of the house.

She glanced through the various camera feeds and soon spotted the culprit, and she relaxed just a little. "A deer," she muttered. "There are dozens of them around, and they often set off the sensors."

Ruston moved closer to her, looking at the laptop screen

as well. So close that she caught his scent. It stirred through her in a totally different way than the adrenaline and nerves.

A bad way.

Because it reminded her of the heat between them.

Reminded her of why they'd landed in bed. That couldn't happen again. Still, it was hard not to notice that face, that body that had drawn her to him in the first place. Ruston was very much the cowboy cop, though his dark brown hair was longer than most cops'. The length was no doubt to go along with his undercover persona. Ditto for the scruff that made him look like an Old West outlaw.

She kept her attention on the screen, looking for anyone or anything else that the deer's movements could have masked. When she'd set up the security, it had occurred to her that an intruder could sneak in behind a deer or some other animal, so she always looked for that. Always.

The seconds crawled by, turning into minutes, and she still didn't see any signs of an intruder. Gracelyn couldn't breathe easier, though. Not with Ruston standing next to her. She had to get rid of him fast so she could get out of there with the baby.

"I read about what happened to your father," she said to jump-start the conversation. Jump-start and then finish it as soon as she got any and all info from him.

He nodded, and she saw the pain flood his cool gray eyes. Pain because his father, Cliff, had been murdered seven months earlier. Gunned down by an unknown assailant. Since his dad had also been the sheriff of Saddle Ridge, Texas, the speculation around his murder centered on his investigations.

And his wife.

Sandra McCullough had left Saddle Ridge just hours before her husband's murder, and she hadn't returned. Of course, Ruston and his siblings, who were all lawmen, wanted to find her. To question her, too. But there was also the fear that she couldn't be found because she was dead. Or because she'd had some part in her husband's death and was now on the run.

"Among other things, your father was investigating the kidnapping of two pregnant women," Gracelyn continued. "According to what I've read, he thought that maybe the kidnappings were possibly connected to the baby farm where we were nearly killed." She stopped and waited for him to confirm or deny that.

Ruston was clearly still working through the horrible memories of losing his father and his missing mother, but he finally nodded. "He was investigating that. What no one has been able to do is link his murder to that case."

"Do you believe there's a link?" she came out and asked.

He didn't get a chance to answer though because his phone vibrated in his pocket. Ruston frowned when he looked at the caller. "It's Marty."

She didn't have to encourage Ruston to take the call. He wanted answers just as much as she did, and this Marty just might be able to give them some. It sickened her though to have to deal with the devil, but Gracelyn was willing to do whatever it took to keep the baby safe.

"Yeah," Ruston said when he answered, and he put the call on speaker. A sign that he had likely been up-front as to why he was here and had nothing to hide.

Unlike her.

Gracelyn wanted those answers. Desperately wanted them. But she also had to get Ruston out of there.

"Steve," the caller said, obviously calling Ruston by his cover name, "I need you to move things up. Get out to the woman's place right now and take her and the kid."

That tightened every muscle in her body. Judging from the way Ruston pulled back his shoulders, he was having a similar reaction.

"Why?" Ruston asked. "What's wrong?"

"I just need her sooner than expected. I've had to work around some transportation issues."

Marty had said that so calmly, all business. There was no hint that he even thought of her and Abigail as anything more than objects.

"Transportation issues," Ruston repeated. "Am I still supposed to take her and the baby to the warehouse in San Antonio?"

"You are, but the people picking her up want her there earlier than planned. Make it happen," Marty insisted.

People. So, maybe Marty was just the middleman on this. Still, middlemen often knew who'd hired them.

"You didn't say, but why do you want this particular woman?" Ruston pressed.

"That's none of your business," Marty snapped, punctuating that with some profanity. "I didn't pay you to ask questions. If you can't take the woman and the kid, then I'll send someone else to do the job, and you'll pay me back every penny of the advance I gave you."

Gracelyn figured that wouldn't be all, that Marty would try to silence Ruston so he wouldn't blow the whistle on him.

"I said I'll get her and the baby and I will." Ruston's voice was a snap, too. "It just makes me uneasy when plans change. I don't want to grab them, show up at the warehouse and then have nobody there waiting to take them off my hands."

"Somebody will be waiting there for you," Marty growled.

"Now, get them and finish this." With that barked order, Marty ended the call.

Ruston stared at the phone a few seconds and shook his head. "I'd planned on dropping you and your baby at a safe house and then driving out to the warehouse with decoys."

Gracelyn had been so shocked at Ruston's arrival that she hadn't had a chance to ask him how he'd planned for all of this to play out. "Decoys?" she questioned.

He nodded. "Charla Burke," he said, referring to an SAPD detective they'd both worked with. "And a dummy baby. Obviously, Charla and I would both be armed, and we'd planned on arresting whoever was waiting in that warehouse. Other cops would be moving to take Marty at the same time." He paused a heartbeat. "I need to let Franklin know about this."

Lieutenant Tony Franklin, the senior officer in charge of undercover assignments in the SAPD Special Victims Unit. Gracelyn didn't have any reason to distrust Franklin or Charla, but she didn't care for them knowing her current location. Then again, Marty obviously knew, too, which meant heaven knew how many others did as well.

Yes, it was definitely well past time for her to leave.

"I have my own safe house already in place," Gracelyn said, and it got the reaction from Ruston that she expected.

His forehead bunched up, and he huffed. Obviously, he knew she could handle herself—most of the time, anyway— but he was probably still concerned. Heck, so was she.

"I don't want police protection," Gracelyn spelled out to him and left it at that.

No need for her to remind him that being a cop hadn't helped either of them on their last assignment. Yes, they'd both gotten out of there alive, barcly, but that'd been more luck than training. At least two dozen bullets had been fired at them during their escape, and they'd received only minor injuries.

Well, minor *physical* injuries, anyway.

Gracelyn was still living with the nightmare of nearly being gunned down, and she figured it was the same for Ruston. Except Ruston had been able to go back to the job. She hadn't been.

A soft sound shot through the room. Not the security system this time, but a kitten-like cry that had come from the baby monitor. Gracelyn immediately looked and saw Abigail was squirming in her crib. That was her cue to get Ruston moving.

"You can leave now," she insisted, going to the bottom drawer beneath the stove and pulling out a go bag that had cash, fake IDs and a gun. She already had other supplies stashed in her SUV in the garage.

Ruston didn't budge. "I hate to see you on your own like this. I know you don't trust me, but I can help you."

She was ready to assure him that she didn't need his help, but the baby's fussing turned into a full cry. Gracelyn checked her watch, even though she knew it wasn't time for a bottle. She'd fed Abigail less than a half hour before Ruston had arrived.

"I'll be fine," Gracelyn said, and she hoped that was true.

She'd been so careful, and here at least four other people knew her current location. Ruston, Marty, Lieutenant Franklin and Charla. Soon, Gracelyn would want to dig into how Marty and his cohorts had found her. And why he wanted her and Abigail. For now, though, she had to move.

When the crying went up a significant notch, Gracelyn

hooked the go bag over her shoulder and headed to the nursery. "I'll get Abigail and leave. Goodbye, Ruston."

"Abigail," he repeated. "You named her after your late mother."

She nodded. Then scowled when he followed her. "No need for you to lock up when you go," she insisted, stopping outside the nursery door to stare at him. "I'll be out of here within minutes."

Ruston stared back. And stared. Then he muttered some profanity under his breath, reached around her and opened the nursery door. He maneuvered around her before she could stop him, and he made a beeline to the crib.

Gracelyn's heart went to her knees.

Somehow, she managed to get her legs working, and she hurried to scoop up the baby. But not before Ruston got a good look at her.

Ruston didn't say anything for several long moments, and even though the only illumination in the room was from a night-light, Gracelyn saw his jaw muscles turn to iron.

"Abigail isn't two weeks old," he said, his voice a low, dangerous snarl.

"No. She's eight weeks old." And Gracelyn quickly tacked on a huge detail that Ruston needed to hear. "She's not our baby."

Ruston had already opened his mouth, no doubt to accuse her of not telling him that he'd gotten her pregnant, but her comment stopped him. Temporarily, anyway. He stared at her, and stared, clearly trying to figure out if she was telling him the truth.

She was.

"Abigail's not my baby either," she added.

Again, Ruston had clearly been gearing up to accuse her of all sorts of things that she wouldn't have done. Yes, she was desperate. Still was. But if she'd had Ruston's baby, she would have figured out a way to tell him about it.

"Then whose child is she?" he demanded. "Because she looks like you." He stopped again. "Is she Allie's? Is she your niece?"

Gracelyn nodded. Of course, that confirmation was going to lead to a whole bunch of other questions. Questions that she couldn't answer. Still, she was going to have to give Ruston something or he'd never leave. Best to start at the beginning, which ironically had been at the end of her career as a cop.

"We didn't catch those people who were running the baby farm," she went on. "They were after us, and I couldn't dissolve into the background by taking on another undercover persona. Because I couldn't be a cop. So, I planned on… running. Hiding. Staying safe."

"You could have come to me," he insisted.

"No, I couldn't have." It was a truth that was going to cut him to the bone, but he had to hear it. "You still trusted the cops. I didn't. I knew you weren't dirty, but someone blew our cover at that baby farm, and that someone could have been another cop."

That was a reminder for her to get out of there with Abigail, since two cops she wasn't 100 percent certain she could trust—Charla and Lieutenant Franklin—knew her location. Well, they knew the location of Lizzy Martin, anyway. But it was possible that they knew it was an alias she'd been using.

"How'd you end up with Allie's baby?" Ruston asked.

Gracelyn gathered the long breath that she'd need. "Allie showed up shortly after I turned in my badge, just as I was about to go on the run. She was scared." And sporting a black eye and bruises on her arms. "She told me her boyfriend was abusive. And that she'd just taken a pregnancy test and was about two or three weeks pregnant. So, I took Allie with me."

She'd had no choice about that. Allie could be flighty and restless, but there was no way Gracelyn could have abandoned the child and her.

"Using an alias I'd set up for her, Allie gave birth to Abigail eight weeks ago in Houston," Gracelyn went on. "Then, a week later, Allie disappeared. She left me a note, asking me to take care of Abigail, but that she wanted to try to make amends with Abigail's bio-dad, Devin Blackburn. He's bad news, Ruston."

She didn't get into the details of that, but Devin Blackburn had money and connections—and three restraining orders from previous relationships. He'd been arrested twice for assault and computer hacking, but the money and connections had kept him from doing any time in a cage.

However, there was one connection Ruston needed to know about. Except she could tell from his expression that he'd already figured it out.

"Devin Blackburn," he repeated. "He was one of the names that came up during the baby-farm investigation."

She nodded. There'd been dozens involved in that case, maybe hundreds, but Devin's name had popped up because he had known associations with a baby broker who'd worked for the farm. Since that particular broker had turned up dead, the cops hadn't been able to learn if Devin's association had led to anything criminal.

"I obviously couldn't risk Allie bringing Devin to the house in Houston, because I didn't know who else he'd let know I was there, so I brought Abigail here," Gracelyn added. "I keep a burner phone and a private Facebook account that Allie could have used to get in touch with me so I could let her know where I was." She paused. Had to.

"But she hasn't contacted me, and I haven't been able to get in touch with her."

He shook his head. "If you'd come to me, I could have helped keep Allie, you and the baby safe," he insisted.

"You would have tried, but it would have meant giving up your badge," she insisted right back. "All four of us would have been in hiding until the people responsible for the danger are caught." She paused again, then drew in a long breath. "I think I'm close to finding those people."

That got his attention, and his glare morphed into a puzzled look. "Who? Is it Marty?"

She shook her head. "I don't have names. I have computer identities that I found on a website that's basically an auction site for babies. One of the identities is Green Eagle."

Gracelyn didn't have to explain why that was important. Ruston would recall it was what the person running the baby farm had called himself or herself.

"That can't be a coincidence," she added.

He made a sound that could have meant anything. Ruston certainly didn't jump to agree to that. "I looked for leaks in SAPD. For any signs that someone had ratted us out. I found nothing."

Gracelyn had known he would look, and if he had indeed found the culprit—if there was a dirty cop to find, that was—Ruston would have already told her.

"I did what I believed was necessary to keep Abigail safe," Gracelyn went on. "And if I had learned the identity of Green Eagle, I'd planned to contact you and give you the name so you could arrest him or her."

He went quiet again, but his gaze stayed intense. "We're going to talk more about Abigail and Allie," he said like a demand. "But for now, I want to know everything you have on Green Eagle and the baby auction."

She nodded. "Not here, though," she said and would have reminded him that it was too dangerous to stay here.

A sound stopped her.

It was that punch-to-the-gut beep from her security system, and even though it was possibly another deer, she whipped out her phone from her pocket and looked at the screen.

The slam of adrenaline knocked the breath out of her.

Because it wasn't a deer. In the milky haze of moonlight, Gracelyn saw the shadowy figure coming straight toward the house.

Chapter Three

Even though Gracelyn didn't say anything, Ruston instantly knew from the change in her body language that something was wrong.

She thrust out her phone screen so he could see what had put that alarm on her face. One look at the person in dark clothes, and Ruston was certain he was sporting plenty of alarm of his own.

He drew his gun and braced for an attack.

Ruston also took a harder look at the intruder to see if he recognized him, but he couldn't see the person's face because it was covered with a mask. He couldn't even be sure if it was a man or woman. He definitely couldn't rule out this being Marty. Or one of his hired guns.

But if Marty had come after him like this, then why not just take him when they'd had their initial meeting? They'd been alone for that with no obvious witnesses. Why wait until Ruston was here?

Unless both Gracelyn and he were targets.

Or maybe the target was the baby.

If so, that pointed right back to the baby farm and this mystery person, Green Eagle. And unfortunately, it could point right back to Ruston himself.

"I was careful," Ruston muttered to Gracelyn. "I didn't see anyone following me here."

That didn't mean, though, that someone hadn't managed to tail him. That caused him to mentally curse. Because, hell, everything about this could have been a setup.

"The windows aren't bulletproof," she whispered, grabbing a blanket from the chair next to the crib.

Gracelyn scooped up the baby, automatically trying to soothe her with gentle rocking motions and murmurs. A necessity, since any sound would alert an intruder to their specific location in the house.

"I have to get her to my SUV," Gracelyn added.

Gracelyn didn't invite Ruston to come along, but he did anyway. He had no intention of letting them out of his sight.

"Are the windows of your SUV bullet resistant?" he asked, following her out of the nursery.

"They are," Gracelyn answered, hurrying into the hall.

She had her hands full, literally, what with holding both the phone and Abigail. Plus, she had a backpack hooked over her shoulder, but she waved off Ruston when he tried to help her.

They'd barely made it another step, though, when they heard the sound. Definitely not something Ruston wanted to hear either.

A gunshot blasted through one the windows.

Ruston muttered some profanity and stepped in front of Gracelyn and the baby. They hunkered down seconds before the next shot. There was the sound of shattering glass falling on the floor, but Ruston didn't see any bullets coming through the wall near them.

"Give me your phone," he insisted. "I can see if he's alone and if he's using any kind of infrared." Infrared that would allow the person to track their every movement inside the house.

She passed her phone to him right as the third shot came, and while Ruston listened for any sounds of the person trying to break in, he also studied the various frames from the camera.

And he saw something he definitely didn't like.

"There are two of them," he relayed to her. "No infrared device that I can see, but one is shooting at the windows in your living room, and the other is on the front porch. How hard will it be for him to get through the door?"

Gracelyn's groan was soft but heavy with fear. "Not hard enough," she answered. "It's reinforced, but if he shoots the locks..."

She didn't finish that. No need. It told Ruston everything he needed to know. He debated making a stand since there were only two of them, and if one of them came through the door, Ruston would be able to take the guy out before he managed to get inside. But it was a huge risk. If the intruder managed to get off even a single shot, it could hit Gracelyn or the baby.

And that meant they had to move now.

Ruston took the bag from her shoulder and shifted it to his so Gracelyn wouldn't have anything to slow her down. He also pictured the location of the interior door that led to the garage. It was just on the other side of the fridge. Not ideal, since there was a window over the kitchen sink and because the second attacker could be at the back door in a matter of seconds.

Still, there weren't a lot of options here, and having the baby in a bullet-resistant vehicle was better than staying in the house that was currently under attack from two directions.

"Stay low and close to me," he instructed, though he knew it wasn't necessary to tell her that.

Gracelyn had been a damn good cop, and she knew how to stay alive. He hoped their combined skills would be enough to keep her infant niece safe.

They moved fast. Well, as fast as they could, considering they were crouching, and they'd just made it to the kitchen when the front doorknob rattled. Of course, it was locked. And as expected, the intruder was having none of that.

The next shot blasted into the lock.

And sent Abigail wailing.

The baby was clearly startled. And terrified. Ruston wanted to punch the intruder for doing that, for putting an innocent baby through this nightmarish ordeal.

Despite the baby's cries, Gracelyn and he kept moving. It seemed to take an eternity to go the twelve feet or so from the hall and into the kitchen, but they finally made it.

Only to hear another shot to the front lock.

And worse, someone jiggling the knob of the back door.

Clearly, these two thugs were going for a coordinated double attack. An attack where they no doubt would try to sandwich Gracelyn and him in, either to try to gun them down or force them to surrender.

Ruston felt a fresh surge of adrenaline. It was mixed with a fresh round of terror, but everything inside him managed to stay still. He relied on his training. On his instincts. And he shifted places with Gracelyn and the baby when they reached the garage door.

He hated sending her out to the garage ahead of him, but again, they didn't have a lot of options here. His shooting hand was free, and he needed to be able to return fire if those two thugs broke through the doors. Also, thankfully, there'd been no indications that someone had managed to sneak into the garage.

Gracelyn had to shift the crying baby in her arms, but the moment she opened the door, she moved into the garage. Ruston stayed put to give Gracelyn a chance to get the baby in the car seat. Once she'd finished that, he would hurry to the SUV as well.

There was a third shot to the front door, followed by what Ruston was certain was a kick and a swooshing sound. Then a single footstep. The intruder was inside.

Ruston glanced over his shoulder to see that Gracelyn was in the back seat of a black SUV and was struggling to get the baby into the infant seat. He couldn't wait any longer. He levered himself up from his crouch just enough to fire a shot in the direction of the front door. When he pulled the trigger, he heard exactly what he wanted.

Some cursing, and the sound of the guy staggering back.

Maybe he was hit, maybe he was merely scrambling to get out of the line of fire. Either way, this should give Gracelyn and him some extra seconds to escape.

Ruston aimed another shot in the direction of the back door, hoping it'd do the same to the intruder who was trying to get in there. But he didn't wait around to see or hear the results of his two shots. He bolted into the garage, hurrying to get behind the wheel.

"Stay in the back seat with the baby," Ruston told Gracelyn.

Since the keys were in the holder below the dash, Ruston was able to use the automatic starter to fire up the engine. In the same motion, he hit the remote on the visor to open the garage door.

"Stay down," he repeated to Gracelyn.

He caught only a glimpse of her face before she did just

that. There was no argument in her expression, only the fear. Something he'd rarely seen in her when she'd been a cop. But this time the fear wasn't for herself or him but rather for the baby.

As soon as Ruston had enough clearance, he put the SUV into Reverse and gunned the engine. He truly hoped the thugs weren't parked nearby. Because if they had to run to their vehicles, that upped Ruston's chances of getting Gracelyn and the baby out of there.

Ruston made it out of the garage, but as he was shifting into Drive, a bullet slammed into the windshield of the SUV. It'd come from the gunman on the front porch, who was obviously very much alive. So was his partner, because Ruston caught a glimpse of the second one hurrying around the side of the house. Like his comrade, this one lifted his gun and took aim.

Two shots tore from their weapons.

Both hit the body of the SUV, causing Ruston's heart to drop. He prayed the bullets hadn't gotten through to Gracelyn and the baby. Still, he couldn't risk checking to see if they were all right. He just slammed his foot on the accelerator and got them the hell out of there.

The gunmen came after them.

Not in vehicles. Ruston didn't see any nearby. But the two men ran after the SUV with both guns blasting out nonstop shots. Most of the bullets slammed into the back window, and Ruston glanced to make sure the safety glass had held. Thankfully, it had.

He also managed to catch a glimpse of Gracelyn.

She'd gotten the crying baby in the infant seat and had positioned her body over the child. A human shield. Of course, that put Gracelyn at greater risk, but he couldn't fault her for it. If their positions had been reversed, he would have done the same.

Ruston sped to the end of the driveway, and with the tires squealing in protest, he turned right onto the narrow country road. Behind them, the shots finally stopped, but Ruston figured that wasn't great news. It likely just meant the gunmen were running to their vehicle and would come in pursuit.

Even at the too-fast speed he was going, he was still ten minutes away from the nearest town, which happened to be Saddle Ridge. No way would backup reach them before that, even though Ruston would have loved to have a dozen police cruisers around right now. Not only would it prevent these gunmen from attacking them again, but backup would mean the thugs stood a chance of being apprehended.

And then Ruston could figure out who had hired them.

That was for later, though. For now, he focused on getting Gracelyn and the baby to safety. That started with contacting someone, and he was pleased to see that the SUV Bluetooth paired quickly with his cell so he could make a hands-free call.

He ruled out calling his sister Deputy Joelle McCullough, because she was seven months pregnant. Instead, Ruston called his brother, Slater, who was also a deputy in the Saddle Ridge Sheriff's Office. Ruston said a short prayer of relief when his brother answered on the first ring.

"Long story short," Ruston immediately said. "Get anyone you can out to the old Henderson Road. Have them head east. I want lights flashing and sirens blaring."

Slater had been a cop for a long time, and that was maybe why he didn't fire off any questions as to why Ruston would need such things. Within a couple of seconds, Ruston heard his brother make a call to Dispatch to request immediate backup and followed that by relaying the location that Ruston had given him.

"I'm on my way," Slater assured Ruston. "How far out are you from town?"

"Too far. Nine minutes." Which was an eternity. "Someone's trying to kill Gracelyn and me, and we have a baby with us."

No need for him to explain who Gracelyn was, because when Gracelyn had been his partner, he'd brought her to their family ranch several times.

"A baby," Slater muttered, and he added some ripe profanity to that. "Is anyone hurt? Do you need an ambulance?"

"No, not hurt." Ruston needed to keep it that way. "Two armed men attacked us at Gracelyn's place and will shortly be in pursuit of us again."

Ruston had barely gotten out the words when he glanced in the side mirror and saw the headlights of the vehicle barreling toward them.

"Correction," Ruston said. "The gunmen are in pursuit *now.*"

That had Gracelyn shifting her position. She was still sheltering the baby, but she moved so she'd be able to use her gun.

"If they shoot out the safety glass, I'll return fire to try to get them to back off," she explained.

Ruston didn't like that plan at all, but if the bulletproof glass didn't hold, then the gunfire could get through to the baby. Having someone like Gracelyn—who was a darn good shot—returning fire could maybe get them to back off. And if she got lucky enough, she'd be able to take out the driver.

"You want to stay on the phone with me while I'm en route to you?" Slater asked him.

Ruston didn't want the distraction. He also didn't add for

his brother to get there fast, because he knew Slater would. "No," he answered, and he ended the call so he could focus on the road.

Since Ruston didn't want to risk wrecking the car, he couldn't try to return fire as well, but he could do something to prevent these thugs from pulling up on the driver's side of the SUV and having an easier shot. He maneuvered into the center of the road. He should be able to see the headlights of any vehicle coming toward them and get out of the way in time.

He hoped.

Ruston kept up the pressure on the accelerator, but the gunmen must have had a more powerful engine in the big silver truck they were using, because they not only kept up, but they also gained ground. Their headlights were getting closer and closer. Worse, Ruston saw one of the thugs lean out from the passenger's window.

And take aim at the SUV.

"They're about to shoot at us," Ruston relayed to Gracelyn, hoping that would cause her to get back down.

His warning came a split second before the shot blasted into the rear window. The bulk of the glass continued to hold, but this bullet had created a fist-sized hole. It didn't seem nearly big enough for Gracelyn to get off a shot, but that didn't stop her.

She took aim. And fired. Not once. But four times.

The sound of each shot ripped through the SUV, causing the baby to wail again, but Ruston saw something positive. The truck swerved, the headlights slashing through the darkness. Gracelyn fired again. And again. Emptying the magazine.

She must have hit the driver, because the truck didn't

just swerve this time. It practically flew off the road and crashed into a pasture fence.

Ruston felt some of the tightness ease up in his chest. Part of him wanted to go back and confront these SOBs, to make them pay for endangering Gracelyn and the baby. But he couldn't risk that. He just kept on driving and was about to use the hands-free system to call Slater to let him know what was going on. However, before he could do that, his phone rang.

"It's Charla," Ruston muttered when he saw the cop's name pop up on the dash screen.

"Don't tell her where we are," Gracelyn was quick to say.

She was still keeping watch out the hole in the back window but was also trying to soothe the baby. The soothing was working or else Abigail had just exhausted herself from crying, because her wails were now just a soft whimper.

"Don't tell Charla where we are," Gracelyn repeated, this time with even more emphasis.

Ruston wanted to bristle at the notion of not trusting a fellow cop. But Gracelyn was right. Someone had set him up, and only a handful of people could have managed that.

Charla was one of them.

Even though the woman had never given him a single reason not to trust her, Ruston was going to err on the side of caution here.

"What happened?" Charla demanded the moment Ruston answered the call.

Since that question could encompass a whole lot of things, Ruston took the safe route with this as well. "My cover was blown. Again. Any idea how that happened?"

There was silence for a long time, and then Charla cursed. "Blown? How? Are you hurt?"

Ruston didn't answer any of those questions but instead

went with two of his own. "Why did you ask what'd happened? Why did you suspect something was wrong?"

That brought on more muttered profanity from Charla. "Because I've got a dead body on my hands. And judging from the crime scene, someone's trying to set you up for the murder."

Chapter Four

Gracelyn's heartbeat was still pounding in her ears, but she had no trouble hearing what Charla had just said.

Dead body.

Gracelyn had to choke back a sob because her mind instantly jumped to whose body that might be. Her sister's.

Sweet heaven, had Allie been murdered?

That was her first thought. Because if someone had come after Allie's baby and her, then they might have gone after Allie as well. Gracelyn needed to know the answer, but she wasn't sure she could handle it right now. Not coming on the heels of this attack that could have killed Ruston, Abigail and her.

"Who's dead?" Ruston asked.

Since Gracelyn didn't want Charla to know she was in the vehicle with Ruston, she stayed quiet. Waiting and praying.

"Marty Bennett," Charla provided. "He was found dead at his house in San Antonio. A single gunshot wound to the head."

Gracelyn felt the relicf wash over her, but it didn't last. Yes, she was so thankful it hadn't been Allie, but Marty Bennett was the man who'd hired Ruston to kidnap Abigail and her.

Why was he dead?

Since he was a criminal, there could be plenty of reasons for his murder, but Gracelyn figured the man's death wasn't a coincidence. It had to be connected to this attack by those two thugs in the truck.

"Are you there, Ruston?" Charla asked.

"Yeah," he confirmed, and Gracelyn saw that, like her, he was still keeping watch around them while he drove. "I didn't kill him. Why do you think someone's trying to make it look as if I did?"

"Because whoever did kill him left your badge at the scene," Charla was quick to reply.

Ruston cursed under his breath. "My actual badge or a fake?"

"Looks like the real deal to me. Where did you last see it?"

He muttered yet more profanity. "In my apartment in San Antonio. Not the one I rent under my current cover, but my actual apartment under my real name. It's nowhere near the one I use for cover, and there are only a handful of people who know about it."

Gracelyn wondered if one of those people was Charla. Or any other cops. If not, it still meant the person behind this knew way too much about Ruston.

"I have a decent security system at the apartment," Ruston went on, "and I didn't get an alert that it'd been triggered."

"Do you have security cams?" Charla asked.

"No, but there are some on the street in front and back of the building."

"They'll be checked," Charla assured him. "I'll send someone over there now."

"No," Ruston said firmly. "Hold off on that. Uh, I'm not

sure who to trust on this. With my cover blown, there could be some kind of leak."

Gracelyn hoped that his distrust extended to Charla. And maybe it did. Her distrust for Charla was certainly there. But it was possible Ruston was simply being cautious. There were plenty of reasons for that.

Maybe Ruston wanted to send up someone he'd be sure wouldn't plant anything or take something else. Then again, since the break-in had already happened, Gracelyn was betting any planting or taking had already happened.

"Where are you, Ruston?" Charla pressed a moment later.

"I'll get back to you on that," he said and ended the call.

Charla must not have cared for that abrupt dismissal, because she immediately tried to call him back, but Ruston declined it.

He looked in the rearview mirror to meet Gracelyn's gaze. "I don't know what's going on," Ruston said before he turned his attention back to their surroundings. "Do you?"

"No." And she wished her head would clear enough so she could think straight. Everything was still racing inside her, and it was hard to sort through the details when she wasn't even sure they were safe.

"Marty hired you to come after Abigail and me," Gracelyn spelled out, hoping that just going through the obvious would help them piece this together. "Then someone murdered him and tried to set you up. That someone killed Marty about the same time two gunmen were trying to kill us."

Saying it aloud worked. Something flashed in her mind. It must have come through in Ruston's, too, because he voiced what she was thinking.

"If the gunmen had killed me, then there's no way Marty's murder could have been pinned on me," he reasoned. "I spoke to Marty on the phone just minutes before the attack, which means it was probably minutes before he was murdered. I was at least fifty miles from Marty. So, the badge wasn't to set me up."

Gracelyn made a sound of agreement. "Maybe it was left to taunt you? To blow any future cover you might have?" If so, it would take Ruston off the market, so to speak. Since his face would be recognizable, he wouldn't be able to go back undercover.

Why would someone want that?

Again, Ruston supplied the answer. "This could have been done to discredit me with both the cops and the criminals." He stopped, shook his head. "And it just might work."

Yes, it possibly would, because even if Ruston had an alibi for Marty's murder, there'd still have to be an investigation. Gracelyn was betting that Ruston would be doing his own investigation, too. She certainly would be as well, since she didn't want another of these attacks.

"Either Charla or Tony could be dirty," she told him. "Of course, that's true about some other cops, but those two were in on every detail of our last assignment. And they were almost certainly in on every detail of your dealings with Marty. I've been digging into their backgrounds, and I believe there are some possible red flags for both Charla and Tony."

Thanks to the rearview mirror, she saw the concern flash in Ruston's eyes. Gracelyn didn't get to say any more, though, since there was the howl of sirens, and just ahead lights slashed across the dark road. Not solo ones either. There were at least three cruisers. In the same instant Gracelyn spotted them, Ruston's phone rang again, and this time it was Slater's name on the screen.

"Is that you coming my way in the black SUV?" Slater asked the moment Ruston answered.

"It is," Ruston verified. "We're not injured, but the SUV is shot up courtesy of two gunmen in a silver truck. They went off the road about four miles back. It's possible one of them is injured, but they're dangerous, Slater. And they need to be caught so we can find out why they did this."

"Understood," Slater said. "Woodrow's right behind me, and the two of us will go after the gunmen. Carmen's in the third cruiser, and I'll alert her to turn around and shadow you."

Gracelyn didn't know who Woodrow and Carmen were, but she was guessing they were deputies. She was also guessing they'd come in separate cruisers to create that "lights flashing and sirens blaring" effect that Ruston had wanted. He'd gotten it, and it might be enough to put off any attackers who were nearby and ready to strike. Hopefully, though, those attackers didn't have a way to escape since they'd crashed their truck.

"Are you going to your place or the ranch?" Slater asked a second later.

"The ranch," Ruston verified, and he ended the call just as Slater and one of the other cruisers went past them.

Slater slowed just a little, probably so he could make brief eye contact with his brother and see for himself that Ruston wasn't hurt. Apparently satisfied with what he saw, Slater went off in pursuit of those gunmen with the second cruiser right behind him. The deputy in the third cruiser waited until Ruston had passed before she executed a U-turn so she could follow them.

"To the ranch?" Gracelyn questioned.

Ruston did another glance in the rearview, and he no doubt saw the concern on her face. And she didn't have to spell out why that concern was there. His father had been gunned down on the family ranch seven months ago, and Gracelyn didn't want to jump out of the frying pan and into the fire.

"We've upgraded security since my father was killed," Ruston said.

Good, because she didn't want a killer to come waltzing in and try to finish what those two gunmen had started. Then again, she'd done plenty of security upgrades and look what'd happened. Still, there had to be a way to keep out a killer, and for Abigail's safety, she had to find it.

Had to.

Abigail wasn't her biological child, but Gracelyn couldn't have possibly loved her more. Of course, when and if Allie returned, her sister might take the baby. Or rather she would try, but Gracelyn couldn't let her do that unless she was certain the little girl was safe. At the moment, she wasn't.

Then again, maybe Allie wasn't either.

Gracelyn quickly had to shove that thought aside. No way could she let that fear take over her thoughts. She needed a clear head to keep watch. Because even though Ruston and she now had backup, they weren't out of the woods just yet.

"Red flags?" Ruston asked.

It took Gracelyn a moment to realize why he'd said that. Before Slater and the other deputies had arrived, she'd been telling him, or rather warning him, about her concerns about both Charla and Tony.

"Possible red flags," she emphasized. "It could be nothing, but I don't want to dismiss them and then have them turn out to be something." She paused a moment to gather her breath. "After our covers were blown, I did some research and found out that Charla's mother was a junkie and had a record for prostitution. When Charla was eight, her mother sold Charla's infant half brother to what was essentially a baby broker. Her mom did it again two years later with a baby girl but was caught and arrested. That's when Charla ended up in foster care."

She paused again to give Ruston a moment to digest that. It definitely fell into the "possible" red flag category, since it wasn't a strong connection to the baby farm that had come into existence some thirty years later.

"Is her mother still alive?" Ruston wanted to know.

"No. She died two years ago."

Which would have maybe been about the time of the start of the baby farm that Ruston and she had ended up investigating. Her mother's death could have been a trigger to start her on a very bad path.

Gracelyn went ahead and added the rest. "And, no, I don't have any proof that Charla stayed in touch with her mother and that the woman passed along her contacts for baby brokers to Charla. Even if she had, I know that doesn't mean Charla used those contacts to become the Green Eagle and start her own business."

Ruston muttered an agreement. What he didn't do was dismiss the possibility that it was exactly what'd happened. "And Tony? What do you have on him?"

"He was in serious debt. Not enough to draw the attention of Internal Affairs, but he'd gotten burned in a divorce settlement and was barely keeping his head above water. Until two and a half years ago, when his debts disappeared. The money appears to have come from an old army buddy of his who passed away, but I think the inheritance paperwork could be bogus."

Ruston met her gaze again. "You hacked into Tony's financials?"

Gracelyn knew she was about to admit to a crime. A

crime that Ruston could use to have her arrested. But she wanted him to have the full picture here. And that picture was anything she'd learned about Tony's funds couldn't be used to launch an investigation.

"I didn't personally do the hacking," she admitted. "I don't have that particular skill set, but I hired someone to do it. An old friend of Allie's, Simon Milbrath, did it. I didn't use my real name when I contacted him. I set up an identity that I used just for my contact with him, and I never met with Simon in person."

Ruston muttered more profanity and took the turnoff to the main road. A road she knew would lead to his family's ranch.

"Simon Milbrath," he repeated as if committing that name to memory. "And Charla?" he pressed. "How did you find the info on her?"

"Not with any hacking," Gracelyn said right off the bat. "I dug through her background and found old newspaper articles about her mother's arrest. Then, using a cover that I was a reporter doing a story, I emailed the now-retired officer who arrested her mother. He was able to tell me that he had suspicions that Charla's mom had helped some of her junkie friends sell their babies through this broker. He also recalled Charla being furious when her mom was taken away."

"Did this retired cop have any computer expertise?" he asked after a short pause. "I'm just trying to get an idea of who could have found your location and then passed it along to Marty, who in turn gave it to me."

Gracelyn wanted to know the same thing, but she didn't have to consider his question for long. "I did a thorough check on the retired cop, Archie Ingram, before I ever contacted him. He's in his late seventies, and there's nothing in his background to indicate he's a computer whiz or that he was dirty. Just the opposite. He had a stellar record…"

Her words trailed off when the ranch came into view. She'd been here two other times when Ruston and she had still been partners, and it'd had a picture-postcard feel to it then, with its acres of pastures and the pretty pale yellow Victorian house. In the milky moonlight, it was still pretty, but she immediately spotted sensors on the fences, and the driveway along with the front and sides of the house had perimeter lighting. She was betting the back did, too.

"Who lives here now?" she asked. As he drove, even more lights flared on, obviously triggered by motion.

"My sister Joelle and her husband, Sheriff Duncan Holder."

She knew that Joelle was a deputy, so there'd be three cops. Maybe four if Carmen stayed. In some ways, even that didn't feel like enough protection. In other ways, it felt like too much, since Gracelyn figured she would be plenty uncomfortable around, well, anyone. That included Ruston's family.

"Do Joelle and the sheriff know we could be bringing danger right to their doorstep?" Gracelyn asked.

"They know. Slater would have told them."

She saw the tall man in the front window. Saw that he was armed, too. Duncan, no doubt, and Gracelyn recalled meeting him as well on one of her trips to Saddle Ridge. He'd been a deputy then and had obviously become the sheriff after Ruston's father had been murdered.

"A couple of months ago, there was trouble here," Ruston went on, stopping in front of the house. "Trouble at Duncan's and Joelle's houses, too. After it was over, they decided to move here and beef up security. Joelle's seven months pregnant, and they wanted to take precautions." He turned in the seat and looked at her. "They'll help us take precautions for Abigail, too."

She nodded and hoped any and all precautions would be enough. "Thank you. And thank you for helping Abigail and me to get away from those gunmen."

The corner of his mouth lifted just a little. "I suspect you could have gotten away from them yourself." The almost smile vanished. "Now, I need to figure out if I led those men to you or if they were already lying in wait to take both of us."

Yes, that was the million-dollar question, all right, but either way, the danger was still there. It could return. And despite what Ruston had just said, she wasn't so sure at all that she could have gotten away by herself.

The only reason she'd been able to return fire and cause the gunmen's truck to crash was because Ruston had been driving. If she'd been alone with Abigail and behind the wheel, it was entirely possible those thugs would have managed to overtake her and force her off the road.

When Ruston stepped out of the SUV, Duncan came out of the house, providing cover. Ruston moved fast, throwing open the back door so he could help her get Abigail unstrapped from the infant seat. The moment they'd done that, Ruston scooped up the baby. Gracelyn grabbed her go bag, and scrambling out right behind him, she hurriedly followed him into the house.

Once they were all inside, Duncan closed and locked the door. He used his phone to rearm the security system and then to make a quick call to Carmen to tell her to assist Slater. As much as Gracelyn wanted the extra backup here, it was best for Slater to have more help. That way, there was a better chance that the two gunmen would be caught.

Joelle was there in the foyer, and she was also armed.

Despite being mega-pregnant, Ruston's sister still looked more than capable of defending her family home.

"Gracelyn," Joelle said and didn't add the customary *it's good to see you*. Still, the woman didn't look upset or angry at the intrusion. Just the opposite. Joelle's face turned a little dreamy when her attention landed on the baby.

Dreamy and then suspicious. She aimed her suspicion at her brother.

"She's not our child," Ruston was quick to explain. "This is Abigail, and she's Gracelyn's niece."

Joelle seemed a little disappointed about that, and then her expression morphed again. She became all cop. "Slater said someone fired shots at you?"

Since the question seemed to be directed at Gracelyn, she nodded and hooked her go bag over her shoulder. "Two armed men. Slater and Woodrow and now Carmen are looking for them."

"I'll fill you in on the attack," Ruston added, aiming glances at both his sister and Duncan. "Any reports from Slater yet?"

Duncan shook his head. "But I've sent them out some more backup, and I've got a half dozen ranch hands patrolling the grounds."

Gracelyn was once again thankful for all these measures, but she wouldn't breathe easier until the two men were caught. Caught and questioned. Hopefully, they'd make some confessions, too.

"Any chance the baby's parents are responsible for the attack?" Duncan asked, aiming the question at Gracelyn.

She wanted to be able to say no, to deny that Allie could have had any part in this. But she couldn't. "I don't know where my sister is," Gracelyn admitted. "And Allie has a bad history with Abigail's father, Devin Blackburn."

Duncan jumped right on that. "Bad? How?"

"An arrest for assault and another for computer hacking. He also has several restraining orders from previous relationships. No jail time, though. When Allie disappeared a few weeks ago, she left me a note saying she was going back to Devin."

"Did she?" Duncan pressed.

"I'm not sure. I've been monitoring Devin's social media accounts, and there's no mention of Allie." That didn't mean, though, that Allie wasn't with him.

"Devin was also interviewed during the baby-farm investigation," Ruston supplied. "Interviewed after Gracelyn and I were attacked there," he clarified. "There was no evidence to charge him with anything."

"But you think he could be guilty," Duncan stated.

"I want to go back through the report of the interview, but Devin has the right skill set to have been involved. Computer hacker, money to set up an operation like that and a connection to a known baby broker."

Duncan nodded. "I'd like to read that report, too."

"I've gone through it many times," Gracelyn admitted. "Especially after my sister got involved with Devin."

"Was that involvement before or after the baby-farm investigation began?" Ruston asked.

"During," Gracelyn answered. "I pressed Allie about the timing, and she said she'd known Devin for years before they became lovers, and that their involvement had nothing to do with the farm. Or what happened to Ruston and me." She paused. "I don't know what's true and what's not."

But she needed to find that out fast.

Abigail whimpered, her arms flinging up in the air as if startled. Maybe from a nightmare. If so, Gracelyn hoped it was a nightmare the baby would soon forget. Still, she went to her and eased her out of Ruston's arms and into her own so she could try to soothe her.

"The nursery is already set up," Joelle explained, "so you can use that, or there's a playpen that I've already put in the guest room if you don't want to be away from her."

Gracelyn didn't even have to think about this. "The playpen." It was basically a portable enclosure that could also be used for sleeping. And it would keep Abigail with her.

Joelle nodded. "It's there and already set up. I can also have whatever you need delivered."

"Thank you, but I have some formula and diapers in my bag and there's more in the SUV." Well, unless that stash had been damaged in the gunfire. Even if it had, though, there was enough in the go bag to last for at least a couple of days.

Enough cash, too, along with a fake ID, a gun and a change of clothes for Gracelyn as well.

"Good," Joelle muttered. "But if you think of anything else, just let me know. Do you want to take her to the guest room now?"

Guest room. Not plural. And it made Gracelyn wonder if Ruston and she would be sharing it. Part of her hoped they would be. It wouldn't be especially comfortable to be in such close quarters with a man who'd once been her lover.

A onetime lover, anyway.

No, not very comfortable, but the discomfort would turn to something much worse—fear—if there wasn't enough protection for Abigail.

"I'll go ahead and take Gracelyn and the baby upstairs," Ruston offered. "Once they're settled, I'll help in any way I can with the investigation."

"I'll help, too," Gracelyn said. "I can get Abigail in the playpen and then make phone calls or anything else you need. I don't want her out of my sight, but I need to do something to help. And please don't say I should get some rest. That's not happening tonight, not after what we've been through."

No one disputed that. In fact, there were sounds of agreement all the way around, and one of those sounds was from Ruston as he led her up the stairs. The guest room was large and just off the right of the landing, and even though the playpen was indeed there, the lights were off. Gracelyn kept them that way. No reason to alert anyone outside that someone was in the room.

"I need to make a call," Ruston said, stepping to the side of the room while she put Abigail in the playpen. "I have to talk to a cop friend."

That gave her a shot of instant alarm, and it must have shown on her face.

"A cop I can trust," he added, already taking out his phone and pressing a contact number. "Noah Ryland."

She immediately relaxed. She'd worked with Detective Noah Ryland at SAPD and believed he was trustworthy. Since Noah was assigned to Homicide, Gracelyn figured that was why Ruston had chosen to call him.

"Noah," Ruston greeted once the detective answered. "I need two favors, and both are huge. I want you to secure any and all files from Marty Bennett's residence and office. He was murdered earlier tonight, and I don't want anything to go missing before it's had a chance to be examined."

She couldn't hear Noah's response to that, but after a few moments, Ruston added, "Yeah, Marty was connected to my current undercover." Another pause. "You heard right. Someone tried to kill me and also planted my badge at the scene of Marty's murder."

More silence, and since she couldn't even hear any immediate murmurings from the other end of the line, she figured Noah was sorting through that info.

"Good," Ruston said after Noah finally spoke. "The second favor involves Gracelyn Wallace… Yes, the former cop… No, she didn't have a part in Marty's murder either," Ruston explained when Noah must have asked about it. "She has a solid alibi. In fact, she was with me at the time of the murder."

He paused when Noah commented on that. "Yes, with me. And that leads me to my next favor. I want to try to stop anyone from going after her again, and I need answers. Gracelyn had contact with a computer hacker named Simon Milbrath and a retired cop, Archie Ingram. It's possible one of them leaked information to Marty or someone who ended up killing Marty. So, I'd like to know if there are any known connections between Marty and them. It's possible there'll be something at Marty's residence to verify those connections if they exist."

Again, she heard Noah murmur something that had Ruston's tight jaw relaxing a bit.

"I owe you," Ruston told the detective. He thanked him, ended the call and turned to her as he put his phone away. "Noah will secure Marty's things…if they haven't already been compromised, that is."

The odds were they probably had been, but maybe the killer had gotten sloppy. If the crime had been premeditated, though, she doubted it. Still, sometimes killers made mistakes.

"Along with looking for any connections between Marty and the hacker and retired cop, Noah's also going to get the surveillance from any security cameras outside my apartment," Ruston explained. "He won't have to do it under the table, so to speak, since he's gotten approval from his lieutenant for me to view the footage in case I see something on it that'll help with the investigation."

"Good." She was glad the lieutenant hadn't tried to stonewall this. Technically, Homicide could have kept this close to the vest, but that wouldn't have benefited anyone.

Ruston scrubbed his hand over his face. "Maybe the surveillance footage hasn't been tampered with."

Again, that was a strong possibility, but unlike removing documents from Marty's home, or planting incriminating ones, it'd be trickier to alter or erase footage from traffic and security cameras.

A cop could do it, of course.

"If I caused all of this to happen, I'm sorry," Ruston muttered.

Even though she had no idea who was responsible, Gracelyn didn't intend to let Ruston fall on his sword for this. "You asked Noah to look at Simon Milbrath and Archie Ingram, and that means you think the leak of my location could have come from one of them. And it could have," she emphasized.

He made a sound of agreement, but the guilt stayed in his eyes. Ruston didn't get a chance, though, to continue voicing that guilt, because his phone rang.

"Slater," he relayed to her and immediately answered it.

Again, he didn't put the call on speaker, maybe because he thought it would wake the baby. But after only a few seconds, Gracelyn knew that Ruston was hearing bad news from his brother.

That churned up the adrenaline again and caused the mother lode of flashbacks to come at her. Not just of this attack tonight but of the one from nearly a year ago. She had to fight hard to push all of that away just so she could try to steel herself up for whatever Ruston had just learned.

It took some effort, lots of it, but she'd just managed to re-gather her breath when Ruston hung up and looked at her.

"Slater found the truck. The license plates are bogus, and the gunmen weren't inside," he relayed. "They were nowhere in sight. Slater and the others will keep looking for them," Ruston added when she groaned. "A CSI team is heading out to examine the truck now and take a sample of the blood drops that Slater spotted. I guess I was right about one of them being injured."

Good, because the blood could lead to a DNA match. She hoped the injury was so serious that it meant this snake couldn't come after them again.

"Slater said it appears the gunmen ran from the truck on foot," Slater went on. "They left a lot of stuff behind."

There was something in the way he said the last part that put her back on full alert. She waited, fighting for her breath again, while Ruston spelled it out.

"Slater had a cursory look of the inside of the truck and found my wallet," Ruston added to his account. "He fig-ures it was taken the same time my badge was. The gun-men's plan was probably to kill you and then set me up for your murder."

Gracelyn tried to mentally work her way through that. Yes, that could have indeed been the thugs' plan. They could have waited out of sight, out of range of her cameras, until Ruston had arrived and was inside. Then they could have broken in and tried to make it look as if some kind of gun-fight had gone on between Ruston and her.

"But why would they want to set you up for my mur-der?" she asked.

Ruston shook his head. "I'm not sure," he said and then paused again. "But there was also an infant seat in the truck. And baby things."

Gracelyn felt everything inside her tighten into a knot. "They were going to kidnap Abigail." Her voice broke. "She was the target."

Ruston came closer, met her gaze, and he took hold of her hand. Probably because spelling it out like that had shaken Gracelyn to the core, and he'd no doubt seen that. His gentle grip helped steady her. More than Gracelyn wanted.

And that was why she stepped back.

She couldn't do this, not with the nightmares pressing so close to her that she could feel them. Memories of coming so close to them being killed ten and a half months ago.

Ruston didn't move back toward her, but their gazes stayed locked. At least they did until his phone rang again. "It's Noah," he muttered when he glanced at the screen. This time, he turned down the volume and put the call on speaker.

"Is something wrong?" Ruston asked the moment he answered.

"Yeah," Noah confirmed. "Something's very wrong. On the drive to Marty's, I made a call to a computer tech I trust so I could get a background check on Archie Ingram and Simon Milbrath." He paused. "They're both dead, Ruston. Someone murdered them."

Chapter Five

Ruston sat in one of the chairs in the guest room and, well, multitasked. He was watching the sleeping baby while Gracelyn showered in the adjoining bath. But he was also working on a laptop while drinking coffee and hoping for a miracle.

One miracle was that the caffeine would perform some magic and make him feel as if he'd gotten a decent night's sleep and now had a clear head. He'd slept some in this very chair, but that nowhere near qualified as anything decent, and so far, his head was nowhere near being clear.

Judging from the glimpse of Gracelyn's bleary eyes as she'd headed for the shower, she was in the same boat. No surprise about that. Like him, not only had she been dealing with the aftermath of the attack on them but also the flood of information they'd gotten since arriving at the ranch.

Three murders.

And all of them people who'd had a connection to either Gracelyn or him. People who could have ultimately given them the identity of the person responsible for this nightmare.

Someone was clearly cleaning up after themselves. Tying up loose ends. And Ruston needed to find something, *any-*

thing, that would give them a break so he could learn who wanted them dead.

Unfortunately, scouring the steady stream of reports coming in and going over Devin's old interview wasn't giving him anything he could use. He figured Duncan was no doubt going through those same reports in his home office, along with coordinating this end of the investigation. That included the CSI search of the gunmen's truck and the search of the grounds of the rental where Gracelyn had been staying.

Detective Noah Ryland was keeping both Duncan and him updated about the active cases there: the three murders and the break-in at Ruston's apartment. Noah had also managed not only to get himself assigned as one of the detectives on the murders, but also to secure Marty's laptop since there hadn't been any actual paperwork in the dead man's office. The laptop was now in the hands of the IT specialist that Noah trusted.

So far, the updates from Duncan, Slater and Noah had been disappointing. And outright frustrating. Someone, somewhere, had to know something that would help make sense of all this, but for now, there were still a whole lot of questions and very few answers.

He hoped some of those questions were about to be answered when his phone dinged with a text. But it wasn't from Duncan, Slater or Noah. It was from Charla.

Where are you? Charla texted. Tony wants you at headquarters right away.

Ruston frowned and then mentally cursed. Eventually, he was going to have to meet with Tony, but he didn't want that to happen until he learned who was trying to kill Gracelyn and him.

Tony wants Gracelyn in as well, Charla added a few seconds later. You'll both need to give a statement about the attack last night.

I emailed Tony a statement, Ruston quickly pointed out, knowing what he'd given wouldn't be nearly enough. It had been the bare-bones details.

You know how this works, Charla insisted. You need to be interviewed in person.

Ruston had a quick comeback for that, too. The attack wasn't in SAPD's jurisdiction. Technically, that would fall under the duties of the county sheriff, but Duncan had already spoken to him, and he'd relinquished authority to Duncan. Charla almost certainly knew that.

Again, he didn't respond, and a few moments crawled by before Charla attempted to call him. So that the sound wouldn't wake up the baby, he'd put his phone on vibrate, and it rattled in his hand. Shortly after the rattling had stopped, he got the ding for a voicemail and listened to it.

"Damn it, Ruston, talk to me. This is important." In the voicemail, Charla huffed. "We got an anonymous tip that Marty was Green Eagle. We could finally be close to solving the case about the baby farm, and I know you want to be in on that. Call me," she demanded.

"Anonymous tip," he muttered, and, yeah, there was plenty of sarcasm in his voice.

If such a tip had indeed been phoned in, it had likely come from Marty's killer. Or someone connected to the murder, anyway. Then again, if Charla was behind this, the tip could be a lie, a ruse to try to tie all of this up.

Ruston's attention zoomed to the makeshift crib when the baby whimpered. Gracelyn had fed her less than thirty minutes earlier, before she'd gone in to take her shower, and the baby had fallen asleep during the burping process. That was when Ruston had gone down to the kitchen to get himself and Gracelyn some coffee.

The burping and so-called uptime, which Gracelyn had explained was to minimize baby reflux, had just been coming to an end by the time he'd returned, and Abigail hadn't stirred when Gracelyn had placed her in the crib. However, she continued to squirm now, prompting Ruston to get up and move closer.

The baby still had her eyes closed but was smiling.

That made Ruston smile, too, even though he'd read somewhere that babies this age didn't actually sport that particular expression. It certainly looked like the real deal to him.

The bathroom door opened, and before he could even glance in that direction, Gracelyn blurted out, "What's wrong?"

"She's fine," Ruston assured her.

Or rather that was what he tried to do. It was obvious the reassurance hadn't worked one bit. Gracelyn ran to the baby, practically pushing him aside.

"She was just moving around a little and smiling," he added to his explanation. In fact, that smile was still on her tiny mouth.

Gracelyn released an audible breath of relief, and he could see she had to work to rein in whatever emotion had sent her running to the baby. Fear, no doubt, mixed with a whole boatload of worry.

"Sorry," she muttered. "Nerves on edge."

"No apology needed." He attempted more reassurance by giving her what he hoped would be a soothing look. This time, he was the one who failed when he saw the blood on her forehead. "You're bleeding."

She immediately pressed her fingers to a spot just inside her hairline. A spot he hadn't noticed the night before since her hair hadn't been swept away from her face the way it was now.

"It's just a small cut that I must have gotten when the safety glass was shot out in the SUV. It's okay," she insisted, taking out a tissue from the pocket of her jeans and pressing it to the wound. "I must have aggravated it when I was trying to brush my hair."

"Do you have any other cuts?" He immediately wanted to know.

"I think there's one other," she said, turning and lifting her hair so he could see the already scabbed spot on the back of her neck.

He wanted to curse. Wanted to beat those gunmen to a pulp. Yes, an extreme reaction to seeing two small cuts, but they were reminders that they could have easily been gunshot wounds.

She turned back to face him and muttered, "Yes." Gracelyn knew exactly how close they had come to dying.

He was about to fill her in on the three texts and voicemail he'd gotten from Charla, but she continued before he could do that.

"If their plan was to kidnap Abigail," she said, "those men took a huge risk shooting into the SUV."

They had indeed, and thinking about that had been a big contributor to Ruston's lack of sleep. "Maybe they did that because they panicked?" He threw the idea out there. That was one of his theories, anyway. "Or maybe because their orders were to eliminate you and me at all costs?"

It sickened him to think that the "cost" could have been the precious baby.

"The men had the infant seat in their truck," he reminded

her. "And if the plan wasn't to take Abigail, then they could have just blown up the house or set it on fire with us inside."

She made a sound of agreement. "How long had you known my address before you showed up?"

"About five hours." He'd already given this plenty of thought as well. "So, maybe those men learned when I did. Perhaps Marty told them, or they found out through a mole or some kind of listening device. Either way, they would have had those five hours to figure out how to come after you." He paused. "Did you do your own security or hire someone else to set it up?"

"I did it," she answered, "with items I bought with cash the day I decided to disappear nearly a year ago. In fact, I've lived mainly off cash since then. Both Allie and I got a share of our parents' life insurance money after they died in a car crash. Allie blew through hers, but I saved mine and have been living off it since my resignation." She shook her head. "Those thugs didn't locate me through the security system, and that takes us back to Marty or someone connected to him."

Gracelyn seemed to settle a little. Ironic, since they were talking about the attack. But they were doing more than that. They were looking at this like cops and not intended victims.

"Did you get any calls or new reports when I was in the shower?" she asked.

"A few," he verified, "and basically all said the same thing. Everything is still being processed and looked at. Including Simon's and Archie's murders. Times of death for those two are about an hour apart, so the same person could have killed them both and then gone after Marty." He stopped and went through the mental checklist. "I also got three texts and a call from Charla."

The worry returned to her eyes. "She's demanding you come in?"

He nodded. "And you."

"Me? How did she know about…?" Gracelyn stopped. "Duncan would have had to do a report, and she could have accessed it. Of course, she wouldn't have needed to access it if she already knew I was an intended target."

"Bingo." It still didn't sit well with him to think of a fellow cop as being responsible for this, but there were bad apples in every career field, and she might be one of them. "Charla says they got an anonymous tip, claiming that Marty was Green Eagle."

Gracelyn's eyes narrowed. "That's convenient."

"Isn't it, though?" he quickly agreed. "It works both ways in the killer's favor. If Marty was indeed Green Eagle, then he can't spill about anyone else who was involved in the baby-farm operation. If Marty wasn't Green Eagle, then someone wanted to set him up, probably with the hopes that setting him up would end any further investigation."

"That's one neat little package," Gracelyn muttered. "Too neat for my liking."

Ruston couldn't agree fast enough. "Let's see how this neat little package plays out. Charla will likely say that because Marty was Green Eagle, he wanted the baby for his still-ongoing business."

Gracelyn picked up on that scenario. "And that Marty wanted to get back at us for infiltrating the baby farm and causing him to have to move locations. Probably costing him a lot of money because of that. So, Marty hired you, somehow already knowing who you were. You and I were supposed to die, with you being set up for my murder."

He nodded. "But it's equally possible that Marty didn't actually orchestrate the attack against us. He could have been merely a middleman who had no connection to the baby farm or to us before someone used or hired him to set up yours and Abigail's kidnappings. He might not have had a clue how someone else was intending for this to play out. In the meantime, the cops will focus on Marty, and the real killer could just fade into the background."

"Or come after us again," Gracelyn muttered, her voice barely louder than a whisper. He saw the punch of emotion hit her, but then she quickly shook it off. "And that brings us back to Charla and Tony. Maybe," she amended. "And maybe they're clean. If so, that leaves Allie and Abigail's bio-father, Devin Blackburn."

Yes, because those two were the only other known players in this potentially lethal puzzle. Ruston had to ask, though he knew it was going to give Gracelyn another of those emotional jabs. "Could Allie have been in on the attack? Does she have a motive?"

"Trust me, I've been giving this a lot of thought," she muttered.

Of course she had. Gracelyn was still a cop at the core, and motherhood was an obvious connection they couldn't overlook.

"There'd be no obvious reason for Allie to kidnap the baby and kill us," Gracelyn said. "Obvious," she repeated. "If she wanted Abigail back, Allie knows how to get in touch with me. She could have called or texted the burner phone in my go bag. I check it often, and there was no contact from her."

Ruston figured Gracelyn had already thought of one possibility, so he voiced it. "What if Allie believed that you wouldn't give Abigail back to her? What if she thought, or someone convinced her, that kidnapping the baby was the only way she'd get her child back?"

Gracelyn's groan was soft, but it seemed to rumble through her entire body. "I wouldn't have just handed Abigail over to Allie. Not until I was certain she wouldn't do anything else reckless. And not as long as she was involved with a man like Devin Blackburn. So, yes, Allie might have known that, and Devin might have convinced her to go along with the kidnapping."

"And our murders?" he asked.

She shook her head. "Allie wouldn't have agreed to that. And, no, I'm not saying that because I'm her sister. I'm saying it because Allie isn't violent. She's, uh, more of a doormat. A very pliable, easily swayed one who Devin could have used to help him set up the kidnapping. Allie would have known what kind of security I was using, and there's a slim chance she might have even had an idea of where I was."

Ruston jumped right on that. "How?"

"I had notes on my tablet," she admitted, her forehead bunching up. That in turn caused her to wince a little, and she dabbed at the cut again. "Notes about possible rentals that I could use to make quick moves. My tablet is password protected, but there's a chance that Allie could have seen me typing and then accessed the notes without me knowing."

"Why would she have done that?" he pressed.

"Not specifically to find the notes," Gracelyn assured him. "But maybe to try to contact Devin. Or to check his social media posts." She stopped and sighed in frustration. "One minute Allie would be cursing Devin for the way he treated her, and the next, she'd be going on about forgiving him. Right before she left, she had convinced herself that she was responsible for him hitting her."

That was classic battered woman syndrome, and apparently the urge to forgive him and reunite had won out. Or maybe it had.

"You're sure Allie voluntarily left to go to Devin?" he asked.

Gracelyn opened her mouth and then immediately closed it, obviously rethinking what she'd been about to say. "You're thinking he somehow lured Allie away?" She paused, then groaned again. "It's possible. That could go back to Allie using my tablet to get in touch with him. If she did, though, she didn't leave a trace of that contact. No copies of emails in the Sent folder or trash."

"Allie could have deleted them. Or Devin could have instructed her to delete them. You said he had an arrest for computer hacking, so he'd certainly know how to do something that simple."

"Yes," she muttered, and a moment later she repeated it while she was obviously working through this theory.

Because he was watching her, he saw the exact second she followed the theory to one possible conclusion. A bad one.

She nodded, swallowed hard. "Devin has a violent temper, and he could have lured Allie to him in order to punish her for leaving him. He could have already killed her."

Yeah. That was a bad possible conclusion, all right. Abusers could escalate. Hits and slaps could turn into something deadly.

"Oh, mercy," Gracelyn whispered, and the emotion took over.

Ruston went to her, pulling her into his arms, and she didn't resist. Gracelyn just let him hold her. Let herself lean on him while she dealt with the sickening realization that her sister could be dead. Unfortunately, that might not be the end of this scenario.

He gave Gracelyn a minute. Then two. And he just kept holding her. Definitely not a chore. In fact, it felt good to have her close like this. It stirred memories, of course. Of the heat. Of the one time they'd been together when a hug of comfort had turned into a kiss.

And then so much more.

Obviously, Gracelyn hadn't been able to deal with that *more* since she'd left the following day. That was the reason Ruston couldn't do what his body was urging him to do and push this contact further. He darn sure couldn't kiss her. That would risk her going on the run again, and he didn't want to lose her.

"If Allie is dead, if Devin killed her, then he might want to get Abigail," Ruston said. He was whispering now, too, because even though Abigail was way too young to understand, he didn't want her to hear any of this. "He might not want any DNA evidence to link him to Allie, and the baby would do that."

He felt Gracelyn's muscles tighten. "I could link him," she muttered.

Ruston eased back enough to meet her gaze. "And that leaves me. Until you told me about Allie and Devin, I had no idea about that connection."

She made a sound of agreement. "It's possible Devin contacted Marty to arrange the kidnapping, and Marty hired you." She stopped. "So, if Marty was indeed Green Eagle and knew your real identity, he could have used this opportunity to get rid of both of us and get payment from Devin for the baby."

Ruston was about to continue that line of thought, but his phone vibrated again, and he saw Noah's name on the screen. He showed it to Gracelyn, and he answered the call.

"Noah," he said, "I have Gracelyn here with me, and I'm

putting you on speaker." That would save Ruston from re-peating any info Noah was about to give them. And hope-fully, that info would be useful and not simply more bad news. They'd filled their bad-news quota for a while.

"Good," Noah replied, "because I had a question for her. Do you recall when you contacted retired sergeant Archie Ingram?"

"About two weeks ago," she quickly provided. "If you need the exact date, I can get it."

"Probably not necessary," Noah assured her, "but you should know that thirteen days ago, Archie called SAPD headquarters and asked to speak to Lieutenant Tony Frank-lin. Tony wasn't available, so Archie left a message, saying it was important, that some reporter was asking about the baby-farm investigation."

Gracelyn and Ruston exchanged glances, and she was probably thinking what he was. That this could indeed be important. If Tony had gotten concerned about a reporter, then he could have attempted to nip it in the bud. But for that to fit meant that Archie, or Tony, had figured out that Gracelyn was the bogus reporter.

"Did Tony call him back?" Ruston wanted to know.

"I'm not sure, but it's something you might want to ask him. He's on his way to Saddle Ridge, Ruston. I suspect he'll find his way to wherever you're staying."

Ruston wasn't sure whose groan was louder, his or Grace-lyn's, but he thought he was the winner. "Any idea when he'll be here?"

"My guess is soon. I saw him hurrying out of his office about twenty minutes ago. Emphasis on *hurrying*."

That would have been about the time Ruston had ended his call with Charla, and he wondered if Charla had said something to Tony to make him rush out to Saddle Ridge.

Probably.

Even if Tony didn't know where the family ranch was, he'd soon find out, and that could mean he'd be here in as soon as ten minutes. Too bad his other sister, Bree, wasn't home. Bree was a high-profile lawyer for the Texas Rangers and could create legal walls in a blink to stop Tony from getting near the ranch.

But Ruston immediately rethought that.

He didn't want to hide behind Bree and legal walls anyway. He'd talk to Tony, give whatever statement was necessary, all the while watching for any signs that the lieutenant could be a cold-blooded killer.

There was a knock at the door, and for a moment, Ruston thought that meeting with Tony would be even sooner than he'd thought. But it was Slater.

"It's me," Slater said, keeping his voice low, no doubt because of the baby.

"Thanks for the info," Ruston told Noah, and he ended the call before he opened the door.

His brother was indeed there and not alone. Joelle was with him, and she had a tray of breakfast items. Fruit bowls, pastries and some juice. "You're probably not hungry," she immediately said. "But I decided to bring it up anyway."

Ruston checked the time. Just past nine, so not late, but he realized he should have already gotten Gracelyn and himself something to eat since neither of them had had dinner the night before. And, yeah, they wouldn't be hungry, but they should still try to eat.

He thanked his sister, who had already set down the tray and was making her way to look at the baby. "How did she sleep?" Joelle asked.

"Pretty good," Gracelyn supplied. "She had a four-hour stretch before she woke up for a bottle. And now she's about an hour into a nap. She might nap for another three hours before I have to feed her again."

"Speaking of feeding," Slater said, handing Ruston a large canvas shopping bag. "Extra diapers and formula," he explained. "Joelle arranged to have it delivered."

"But I made a point of telling the store clerk I was having some serious nesting urges and that I wanted the items for the nursery," Joelle added. "That way, no one is blabbing about a baby being here at the ranch."

Gracelyn added her own thanks to Joelle. It was possible the ranch hands were aware that Abigail was here, but the fewer people who knew, the better.

They shifted their attention to Slater. Everything about Slater's expression conveyed that he didn't have good news.

"Did you find the gunmen?" Ruston came out and asked. He set the canvas bag in the chair where he'd slept.

"No, but we think we know who one of them is. The blood is at the lab, and that might take a while to process, but there was a single partial fingerprint on the passenger's-side door handle. The handle had been wiped down, but he must have missed this one. Probably because he was in a hurry to get out of there. Anyway, the CSIs ran the partial, and they got an immediate hit for a man named Terry Zimmer."

Ruston tested out the name by repeating it a couple of times, but it wasn't familiar. "Zimmer has a record? Is that why his prints were on file?"

Slater shook his head. "He was a cop in Austin and resigned after some complaints about excessive force. That was three years ago, and afterward he supposedly worked for a company that provides security for large parties, weddings and corporate events."

Ruston latched on to one word. *"Supposedly?"*

"He did work there, part-time," Slater confirmed, "but

he quit a little over a year ago, and no one at the company has heard from or seen him since." He paused a moment. "The CSIs found something when they ran facial recognition on him."

Slater took out his phone, and Gracelyn and Ruston stepped closer to look at the picture. It was a grainy shot but still clear enough for Ruston to realize what he was seeing. The sprawling Victorian house that had once been a small hotel. That'd been its purpose fifty years ago, anyway. But it had been converted into something else.

The baby farm.

This had been the place Gracelyn and he had infiltrated. The place where they'd nearly died.

Gracelyn had no trouble recognizing it either, it seemed, because Ruston heard her quick intake of breath. Despite the god-awful memories it held, though, she didn't back away. Neither did Ruston. That was because the house wasn't the only thing in the picture. There was a man dressed in dark camo, and he was armed. His stance suggested he was standing guard.

Slater zoomed in on the man's face. "This was a picture taken shortly before Gracelyn and you arrived there under-cover. And that's Terry Zimmer."

Ruston's mind began to whirl with thoughts of what this might mean. One immediate question came to mind. Was this Green Eagle? Ruston's guess was no. The boss of an operation that made millions of dollars probably wouldn't have been doing guard duty.

"Why wasn't this match made after the attack?" Gracelyn wanted to know. "Why did it take so long to identify him in this picture?"

"Apparently, because there are hundreds of photos that were taken over a monthlong period when the San Antonio cops had the place under surveillance," Slater explained. "Or that's what the CSIs told me, anyway. Hundreds that are still in queues waiting to be processed. This picture was one of them, and it popped because it'd been scanned into the system, but that's about all that had been done with it."

Ruston knew it wasn't that unusual for evidence to take months to process. He only hoped that someone, like a dirty cop, hadn't purposely delayed the examination of this photo.

"Does Duncan know all of this?" Ruston asked.

Slater nodded. "I filled him in before I came up to tell you." He paused. "While I had the CSI on the phone, I asked for a quick background on Zimmer, and I got his employment history. As a rookie cop in Austin, he worked with your lieutenant."

"Tony knows him," Gracelyn muttered, sounding just as rocked by that tidbit as Ruston was.

Of course, just because Tony knew Zimmer, it didn't mean they'd stayed in contact with each other. Still, it was a connection that made Ruston very uneasy.

"Now that we have a name and a face," Slater went on, "we can put out an APB. The more lawmen looking for Zimmer, the sooner he'll be found." He locked gazes with Ruston. "Of course, the person who hired Zimmer could be sheltering him. Or trying to silence him."

Yeah, and either one of those wasn't good. Ruston didn't want Zimmer to disappear or die. He wanted answers, and after that, he wanted him in a cage for the rest of his miserable life.

"Text me a copy of that picture," Ruston said.

Slater did that before he continued. "The CSIs will continue to process the other prints they retrieved from the truck," Slater went on. But he stopped. All of them did. They froze.

Outside, Ruston heard something that tightened every muscle in his body.

A gunshot.

Chapter Six

The moment Gracelyn heard the sound, she hurried to the baby, scooped her up and scrambled away from the windows. Even though the drapes and blinds were closed, that wouldn't stop a bullet.

Part of her, the former-cop part, wanted to grab a gun and be ready to return fire, but the baby had to come first. She couldn't protect Abigail if she was doing what Slater and Ruston were doing. They had already drawn their weapons, and Ruston had hurried to one window while Slater had gone to the other. They both lifted a few slats of the blinds so they could look out.

Joelle pulled out a gun, too, from the back waist of her jeans, but instead of the window, she maneuvered herself in front of Gracelyn and the baby.

There was the popping sound of another gunshot. It didn't sound close, and neither bullet had slammed into the house. Maybe that meant the shots had come from a hunter or someone who was trying to scare off a wild animal. Gracelyn wanted to hang on to that hope, but after what'd happened the night before, this was most likely another attempt to come after all three of them.

It was an incredibly risky move.

The ranch had four cops and ranch hands, all armed.

Then again, these shots were likely coming from a sniper and it wasn't a close-range attack. It was possible the shooter thought he could pick off some of them before moving in to finish the job he'd started.

"Is everyone all right?" Duncan called out. Judging from the sound of his voice, he was downstairs.

"So far," Joelle answered. "Can you see the shooter?"

"No," Duncan replied quickly. "But it's not any of the hands." He paused a heartbeat. "Someone's coming."

Duncan added that last part just as there was a third round of gunfire. And just as Ruston muttered some profanity. "It's an SAPD cruiser," Ruston snarled. "Probably Tony."

Gracelyn shook her head. "He's not the one firing those shots."

"No," Ruston agreed. "It appears he's the one being shot at."

That definitely didn't tamp down any of Gracelyn's worries since the gunman could change targets at any second. But it did punch some holes in one of her theories that Tony might be behind the attacks.

She heard the sound of the vehicle then. The sharp squeal of brakes as it came to a stop.

"The cruiser isn't in front of the house," Ruston relayed, glancing back at her to make very brief eye contact. "He's stopped at the end of the driveway."

Gracelyn nearly asked if that was because the driver had been hit. The cruiser was bullet resistant, but that didn't mean shots couldn't get through. So, if this was indeed Tony, he could be hurt. Then again, it was also possible he hadn't wanted to come closer since the gunshots could endanger those inside.

The silence came, and it seemed to her that everyone was holding their breaths. Even Abigail wasn't making a sound.

Then Ruston's phone vibrated.

It barely made a sound, but it cut right through the silence. While he continued to volley glances out the window, he took out his phone. "Tony," he said, and he answered it on speaker. "Are you in the cruiser at the end of the driveway?" Ruston demanded.

"Yeah," Tony immediately verified. "Who's shooting at us?" There were hitches in his breath, and the question rushed out.

"I was about to ask you the same thing," Ruston countered. *"Us?"* he questioned. "Who's with you?"

"It's me," Charla said. So, their call was on speaker as well. "Are the shots maybe coming from one of the local lawmen or a ranch hand?"

"No." He huffed, and when he repeated it, there was plenty of frustration in his voice. "I think the shots came from the west. There are a lot of trees in that area, so check and see if you can spot a sniper."

Because Gracelyn was watching Ruston so closely, she saw when he shifted his attention in the direction of the road. "A Saddle Ridge cruiser is coming," Ruston relayed to everyone just as his phone dinged with a text. "Duncan says it's Luca. Deputy Luca Vanetti," he spelled out, no doubt to inform Charla and Tony. "And Duncan is Sheriff Holder. He's here inside the house."

"I don't see a sniper," Tony said. "In fact, the only people I see are the deputy in the cruiser and some cowboys with rifles back behind the house. You're sure they're not the ones who shot at us?"

"I'm sure," Ruston snapped, and this time there was some anger in his voice. "I'm not a dirty cop, and I didn't set anyone up to be murdered."

Before Ruston could add anything to that, he got a text.

"Duncan says one of the hands spotted someone in that area by the trees. It's probably the sniper, so the hands are going in pursuit."

That gave Gracelyn a jolt of both hope and fear. She wanted the ranch hands to catch the guy, but they weren't cops. And they weren't killers like the sniper almost certainly was. The ranch hands could be hurt. Or worse. Still, if they managed to capture him, then they might learn why these attacks were happening.

Or if this was actually an attack.

After everything that had happened, Gracelyn wasn't about to dole out any automatic trust to Charla and Tony simply because they'd been shot at. One of them could have arranged this, knowing their odds of being hurt while sitting in a cruiser were slim.

Slater got another text. "Luca will escort the two SAPD cops to the house. They'll stay downstairs," Slater added, glancing at Gracelyn, probably to try to reassure her that Charla and Tony wouldn't be a threat.

And they probably wouldn't be, in a house surrounded by lawmen. No, this wouldn't be an optimal time for them to try to tie up loose ends. If that was what one of them was actually trying to do, that was. But Gracelyn very much wanted to see their faces so she could maybe tell if they were trying to hide their guilt.

"We'll talk once Charla and you are inside," Ruston said to Tony, and he ended the call.

Gracelyn turned to Joelle. "Would you be able to stay up here with the baby?" she asked.

Joelle didn't jump to say yes. She looked at Ruston, and he gave her a nod. Only then did Joelle ease Abigail into her arms.

"I'll stay up here with Joelle," Slater immediately volun-

teered, "but if things get dicey downstairs, let me know."
He looked Ruston straight in the eyes. "Are those two cops
killers?"

Ruston held his brother's gaze. "I don't know. They might
both be clean, but I can't trust either of them until I know
for certain they aren't behind this. Right now, I'm nowhere
near certain."

Slater nodded. "Let me know if you need help," he repeated.

Ruston turned to Gracelyn, studying her, and she thought
maybe he was looking for any sign that she, too, wanted to
stay put. She didn't.

"I'm armed," she let him know. "And I want to hear what
they have to say."

He didn't try to talk her out of it. Probably because he
understood she needed to do this as much as he did. "We
shouldn't accuse Charla or Tony of anything right now.
Nothing to put them on the defensive. Agreed?"

Gracelyn huffed. She did agree, since the pair were more
likely to talk if they thought they were all on the same side.
"All right," she finally said. "I'll play nice if they do."

Ruston didn't challenge that either. "I'll text Duncan and
let him know that, while both Charla and Tony are suspects,
we don't have anything concrete on them. Not enough to
treat them like criminals, anyway." He stopped. "I'll ask
Duncan if he wants to go tough on them to try to get some
answers. Duncan's instincts are good," he added. "If he
senses trouble, he'll shut it down."

That was a lot of trust to put in Duncan's hands, but she
reminded herself that if Ruston believed in the sheriff, then
she should, too. Plus, there was that whole deal about this
being a bad time for Charla or Tony to try to come after
Ruston and her.

Ruston sent the text and then motioned for her to follow him. After she brushed a kiss on the baby's head, Gracelyn did just that.

Ruston didn't put away his gun as they started down the stairs, and Gracelyn kept her hand on her own weapon. There were some footsteps and movements in the foyer, and she heard Duncan.

Ruston and she followed the sound of his voice and those footsteps and found Duncan, their two visitors and a black-haired man she figured was Deputy Luca Vanetti. All four still had their weapons drawn, and it gave Gracelyn an immediate jolt. Her instincts were to take out her own gun, to be ready to defend herself, but she forced herself to stay calm.

Both Charla and Tony immediately turned to Ruston and her, and Gracelyn tried to interpret their expressions. They were both a little wild-eyed, perhaps cranked up on adrenaline from the attack. Of course, it could be a pretense, and Gracelyn wished she knew for sure.

Both Charla and Tony were what many people would call average and nondescript. Charla was five foot six with brown hair and brown eyes. Slim but not overly thin. Attractive but not beautiful. Tony was about five foot ten and had sandy-blond hair and a face that sported no scars and no unusual features.

Nothing about them stood out, which was an advantage in undercover work, something Charla still did. Tony, however, with his promotion to lieutenant, was a "suit" these days and didn't do fieldwork.

Gracelyn had always felt as if she, too, fit into that average and nondescript category. But not Ruston. No, he had one of those faces that people definitely noticed. Handsome. Hot. That should have been a disadvantage for him, but it hadn't been. He'd always managed to alter his looks just enough for undercover work, and sometimes, he'd even used those good looks to coax his way into places and situations.

"Gracelyn," Tony muttered as a greeting, and he shifted his attention to Ruston and said his name as well. "Are you two all right? Were there shots fired into the house?"

"The shots didn't come into the house," Ruston stated. "They all seemed to be aimed at your cruiser."

Ruston hadn't emphasized the word *seemed*, but Gracelyn thought it was a good addition to his explanation. Because if Charla or Tony had indeed orchestrated this, then maybe the shots hadn't even come near them.

"I heard you say the ranch hands spotted the sniper and were in pursuit," Charla piped in.

She, too, was still gulping in her breath and looking a little shell-shocked. But Gracelyn had had to do that a time or two herself when undercover and playing a role. Undercover cops had to be good actors, and that could be exactly what Tony or Charla were doing now.

It was Duncan who answered. "Yes, the hands are looking now," he confirmed, "but I have other deputies on the way. They'll set up roadblocks. We might get lucky if the shooter's still in the area."

Tony nodded, and he was visibly steadier when he looked at Ruston and her again. "We have a lot to talk about," he said, sounding very much like a boss now.

"If you're here to demand I come into headquarters—" Ruston started.

"I'm not," Tony interrupted. "Well, I was, but I'm sure as hell not demanding it now. It's obviously not safe to try to get you into San Antonio. You either," he added to Gracelyn. "How's the baby? Is she safe?"

"She's with two cops," Gracelyn answered, rather than

spell out that the baby was in the house. If Abigail was indeed the target, then there was no need to advertise her whereabouts. "Cops that I trust," she couldn't help but add.

Something flashed in Charla's eyes. Anger, maybe. And she looked ready to demand to know if that was some kind of dig. It was, of course. But Tony spoke before she could.

"I understand your distrust of the police after what happened on your last assignment," he said. His voice was oh so sympathetic. Perhaps too much so. "But we need to talk to you about the attack last night. Ruston emailed me a brief report, but we'll need your account, too."

Charla took up the explanation from there, turning toward Duncan. "We understand that this is your jurisdiction," she said to Duncan, "but we have three dead bodies, and that needs to be investigated."

Duncan glanced at Ruston, and Ruston nodded. That was apparently the only cue Duncan needed.

"We can do the interviews here," Duncan said, speaking boss-to-boss with Tony. He motioned for them to all take a seat. "And since the investigations overlap, it'd be a good time for you and your detective to answer some of my questions, too." That wasn't a suggestion. Duncan was in all-cop mode now.

Charla opened her mouth, and Gracelyn was betting she was about to protest, but she hushed when she met Tony's gaze. Apparently, Charla also responded to subtle cues.

"All right," she said, holstering her gun and reaching into her pocket.

That had Gracelyn reaching for her gun. And Charla noticed. Her eyes widened, then narrowed. "Really?" Charla snarled.

"Really," Gracelyn snarled right back. She didn't add more because she didn't want this to turn into a sniping contest. Not when she wanted those answers from Charla and Tony.

Charla made a show of taking her phone from her pocket and holding it up for Gracelyn to see. "I need to record this interview."

Duncan holstered his own gun, took out his phone and sat in one of the chairs. "And I'll record your responses." He clicked on the record function. "In fact, I'd like to start. Sheriff Duncan Holder conducting interview of... State your names for the record," he insisted.

Charla and Tony were clearly not pleased to be on the other end of what would likely turn out to be an interrogation, but they both gave their names and sat on the sofa across from Duncan.

Duncan stated the date and time and continued. "Someone blew Detective Ruston McCullough's cover while he was on assignment at a house in my jurisdiction, and it nearly got him and Gracelyn Wallace killed. Who did that? Who's responsible for not securing the location of an undercover officer?"

Gracelyn had to suppress a smile. She was so glad Duncan had taken over the bad-cop role, and he'd almost certainly done that on purpose so that Tony and Charla's venom would be aimed at him. Of course, some of that venom would no doubt still come at Ruston and her. And she welcomed it. Because angry people often let things slip.

"That's being investigated," Tony answered. Yes, there was ire, all right. "We're still in the preliminary stages of that, but it's my theory that no one in my department was responsible. I trust the cops who work for me."

"Including Ruston?" Duncan asked.

Tony blinked. "Of course."

"Then that means you don't believe he was responsible in any way for his cover being blown," Duncan quickly concluded.

Tony shook his head, maybe objecting to the *in any way* part, but Duncan didn't give him a chance to voice that.

"For the record, Lieutenant Franklin indicated nonverbally that he did not believe Detective Ruston McCullough compromised his undercover identity. Is that right?"

"That's right," Tony muttered.

"Good. So, if Ruston didn't tell anyone who and where he was," Duncan went on, "then who did? What's your theory?"

Charla huffed. "That the leak came from Marty Bennett, the man who hired Ruston's undercover persona."

"Marty, who's now dead," Duncan stated in a way that made it sound like "isn't that convenient" sarcasm. "And how would Marty have learned Ruston was a cop?"

"We don't know," Tony jumped in. He met Ruston's gaze. "Not yet. But we'll find out. That's why we're here. I need to know if there's any possibility that you gave Marty some information, no matter how small, that made him believe you were undercover and that this was a sting operation."

Now it was Ruston who huffed. "So, you do think I was responsible for the leak. Trust me, I wasn't. My life was on the line. Gracelyn's life and the baby's, too. No way would I have risked letting anyone know. Especially a lowlife like Marty."

Duncan sat back, and Gracelyn took that as another of those subtle cues that he was relinquishing the interview to Ruston and her. Gracelyn went with it.

"I certainly didn't leak my location to anyone," Gracelyn stated, easing down onto the love seat that was positioned adjacent to the sofa and the chair where Duncan was seated.

"And until Ruston showed up, I had no idea he was even coming. But those two gunmen who tried to kill us, they knew. They knew my exact location."

"Which they could have gotten from Marty," Charla interjected.

"And that leads us right back to the question of who told Marty," Ruston said, sitting next to Gracelyn. "It's not just Gracelyn's location either, but considering the break-in at my apartment, someone would have told either Marty or his killer about that, too. That's a lot of information for someone outside of SAPD to have."

"We're looking into that," Tony insisted, and he shifted his attention to Gracelyn. "Is it possible you alerted someone to Ruston's identity—"

"No," she interrupted, "because I didn't know his undercover identity."

"But you knew the location of his apartment," Charla quickly inferred. There was something in her tone that suggested Charla had guessed that Ruston and she had gone there because they'd been lovers.

"No," Gracelyn repeated. "I didn't."

Charla pulled back her shoulders, and it seemed as if she wanted to challenge that. "But you came here with him. Before last night, I mean. You visited Ruston here in Saddle Ridge."

Gracelyn let her smile come. "That wouldn't have been in any report, Charla. How would you know that?"

"I must have heard it somewhere," Charla muttered, but her eyes were narrowed now. "What is this about?" she demanded. "You can't possibly think Tony and I had something to do with what happened?"

"Did you?" Ruston asked, and he used some of Tony's wording to phrase his next question. "Is there any possibility that you gave Marty information, no matter how small, that ended up blowing my cover?"

"Absolutely not," Tony insisted.

Ruston didn't miss a beat. He took out his phone, brought up the photo he'd gotten from Slater and held it out for Tony to see.

"This is one of the gunmen who tried to kill us," Ruston spelled out. "Recognize him?" His tone indicated he already knew the answer.

A muscle tightened in Tony's jaw. "Terry Zimmer. How the hell do you know he was involved?"

"Evidence gathered from the vehicle used in the attack," Duncan supplied. He checked the time. "It's been less than fifteen hours since that attack, and we—a small-town sheriff's office with limited resources—have identified a former cop who you personally not only know, but one who also tried to murder Ruston and Gracelyn. And he was connected to the baby farm. You know the one I'm talking about. Gracelyn and Ruston were nearly killed then, too."

"How do you know that?" Tony demanded, but then he waved off the question. "I haven't seen or spoken to Zimmer in over a decade."

"Good," Duncan said, and he breezed right on. "Because as we speak, I have the Texas Rangers doing a deep background check on Zimmer. Deep," he emphasized. "So, you want to rethink that answer?"

"No." Tony spoke through clenched teeth now. "And there was no reason to involve the Rangers."

"Beg to differ," Duncan argued. "I have a high-ranking cop in SAPD—that would be you—with connections to a man involved in both an illegal black-market baby operation and the two attempted murders of police officers. I don't want this swept under any rug. I want everything out in the open."

The anger came, flaring through Tony's eyes, and he whipped out his phone, his movement so fast that it had Luca, Duncan, Ruston and Gracelyn all drawing their weapons. That caused Tony to scowl.

"Since you've brought in the Rangers," Tony said, his tone icy now, "you'll want to let them know about Gracelyn's involvement in this. And, no, I don't mean the so-called attempts to kill her. I mean her involvement."

Gracelyn flashed him her own scowl, but the uneasiness fell on her like a dead weight. She didn't ask what Tony meant by that, but it was obvious he had something up his sleeve. Or rather on his phone, because he thrust it out for her to see.

She leaned in closer, looking at the image that was just as grainy as the one they had of Zimmer.

"This was taken from the security camera just up the street from Marty's house," Tony explained, keeping his steely stare on Gracelyn. "Notice the time stamp."

She did. It would have been around the time that Marty had been murdered. There was the vague image of someone dressed in dark clothes.

Tony enlarged the image and showed it to her. Gracelyn leaned in again. And saw the face. She managed to choke back a gasp. Barely. But inside, a firestorm of emotions came at her.

Because she was looking at her sister's face.

Chapter Seven

Ruston wanted to curse. Something that Gracelyn likely wanted to do as well, and like him, she was no doubt trying to absorb the shock of what they were seeing.

Allie.

Near a murder scene.

No way could Ruston convince anyone, including himself, that Allie had simply been in the wrong place at the wrong time. That would be way too much of a coincidence.

"That's your sister, right?" Tony asked.

Gracelyn nodded. "Yes, that's Allie."

Both Tony and Charla had smug looks on their faces. "And what was she doing there?" Charla demanded.

Gracelyn shook her head. "I don't know. I haven't heard from her in a while, so I didn't know where she was."

"Well, clearly she was at the house, or at least near the house, of a man who was murdered," Charla said. "So, it's highly likely that she's the one who compromised Ruston's identity."

"No," Ruston was quick to argue. "There's nothing highly likely about that scenario. I had absolutely no indication from Marty that Allie was involved with this."

Of course, Marty wouldn't have mentioned that if she had been, but the premise was still way off.

He hoped.

Because if Allie was truly involved, this was going to crush Gracelyn. However, it might not be that much of a shock once it all sank in, and Gracelyn would likely come to some conclusions.

There was one way this could have all fit.

One way to explain why Allie had been there.

Ruston, though, had no intentions of voicing it in front of Charla and Tony. Thankfully, he didn't have to, because Tony's phone rang, and he saw Captain Katelyn O'Malley's name on the screen. Tony's boss. That wiped any trace of a smirk off Tony's face, and he stood, stepping to the side and muttering something about having to take the call.

"Why was your sister there?" Charla demanded, obviously trying to continue this interview.

But Tony's call only lasted a couple of seconds, and when he turned back around, Ruston thought the lieutenant looked even more riled than when they'd been peppering him with questions.

"I have to go," Tony said, motioning for Charla to stand. He aimed those anger-filled eyes at Duncan and then Ruston. "Captain O'Malley got a call from the Texas Rangers, and they want to talk to me about my association with Zimmer. And it apparently can't wait."

Ruston could have managed his own smirk, but he didn't. He just considered this progress, because if there was something dirty going on with Tony's connection with Zimmer, maybe the Rangers could find it.

Charla clearly wasn't pleased with any of this, and she huffed. "The sniper could still be out there," she reminded Tony.

"Then we'll be careful." Tony looked at Ruston again.

"But it might not be necessary. The shots could have just been a way to try to ward us off."

Tony was obviously suggesting that Ruston and his family were behind the shooting. Of course, they weren't, but the gunfire could have indeed been a warning. The killer might want to discourage police interference if he wasn't linked to Tony or Charla.

And that brought him back to Allie.

Tony got Charla moving, and despite the intense exchange that had gone on during the interviews, Luca, Duncan and Ruston all provided cover as Tony and Charla hurried down the porch steps and to the waiting cruiser. Gracelyn drew her weapon as well, but thankfully stayed in the door.

Ruston held his breath when no shots came, and he rushed back in, mainly so he could get Gracelyn fully back inside. He expected her to still have that shell-shocked look on her face, but she had shaken that off.

"I need to try to call Allie," she insisted.

"You know how to get in touch with her?" Duncan asked, shutting the door and resetting the security system.

Gracelyn nodded, then lifted her shoulder as if not so certain of her response. "I gave her a burner before she left and told her if I needed to contact her, I'd call her with a burner I keep in my go bag. Or that I'd message her through a private Facebook page I'd set up. I'll try the phone first."

"I'll get your go bag," Duncan offered when she started for the stairs. "I want to check on Joelle anyway."

"And I need to text one of the ranch hands to see where they are in their search for the sniper," Luca explained, taking out his phone and moving away from them.

Ruston had no doubts that Duncan did want to check on Joelle and that Luca needed to make contact with the ranch hands, but he also figured this was about giving Gracelyn and him a moment alone. Gracelyn clearly needed it, because she went straight into his arms.

"Oh, God," she muttered. "I'm so sorry."

He'd expected this from her, but it still riled him. "You aren't going to take the blame for anything your sister might have done. If she did anything at all," he tacked on to that. "Someone could have lured her there to Marty's."

Gracelyn made a half-hearted sound of agreement. "But even if she had been lured, it means someone used her to get to you. To try to kill you."

"And you," he pointed out. As good as it felt to hold her, and it felt darn good, he pulled back just enough so he could look her straight in the eyes. "Play this through while thinking like a cop and not like the sister of a woman who's screwed up time and time again."

She stared at him, and he saw the shift. He saw Gracelyn tucking away some of the raw emotion that had to be eating away at her. "All right." She repeated that several times. "I don't recall Allie ever mentioning anyone named Marty, so she might not have even known him." She paused. "And she might not have been in that area because of him."

Bingo. "Where does Devin Blackburn live?" he asked.

"One of those upscale apartments on the River Walk in San Antonio. I've never been there, and he also owns a house in a gated community on the north side of the city. I've never been to it either," she was quick to add. "But after Allie told me some of the things he's done, I researched him."

"Are either of those two places anywhere near Marty's?" He pulled out his phone and showed her first the location of Marty's office and then the man's house, where he'd been murdered.

She looked at the addresses on the map, sighed and shook her head. "No."

"But maybe Allie is staying near there," he pointed out. "You don't know for certain she's with Devin."

That put some hope in her eyes. "True. Things might not have worked out between them." She paused, huffed. "Of course, that doesn't explain why Allie wouldn't have tried to come back to get Abigail."

No, it didn't. But there was something else that had to give Gracelyn hope. "Allie's alive, and she didn't appear to be hurt." He wanted to see the actual surveillance footage, though, so he could try to determine what direction she'd come from and if anyone had been with her.

Since Noah was one of the detectives investigating Marty's murder, Ruston sent him a text to request a copy of the security feed. Of course, Noah would almost certainly scour that feed for himself, looking for anything that would help him find Marty's killer.

"I swear, I won't fall apart," Gracelyn muttered.

Ruston looked down at her. They were still close. Very close with their bodies touching. "I never thought you would," he let her know.

She shook her head. "I fell apart nearly a year ago when we were almost killed."

"No." He pulled her back into his arms, creating even more contact, but hopefully giving Gracelyn something she needed right now. "You never fell apart. If you had, you wouldn't have been able to put together a plan to disappear the way you did."

Even though he could no longer see her face, Ruston suspected she was sporting a very skeptical expression. "I disappeared," she stated.

"Because you needed time to process what'd happened,"

he spelled out. "And while I would have preferred you process that with me around, I understand why you had to have that time, that space."

She lifted her head and looked up at him as he looked down at her. "Yes," she muttered. "You understand because of your father."

Yeah, he did. And Ruston was well aware that his father's life had ended just a few yards from where they were standing right now. Ruston had done his own version of disappearing in the weeks following that. He'd thrown himself into the investigation. He'd become obsessed with finding his father's killer. That obsession was still there. Maybe it always would be until his dad finally got the justice he deserved.

First, though, he had to unravel who was after Gracelyn and him. That was the only way to keep the baby and her safe.

She groaned softly, causing Ruston to look at her again. Not that his attention had strayed too far. And it didn't stray now either. With their gazes locked, things passed between them. The worry. The urgency to find their attacker.

The heat.

Yeah, it was there, all right, and it felt like a gut punch of a different kind. It was also a complication. One that he knew he shouldn't act on. But he did anyway.

Ruston dipped his head and kissed her.

Since he hadn't actually planned it, he wasn't sure if this was for comfort or if the heat was calling the shots here. When the taste of her jolted through him, he had his answer.

The heat was in charge.

That definitely wasn't a good sign, and he figured Gracelyn would realize that and push him away. She didn't. She sank right into the kiss, pressing her mouth harder against his. Deepening it, too, and skyrocketing the fire. Making every inch of him want every inch of her.

The sound of approaching footsteps had Gracelyn and him practically jumping away from each other. Not in time, though, for Duncan to miss what'd been going on. Duncan didn't question it, not verbally, but Ruston figured the look Duncan gave him was sort of a caution. *You're playing with fire.*

Ruston knew that was the truth. This heat between Gracelyn and him was strong and hot. It was also a distraction. One that could ultimately cause him to lose focus at a time when that could turn out to be a fatal mistake. Still, Ruston couldn't just flip a switch and put an end to the heat. He just needed to try to keep it in check until Gracelyn and the baby were no longer in danger.

Duncan handed Gracelyn the go bag. "Joelle says she'll stay with the baby as long as needed," he said while Gracelyn began to dig through the bag for the burner phone. "I'm hoping you'll let her do that."

Gracelyn looked up at him, and Duncan huffed. "I'm worried about her. She's a cop to the bone, but she's also pregnant. I'd rather her be with Abigail than facing down murder suspects."

Since Joelle was his sister, Ruston felt the same way. It was even more of a reason for them to find the killer and put a stop to the danger.

"With Allic on that surveillance footage, SAPD will bring her in for questioning," Ruston told Duncan. "If they can find her, that is."

"I'd like to question her, too," Duncan insisted. "And her boyfriend, Devin Blackburn."

That was exactly what Ruston had hoped he would say.

First, though, they had to locate Allie, and that started with the phone call.

"You'll probably want to record this in case Allie answers," Gracelyn said.

She waited until Ruston had hit the recording app on his phone before she used the burner to dial the only number in its contacts. Gracelyn then put it on speaker just as it rang.

And rang.

After what felt like an eternity, it went to voicemail, but there was no personal recorded greeting to invite the caller to leave a message. Just the beep.

"It's me," Gracelyn said. Ruston figured she purposely didn't leave her name in case someone other than Allie had access to the burner. "We need to talk. It's important."

She ended the call, slipped the burner into the pocket of her jeans and took out her other phone. "I'll leave a message on the private Facebook page, too," she added and did that as soon as she pulled up the app.

When Ruston heard the ringing, he at first thought it was Allie returning her sister's call, but it was his own phone.

"Noah," he relayed to Gracelyn and Duncan, and he took the call on speaker. Gracelyn stopped what she was doing and moved closer to listen.

"I just heard someone shot at Tony and Charla," Noah said right off the bat.

Ruston realized he should have added that to the text he'd sent to Noah earlier. "Yeah," he verified. "They're both okay. The sniper hasn't been found, but Tony and Charla are headed back to San Antonio."

"Glad to hear they weren't hurt. Does their departure have anything to do with the Texas Rangers being in Captain O'Malley's office?" Noah asked.

"It does." And this was yet something else he should

have told Noah about. "There was a fingerprint in our attackers' truck that belonged to former cop Terry Zimmer.
He was also connected to the baby farm. And Tony. They
were rookies together in Austin."

Noah said a few words of choice profanity. "Yeah, that
would get him in the captain's office." He paused a second.
"You really think Tony could be dirty?"

Ruston didn't want to think it, but there was no way he
could deny the possibility. "Either that or someone came by
a whole lot of information that shouldn't have been available to anyone but cops."

Noah made a sound of agreement. "Terry Zimmer," he
repeated. "I'm plugging his name into a search engine I put
together. It's sort of a cop's form of Google that taps into
data pools of arrest histories, police reports and witness
statements. I'll let that run while I tell you the main reason
I'm calling." He paused. "There's a problem with Marty's
computer files."

Now it was Ruston who cursed, and Gracelyn wasn't far
behind him on that particular reaction. "What happened?
Did they go missing?" Ruston asked.

"No, but they might as well have." There was plenty of
frustration in Noah's voice. "The techs say it was some kind
of complex computer virus that corrupted every file on the
laptop. They'll see if they can get anything from the corrupted data, but it doesn't look promising."

Hell. Of course, Marty would put some kind of mea-
sure like this in place. Except Ruston rethought that. "Any
chance the virus was added after the laptop was taken into
custody?"

"I asked the techs about that, and they say the virus
doesn't appear to have been uploaded remotely, that they
think it was already on the computer."

So, the killer likely hadn't done that. If he'd gotten access to Marty's laptop, he could have just destroyed it. Unless… "Any chance those files were backed up on a storage cloud?"

"Yes," Noah verified, "and those copies were corrupted, too." He stopped, muttered something that Ruston didn't catch. "Hold on a second," Noah added. Then he cursed again. "You said Tony knows Zimmer, but you didn't mention that Charla does, too."

Ruston saw the surprise register on Gracelyn's face and figured it was on his as well. "Because I had no idea. And she didn't say a word about it."

"Well, she knows him, all right. According to a report Charla filed last year, Zimmer was her confidential informant."

Ruston went still. "Give me the details on that, please." He wanted one bit of info in particular. "Was it connected to the baby farm?"

"I'll read it thoroughly but just scanning through for now," Noah let him know. "But, no, it doesn't appear to have anything to do with the baby farm. This report was filed about a month after the attack on you and Gracelyn. Charla was undercover to investigate some illegal weapons being moved through and stored in a warehouse. The weapons were found, and Charla noted that Zimmer had provided her with info for which he was paid."

So, that might be why Zimmer had been actually named. The payment would have required an invoice.

"Anything in that report about Charla investigating Zimmer before she used his info?" Ruston asked. Because if Charla had run a deep background check, she might have found a photo of him at the baby farm.

"Nothing that I can see," Noah answered. "But like I said, I'm skimming. I'll go through this line by line, and I'll keep running the search engines. If I find anything, I'll let you know. Oh, and you'll be getting a copy of the surveillance feed sometime today."

Ruston thanked him and ended the call just as another phone rang. The burner this time. Gracelyn yanked it from her pocket but didn't answer it on speaker until Ruston had the recording app going.

"I understand you want to talk to Allie," the man said.

"Who is this?" Gracelyn demanded.

"Devin Blackburn," he said without hesitation.

Ruston didn't like this one bit. Clearly, neither did Gracelyn. "Where's Allie? Why are you using her phone?"

Devin countered that with a question of his own. "Are you Gracelyn?"

Gracelyn hesitated but finally said, "Yes. Where's Allie?" she repeated.

Devin's sigh was loud and long. "That's what I was hoping you could tell me. I don't know where your sister is."

"But you have her phone," Gracelyn quickly pointed out.

"No, I have a phone that I found in her purse. It's not the one she usually uses. When I heard it ringing, I didn't get to it in time to answer it, but I listened to your voicemail. I figured from your tone that you're worried about her. Well, so am I. Do you have any idea where Allie is?"

The image of Allie on the security footage flashed into Ruston's head, and he was certain the same image was going through Gracelyn's.

"When is the last time you saw my sister?" Gracelyn pressed.

"Two days ago." Devin didn't hesitate, but then he sighed again. "I'm afraid Allie has gotten into serious trouble."

Some of the color drained from Gracelyn's face. "What do you mean?"

Devin wasn't so quick to answer this time. "We have to talk, and it should be in person. You can either come to me, or I can meet you somewhere."

Gracelyn paused, too. "Meet me at the Saddle Ridge Sheriff's Office."

Ruston expected Devin to balk about the location. He didn't. "Saddle Ridge Sheriff's Office," he confirmed. "I can be there in an hour. See you then."

"Wait," Gracelyn said before he could hang up. "What kind of trouble is Allie in?"

No sigh this time but rather a soft groan. "The kind that can get her killed. Let's see if we can prevent that from happening."

Chapter Eight

Gracelyn was fully aware this wasn't the safest thing to do. Meeting Devin meant leaving the ranch. Leaving Abigail. And Ruston and her going outside when there was a sniper still at large. But after talking it over with Ruston, they had decided it was a risk they had to take.

Because they needed to hear what Devin had to say.

And they didn't want to do the interview at the ranch. Better to have some distance between Abigail and him, even if that distance meant more of a risk to Ruston and her. A risk, though, that didn't compromise Abigail's safety.

That was why Ruston and she had arranged for plenty of protection, with Slater, Luca and Joelle all staying with the baby while the armed ranch hands patrolled the grounds. A sniper could still return to fire more shots, but any gunfire was more likely to be aimed at Ruston and her. That was why they were all keeping watch as Duncan drove them to the sheriff's office.

A drive that hopefully wouldn't turn out to be a huge mistake.

Gracelyn needed to know what was going on with Allie, and Devin might be able to give her answers. And if she was to believe what Devin had said, they were answers that might help save Allie's life. She wasn't close to her sister, wasn't even sure she could say she actually loved her, but Gracelyn certainly didn't want Allie hurt or dead.

What she wanted, though, was to talk to Allie. That was critical. And Gracelyn hadn't given up hope of that happening. It was the reason she'd brought the burner with her, and she'd also left a message for Allie on that private Facebook page. Since Allie didn't have the burner Gracelyn had given her—Devin did—maybe Allie would use her regular phone, see the Facebook message and get in touch with her.

Because Ruston and she were in the back seat of the cruiser, Gracelyn had turned to keep watch behind them. To make sure they weren't being followed. Ruston was watching the sides of the narrow road while Duncan focused on the driving and what was ahead. All of them were primed for an attack, and they stayed that way during the entire ten-minute drive, even though they didn't see another vehicle until they were in town.

Duncan parked, and they used the side door to enter the building to get to his office. Gracelyn had been here before, too, when Ruston's father was sheriff, and it appeared that Duncan had kept things exactly the same, down to the Texas landscape art on the walls.

His office front was all glass, so she had no trouble seeing into the large bullpen and reception area, where she immediately spotted two deputies. She was pretty sure they were Carmen Gonzales and Woodrow Leonard, and both were on the phone while Carmen was also using her computer. However, the moment she noticed Duncan, she ended the call and stood.

"Devin Blackburn's not here yet," she relayed to Duncan. "And we're still waiting on those two officers to come down and pick up the prisoner."

"What prisoner?" Ruston asked.

"A guy named Brent Litton," Duncan supplied. "Woodrow pulled him over for speeding, and when he ran the plates, it came up there was an outstanding warrant on him for a string of burglaries in Austin. Austin PD is supposed to come and get him sometime today." He looked at Gracelyn and must have seen the concern on her face. "This guy isn't the sniper. He's been behind bars since about ten last night."

Gracelyn wished he had been the sniper so they could have questioned him. Additionally, he would have no longer been a threat.

"I need you to sign some reports," Carmen continued, still speaking to Duncan.

The deputy picked up a folder and started toward him, but Duncan went to her in the bullpen. Again, Gracelyn thought he'd maybe done that to give Ruston and her a little privacy so she could settle her nerves. But there wasn't any time for that because Ruston's phone rang, and when he took it from his pocket, she saw Noah's name on the screen.

"Devin's not here yet," Ruston told Noah the moment he answered. Ruston had already filled Noah in on Devin's phone call, and Noah had to be just as anxious as they were to find out what the man had to say.

"I hope he hasn't had second thoughts," Noah muttered. "Up to now, he's been dodging my calls and requests to come in for an interview. And I don't have enough for a warrant. In fact, I don't have anything on him except his involvement with Allie."

Yes, and that was why they had to get more. Well, if there was more to get, that was. It was entirely possible that Devin had nothing to do with any of this.

"I'm about to email you the surveillance footage of Gracelyn's sister," Noah continued a moment later. "I wanted to take care of that because I think Tony's trying to have me taken off Marty's murder. He's pissed off, Ruston, and he knows we're friends."

"He also knows you're a good cop," Ruston snarled. "Is he purposely trying to compromise the investigation?"

"I hope not, but the possibility has occurred to me. I don't think he'll succeed in getting me removed," Noah added. "He's having to deal with both the Rangers and Internal Affairs. This is gossip, but word is there are some inconsistencies in his finances and that he'll be put on paid leave for a couple of days."

That definitely wouldn't make Tony happy, but Gracelyn was thankful this was being done. Because there were inconsistencies, and if they had anything to do with the murders and attacks, then that should come to light.

"What about Charla?" Gracelyn asked. "Is Internal Affairs looking at her, too?"

"Not that I know of, and she wasn't in the meeting with the captain and the Rangers." Noah paused. "Is Charla aware that the two of you know about her connection to Zimmer?"

"Not yet," Ruston answered. "I wanted to confront her with that myself to see her reaction, and then I'll pass the info along."

Normally, the passing along meant her boss would be the one who got that info, but since her boss was Tony, that would likely be elevated to the captain.

The front door opened, and a dark-haired man came in. Devin. She recognized him from his photos.

"Gotta go," Ruston told Noah. "Allie's boyfriend just showed up."

"Good. Let me know if he spills anything I can use," Noah added right before he ended the call.

Gracelyn's first impression of Devin was that he didn't look the sort to spill anything that wouldn't paint himself in a good light. But that left plenty of other areas where he might be helpful. First, though, she had to get past that initial feeling of disdain. This was a man who'd assaulted and stalked women. That made him slime in her book, but if she hadn't known his history, she might not have seen the sliminess.

He was dressed like a rock star in his designer jeans with rips in all the trendy places. He'd paired them with a black tee that she was betting he hadn't bought off the rack. Expensive boots and sunglasses completed the outfit.

Woodrow went to Devin, first checking his ID and then sending him through the metal detector. No alarms sounded, but then, Devin would have been a fool to come to a sheriff's office armed.

"Gracelyn?" Devin questioned once he'd cleared security. When she nodded, he thrust out his hand for her to shake. She did that while keeping her gaze pinned to him.

"We can use interview room one," Duncan said, and he introduced both himself and Ruston.

"We?" Devin challenged. "I thought it'd be just Gracelyn and me talking."

"Then you thought wrong," Duncan quickly replied.

Devin didn't scowl at that remark. In fact, the little twist of his mouth seemed to convey that he'd expected this to be an official interview with the cops.

"Detective Noah Ryland from SAPD has been trying to get in touch with you," Ruston said to Devin as they walked to the room.

"Really?" Devin said, and he checked his phone. "No messages from him. Oh," he added as if something had just occurred to him. "I have a new number. Guess he's probably been trying to reach me at the old one. Detective Ryland, you said?"

Ruston nodded. He, too, had a hard look in his eyes.

"All right, I'll call Ryland when I'm done here," Devin said once they were in the interview room. "I'm guessing he wants to talk to me about Allie," he added. "Has she done something else I don't know about?"

None of them answered, but Duncan launched right into reading Devin his rights. That finally erased some of Devin's cockiness.

"Am I under arrest?" Devin asked.

"No. Reading you your rights is for your protection, so that you know what's expected of you," Duncan explained. "And so you're aware you can have a lawyer. We can all wait here if you want to call one."

"That won't be necessary. I didn't do anything wrong," Devin insisted. "In fact, I'm trying to do what's right by coming here." He sat and looked at Gracelyn, who took the seat at the table across from him. Duncan sat next to her while Ruston opted to stand.

Gracelyn didn't waste any time getting the questions started. "On the phone, you said you were afraid my sister had gotten into serious trouble. Explain that."

Devin gathered his breath, and rearranged his expression by bunching up his forehead. "Allie's been using drugs again. Two days ago, I caught her trying to make a deal with one of her old dealers. She didn't even deny it. Didn't deny either that she'd taken money from my wallet to buy the drugs."

Gracelyn tried to ignore the initial emotional punch of that. It certainly wasn't the first time she'd heard someone say Allie was using. In fact, Allie had been arrested twice for drug possession when she'd been a juvenile. Her pattern was to stay clean for about a year, and then she'd have a relapse. Thankfully, she'd been in the clean stage when she was pregnant with Abigail.

"Allie and I had a big argument," Devin went on, "and I told her she had to leave. I've got a record." He added a dry laugh. "But I'm positive you already know that." He put his arms on the table and leaned in toward her. "I don't want to do anything that could land me in jail. Not only would that cause my folks to disown me, but it's not who I am now. New leaf and all that."

Gracelyn figured she failed at totally suppressing a scowl over the way he'd flippantly thrown in that last part. But she was betting he was indeed concerned about being disowned. From everything she'd read about his parents, they fit more of the mold of upstanding citizens.

"Where did Allie go after you argued?" Gracelyn asked.

"I have no idea." He paused, forehead bunching up again. "But she said if I didn't give her the money that she'd get it from you. She figured by now you were attached to the baby and that you'd be willing to pay for the privilege of keeping her."

Gracelyn felt sick to her stomach, and she wanted every word of that to be lies. But she couldn't be sure. When Allie was using, she would resort to anything to get her hands on drugs.

"So, you know about the baby," Ruston commented.

"Yeah, Allie told me about her." Devin stopped, and his eyes widened. "Wait. Is the kid okay? Is she safe?" The concern in his voice appeared to be genuine. *Appeared.*

"She's safe," Gracelyn settled on saying. "What did Allie tell you about the baby?"

"That I'm her father," Devin admitted without hesitation.

"Are you?" Gracelyn pressed, though she thought she already knew the answer. It was the eyes. Abigail's eyes were a genetic copy of Devin's.

Devin shrugged. "It's a good possibility that I am. I mean, the timing fits. Allie and I had been together for a while before she left. Another argument," he tacked on to that.

"Yes, I remember seeing the bruises and her black eye," Gracelyn remarked. She sounded as if she had ice in her blood, but it was all fiery anger.

Devin held up his hands. "She didn't get those from me. Scout's honor." He made a crossing gesture over his heart. "She got those from her dealer."

"She wasn't using when I saw her with the bruises," Gracelyn argued, and this time the anger coated her words.

"No," Devin agreed, "but she'd agreed to sell some product for him and had reneged on the deal. He came after her, and that's why she ran. She didn't think I'd be able to protect her."

Duncan slid a notepad and pen at Devin. "Write down the name of this dealer."

She thought maybe Devin would refuse. He didn't. He scribbled down a name and passed it back to Duncan.

Gracelyn's stomach dropped.

Because he'd written *Terry Zimmer*.

"What?" Devin said, obviously noticing her surprise. "You know that guy?"

Now she was the one who hesitated. "How well do you know him?" Gracelyn countered.

"Not well at all, and I want to keep it that way." He leaned back in his chair. "But Zimmer came round a few times before Allie left that first time. I swear, at first I thought the guy was a cop."

"You didn't check out his background or anything?" Ruston asked. "I mean, since you supposedly have better-than-average computer skills."

Devin's mouth tightened a little. Ruston had obviously managed to get under his skin. A small victory.

"Yeah, I did," Devin admitted. "Former cop turned drug dealer. Talk about a drastic turn in career paths. But other than meeting him a couple of times and checking him on the internet, I don't really know the guy."

"But you saw him with Allie two days ago," Gracelyn reminded him.

"I did, and that's why I wanted to talk to you. I'm worried she's with Zimmer, and if so, God knows what kind of trouble he can get her into."

Gracelyn was worried, too. Especially worried that the trouble involved murder.

"Did you ever hear Allie talk about a man named Marty Bennett?" Gracelyn asked.

"Marty," Devin repeated. "Sure. We both know Marty. Knew," he amended. "I heard he died."

"He was murdered," Ruston provided.

Devin shook his head in an "I'm not surprised" kind of way. "Marty had dealings with a lot of dangerous people."

"So, how did you know him?" Ruston added.

Devin didn't jump to answer this time. "I borrowed money from him twice." He glanced at Gracelyn's raised eyebrow. "I have a trust fund, but sometimes I run short. I paid Marty back every cent, and then some." He paused then. "You think Allie had some kind of run-in with Marty?"

"Did she?" Gracelyn pressed.

"I don't know. Maybe," Devin conceded. Then his eyes widened again. "You don't think she killed him, do you?"

That was the last thing Gracelyn wanted to think. But

she had to consider it. Especially if Allie was truly hooked up with Zimmer.

"Hell," Devin grumbled. "If Allie's gone that far off the rails, I wouldn't let her near the kid. Look, the kid may or may not be mine, but I don't want anything to happen to her, okay?"

"You're not interested in finding out if she actually is your child?" Duncan asked.

Devin shrugged. "If you want me to give you a sample of my DNA, you can check it. I personally don't need the results, but you might want them." He aimed that last part at Gracelyn. "I mean, just in case the kid asks about that sort of thing down the road."

"You don't want to know if she's your daughter?" Gracelyn managed to say, though her throat was very tight now.

"No," Devin insisted. "I'm not exactly the father type. And FYI, I told Allie that when she first suspected she might be pregnant. I told her if she had the kid, it was hers, not mine. I wanted no part of any of that."

Gracelyn hated the way he threw the word *kid* around. Then again, she hated Devin, so it stood to reason she despised anything that came out of his mouth.

"I'll get a DNA test kit," Duncan said, standing.

The surprise flashed through Devin's eyes, but he didn't go back on his offer to give them a sample. Good. This would expedite things. Since Devin had a record, they could go through the database and get his DNA, but this way, his sample could be sent directly to the lab. Then not only could they use the DNA for a paternity test, but they could see if it matched any of the evidence gathered from the multiple crime scenes. It was a long shot, but sometimes long shots paid off.

And that was why she went with another one while Duncan was getting the test.

"Last year your name came up in an investigation that dealt with a black-market baby operation," Gracelyn stated. "You were interviewed because—"

"Because I knew the wrong person," Devin interrupted. He huffed. "Freddy Dundee. I had no idea he was selling babies. And apparently he sold some kids to the so-called baby farm that the cops tried to bust." He stared at her. "You were a cop. Were you involved in the investigation?"

"No," she lied, and she watched his reaction to that. Another of the almost smiles. So, he knew she'd been involved, which meant he likely knew that Ruston had been as well.

"Probably for the best you weren't involved," Devin commented. "I mean, I heard it turned out bad for the cops."

"It turned out bad for the criminals, too," Ruston interjected. "The baby farm was shut down."

"Well, that's good," Devin muttered, and this time there was no reaction at all. Gracelyn wouldn't have wanted to play poker with this guy.

Gracelyn pushed some more. "I'm trying to work out a timeline for Allie and you. When did the two of you become involved?"

"Oh, I've known Allie for years. We met at a party... I'm not sure how long ago. But years, like I said."

"When did you start a romantic relationship with her?" Ruston asked.

Devin shrugged, glanced away. "I'm not sure," he repeated.

"Was it about a year ago?" Ruston pressed. "Longer, shorter?"

Now Devin's eyes hardened. No more poker face. "You're trying to pinpoint if I hooked up with her to get some insider info on the baby-farm investigation. I didn't. And it wasn't a romance. It was sex. Allie tried to make it out to be more than it was." He checked his watch. "Sorry, but I forgot I have another appointment back in San Antonio. Can we wrap this up?"

Gracelyn wanted to continue to push on the baby-farm connection, but Devin seemed right on the edge. She didn't want him walking out, especially before he'd done the DNA test.

"Have you ever had any dealings with Lieutenant Tony Franklin or Detective Charla Burke?" she asked. On the surface, it might seem as if she was changing the subject, but she was just shifting it a little.

Devin repeated the names as if trying to see if they sparked any recognition. He shook his head. "I don't think so, but again, you know I've been arrested." He stopped, smiled. "And I can't recall all the cops involved in every case."

She couldn't tell if he was lying, so she used her phone to pull up photos of both Charla and Tony. And she watched to see if there was any reaction.

Maybe.

There was just a slight tensing of his jaw before he shook his head again. "I don't know them. Why? Are they involved in this mess with Marty?"

Quite possibly. One of them, anyway. But it was equally possible that both Charla and Tony had had nothing to do with the attacks and murders. That could all be on the man sitting directly across from her.

Gracelyn wished there was something they could use to hold Devin while they continued to dig deeper into the investigation. There was his association with Marty. And

Allie. But there wasn't any proof that Duncan or SAPD could use for an arrest.

Not yet, anyway.

Duncan came back into the interview room with the test kit, and he handed it to Devin, instructing him on how to use it. Again, Devin hesitated, but he went through with the cheek swab. He handed it back to Duncan and then checked his watch.

"I need to leave for that other appointment," Devin said, standing. "Do any of you have any more questions for me before I go?"

Ruston, Duncan and Gracelyn volleyed glances at each other. It was Duncan who answered. "If we think of anything else, we'll let you know. You'll need to check in with Detective Ryland," he reminded Devin. And he gave Devin the detective's contact information.

"Right. I'll do that." Devin started for the door but then stopped and tipped his head to the test kit Duncan was still holding. "Do me a favor and keep the results of that to yourself," he insisted. "I really don't want to know one way or another if the kid is mine."

He walked out, and for several moments Duncan, Ruston and she sat in silence. No doubt mentally going over everything Devin had just told them. That was what Gracelyn was doing, anyway.

Duncan went to the door and shut it. "You believe him?"

"No," Gracelyn was quick to say. "My gut says he's lying about something. I just don't know what," she admitted.

Duncan made a sound of agreement. "If any part of what he said was true, it doesn't look good for your sister."

"It doesn't," she admitted. "And that's not exactly a surprise. Allie has a history of drug use, and she can be very impulsive. I still don't believe she's a killer, though, and Devin didn't give us any concrete proof that she is."

Duncan tapped the notepad with Zimmer's name on it. But then he shook his head. "That could be one of Devin's lies. There's no known evidence to indicate Zimmer is a dealer. No known evidence to indicate he's even connected to Allie. I've been digging through Zimmer's background, and nothing about Allie or drugs has come up."

That brought on another round of silence while they obviously thought that through. "So, why would Devin have lied about that?" Gracelyn muttered, and she already had her own theory forming in her head.

"Because Devin might have thought it would make us look at Zimmer and Allie and not him," Ruston threw out. "That way, we might not concentrate on Devin's admission that he knew not only Marty but Zimmer as well."

"And we might not concentrate on the fact that Devin is a known hacker," Duncan spelled out. "A hacker who could have maybe accessed any and all information that was used to murder three people and attack Ruston and you. Added to that, he was interviewed about the baby farm."

All of that was true, but it brought Gracelyn to one very important question. "Why would Devin have killed or hired someone to kill?"

Duncan shrugged. "That's what we need to find out. Maybe this is about money. He worked hard to make it seem as if he wasn't interested in Abigail, but she could be a money source for him. Kidnap her and sell her on the black market. That plan failed, so now he could be in the cover-up mode by implicating Allie." He paused. "But that doesn't explain the two murders of the hacker and retired cop."

Gracelyn could think of an explanation. A bad one.

"Devin could be Green Eagle. That would make everything fit."

"Yes," Ruston muttered, and he took out his phone. "I'm calling Noah. I'm hoping he can get Devin in right away and grill him about Marty. And about any possible connection to the baby farm. Noah might be able to get something out of Devin that we missed."

Ruston called Noah, but the detective didn't answer. As Ruston was leaving a voicemail, his phone dinged with an incoming call.

"It's Slater," he relayed.

Every muscle in Gracelyn's body tightened, and she prayed nothing had gone wrong at the ranch.

Ruston quickly finished the voicemail and took the call from his brother on speaker. "Did something happen?" Ruston immediately asked.

"No, everything is secure here," Slater replied just as quickly. "I just got a call, though, from one of the hands. No sign of the sniper, but he found spent shell casings beneath one of those big oak trees near the road. I'll call the CSIs to come out and collect them."

Gracelyn forced herself to unclench some of the tightness in her chest. She knew the exact area of trees that Slater was talking about, and the location probably hadn't been a coincidence. The sniper had likely chosen it so he could make a quick getaway.

"I'll have the CSIs check the ranch trails nearby," Slater went on. "It's possible the gunman parked on one of those and left some tracks."

True, but a former cop like Zimmer would have known that. Then again, Zimmer had left his prints in the truck, so maybe he wasn't careful. There was a third possibility, though, that Zimmer had been set up.

Maybe by Devin.

That could have been why Devin had been so quick to volunteer Zimmer's name to them.

Gracelyn heard a soft sound come from the small bag she'd brought to the station with her, and it took a couple of seconds for her mind to register what it was.

"It's the alert I set up for messages coming from the private Facebook page," she said, already hurrying to retrieve her phone.

And there it was.

What she'd been waiting for.

It's me, Allie. I don't have the phone you gave me. I must have left it somewhere. Give me your number so I can call you.

Since both Duncan and Ruston had moved closer, she showed them the message, and she fought the urge to fire off a quick response.

"It could be a hoax," she muttered. "Devin or someone else could have gotten access." Still, there was no way she could just ignore this. She typed in her number. And waited.

Gracelyn didn't have to wait long.

Within a couple of seconds, her phone rang, and she saw Unknown Caller on the screen. Holding her breath, she answered it.

"Gracelyn," the caller said, the single word rushing out with a long breath.

"It's Allie," Gracelyn whispered to Duncan and Ruston. The relief came, washing over her. Temporarily, anyway. And then came the worry.

"Allie, where are you?" Gracelyn asked. "Are you all right?"

"No. I'm not all right at all." A hoarse sob tore from her

sister's throat. "I'm here in Saddle Ridge, and I have to see you right now."

Gracelyn had so many questions, but she started with an obvious one. "Why are you in Saddle Ridge?"

"I'll tell you when I see you." Allie sobbed again. "When can we meet? I can come to wherever you are."

Gracelyn debated how to respond, and she went with the truth. "I'm at the sheriff's office." She thought that might get Allie to hang up. Or change her mind about meeting with her.

It didn't.

"Okay," Allie finally said. Her voice broke on that single word. "I'll be there in about thirty minutes. I need help, Gracelyn. I need a deal with the cops. I need immunity."

Gracelyn opened her mouth to ask why Allie would need those things, but her sister had already ended the call.

Chapter Nine

Ruston watched Gracelyn pace across the interview room, and he could practically see the nerves coming off her. He was in the same boat, but he was trying to tamp down the worst of his worries.

That this was some kind of ruse for gunmen to try to murder Gracelyn.

Yes, they were in a police station with at least four cops in the building, but if Allie was desperate—and she was a killer—then she might have come here to try to go after her sister.

Ruston had no intention of letting that happen.

Duncan was on the same page with that, because right after Allie had ended her call, he'd gone to his office to let the other deputies know that Allie would be coming in. Or rather she had said she'd be coming in. If she did arrive, she'd be treated like a dangerous suspect and would be thoroughly searched before she got anywhere near Gracelyn.

"Immunity," Gracelyn muttered.

Yeah, Ruston hadn't missed that part. Immunity probably meant Allie had committed a crime and had useful information that she hoped to trade so the cops could catch a bigger fish. But if this was about murder, immunity probably wasn't going to be an option.

And that meant they might have to arrest Allie on the spot.

That thought had no doubt already occurred to Gracelyn, and it had to be contributing to the nerves.

"Has Allie ever been to Saddle Ridge before today?" Ruston asked, hoping the conversation would help settle her before Allie showed up. That thirty-minute arrival was ticking down fast.

"Not that I know of," Gracelyn said, "but I'm sure she heard me mention you were from here."

Yeah, and that meant Allie had made the connection between Gracelyn and him when such a connection shouldn't have been obvious, since before yesterday, they hadn't seen each other in months. But it might have been obvious to Allie if she'd known they had been attacked and had had to flee with Abigail.

One way Allie could have known that was to be directly involved in the attack, but Ruston was hoping that hadn't happened. That instead she'd come by the information from someone else. Like Devin.

"Even though Devin claimed he doesn't know where Allie is," Ruston pointed out, "he could have been lying. He could have been with her when he arranged the meeting and told Allie he was coming here to see us."

Gracelyn nodded, and she seemed to latch on to that. But the hope didn't stay on her face long. Probably because she was well aware of her sister's checkered past. Also, there were those parts about needing immunity and cutting a deal.

There was a knock at the door, and Ruston steeled himself. But it wasn't Allie. It was Woodrow. "There's a cop here to see you. Detective Charla Burke."

Ruston groaned. They didn't need this now. "What does she want?"

"She wouldn't say. Only said it was important."

Ruston connected with Gracelyn's gaze, and even though she didn't look any happier about this intrusion than he was, she nodded. "Let's give her five minutes."

Ruston turned back to Woodrow. "Bring her back here."

That way, Charla wouldn't be in the front of the building when and if Allie came in. After seeing Allie on that surveillance footage, Charla would almost certainly recognize her, and he didn't want the cop trying to question, or intimidate, Gracelyn's sister.

"Duncan probably told you we're expecting another visitor," Ruston commented.

Woodrow nodded. "Allie Wallace. Duncan is keeping an eye out for her."

Good. That was just as they'd planned it since Duncan hadn't wanted Gracelyn in the front of the building either. The windows were bullet resistant, but if the sniper targeted her and used a powerful enough weapon, he might be able to get a shot through. The interview rooms were the only places in the sheriff's office without windows.

"If Allie comes in while Charla is still here, make sure the women's paths don't cross," Ruston spelled out.

"Will do," Woodrow assured him, and he walked away. It didn't take him long to return with Charla.

One look at her face, and Ruston knew she was riled to the bone.

"Make this quick," Ruston immediately told her.

"Quick," Charla snarled like profanity. "Because you're busy trying to ruin Tony's career."

"No." Ruston stretched that out a few syllables. "I'm trying to find out the truth as to why someone has been murdering people. And shooting at Gracelyn, me and you. I know you didn't forget about the sniper."

No way, but it was possible she knew the sniper wasn't an actual threat to her because he was working for her.

"What Internal Affairs is investigating has nothing to do with that," Charla snapped. "It's about some discrepancy in his finances."

"Which could in turn be linked to the attacks and murders," Gracelyn was quick to say. She huffed. "You're a cop, Charla. You know how this works. If there are funds that Tony can't account for, then that opens the door for an investigation into all aspects of his life. Internal Affairs might not find anything."

The anger, and worry, flashed across Charla's face again. "And if they do, it won't have anything to do with murders or attacks."

Yes, but the funds could still be illegal, and that in turn could indeed cost Tony his career.

"I think someone's setting him up," Charla muttered. She fired glances at both Gracelyn and him. "And it sure as hell better not be either of you."

"Or you," Ruston suggested.

Charla practically snapped to attention. "What does that mean?"

Since time was of the essence, Ruston went with a simple response. "Terry Zimmer."

For a couple of seconds, Charla just looked puzzled. Then she put on her cop's face. "What about him?"

"When we showed Tony and you Zimmer's picture, Tony owned up to knowing him," Ruston spelled out. "You didn't."

"Because I—" She stopped, groaned and pinched her eyes together for a second. "I didn't say anything because Zimmer was a confidential informant. And if I'd admitted that, you would have assumed the worst because of the photograph of Zimmer at the baby farm."

"I did assume the worst," Ruston confirmed. "I wouldn't have necessarily done that if you'd been up-front." That was possibly true. Either way, he would have kept Charla on the suspect lists, but she'd made herself look darn guilty by not owning up to knowing Zimmer.

"I swear, I didn't know Zimmer had any connection to the baby farm," Charla insisted.

"But he did," Ruston argued, "and he has a connection to you."

Charla huffed. "You can't possibly believe I was part of that. Why would I? I have no…" She stopped again. "Oh," she muttered. "This is because of my mother."

Bingo.

Charla laughed, but there was no humor in it. "I see. Because my mother sold babies, you believe I continued the family business. I didn't." She paused again. "The only thing I'm guilty of is not admitting I knew Zimmer."

Ruston decided to go out on a limb here. "And protecting Tony. How long have you known about those mystery funds in his accounts?"

Another bingo. Charla certainly didn't jump to deny it, and the look on her face confirmed she had indeed known. "Go ahead, report me to Internal Affairs. Better yet, I'll save you the trouble and do it myself."

Charla stormed out, and Ruston turned to Gracelyn. He didn't get a chance, though, to get her take on everything the woman had just said. That was because his phone dinged with a text.

"It's from Duncan," he said. "Allie just came in, and Duncan has her in his office."

Ruston didn't need to ask for her take on that. She was

both relieved and anxious, and she immediately headed out of the interview room. He was right behind her.

When they made it to the front of the building, Charla was thankfully nowhere in sight, which meant she likely hadn't seen Allie. Then again, Ruston might not have seen her either if he hadn't been specifically looking for her. Gracelyn's sister was in the corner of Duncan's office, standing away from the large window, and she was wearing a purple hoodie that covered not only her head but a good portion of her face as well. Her shoulders were hunched, her gaze aimed at the floor.

Duncan was standing by his desk, and the moment Gracelyn and Ruston were inside the office, he shut the door.

"She's been frisked," Duncan told them. "No weapons. And I've already Mirandized her."

If Allie had objected to the frisking and Miranda warning, she didn't voice it. However, when she lifted her head and Ruston got a better look at her face, he could see the agitation in her bloodshot eyes. He searched her face, looking for any resemblance between Gracelyn and her. Or her and the baby. But it just wasn't there.

"Gracelyn," Allie muttered, and the tears came. Probably not her first of the day. "You have to help me."

Gracelyn didn't respond, didn't move. She just stood there for several moments and studied her sister. Then, on a sigh, she went to Allie and hugged her. It didn't last long. Allie ended it and stepped away from her.

"Go ahead," Allie said, defensiveness in her voice now. "Ask me if I've been using. That's what you always do."

"Have you been?" Gracelyn obliged.

"No," Allie snarled. "I'm clean." She paused and groaned. "I haven't used anything today," she amended.

That was possibly true. Possibly. And it drilled home for

Ruston that Allie had to be beyond desperate to walk into a sheriff's office and admit that she'd recently used drugs. Something she could be arrested for if they found any illegals in her possession. Then again, she could be arrested for something a whole lot worse.

"You said you wanted immunity," Gracelyn reminded her. "Why? What did you do?"

Allie shook her head and folded her arms over her chest. "First, the immunity, and then I talk."

Gracelyn shook her head. "That's not the way immunity works. You tell us what you know, and then we talk about immunity or a deal."

Allie did more head shaking. "But how do I know you just won't arrest me?" She aimed the question at Duncan.

"You don't, but I could have arrested you the moment you stepped in here, and I didn't," Duncan spelled out. "That's because I want to hear what you have to say. Then I can decide how to help you."

Duncan had clearly sugarcoated that, but Ruston figured if Allie was a victim in all of this, if she had nothing to do with the murders, then Duncan would almost certainly follow through on that "help" if what Allie told them led them to the killer.

"I'll need to record what you say," Duncan added, holding up his phone. "That's for your protection," he said when Allie made a soft gasp. "The district attorney will need to hear your own words before she can work any kind of deal. I can't go to her and just give her a summary."

Not entirely true. Deals happened with summaries. But Duncan wanted anything Allie might say to be on the record. Of course, Allie could lie on the record as well.

"All right," Allie finally said, but she didn't launch into

the reason she was here. She sat there until Gracelyn gave her a prompt.

"The San Antonio police have been looking for you," Gracelyn said. She had likely gone with that rather than a direct question to ease Allie into this.

Allie nodded. "I know." She stopped again, and this time she pressed her fingers to her mouth. Both parts of her were trembling, and she looked on the verge of having a full meltdown. "It's because of Marty, isn't it? Because he's dead, and they want to ask me if I killed him. I didn't. I swear, I didn't."

Duncan went to a small fridge behind his desk and brought out a bottle of water for Allie. He also motioned for her to sit in one of the chairs. She drank some water but remained standing.

"You were spotted on a security camera near Marty's around the same time he was killed," Ruston said, figuring it was something Allie might already know.

She did.

"Devin called and told me. He said that's why the cops wanted to talk to me."

Ruston and Gracelyn exchanged glances, and he saw the question in her eyes. Had SAPD released that info about Allie being on the security feed? He shook his head, though that was something that likely would have happened soon if the cops hadn't been able to locate Allie.

So, how had Devin known?

It was something Ruston would have Noah ask Devin if and when the man came back in to be interviewed.

"Why were you at Marty's?" Gracelyn asked her sister.

"Well, it wasn't to kill him," Allie was quick to say. "That'd be like killing the golden goose." She glanced away.

"I was going to try to get a loan from Marty. I needed money so I could get back on my feet."

Interesting. "And you knew Marty loaned money because he'd done that for Devin?" Ruston wanted to know.

"Devin," Allie spit out. She said the man's name like profanity. "Yeah, Devin owes Marty lots and lots of money. Some kind of investment deal gone wrong," she added in a mutter.

"Really?" Gracelyn asked. "I was under the impression that Devin had paid off his debts to Marty."

"As if," Allie snarled. "And if Devin told you that, he's lying. Then again, he lies about a lot of stuff." The tears came again, and she sank down into one of the chairs. "He told me he loved me, and then he kicked me out."

Gracelyn sat, too, probably so she'd be eye level with Allie. "Why did he do that?"

Allie stayed quiet for so long that Ruston thought she might just clam up, but she finally answered. "He claimed it was because I used just a little to help take the edge off my nerves. He called me names, said I'd never be anything but a screwup, and he kicked me out. That's why I went to Marty."

Ruston didn't like having to rely on hearsay to try to figure out the big picture here, but it was possible that things had played out that way. If Devin did still owe Marty a lot of money and was trying to resolve that in some way, then he might not have wanted a loose cannon like Allie around.

"Tell me what happened when you went to Marty's," Gracelyn pressed.

Allie drank more water and then took several long breaths. "I saw him twice. First, two days ago, and he was fine then." She had fixed her gaze on her thumbnail now and was scraping away some flakes of bright pink polish.

"Then I went back last night to get the money, but Marty was dead when I got there." The water and breaths didn't help. Allie broke into a heavy sob. "He was dead, and there was so much blood. I'd never seen that much blood before."

Ruston got an instant flash of his father's murder. Of the blood. And he relived the shock of seeing that. The crushing pain in his chest that followed. But Ruston shoved that aside. Had to. He had to focus on what Allie was saying to finish creating that mental big picture.

"So, what did you do?" Gracelyn continued.

"I ran, of course," Allie was quick to say. "I got out of there as fast as I could because I thought the killer could still be there. He could have killed me if he thought I was a witness or something."

"He?" Gracelyn questioned. "You thought the killer was a man?"

Allie looked at her and then shook her head. "No. I mean, I didn't know. I just assumed it was a man who'd done something like that. I didn't want to hang around and end up like Marty."

"Or answer questions from the cops who responded to the scene," Duncan commented.

Allie's mouth went into a flat line, but at least she stopped crying. "Or that," she verified, her voice a snap now. "With my record, they would have thought I was responsible, and I'm not."

The cops would have indeed thought that, and Allie would have become their prime suspect with the means and opportunity to have done the kill. But Ruston wasn't sure of her motive.

"Where did you go when you ran from Marty's?" Gracelyn asked.

"To a hotel about six blocks away. I used cash so there wouldn't be a way to trace the room to me."

"Cash?" Gracelyn repeated. "You had cash for a hotel room, but you went to Marty for a loan?"

Allie huffed. "I needed more than what I had on me." She quickly waved that away as if she didn't want to dwell on that particular subject. "With Marty out of the picture, I decided to try to convince Devin to give me some money. I still had a key to his place, and I slipped in. I wanted to make sure he was in a good mood before I asked him for a loan."

Or she'd slipped in to steal from Devin. But since he didn't want to disrupt the flow of her explanation, Ruston kept that to himself for the moment.

"I heard Devin talking on the phone," Allie went on. "And I heard him say he was coming to Saddle Ridge, and he said all that stuff about me being in trouble." The anger increased with each word. "I knew then he was coming to see you, to whine about me using a little."

"And you followed him?" Gracelyn pressed.

Allie nodded. "I took a taxi, and trust me, that ate up a lot of what little cash I have left, but I didn't want Devin to come here and tell you a bunch of lies about me."

"Why would he do that?" Ruston asked.

"Because he's a selfish SOB, that's why," she was quick to say. "He never once asked about our baby."

Ruston checked the time. Allie had been here for going on ten minutes, and this was the first time she'd brought up Abigail. Added to that, she hadn't mentioned her in the phone call she'd made to Gracelyn.

"So, did Devin tell you lies about me?" Allie asked.

Gracelyn shifted closer to her sister, a signal that she was going to deal with this answer. "He said you were using again and that he kicked you out. He thought you'd hooked up with your former drug dealer."

Allie huffed again. "There was no hooking up. I used, yes, but it was from a small stash I'd left at Devin's last year. I guess he didn't find it, because it was still there."

"Terry Zimmer," Gracelyn threw out there, and she no doubt wanted to groan because she couldn't have missed the flicker of surprise in her sister's eyes.

"I don't know who that is," Allie insisted. It was a lie and not a very good one at that.

"I believe you do," Gracelyn said, somehow managing to keep her voice level. "We've already told you that immunity can't even be considered until you tell us the truth about everything."

"I did tell the truth," Allie howled.

"No, you didn't," Gracelyn argued. "You know Zimmer, and you have to tell me if he's connected to the reason you need immunity."

"I don't know him," Allie practically shouted, springing to her feet. "I don't…" She stopped and locked gazes with Gracelyn, who wasn't pulling a visible punch. She was staring at her sister the way she would a murder suspect.

"The truth," Gracelyn repeated. "That's the only chance you have of me helping you. Lie again, and you'll be arrested."

Allie flung gazes at all three of them, and for a moment, she looked like a trapped animal ready to fight her way out of there. Then a sob tore from her throat, and she sank back into the chair.

"I didn't kill Marty. That's the truth," Allie stated. "And Zimmer isn't my dealer. In fact, I'd never met him until two days ago, when I went to see Marty." She lowered her head, shook it. "You're going to be so upset when you hear this.

Really, really upset," she emphasized, "but I swear, at the time I thought it was the only option I had."

Hell. Ruston figured anything that came after this part of the explanation couldn't be good.

"What option?" Gracelyn insisted.

Allie sobbed again, and the tears returned, but thankfully that didn't silence her. "I thought Devin was going to take care of me, but when he didn't, I knew I was going to need some money. A lot of money so I could get away and have a fresh start. I'd heard Marty had connections, so two days ago I went to see him."

Gracelyn pulled in a sharp breath. "Why?" And there was a lot of emotion and strain in that one word.

Allie swallowed hard. "Because I had heard that he sometimes acted as a go-between for people looking to adopt. Good people," she tacked on to that. "I wouldn't want my baby going to just anyone."

Duncan and Ruston both cursed. Hell. She'd planned on selling Abigail.

Gracelyn stayed put in the chair, but her eyes had narrowed. "Say it," she demanded. Not yelling, but there was a dangerous edge to her voice.

"All right." Allie threw an indignant stare right back at her sister. "A couple wanted to adopt the baby, and they were willing to pay my expenses. You know, for carrying her for nine months."

"How much?" Gracelyn asked. That dangerous edge went up a notch.

"Ten thousand," Allie spit out as if she wasn't the least bit ashamed of it. "I knew you wouldn't just hand Abigail over, not without asking me a lot of questions, and I told Marty that. He said there was a way to get her. A fake kidnapping, but it wouldn't actually be a kidnapping because she's my daughter."

Ruston wasn't sure how Gracelyn managed to just sit there and not spew every word of profanity she knew. Maybe because this had shaken her to the core. Allie had been planning on selling that precious baby. And that was just the tip of the iceberg.

Gracelyn held up a hand, maybe to steady herself. Maybe to signal that she wanted to continue the questioning. "How did Marty know where the baby was?"

"I told him. Well, I guessed because I'd seen the file with places where you might be, and I'd taken a picture of it with my phone. You know, just in case I wasn't able to track you down."

So, that was how Marty had gotten the address. Ruston figured Gracelyn was mentally kicking herself for that. All those security precautions down the drain because of Allie.

"You said you saw Zimmer at Marty's," Gracelyn went on a moment later.

"Yes, but not last night, not when I found his body. Zimmer was there on my first visit. I got the impression he worked for Marty. Maybe like an assistant or something."

Ruston was going with the "or something" on this one, and it made him wonder if Zimmer had been around when he'd met with Marty. Maybe. Zimmer certainly hadn't been in the room with them, but it was possible Zimmer had seen him.

"So, how was the fake kidnapping supposed to work?" Duncan asked.

Allie lifted her shoulder. "I'm not sure. Marty said he'd take care of all of that. He just told me to come back when he had the baby and that he'd give me the money. But I didn't want to wait for him to call me. He'd said he'd have the baby last night, so I went to his place to wait."

"Did you know Marty intended for me to be kidnapped as well?" Gracelyn asked.

Allie dismissed that with an eye roll. "That was only so you wouldn't interfere with the men taking the baby. Marty would have let you go."

"Not a chance," Gracelyn muttered. She didn't mutter the rest, though. It came out loud and clear. "You set me up to either die or be sold. You set me up so that I had to fight to save Abigail, Ruston and myself. You did that." She jabbed her index finger at Allie.

Allie huffed once more and got to her feet again. "I did what I had to do to get my daughter. You can't just keep my baby. She's mine, not yours."

Gracelyn stood, too, and, oh, Ruston didn't like that her entire body seemed to make her sister pay. "Yes, biologically you're her mother, and you were planning on selling her. Hear this, Allie—I'll see you locked away for the rest of your miserable life before I let you anywhere near Abigail."

"You can't do that." Allie drew her hand back as if she might slap Gracelyn, but Duncan put a stop to that.

"Sit down and shut up," Duncan ordered Allie.

For a moment, Ruston thought Allie might launch herself at him, but she must have realized that assaulting a cop would only add to the mess she'd gotten herself into.

"I want that deal," Allie snarled. "I want immunity."

"Did you miss that 'shut up' part to my order?" Duncan growled. "Now, sit there and don't say another word until I'm ready for you to talk."

Duncan motioned for them to step out into the bullpen. "You're going to have to turn this over to SAPD, aren't you?" Gracelyn immediately asked him.

"Afraid so." Duncan didn't sound at all pleased about that either. "Every crime she committed, including the most serious ones, are in SAPD's jurisdiction."

Ruston knew that was true, and it was also true that Allie would need to go through this all again with the San Antonio cops. "I'll call Noah," he said. But before he could do that, Woodrow motioned to get his attention.

"You got a call on the station's landline," Woodrow said. "Actually, the caller wants to speak to both Gracelyn and you."

"Who is it?" Ruston asked.

"The guy says he's Terry Zimmer."

Hell. That caused the squad room to go quiet, and there was no need for Ruston to explain to Woodrow who the caller was. Or rather who he was claiming to be. Woodrow and Carmen both knew that was the name of their murder suspect.

"He used your rank, Ruston," Woodrow added. "He knows you're a cop. And he says there are some things you need to know."

Chapter Ten

Zimmer.

Of all the people who she thought might try to contact them, he wasn't one of them. Not unless he wanted to taunt them about the attack. But even if that was Zimmer's intentions, this was a call they had to take.

"Use the landline in the interview room," Duncan offered, glancing back at his office. "And I'll try to have the call traced."

Allie was still in the chair and had moved on to biting her nails instead of just scraping off polish. Just the sight of her made Gracelyn's stomach twist. She would never forgive Allie for trying to sell Abigail. But she'd have to deal with her sister later. For now, she wanted to hear what Zimmer had to say, so Ruston and she headed back to the interview room.

This particular landline had a recording function on it, and Ruston turned that on in the same moment that he answered the call on speaker.

"I'm listening," Ruston said in lieu of a greeting.

"How about Gracelyn?" the man fired back.

Gracelyn didn't think she'd ever heard that voice before. Not a Texas drawl but a quick clip pace that seemed to be void of any accent.

"Gracelyn will especially want to hear what I have to say," the caller insisted.

Ruston motioned for her to stay quiet. And she did. She couldn't think of a good reason to let a murder suspect know her location. It was possible, though, that Woodrow had already done that, but Gracelyn had no intention of confirming it.

"I'll pass along anything you tell me to Gracelyn," Ruston said. "Or you can just turn yourself in, and the three of us can have a face-to-face chat."

Zimmer didn't react to that. "I'm guessing she's there with you," he commented several moments later. "So, I'll just go ahead and direct this to her. And by the way, don't bother with the trace I'm sure you're doing. I'm using a burner."

Gracelyn figured that, but sometimes it was possible to trace the location of a burner. Of course, Zimmer would know that, so he could be either driving around or else planned on leaving the scene as soon as he was done with this call.

"I believe your sister was set up, Gracelyn," Zimmer went on to say. "And, yeah, I know what she tried to do. She wanted to sell her baby. But everything else is a setup."

That could be true. *Could be.* However, the attempt to sell her child and commissioning a double kidnapping wouldn't just end up a slap on the wrist. Allie would be going to jail.

"Did you set Allie up?" Ruston came out and asked.

"No." And there seemed to be genuine frustration in his voice. Zimmer didn't add anything to that, though.

"Then who did?" Ruston demanded.

"I'm not sure. That's the truth," he snapped when Ruston huffed. "At first, I thought it was Marty. I thought maybe he wanted a way out of paying Allie the ten grand he promised her. And maybe it was him and someone then pulled a double cross and put a bullet in his head."

Marty hadn't died from a gunshot to the head but rather to the chest. But Ruston didn't correct Zimmer. It was possible Zimmer already knew that and had doled out some false information so that Ruston and she wouldn't think he was guilty.

Gracelyn didn't buy it, not for a second, and judging from Ruston's expression, neither did he.

"Are you also going to tell me you didn't have any part in trying to kidnap Gracelyn and the baby?" Ruston asked.

Zimmer muttered something she didn't catch. "It's not what you think."

"Then tell me what the hell it was," Ruston snarled.

Gracelyn totally understood the surge of anger in Ruston's voice. The anger raced through her, too, at the thought of how close they had come to dying. And this scumbag was no doubt responsible.

"I've been investigating the baby farm," Zimmer said after a long pause. "Not officially, but I've still got enough cop in me that it doesn't sit well when someone buys and sells babies as if they were merchandise."

"You were working at the baby farm," Ruston pointed out.

"Yeah, so I could dig around and find out who was responsible. I wanted to bring him or her down. I wanted to put an end to it."

Ruston didn't appear ready to tamp down his anger or the sarcasm that went along with it. "You seem awfully dedicated to justice, considering you're a disgraced former cop. Or do you have an excuse for that, too? Maybe someone set you up?"

"No. I used excessive force, and I resigned." There was

some anger in his tone now, too. "And I'm dedicated to justice in this particular matter because when I was a baby, I was sold to a couple in a private adoption. A couple who shouldn't have been given a pet rock, much less a kid."

Ruston used his cell to open the site where records of former police officers could be accessed. He used his password to access it and then handed Gracelyn his phone so she could check and see if there was anything in Zimmer's background to indicate there was a shred of truth in what he was saying.

"Because I wanted to find the person running the baby farm, I managed to get hired as a security guard," Zimmer went on. "Just like Gracelyn and you did."

Oh, that reminder didn't help ease any of Ruston's anger. Nor hers. "Were you the one who tried to kill Gracelyn and me that night, just like you did when you attempted to kidnap the baby and her?"

"No." Zimmer paused and repeated that through what sounded to be clenched teeth. "I don't know who shot at you at the baby farm. And I didn't shoot at you during the kidnapping attempt either. Yes, I fired shots, but I purposely aimed away from you. That was to convince the thug who was with me that he and I were on the same side. If he'd thought I had my own reasons for being there, he would have killed me."

Ruston paused a moment, probably to try to wrap his mind around all of that and figure out if it was true. While he did that, Gracelyn showed him what she'd accessed on Zimmer. There were no accounts of any childhood abuse. No reported accounts, anyway, but Zimmer was a former elementary school counselor, and when he'd been on the force, he'd routinely volunteered to work with troubled kids who'd ended up in juvie.

Another thing stood out, though.

The excessive-force charge had involved a couple who had gotten off child-abuse charges because of a botched investigation. Zimmer had been the investigator.

All of that presented a package of a man who seemed to want to help kids and get them away from scumbag parents. But that didn't mean Zimmer hadn't crossed some very big lines and turned criminal.

"Give me the name of the thug who was with you when you attacked Gracelyn and me," Ruston ordered.

"He used the name Buddy Bradley," Zimmer answered without hesitation. "Marty said Buddy had worked for him for years. I'm guessing the CSIs found his blood in the truck and sent it to the lab. If you don't have confirmation already, you'll soon get it and learn his real name was Robert Radley and that he had a record a mile long."

"Was? Had?" Ruston questioned as Gracelyn started looking for any info on him.

"He's dead. And, no, I didn't kill him," Zimmer insisted. "You did. Or maybe it was Gracelyn. Whoever fired that shot at him through the door. The bullet must have nicked an artery or something, because by the time I got him in the backup vehicle we'd left on one of those ranch trails, he'd bled out."

Gracelyn held up his phone so he could see the quick run she'd just done on Robert Radley. The man was forty-two and did indeed have a long criminal history that included B and E, assault and drug charges. He'd been in and out of jail since he was sixteen.

"I'd never met Buddy before Marty paired us up to do the kidnapping," Zimmer went on. "But it took me about a half of a second to realize he was a dangerous hothead."

"And yet you went through with the job," Ruston reminded him.

Zimmer was quick to answer that, too. "If I hadn't, Marty would have just hired someone else. I figured if I was there, I could keep Buddy in check. Obviously, I failed at that."

"Yeah, you did," Ruston agreed. "Now, tell me why the hell Marty hired you and the hothead when he had already arranged for someone else to kidnap Gracelyn and the baby."

That was the big question, and Gracelyn automatically moved closer to the landline because she didn't want to miss a word of this.

"You," Zimmer said. "Marty hired you to do the kidnapping." He groaned. "I was at Marty's when he called you over. Marty asked that I stay out of sight in a little room he has off his office. He wanted me to listen to the conversation and make sure there were no red flags in anything you were saying. He wasn't sure he could trust you."

The muscles in Ruston's jaw turned to iron. "Did you recognize me?"

"I did," Zimmer admitted. "I'd gotten copies of the reports on the baby-farm attack, and I knew you were there. Gracelyn, too."

"Did your friend Charla get you those copies?" Ruston asked.

"No. I, uh, hired someone for that." Zimmer's voice lowered to a murmur. "A hacker. Simon Milbrath, and yeah, I know it looks bad that he was murdered, but I didn't kill him."

Gracelyn saw the mountain of skepticism in Ruston's expression. She was right there with him. So far, Zimmer had what was called the *categorical trinity*. Means, motive and opportunity. Zimmer could have killed both Marty and Simon to eliminate anyone who could have ratted him out.

And since Zimmer had already admitted to hiring a hacker, that same hacker could have been keeping tabs on anything connected to the baby-farm investigation. The call Archie made to Tony might have fallen into that category.

"You told Marty I was a cop," Ruston said.

"I told him I thought you were an informant for the cops," Zimmer corrected as if that were a good thing. "And I did that, hoping that Marty would pull you off the assignment."

"Why? Because you knew I'd kill you for coming after Gracelyn and the baby?" Ruston's voice was pure ice now.

"No. I did it because I could tell Marty was suspicious of you. Why else have me listen in on the conversation? Marty didn't fully trust you, and I figured it was safer for you to be pulled off the job rather than risk Marty having you killed."

"That's generous of you," Ruston countered. "And why was Marty suspicious of me? Because of something you told him?"

"I think Allie must have said something about you, like maybe you could have helped Gracelyn go into hiding. If Allie had mentioned you, Marty would have looked you up. Hell, Marty had hackers on his payroll, and he could have discovered you were a cop and set you up to die. Marty didn't come out and say that to me, but Buddy was awfully fast on the trigger."

Ruston and she locked gazes, no doubt so he could see what her take was on this. Gracelyn had to shake her head. Like Allie, Zimmer wasn't innocent. He was a criminal, but maybe he hadn't gone to her place with the intention of killing anyone.

"Did Marty break into my apartment?" Ruston asked Zimmer.

"I'm not sure. When I showed up to do the job, Buddy

had your wallet, and he said Marty had told him to leave it at Gracelyn's."

"And my badge?" Ruston added.

"I don't know about that," Zimmer answered. "If Marty or Buddy had it, they didn't share that info with me."

Again, Gracelyn had no idea if that was the truth. She was betting Ruston didn't either.

"Someone fired shots at an SAPD cruiser," Ruston said. "Was that you?"

Zimmer muttered some profanity. "It was," he verified and then paused. "After Marty was murdered, I got a call from a guy who said he was Marty's partner and that he had one last job for me. No, I don't have a name. He wouldn't say, but he told me he had photos and recordings of me with Marty from when I agreed to kidnap Gracelyn and the baby. He said he'd turn that over to the cops if I didn't do one last job."

"The job of trying to shoot the two police officers in that cruiser," Ruston snapped.

"No, the job of firing shots at the cruiser. The man told me to miss. I wouldn't have done it otherwise."

Ruston's gaze met hers. "Was Marty's partner your old friend Tony?" he asked Zimmer.

"No," the man repeated. "That wasn't him on the phone. I think I would have recognized his voice."

"Think?" Ruston challenged.

Zimmer stayed quiet for a while. "I don't believe it was him." Then he stopped and cursed. "Maybe it was. Anyway, I agreed to go through with it with one stipulation. That the so-called partner meet me in person afterward and hand over those photos and recordings. I had to figure the guy would keep copies and would continue trying to use them as leverage for future jobs, but I wanted that meeting to know who I was dealing with."

"And?" Ruston prompted when Zimmer fell silent.

"He didn't show for the meeting. And he hasn't contacted me since."

The partner could be Tony. Or Charla, for that matter, if she'd gotten a man to make that call for her. Devin could have done it as well.

"What is it you want me to do with what you've just told me?" Ruston continued a moment later.

"I want you to find out who killed Marty, Simon and the retired cop," Zimmer was quick to say. "And it wasn't Allie. Find out who it was, and I'll turn myself in. If I do that now, I'll end up dead. Find the killer," he insisted a split second before he ended the call.

Ruston ended the recording, and he immediately called Duncan. "Were you able to get a trace?" he asked.

"No," Gracelyn heard Duncan say.

And then she heard something else. Something that sent her stomach to her knees.

A woman screamed.

"Allie," Gracelyn said, her sister's name rushing out with her breath.

Ruston threw open the interview room door. In the same motion, he put away his phone and started running toward Duncan's office. Gracelyn was right behind him. They raced into the squad room.

And into chaos.

Allie was still in Duncan's office. Still screaming. Gracelyn soon saw why. There were two uniformed officers, and both had their weapons drawn. One of them, a beefy black-haired man, had Deputy Carmen Gonzales in a choke hold, and his Glock was pointed at her head. The other man, a lanky blond guy, was aiming at Allie.

He fired.

Just as Duncan tackled Allie and knocked her to the ground. The shot crashed through the office window, causing the glass to explode, but Gracelyn couldn't tell if the bullet had hit her sister. Or Duncan.

Ruston drew his gun. So did Gracelyn. Just as the lanky blond man turned his weapon toward them. Ruston dragged her to the floor as he fired.

There was the howl of some kind of alarm, loud and blaring, and Gracelyn saw Woodrow beneath his desk, where he'd taken cover. Either Duncan or he must have activated a security alert, and she hoped that brought officers responding to the scene. They might not get there in time.

Another shot came their way, blasting into the wall mere inches above their heads.

Mercy, what was happening? Gracelyn didn't have a full answer to that, but one thing was for certain. These weren't good cops. They might not even be cops at all, and they had probably used their uniforms and badges to gain access to the building.

And Allie, Ruston and she were their targets.

She cursed the call that'd just come from Zimmer. He'd phoned the landline, maybe to make sure they were there so he could send in these goons. If so, it'd been beyond gutsy to have hired guns come into a police station.

Gutsy and maybe extremely effective.

Ruston and she had a small amount of cover since there was a desk in front of them, but if the blond shooter came closer, he'd basically have them pinned down. That was probably why Ruston maneuvered himself in front of her.

Shielding her. And in doing so, he was putting himself in the direct line of fire.

Gracelyn didn't want Ruston sacrificing himself for her, but this wasn't the time for her to question what he was doing. And what he was doing was getting himself into a better position to fire if he got a clean shot. At the moment, he didn't have one since both gunmen were using Carmen as their shield.

"Stop them," Allie yelled. "They're going to kill all of us."

Her sister might be right. If these fake cops had come here to eliminate Ruston, Allie and her, then they weren't likely to leave Duncan, Carmen or Woodrow alive either.

"They've locked the front door," Ruston whispered to her.

That didn't help her tamp down the wild surge of adrenaline. It meant no responders would be coming in that way. But there were other doors to the sheriff's office, and she doubted they'd managed to lock them all.

Around the squad room, phones began to ring, the sounds blending with the loud, pulsing alarm. Responders were probably trying to find out what was going on, but no one answered any of the phones. Well, maybe Duncan did. Gracelyn couldn't see Allie or him.

"If you want to save some lives, step out and let's finish this," the bulky gunman growled.

Gracelyn didn't have any doubts about what he meant. He wanted Ruston, Allie and her to sacrifice themselves. And she might have considered it. Might. But she went back to her original idea. These gunmen had no intentions of letting any of them live.

"Keep watch behind us," Ruston muttered.

That slammed her with more adrenaline, but she turned so she was essentially back-to-back with him. And got the mother lode of flashbacks. To survive the attack at the baby farm, they'd had to do this. They'd had to sit there with the threat of being gunned down and dying.

Gracelyn shook her head, forcing back those images. Forcing back the gut-wrenching emotions that went along with them. She couldn't let those flashbacks play into what was happening now. She just couldn't. Because it could get a whole lot of people killed.

"Five seconds," the gunman warned them. "That's how long you've got before we start shooting the hell out of this place. We won't kill Deputy Gonzales right off, but we'll make her wish she was dead."

Gracelyn couldn't see Carmen's face, but she knew the woman had to be terrified as the gunman started the countdown.

"Five…"

Ruston inched closer to the side of the desk. From Duncan's office, Allie quit screaming, making Gracelyn wonder if she had been hit after all. Or maybe Duncan had just figured out a way to silence her.

"Four…"

Gracelyn kept watch of the hall and the sides of the room, and from the corner of her eye, she saw Woodrow move as well. Like Ruston, he was adjusting his position, preparing for an attack.

"Three… Time's running out," the gunman added as a threat.

Woodrow looked in their direction, and even though Gracelyn couldn't see Ruston's face, he nodded. Woodrow and he had made some kind of silent pact. Maybe to leave cover and try to get that clean shot.

Gracelyn decided to help with that.

"Two," the gunman barked out.

She took off one of her shoes, holding it for a split second in Ruston's line of sight so he'd know what she was doing. Then she hurled it over the desk and in the direction of Carmen and the gunmen.

All hell broke loose.

There were scuffling sounds, and shots rang out. So many shots. With the alarms and the blasts, she couldn't tell what direction the gunfire was coming from, but it seemed to be coming from everywhere at once.

And maybe it was.

She caught a glimpse of Duncan crouched down in the doorway. Ruston and Woodrow had left cover and were both firing. Gracelyn continued to keep watch behind them, but she scrambled around to the side of the desk and saw Carmen on the floor. The deputy didn't appear to have been shot, but she was crawling toward Gracelyn.

The blond gunman pivoted to shoot Carmen, but he didn't get the chance. Gracelyn fired, but she was pretty sure that Woodrow and Ruston did as well. Maybe even Duncan. Multiple shots hit the gunman in the chest, and he dropped like a stone, his weapon clattering to the floor.

The beefy gunman dropped, too, but he wasn't shot. He was coming after Carmen, no doubt to get back his human shield.

He failed.

There was another round of gunfire. Gracelyn couldn't get in on this one because Carmen was in front of her, but her shot wasn't necessary. Bullets slammed into the gunman, and he used his last breath to snarl out some profanity. Gracelyn figured he was dead before he even hit the floor.

Gracelyn continued to hold her breath. Continued to watch for another attacker. Someone, maybe Woodrow, shut off the alarm, but around the office, the phones continued to ring.

"Is anyone hurt?" Duncan called out.

"I'm okay," Carmen answered.

Gracelyn didn't answer. Couldn't. Because she couldn't unclamp her throat enough to speak. She just wanted to hear Ruston's voice. She needed to know he was okay.

"I'm fine." That came from Woodrow. "Are you hurt?"

"No," Duncan confirmed.

"I'm okay," Ruston finally said. "Gracelyn?"

"Okay," she finally managed. The relief came. Well, relief about Ruston and the others, anyway.

"Allie, were you hit?" Gracelyn called out.

Nothing.

No response.

Not for a couple of seconds, anyway, and then she heard Duncan curse. "Allie's not here."

Alarmed, Gracelyn stood, her gaze zooming to Duncan's office. Since the glass was now gone, she had no trouble seeing directly inside. And what she saw was the open side door that her sister had almost certainly used to escape.

Chapter Eleven

Ruston seriously doubted Gracelyn was actually sleeping, but since she wasn't saying anything, he stayed quiet as well.

And replayed every second of the nightmare that'd happened at the sheriff's office.

That'd been over twelve hours ago, and after the shots had ended, both Gracelyn and he had gotten caught up in the investigative whirlwind of trying to piece everything together. That had been both an exhausting and frustrating process that was merely on pause so everyone could get some rest.

In Gracelyn's and his case, they'd chosen for that "rest" to happen at the ranch so she could be with Abigail. Ruston had even managed to get Gracelyn to eat something before they'd gone to bed. Well, she had gone to bed, and he'd taken the chair again. She had offered to share the queen-size bed with him, and that'd been a damn tempting offer, but he didn't have a lot of willpower right now when it came to Gracelyn. What could start as a hug of comfort could turn into a whole lot more, and Gracelyn didn't need that right now.

Like him, she needed some rest so she could approach the investigation with a clear head.

Clearly, Duncan wasn't in the rest mode, because even though it was well past midnight, Ruston's phone lit up with a text from him. Ruston had put his cell on silent, even shutting off the vibration so that it wouldn't wake Gracelyn if she did indeed manage to fall asleep. But she must have seen the flash of light, because she sat up, her gaze racing across the room to him.

"Did they find Allie?" she whispered.

The only light was coming from the ajar bathroom door, but Ruston had no trouble seeing that she was not only wide-awake but that she was just as on edge as he was.

He shook his head. "Duncan got IDs on the two dead fake cops, though. And they were fake," he emphasized, trying to keep his voice as low as possible. Abigail was only an hour into what should be a three-or four-hour stretch of sleep for her, and he didn't want to disturb her.

Apparently, Gracelyn was concerned about disturbing Abigail, too, because she moved as if to get out of bed to come to him. Ruston fixed that by going to her. He sat on the edge of the bed so they could talk, but he hoped this would be a short conversation. He was still hanging on to the hope that Gracelyn might actually get some rest tonight.

She wasn't wearing the pajamas that Joelle had brought in for her but had opted for a loose pair of loaner jogging pants and a T-shirt. Her shoes were right next to the bed beside her freshly restocked go bag. All indications she was ready to get Abigail out of there if necessary.

Ruston was hoping like the devil it wouldn't be necessary.

"The dead men are Eddie Baker and Andre Culpepper," Ruston told her. "Both have criminal records. According to Carmen, when they showed up to escort a prisoner to Austin, she thought there was something suspicious about the paperwork they had. She was about to call Austin PD when one of them grabbed her."

That was a nutshell account of what'd happened. Of

course, the emotional couldn't be put in a nutshell. There'd been an attack at the sheriff's office, and now two men were dead. No wonder Duncan was still at work.

"What about the prisoner they were supposed to transport?" Gracelyn asked. "Was he in on it?"

"Duncan doesn't think so. Austin PD was actually sending down two officers to collect him, but they weren't coming for another two hours."

She stayed quiet for several seconds. "So, these two fake cops would have had access to Austin PD info," she concluded.

"Looks that way," he agreed.

"Zimmer," she muttered. "He could have set all of this up."

She'd get no argument from him about that. In fact, it was possible Zimmer had orchestrated this and everything else that'd happened. The man had sounded somewhat sincere when he'd told them about his quest to catch those involved in the baby farm, but that could have been all smoke. A ruse to confirm Gracelyn and he were at the sheriff's office so he could send in the thugs to attack.

"We were the targets," she said. "Me, you and Allie. They came there to kill us." Her voice broke and she squeezed her eyes shut as if trying to hold back tears.

Cursing and breaking his promise to himself that he wouldn't try to soothe her, Ruston pulled her into his arms. A hug probably wasn't going to do much, but it was all he had. There was no good news to give her. Heck, he couldn't even dispute that part about them being targets. In fact, it all made sense if Zimmer was trying to tie up some loose ends.

"I'm not going to let Allie or Zimmer get to Abigail," she whispered, her words brushing against his neck.

Ruston rethought that notion about a hug not doing much

good because Gracelyn sounded stronger than she had just seconds earlier. Of course, the baby could do that. Ruston would protect the little girl with his own life, and that included not letting Allie or Zimmer get anywhere near her.

"Allie doesn't even love her," Gracelyn went on. "She was going to sell her."

"I know," Ruston murmured. And he knew something else.

That Gracelyn did love the baby.

Heck, so did he. That added even more urgency to the need to keep Gracelyn and her safe.

"Has there been any sign of Allie?" she asked.

"No." And that had given him plenty to think about.

If Allie had told the truth about not having much money, she couldn't have gotten far. Not on her own, anyway. But it was possible Zimmer or another thug was waiting near the sheriff's office and scooped her up after she ran outside. If that hadn't happened, then whoever had hired those two fake cops would no doubt be looking for her.

If they found her, they'd kill her.

Ruston knew Gracelyn was well aware of that. Allie probably was, too, but so far, that hadn't caused Allie to seek out police protection, something she could get with one phone call to either Gracelyn, Duncan or him.

Gracelyn had left a message for Allie encouraging her to do just that. To accept that protection. But so far, there'd been no response from her sister.

She eased back from him, just far enough for her to make eye contact. "You moved in front of me," she said, and he must have looked confused, because she added, "During the shooting."

Oh, that. "Yeah," he admitted. "It has nothing to do with you being a woman. It was just instinct."

Since she wasn't exactly doling out any thanks, he geared up to add an apology to that. And let her know that his instincts would be the same if it happened again.

"You did that at the baby farm, too," she muttered.

Ruston couldn't recall that for certain. Those moments they'd been pinned down by gunfire were a blur. Then again, he'd worked hard to make sure they were. He didn't need images like that in his head.

She sighed. "What's going on here?" Gracelyn asked.

And he didn't think they were talking about gunfire any longer. Nope. There was just enough light for him to see the change in her eyes. Her breath hitched a little. He felt her muscles tense beneath his hands. A reminder that he was still holding her in his arms.

"I think what's going on is a complication," he admitted. "Something we'd like to postpone. But it doesn't seem to want to go away."

"No," she quietly agreed.

They sat there, face-to-face, body-to-body, and it seemed as if everything stopped. Only for a second or two. But in that brief span of time, Ruston managed to have an argument with himself as to why he should move away from her.

An argument he lost.

Gracelyn lost it, too, because she was the one who leaned in and pressed her mouth to his. And just that, just that brief touch of her lips, sent the heat soaring.

He tried to rein in that heat. That need. But it was a lost cause and not one he wanted to win. He wanted to kiss Gracelyn, so that was exactly what he did.

She moaned, the silky sound one of pleasure, and immediately notched up the intensity by deepening the kiss. The taste of her hit him hard again, spearing right through him and instantly making him want more.

He took more.

Ruston tightened his grip on her and brought her closer to him. Until her breasts were against his chest. Until there was no space or distance between them. And even that didn't seem close enough.

Of course, his body was insisting on getting closer to her. His body was urging him on and on. And Gracelyn certainly wasn't putting on the brakes either. So, maybe she was using this to shut out the nightmarish thoughts if even for a minute. Maybe this was a kind of comfort after all.

That notion stayed with him until she skimmed her hand down his back and then snuggled even closer to him, adjusting her position until she was in his lap. The kiss didn't stop. It continued to rage on. So did the touching, and Ruston got in on that. He slid his fingers over her breasts. And enjoyed the hell out of that little hitch that came from her throat.

This was how things had started the night after the baby-farm attack. The hug that had led to a kiss. The kiss that had led to, well, a hot and heavy make-out session that had landed them in bed. Since they were already in bed, they wouldn't have far to go.

But was Gracelyn ready for this?

Physically, yeah, she was. He could feel the unspoken invitation she was offering him. However, going just the physical route here could cause her to have lots of regrets. That was what had happened last time, and it had sent her running. Ruston didn't want that again.

And that was why he pulled back from her.

Not easily. It took every bit of willpower he could muster, and even then, he wasn't sure it was a battle he was going to win with himself. If she'd kissed him again, that would snap the leash on the heat, and they would just have to deal with things like regret later.

But she didn't kiss him.

She didn't move off his lap either, and he was well aware that the center of her body was pressing against his erection.

Gracelyn stared at him. "I want you to know that after the shooting at the baby farm, I didn't leave because of you. I left because of me, because I couldn't stay and deal with what was going on in my head."

"I understand," he assured her. And he did. "There were times after my father was killed when I considered leaving for a while, too."

"But you stayed because of your siblings," she finished for him.

He nodded. Joelle and Bree had taken the murder so hard. Heck, they all had, but they had found strength with each other. Gracelyn hadn't had that with Allie.

"Once this is over and the killer is caught, we should go on a date," she said.

Ruston laughed and then immediately cut off the sound when Abigail squirmed a little. He waited until he was sure she was back asleep before he responded.

"I'd like to go on a date with you," he told her and brushed his mouth over hers again. Not a hungry kiss exactly, but then again, with Gracelyn, hunger was always right beneath the surface.

She snapped it straight to the surface when she leaned in and kissed him again. The real deal kiss.

Nothing held back.

And considering they were both already hot and primed, Ruston knew exactly where this was going.

GRACELYN FIGURED THIS was a huge mistake, but she simply didn't care. She wanted Ruston. Needed him. And she didn't have the willpower to fight off that need any longer.

She just sank into the kiss and let Ruston and his incredible mouth perform some magic.

The magic happened, all right.

She felt the heat race through her, and Gracelyn just let it carry her away. It had been like this on that other night Ruston and she had been together. That one, too, had been fueled with spent adrenaline and need. So much need. And once again, Ruston managed to notch up the heat.

They were already face-to-face, body-to-body, center-to-center, and that made it easier for him to lower his mouth to her neck and light some fires there. He touched, too. Mercy, did he touch. There was an urgency, and a gentleness, in the way he slid his hand down her back.

Gracelyn nearly got lost in the fiery haze, nearly let Ruston carry her away. But she wanted to give as good as she was getting. She wanted to do her own tasting and touching, so she unhooked his shoulder holster, setting the weapon aside on the nightstand, and then rid him of his shirt.

And her version of touching and tasting began.

She lowered her head, kissed his chest, and she felt his muscles stir beneath her mouth. Gracelyn used her tongue. Heard the rumble of pleasure that came deep from within his throat. She kept kissing while she slid her hand to his stomach.

More muscles stirred. He made that sound again. And she just kept pushing, firing up the heat. Until Ruston could seemingly take no more. He pulled off her top and turned the tables on her by touching her breasts. It was an amazing sensation that became so much more when he rid her of her bra.

The urgency escalated. Of course it did. This level of heat couldn't last, and it demanded to be sated now. That was the word pounding through her head—*now*—when she reached for the zipper of his jeans. He stopped her, and Gracelyn muttered some profanity when he moved her off his lap and stood.

For a few horrible moments she thought he was stopping, but Ruston pulled off his boots before he fished through the pocket of his jeans and came out with his wallet. Then a condom.

Gracelyn wanted to curse some more because the heat and need had nearly made her forget the whole safe-sex thing. Thankfully, Ruston hadn't. Also, thankfully, he was prepared.

And naked.

That happened when he shucked off his jeans and boxers. A fully clothed Ruston could fire her up, but a naked one stole her breath. The man was drop-dead hot, and he was hers.

Well, hers for this moment, anyway.

And this moment was enough. Gracelyn wouldn't allow herself to think beyond it. She didn't want to deal with anything but this urgency that was building, building, building in every inch of her.

Ruston moved back toward the bed, anchoring his knee on the edge of the mattress while he leaned in and pulled off her sweatpants. And panties. He didn't lower on top of her, though. But he kissed her. A long, slow slide of his mouth that started at her neck and went lower. To her breasts.

Then lower. To her stomach.

Then lower still. And that was a kiss that had Gracelyn jolting. That had her nearly flying right over the edge of a climax. While she was certain that would be amazing, she didn't want to finish things like this.

She levered herself up, not easily, and took hold of Ruston to pull him down on top of her. She wanted his body on hers. And that was what she got. She wanted him to be as mindless and ready as she was, and she got that, too, when she wrapped her hand around his erection.

Judging from the profanity he grumbled, that was the best kind of torture for him, and it caused him to hurry to get the condom on.

They were face-to-face again when he pushed inside her. Face-to-face when the thrusts turned from gentle and testing to deep and demanding. Face-to-face when those thrusts made it impossible for her to hang on any longer.

Gracelyn let him finish her. She let Ruston take her to the only place she wanted to go.

With the climax rippling through her, they were face-to-face when she kissed him and took Ruston right along with her.

Chapter Twelve

Ruston lay next to Gracelyn while she slept. And she was indeed sleeping. He could tell from the now gentle, even rhythm of her breathing. Nothing like the urgent pace that'd happened when they were having sex. Then again, there were many things that took on that level of heat and need.

There weren't many things that could make him forget that a killer was after them. Temporarily forget, anyway. Now that the fire had been cooled for the moment, he remembered.

And he worried.

How the hell was he going to keep Abigail and Gracelyn safe?

For the moment they didn't have anyone trying to gun them down, but Ruston also knew they couldn't stay holed up like this. It was like being undercover. With a baby, no less. That had to stop.

But how?

He didn't even know who was trying to kill them, much less how to draw the person out in a way that didn't involve putting Gracelyn or Abigail in even more danger than they already were.

There was one bright thing in all of this. Gracelyn and he were fully on the same side now. They were together, and while he wasn't going to try to figure out what that meant for the future, Ruston knew they'd be working together to protect Abigail.

"I can practically hear you thinking," Gracelyn muttered.

Ruston silently cursed when he looked down and saw she was now wide-awake. He silently cursed again at the heat that instantly notched up inside him just by looking at her.

"I was hoping you'd get more than an hour's sleep," he said, and because he couldn't stop himself, he kissed her.

Gracelyn kissed him right back and made that amazing sound of pleasure that took the hunger up even more. And while his body was all for revving up, it wasn't a good idea.

"I don't have a second condom," he told her.

She winced a little, then smiled. A wistful kind of smile that had an edge to it. The kind of edgy vibe that lovers threw off when the heat was strong and wouldn't just go away.

Using a single finger, she slid a strand of hair off his forehead. That shouldn't have felt like foreplay. It did. Then again, at the moment her breathing felt like foreplay, too.

He kissed her, way too long, way too deep. Enough to fire them both up. He would have taken that heat to the center of her body for some very pleasurable kisses. But a flash of light stopped him.

It hadn't come from the window, so it wasn't headlights. It took him a second to realize it was the phone. It was on the floor mixed with their discarded clothes. And it grabbed his attention, all right. It grabbed Gracelyn's, too, because she tensed, clearly bracing for the worst.

He scrambled off the bed, located the phone and saw the name on the screen. "It's a text from Luca," he relayed to her.

Apparently, Luca wasn't getting any sleep tonight either.

Ruston read the message and quickly told her so she could release the breath she was holding.

"The search team found the dead man, Buddy, who Zimmer told us about," Ruston explained. "The body was just off one of the ranch trails. The medical examiner will get the body and give us a cause of death, but Luca says it appears the guy did bleed out. So, Zimmer hadn't lied about that."

But Ruston immediately rethought that.

"Zimmer could have been the one to kill him," Ruston amended. "I could have shot Buddy when he was at the front door of your house, but Zimmer could have finished him off. Zimmer might not have wanted to leave behind a loose end, especially one who's a hothead."

Obviously, that hadn't occurred to Gracelyn yet, but it would have soon enough. Zimmer could have told them only the details that would paint him in the best light possible. The bottom line, though, was Zimmer could be a cold-blooded killer.

"Duncan will look for any connection between Zimmer and the dead fake cops," Ruston assured her. Since it didn't feel right to be discussing this while he was naked, he began to dress. "But my guess is if there is one, it won't be obvious. Whoever set this up had to know it was risky."

She made a sound of agreement and must have felt the same way he did, because she got up and started dressing as well. "And yet he went through with the plan anyway." Gracelyn sighed. "That tells me the attacks aren't going to stop." She pulled on her top, and when she'd gotten her head through the neck opening, she looked him straight in the eyes. "You and I are the ultimate loose ends because the killer has to know we won't stop until he's caught."

Ruston couldn't argue with any of that, but he had a bad

feeling about where Gracelyn was going with this. Still, he sat there and heard her out.

"Before today, I thought Abigail was the target," she continued. She pulled on her panties and then the jogging pants. "But I think they wanted her only because they could sell her. They didn't come after her here at the ranch. Thank God," she added in a mutter. "They came after us instead. So, we're their priority."

Again, he couldn't argue. In fact, he could take this line of thought one step further. "You're thinking Abigail would be safer away from us."

She nodded, but he saw the dread that was causing. For all intents and purposes, Gracelyn had become Abigail's mother, and it would crush her to have to leave the baby. Still, it would crush her even more if Abigail was hurt because some thugs were coming after Ruston and her.

But there was even more to this.

More that had Ruston muttering some profanity.

"You're thinking of making ourselves bait," he spelled out. He cursed while he finished putting on his clothes and his shoulder holster.

"Bait with a plan," she said, and she continued talking despite his groan. "We could leave Abigail here with lots of protection. Lots," she emphasized. "I mean security that's so tight, there's no way anyone can get to her. Then you and I could draw out the killer. Because as you know, we'll never be safe until the killer is caught."

He did know that. But there was a part of this plan he didn't like, and that was a huge understatement.

"You could have that same airtight security," Ruston insisted. "You could be here with Abigail, and I could become the bait."

She stared at him and took hold of his shoulders. "They

want both of us, Ruston. If I'm here, they could come here. Or they just wait until something draws me out. I can't stay holed up in here forever, and they know that."

Ruston wanted to argue with her. Mercy, he did. Because he wanted to keep Gracelyn safe. He didn't want her anywhere near the line of fire again.

"We've done undercover together before," she added a moment later, "and this would be very similar."

"Yeah, and the last time we were undercover together, we nearly died," he reminded her.

"Because someone betrayed us or made us as cops. Maybe Zimmer. Maybe Charla or Tony. Heck, maybe it was Devin, since he seems to be connected to everything that's happening. But for this, we make the plan. This time, only people we trust will know what's going on."

That would be a given, but he still wasn't on board. "So, what? We set up somewhere and lure the killer to us? Because he won't be alone. And, heck, might not come at all. He could send more hired thugs like he did at the sheriff's office."

"He might be running out of hired thugs," she muttered. "But if he's not, then the plan should include capturing at least one of them and getting him to talk."

Ruston huffed because there were so many things that could go wrong with this plan, and Gracelyn no doubt saw the skepticism that was still all over his face.

"Let's map it out like an op," she went on. "Then we can identify any weak spots and fix them. Only then do we go in. Only then do we put this into motion."

"And what if the op is mapped out, and there are weak spots we can't eliminate?" he asked.

"Then we come up with another plan, one where we can make it as safe as possible."

Which wouldn't be very safe if they were literally putting themselves out there as bait. Unfortunately, he thought the bait would work. The killer seemed desperate to eliminate them. Still…

His phone lit up again, and this time, it was Slater's name on the screen. Yeah, no one other than Abigail was getting much sleep tonight. Slater hadn't sent a text but was calling instead.

Hell.

This couldn't be good, and he hoped the killer hadn't already launched an attack here at the ranch.

Since Ruston didn't want the sound of Slater's voice waking the baby, he didn't put the call on speaker. "Slater," he whispered. "What's wrong?"

"I just got a report that SAPD found another body," Slater said.

That caused everything inside him to clench. "Is it Allie?" he asked.

"No," Slater was quick to answer.

Even though he hadn't put the call on speaker, Gracelyn obviously heard that, and she made a sharp sound of relief.

"SAPD thinks this one is a suicide. Or at least it was set up to look that way, with a single gunshot wound to the head," Slater explained. "The dead guy is Zimmer."

Chapter Thirteen

Gracelyn sat in the family room at the McCullough ranch, holding Abigail and waiting while Duncan was talking on the phone to Noah about the latest updates in the investigation. She felt drained. Numb. But she knew those feelings would have been much worse had it been her sister's body that was found.

That was what she'd first thought when Slater had called hours earlier to tell them what had happened. Gracelyn had thought that Zimmer had gotten to Allie and had silenced her for good.

Instead, Zimmer was the one who was dead.

Gracelyn had read the preliminary report that Noah had done, and someone out walking their dog had spotted Zimmer slumped behind the wheel of his truck that was parked outside a long-stay motel. As Slater had said, he'd died from a gunshot wound to the head that appeared to be self-inflicted.

She wasn't buying that.

And apparently neither was Ruston, Joelle, Duncan, Slater or Noah. Like her, they were all convinced that Zimmer had been murdered. Probably by the same person who'd already murdered at least three other people and had hired those fake cops to come after Ruston and her.

"You should eat," Ruston said, tipping his head to the breakfast sandwich that was on the end table to her right. It was one of many sandwiches that Luca had dropped off from the diner.

Ruston leaned in and smiled at Abigail. "Hey, sweet girl." He brushed a kiss on her cheek.

Abigail turned her head toward him, something she'd only recently started doing, and she studied Ruston for a couple of seconds before her tiny mouth bowed into a smile. The baby's attention then shifted to his badge that he had pinned to his shirt. It was shiny, since it was new and had been delivered earlier, courtesy of Captain O'Malley. Gracelyn was glad the captain had made that kind of effort, because it showed she still had plenty of faith in Ruston as a cop.

"Want me to hold Abigail while you eat?" Ruston asked.

Gracelyn wasn't sure her stomach was settled enough to handle any food, but it was obvious Ruston was concerned about her. Added to that, she really did need to try to eat something, since she couldn't even remember when her last meal had been. So, she handed him the baby and picked up the sandwich. Just as Duncan finished his latest phone call.

"Time of death for Zimmer was about ten last night. The medical examiner agrees that it's not suicide," Duncan said right off. "The angle of the shot is off. Good, but off."

"Close range or from a distance?" Joelle asked. She was in the chair next to Duncan and was eating a bagel that had been slathered with cream cheese.

"Close range but not point-blank," Duncan supplied. "Noah believes Zimmer's killer was waiting for him, and when Zimmer parked in front of his motel room, the killer shot him. Not through the glass. Zimmer had apparently lowered his windows."

"Because he knew his killer and was going to talk to him or her?" Ruston wanted to know.

"Maybe. Noah said the AC wasn't working in Zimmer's truck, so both the driver's and passenger's windows were down. He was shot through the passenger's window. The killer could have simply walked up to him, fired and then placed the gun in Zimmer's hand to try to make it look as if he'd pulled the trigger."

Gracelyn took a moment, fixing that scenario in her mind. "Is the gun registered to Zimmer?"

Duncan shook his head. "It was reported stolen about a year ago, so no way to trace it. Zimmer had a slide holster in the back of his jeans, but there was no gun inside it."

"Which meant the killer likely took it," Ruston said, shaking his head. "Was the motel parking lot well lit? And please tell me there are security cameras nearby."

Duncan's sigh said it all. "No cameras, bad lighting, and in a neighborhood where it's rare for someone to come forward and report what they saw."

The killer would have known all of that. Added to that, it'd been night, and the darkness would have given him an advantage.

Duncan washed down a bite of his breakfast burrito with some coffee and shifted his attention to Gracelyn. "There's been no sign of your sister. Why don't you go ahead and leave her another message on the private Facebook page? Tell her I want to talk to her about that deal she was looking to make."

"I will," Gracelyn said, taking out her phone to do that. "But I doubt she'll believe that."

"Probably not, but we need to find her. And, yeah, there's a slim-to-none chance of a deal, but if she cooperates, the DA might show some leniency."

Gracelyn didn't say aloud that Allie didn't deserve leniency. Not after what she'd tried to do to Abigail, but that wasn't for her to decide. Right now, Allie just needed to turn herself in or she would likely end up dead like Zimmer.

She left the message for Allie just as Duncan's phone rang. "It's Hank, one of the ranch hands," he relayed.

Gracelyn couldn't hear what the hand said, but whatever it was caused Duncan to get to his feet and make a beeline toward the front window. "We have a visitor," Duncan explained. "It's Tony. He said he's here to make a confession."

"A confession?" Ruston and she repeated in unison.

Mercy. Gracelyn hadn't seen this coming. Then again, maybe this was just another ruse to get close to Ruston and her so he could kill them.

Duncan must have had the same concerns, because he glanced back at Joelle. "Why don't Slater and you go ahead and take the baby upstairs?"

Joelle nodded, immediately got up and took Abigail from Ruston. Gracelyn figured Duncan was about to tell her to go with them, but he didn't.

"Tony's still at the end of the road, and the hands can and will block him from coming closer. It's up to you whether or not you want to see him," Duncan explained, looking at both Ruston and her. He listened to something else Hank said. "Tony's alone and volunteered to be disarmed before he comes in the house."

Before Duncan had added that last part, Gracelyn had figured they would be having this conversation with Tony on the porch and Ruston and she would be tucked back in the foyer.

"We'll talk to him," Gracelyn agreed after she got a nod from Ruston. "I want to hear what he has to say."

They had a lot of information about the murders and attacks. Info from plenty of sources that might or might not be reliable. Zimmer, Allie, Charla and Devin. If Tony was truly here to confess, then all of those pieces of info might actually fit. They might be able to make an arrest and put a stop to any other murders or attacks.

"Frisk him thoroughly," Duncan told the ranch hand on the phone. "Hold on to any weapons he has and then drive him to the house in your truck. If this is some kind of last-ditch effort, Tony's vehicle could be rigged with explosives."

Gracelyn hadn't even considered that, a reminder that she really needed to try to keep a clear head. If Tony was desperate enough to make a confession, then he might want to first do as much damage as possible.

Since Ruston and Duncan were already at the front windows and had their weapons drawn, Gracelyn moved to the side one and took out her gun as well. The ranch hands were keeping an eye on the yard to make sure no one tried to sneak into the house, but she needed to do something to make sure they weren't attacked.

It was a good five minutes before Gracelyn saw the truck coming up the road, and she lost sight of it when it turned down the driveway toward the house. Both Duncan and Ruston stayed in place until the driver turned off the engine, and then they went to the door.

"Hang back until we have Tony inside," Duncan told her. "I've got to turn off the security system for just a couple of seconds. Once Tony is inside, I'll turn it back on."

Gracelyn muttered an agreement and continued to keep watch out the side window, especially since there'd be that short pause for the security. It wasn't long before the footsteps on the porch had her turning in that direction. Tony stepped in, and while he frowned at Duncan and Ruston basically holding him at gunpoint, he didn't protest.

"I won't take much of your time," Tony insisted, spearing Ruston with his gaze before he did the same to her.

Duncan maneuvered Tony into the foyer so he could shut the door, and Gracelyn saw him rearm the security system. Only then did Gracelyn give Tony her full attention. He looked disheveled, with his clothes wrinkled and stubble that was well past the fashionable stage. Like the rest of them, Tony didn't appear to have gotten much sleep.

"I'm resigning from SAPD today," Tony stated. He'd somehow managed to keep the emotion out of his flat tone, but the emotion was there in his eyes. A mix of anger and frustration. And guilt.

"You said you were here to make a confession," Ruston pressed. No flat tone for him. There was a "get on with this" edge to his voice.

Tony nodded. "Internal Affairs is examining my financials, and it won't take them long to discover that I accepted money from Marty. Payment in exchange for redirecting investigations so they didn't lead to him."

Ruston uttered a single raw word of profanity. "You sold out Gracelyn and me at the baby farm?"

"No," Tony was quick to say. "Hell, no. Nothing like that." He groaned and shook his head. "I was broke and behind in my child support. My ex was going to report me, and I would have maybe ended up losing my job, so I borrowed money from Marty. I know it was stupid," he quickly added, "but I was desperate."

"Desperate enough to sell out your badge," Ruston snapped, taking the words right out of Gracelyn's mouth.

Tony sighed. "Yes, but I didn't see it as selling out. I thought, stupidly thought," he amended, "that I could get my ex off my back and find another way to pay Marty what I owed him." He paused. "But Marty didn't want payback in the form of money. He wanted a cop in his pocket. He got one, but I never compromised the safety of any officers. Like I said, I only redirected investigations away from Marty."

The anger and disgust rolled through her, and Gracelyn had to tamp some of that down before she could speak. "Did you tell Internal Affairs this?"

"No, but I will. I wanted to tell Ruston and you first, and then I'll talk to Charla. Then I'll turn myself in."

"Charla doesn't know what you've done?" Gracelyn asked.

"No, and she'll be crushed," Tony concluded.

Maybe. But if Charla was the killer, then she might be pleased about this development, because in a way, it took some of the focus off the person behind the attacks and murders.

Tony pulled in a long breath. "I didn't directly do anything to put the two of you in danger, but by protecting Marty, the danger happened anyway."

Yes, it had. And Internal Affairs would no doubt question him about that once he told them what he'd done.

If he told them, that was.

It occurred to her that Tony might be planning to go on the run. But if so, why come here first? Was this actually some kind of ploy to distract them? That thought flashed in her head just as Duncan's phone rang.

"It's Hank," Duncan muttered, keeping his gaze on Tony while he took the call. Gracelyn couldn't hear what the hand said, but whatever it was prompted Duncan to mutter his own word of profanity, and he shook his head. "No, search them and bring them up. I'll call for every available deputy to respond." And Duncan proceeded to contact Dispatch.

Gracelyn's stomach dropped. "Are we about to be attacked?" she asked Duncan the second he finished the call.

"I don't think so. Hank said that Devin just arrived," Duncan explained. "And he has Allie with him. Devin wants me to arrest her."

"Allie," Gracelyn murmured, and she looked at Ruston to get his take on this.

He was apparently on the same wavelength, because she could see the uneasiness in his eyes. Then again, that feeling had already been there for both of them with Tony's arrival. Now it was skyrocketing.

It could be a coincidence that two of their suspects, Tony and Devin, were there at the same time, but Gracelyn didn't like coincidences. Maybe Tony and Devin were working together. This could be the start of another attack.

Part of her was relieved her sister was alive. But there was no relief whatsoever in the fact that Devin was the one bringing her in. Well, supposedly he was, anyway. Gracelyn didn't trust Devin any more than she did Tony or her sister.

Or Charla.

Since Charla was the only one of their suspects who hadn't shown up, that made Gracelyn wonder where she was. Was she standing back, watching this all play out after she'd set it in motion?

Perhaps.

Or Devin could be the one playing games here. But if he was the one responsible for the murders and attacks, then why hadn't he just killed Allie? That didn't help settle Gracelyn's worries about Devin, since this could be a sort of reverse psychology. A way to try to make himself look innocent by keeping one loose end alive.

"I don't want Allie in the house," Ruston insisted. "She might try to go after Abigail."

Gracelyn was in complete agreement, and apparently so was Duncan since he didn't protest that. "Hank, let me speak to Devin," Duncan told the ranch hand. "I'm putting the call on speaker."

The downside to that was Tony was standing right there and would be able to hear everything, but that was better than the alternative of bringing Devin and Allie to the house. Or sending Tony on his way. If Tony had hooked up with Devin to do another attack, Gracelyn thought it would be best if they weren't together. Then again, it was possible Devin was counting on Tony to be his inside man in whatever might be about to happen. That was why Gracelyn kept her attention pinned to Tony.

"Don't," she warned Tony when he reached for something in his pocket.

Tony huffed, clearly annoyed at her warning. "I just want to call SAPD and get you some help out here."

"No calls," Duncan ordered, muting his phone so that Devin wouldn't be able to hear any of this. "Just stand there and don't say anything."

Tony's eyes narrowed, but he held up his hands as if in mock surrender. Oh, yes. Gracelyn was definitely going to watch him.

Duncan's phone began to ding with a series of texts, and Gracelyn caught glimpses of his screen. Carmen, Luca and Woodrow were on their way.

"Sheriff Holder," Devin said the moment he was on the phone. "I've got Allie with me."

"So I heard. How did you know I was here?" Duncan asked.

Devin seemed to hesitate as if he hadn't expected the question. "Allie told me about the shooting at the sheriff's office, and I figured the place was a giant crime scene right now."

It was, and since the CSIs were working the scene, the

building was temporarily closed, and Duncan and the other deputies were working from home.

"I guessed you'd come back here with Gracelyn," Devin tacked on to his explanation.

"And you decided to bring Allie with you." The remark was heavy with skepticism.

"He brought me here against my will," Allie shouted. "He tied my hands and kidnapped me."

"I found her trying to sneak into my house," Devin countered. "I'd changed the locks, and she'd broken a window. When I confronted her, she tried to punch me. Then bite me. Then scratch me." He sounded riled about that. "I brought her here so you can arrest her."

"SAPD could have done that much faster," Duncan was quick to point out.

More silence from Devin. But not from Allie. She continued to curse and yell, and Gracelyn hoped she didn't break out of whatever restraints were on her.

"I thought you'd want to handle the arrest," Devin finally said. "SAPD might not turn her over to you to answer for what she did, and I know Gracelyn especially will want her sister punished."

"Abigail is mine." That came as another shout from Allie. "I can do with her what I want."

The words hit Gracelyn like a heavyweight's fists. Allie could be just ranting out of rage, but that sounded very much like the threat that it was. If Allie got her hands on Abigail, there was no telling what she'd do to the child.

Duncan sighed and scrubbed his hand over his face, and he checked the text messages that were lighting up his phone. "Stay put at the end of the road. Deputies Vanetti and Leonard will be there in just a few minutes. They can take custody of Allie and transport her to the county jail."

That brought out even louder shouts and cursing from Allie. "Gracelyn?" her sister called out. "I know you're there. Help me. Help your sister. Please," Allie begged. "Stop the deputies from taking me."

Gracelyn nearly spoke, not to give Allie any assurance she would stop the deputies, though. But to tell Allie that she would arrange for a lawyer to represent her.

"Gracelyn," Allie went on, and this time she spoke her name as if coated with venom. "So much for sisterly love, huh? You won't even help me. Well, to hell with you, Gracelyn. I wish the gunmen would have killed you. I wish you were dead." She was shrieking by the time she got out those last words.

Gracelyn wanted to be immune to them. But she wasn't. The words and her sister's hatred sliced her to the bone.

"Hell, Allie managed to get out of the car," Devin snarled.

Through the phone, Gracelyn heard Devin shouting her sister's name just as there was the squeal of brakes.

And the deadly-sounding thud that followed.

Chapter Fourteen

Ruston finished his latest phone call, this one an update from Slater. A call he purposely hadn't put on speaker since Gracelyn was talking with one of the ER nurses, Eileen Parsons, and he hadn't wanted Eileen to hear anything that might then end up as gossip. Added to that, if Slater had doled out some bad news, Ruston had wanted the chance to soften that news before passing it along to Gracelyn.

Gracelyn didn't look on the verge of falling apart, but he didn't want to add anything else to this already bad situation. Allie was now out of nearly seven hours of surgery, but she was critical. The surgeon had already told Gracelyn and him that Allie's chances of survival weren't good.

Ruston hadn't actually seen Allie since she'd bolted into the road and been hit by a rancher who just happened to be driving by at the time. But he'd heard the sound of the impact. He'd heard the urgency in Hank's voice, too, when he'd shouted for Devin to call an ambulance.

And Ruston had seen the blood on the road.

Gracelyn had seen it as well. No way to avoid it since Duncan, Ruston and she had left the ranch in a cruiser to come to the hospital, and they'd had to drive right past the spot where Allie had been hit.

Ruston had dreaded that drive for a lot of reasons, but

it hadn't been optional. Not after the hospital had called Gracelyn to ask her to come in and donate the rare AB negative blood that Allie and she shared. Gracelyn had done that, and now, ten hours later, they were waiting to see if it would save her sister's life.

Even though Allie's last words to Gracelyn had been to wish her dead, Gracelyn clearly didn't feel the same way about Allie. No way was she pleased with pretty much anything Allie had done, but Ruston understood her need to be here. Her need to do whatever she could to keep Allie alive.

Later, if Allie made it, she'd have to answer for the horrible crimes she'd committed. But *later* would have to wait.

Eileen looked over at him when Ruston put his phone away and made his way back toward Gracelyn and her. Not that he had gone far. For one thing, he wouldn't have let Gracelyn out of his sight, and for another, this particular waiting room was small, not much larger than a normal-sized kitchen.

Not many places to have a private conversation.

It was at the other end of the hospital from the much larger ER waiting room, which not only had way too many windows for Ruston's liking but also multiple points of entry. That was why Duncan and he had insisted on using this area, which had been set up for families to wait for surgical patients. No windows. Only one way in and out, and Duncan was guarding that.

Literally.

Duncan was pacing up and down the hall in front of the open archway entrance while he was on the phone, dealing with all the various moving parts of multiple investigations. That included making sure the hospital itself was secure. Duncan had brought in reserve deputies for that as well, but there was always the concern that someone could slip in.

Or had already slipped in.

There had been well over a two-hour gap between the time that Gracelyn had gotten the call to ask if she'd donate blood and their arrival here at the hospital. There'd been no reserve deputies on the doors during that gap, so someone could have gotten in then.

"Any news about Allie?" Ruston asked Eileen.

The nurse had come in just as Ruston had gotten the call from Slater, so he hadn't heard anything of what she'd come to tell Gracelyn. But Ruston figured Eileen wasn't there to deliver the news that Allie was dead. That would almost certainly come from a doctor.

Eileen nodded. "They had to take her back into surgery to try to stop some internal bleeding. We're not sure how long the procedure will take." She sighed, checked her watch. "You guys have been here a long time, and I just wanted to check on the two of you and see if you needed anything."

Yeah, he needed a safe place for Gracelyn. Safer than here, anyway. But that wasn't something Eileen could fix.

Ruston looked at Gracelyn to see if she intended to take Eileen up on her offer, but she shook her head. "We're fine for now, but thanks," Ruston told the nurse, and he went to Gracelyn to pull her into his arms.

"What did Slater tell you?" she immediately asked. "Is Abigail all right?"

"She's fine. All the security measures are still in place."

All was a lot. Joelle, Slater and Luca were inside the locked-down ranch house with Abigail, and Slater had brought in his ranch hands to patrol the grounds with the other hands already keeping watch. A reserve deputy was at the end of the road to stop anyone from driving up to the house.

That included Tony or Devin. Ruston hadn't wanted them

hanging around, so he'd sent them both on their way, though Devin would have to come in and give a statement about why he'd brought Allie to the ranch in the first place. But that would have to wait.

Part of Ruston had wanted to haul Devin in if only so he could keep him under a careful watch for a while, but the deputies and Duncan were already stretched thin. Added to that, the sheriff's office was still shut down, and with Duncan on guard duty, it would have meant bringing Devin to the hospital. Since that wouldn't have pleased anyone, Duncan had sent Devin home.

Hopefully that wouldn't turn out to be a fatal mistake.

"Slater said no one has gotten onto the ranch," Ruston emphasized before he told her the rest. "But one of the hands did see a vehicle driving slowly on the road that leads to the turnoff to the ranch. He didn't recognize the car, so he got the license plate and phoned Slater. When Slater ran it, he learned the vehicle belongs to Charla."

Gracelyn huffed. "What was she doing there?"

"I'm not sure. And it might not have been her behind the wheel. The hand thought the driver was a man."

"A hired gun?" But she immediately dismissed that with a head shake. "No, Charla wouldn't have let a hired gun use her car."

"Probably not," he agreed. "If she's not behind the attacks, someone could have stolen her car to make it look as if she was in the area."

He thought of another possibility, though. That Charla had hoped this mystery driver would be mistaken for her and therefore give her some kind of alibi.

"Slater did try to call her," Ruston added, "but it went straight to voicemail, so he left a message for Charla to contact either him or me."

Whether or not Charla would call back was anyone's guess. Ditto for her revealing what she was actually doing there. She could have been setting up another attack. Or she could have simply been looking for Tony. Ruston had no idea where he was. Then again, he could say that about all of their suspects except for Allie.

"You're thinking how vulnerable we are here at the hospital," Gracelyn muttered, and when he pulled himself out of his own thoughts, he realized she was staring up at him.

Ruston nodded. "Vulnerable here and anywhere else we happen to go," he admitted.

Gracelyn matched his nod. "Once Allie's out of surgery and we're back at the ranch, we should talk about that plan for us as bait. And, no, I don't like it any more than you do," she was quick to add. "But the truth is, we're no closer to catching this killer than we were two days ago. You and I are what he or she wants. We're what could cause the killer to slip up and get caught."

Every word of that was true, but it didn't minimize the risks they'd be taking. That was why he tried again to offer her a plan B. "I can be the bait, and you can be part of the security setup. You can be the one to help pen in the killer."

Ruston could tell from the look in her eyes that she was going to argue with that. She didn't want to be tucked away somewhere while he was basically dealing with a serial killer. But she didn't get a chance to voice that because of the sound of footsteps.

Both Gracelyn and he put their hands over their guns, proof of just how on edge they were, but it was Duncan who stepped into the doorway.

"Anything on Allie?" he immediately asked.

"She's back in surgery," Gracelyn answered. "Internal bleeding. It doesn't sound good."

Duncan muttered an "I'm sorry" and then paused. "The medical examiner found something on Zimmer's body."

That got their attention, and they pinned their gazes on Duncan.

"Zimmer had homemade tats between his toes," Duncan explained. "Recent ones. It appears to be a username and password. For what, we don't know, but I just got off the phone with the tech guys who are going to try to find out what they could mean."

Ruston thought back through all the things Zimmer had told Gracelyn and him in that phone conversation. "If Zimmer wasn't lying about investigating the baby farm, this could be his notes or something. Heck, it could give us the name of the killer."

"Yeah," Duncan muttered, not sounding overly hopeful, yet there was some hope there. Maybe because they didn't have any other leads.

"Did Slater tell you about Charla's vehicle being spotted near the ranch?" Ruston asked him.

"He did," Duncan verified. "Any chance your pal Noah Ryland can locate her and ask her about that?"

"I'll check," Ruston said, taking out his phone. "While I'm at it, I'll see if he can get any feed from security cameras near Devin's. It'd be interesting to see if his story about Allie trying to break in meshes with what shows up on the cameras."

Ruston started the text but then glanced up when the lights flickered. He frowned because there wasn't a storm to cause any interference. Frowned, too, because any and everything that wasn't normal was suspicious.

His suspicions skyrocketed.

The lights went out, and the room was plunged into total darkness.

GRACELYN HEARD HERSELF GASP, and she thought maybe her heart had skipped a beat or two. She immediately fumbled for her phone, but before she could take it out, a light came on. Not the overhead ones. This was a much dimmer one that was fixed on the wall.

"The generator kicked in," she heard Ruston say.

Obviously, he didn't think the loss of power was a fluke, because he'd stepped into the doorway next to Duncan and had already drawn his gun. Duncan and she did the same.

And they waited.

Her heartbeat started to race and thud as she thought of all the things that could go wrong. The killer could be coming after them. Right now. He could be using the dim lights as a way to get closer. But Ruston, Duncan and she were ready for that.

She hoped.

Gracelyn prayed the killer hadn't come up with a way to get to them that they couldn't stop. Or a way to crush her without even being near her.

"Abigail," she muttered, and the fear came, soaring.

Because if the killer had arranged for this, there could be an attack at the ranch. Her hands were far from being steady when she took out her phone and made a call to Joelle.

More waiting. Each fraction of a second seemed to take an eternity, but Joelle finally answered.

"Is everything okay?" Joelle and Gracelyn blurted out at the same time.

Apparently, Joelle was just as much on edge as she was. "The power went out at the hospital," Gracelyn explained. "We're okay, though," she quickly added when Duncan shot her a pleading glance. He obviously didn't want his pregnant wife to worry about him. "I just wanted to make sure everything was all right there."

"We're okay here, too," Joelle assured her. "No power outages. No signs of anyone trying to get near the house. Abigail just had a bottle and is asleep." She paused a moment. "Is Allie out of surgery?"

"Not yet."

"Okay, keep me posted," Joelle said, and she paused again. "You think the killer messed with the power, don't you?"

Gracelyn considered lying, but Joelle was a cop and would likely see right through that. "It's something we're considering. But the three of us are together, and we'll stay that way to give each other plenty of backup."

"All right." Joelle's voice was more than a little shaky now. "Just be careful, and tell Duncan I love him. Wait, don't do that," she quickly amended. "Because that sounds like a goodbye. Tell him to come home when he can."

"I will," Gracelyn assured her. She ended the call and relayed the message. "Joelle says to come home when you can."

Duncan made a sound of agreement, but heaven knew when that would be. For the moment, though, they weren't going anywhere. If the killer was indeed in the building, then it was best to stay put and have him or her come to them. Three against one. Well, three against an army, if the killer had backup.

But Gracelyn had to pray that wouldn't happen.

Duncan was looking to the left of the hall while Ruston was keeping an eye on the right. Gracelyn was between them and volleyed glances in both directions and at a stained glass window high on the wall across from them. She seriously doubted it would open, but it was possible someone could shoot their way through it. If that happened, she'd have a fairly good shot to stop anyone coming in that way.

A phone rang, the sound slicing through the silence, and Gracelyn saw the screen of Duncan's cell light up. "It's Anita Denny," he said, referring to one of the reserve deputies he'd posted around the hospital.

Duncan answered it, sandwiching the phone between his ear and shoulder while he continued to keep watch in the hall. He hadn't put the call on speaker, probably because he didn't want the sound of the deputy's voice to interfere with the sound of any approaching footsteps. That, and he likely didn't want Anita to give away anything that might help a killer pinpoint their location.

"Are you okay?" Duncan asked, and there was plenty of alarm in his voice.

Oh, mercy. Something had happened.

"Describe him," Duncan insisted a moment later, and then he paused, no doubt to listen to what Anita was telling him. "And you're sure it was a man?" Another pause, followed by some muttered profanity. "All right. Stay put, and I'll get someone to you," he said, ending the call.

"Who do you need me to call or text?" Ruston immediately wanted to know.

"Text Woodrow," Duncan was quick to say. "He's with the medical examiner and can be here in about fifteen minutes. I want him to go to the east side of the hospital to check on Anita. She says she's okay, but I'm not convinced."

"What happened to her?" Ruston asked Duncan while he sent the message to Woodrow.

"Someone tossed some rocks from the roof of the hospital. A few of them hit her, and when Anita looked up, she saw a man looming over the side. Just the top of his head, though, not his actual face. Anita called out to him, but he disappeared from sight."

So, it could be either Devin or Tony. Or someone that Charla had hired.

Or none of the above.

Gracelyn wanted to believe this was some kind of prank. But it didn't feel like one at all.

"Who can I call to get someone onto the roof?" Gracelyn wanted to know.

"Anita's already done it," Duncan explained. "Two hospital security guards are headed up there now. I'm contacting Dispatch to see who they can get up there to help them."

Gracelyn had no idea if the guards could handle something like confronting a killer, but she suspected the confrontation wouldn't happen. The killer wanted Ruston and her, not the guards. So, maybe this was some kind of distraction? Certainly, the killer wasn't hoping to lure them up to the roof, too?

But maybe that would work.

Partially, anyway.

If the killer managed to hold the security guards hostage, Duncan might go up there. Might. And that would leave Ruston and her alone. But even then, they certainly weren't defenseless.

Duncan had just made his call to the dispatcher when Gracelyn heard something that had them all stopping cold.

A gasp.

It had come from the direction of the nurses' station just up the hall, and they all turned in that direction, each of them bringing up their guns. The light was dim in that area, too, but not so dim that Gracelyn didn't see the nurse lying face down on the floor. For a horrifying moment, Gracelyn thought she was dead, but the woman lifted her head and then tried to scramble away from something.

Or rather someone.

There, in the shadows, Gracelyn saw a figure wearing all black who was crouched down behind the nurse. Gracelyn couldn't see his face. Heck, couldn't even tell if it was a man.

Like Ruston and Duncan, Gracelyn took aim at him, but none of them had a clean shot because the person grabbed the nurse, hooked an arm around her neck and used her as a shield. That was when Gracelyn realized why she couldn't see the person's face.

Because there was a gas mask covering it.

A split second later, there was the thudding sound of something hitting the floor. A small canister, and white smoke immediately spewed from it. One whiff, though, and Gracelyn knew it wasn't smoke.

It was tear gas.

Her eyes started to burn like fire, and she began to cough. She tried to bat the gas away from her face but couldn't. It was everywhere, engulfing them in the thick cloud, and it was having the same effect on Ruston and Duncan, too, because they were coughing as well.

Not the killer, though.

That thought was loud and clear in her head. The killer had on that mask, which meant he could walk right through the gas and get to them.

Gracelyn tried to run. Tried to get to some fresh air so she'd have enough breath to fight back. To protect anyone who was now in this killer's path. But the coughing overtook everything, and she couldn't see. She had no choice but to drop to her knees.

Gracelyn felt someone take hold of her arm. Not a gentle grip. A hard, wrenching one that dragged her to her feet and ripped the gun from her hand.

"Move," the voice snarled.

The person's crushing grip made sure she did that. Moving her away from the waiting room. And toward the exit. That was when Gracelyn realized what was happening.

She was being kidnapped.

Chapter Fifteen

With his pulse racing and adrenaline firing on all cylinders, Ruston could hear the sounds around him. Footsteps, coughing, gasps for breath. He was doing plenty of coughing and gasping of his own, and he was on his knees. He couldn't see anything but the ghost-white tear gas.

He couldn't see the person who'd set off the canister.

Ruston figured the guy was there, though, and had done this so he could kill Gracelyn and him. The tear gas would make that easier for him to do that since he was wearing a mask, but first he'd have to get to them, and Ruston needed to do something to prevent that from happening.

Hard to do anything when his throat and lungs were on fire, and the coughing was making it impossible to do much of anything. He tried to call out to Gracelyn, to tell her to stay right next to him. However, he failed. Everything inside him was yelling for him to get away, to breathe in some fresh air. But he also needed to protect Gracelyn, and at the moment, he clearly couldn't do that.

Ruston wasn't even sure where she was.

He tried to move. Tried to listen. And he could hear more of the shuffling of footsteps mixed in with the other sounds. What he couldn't hear was Gracelyn or Duncan.

Along with essentially blinding him and sending him

into a coughing fit, Ruston was disoriented and couldn't tell exactly where he was. He kept his gun gripped in his right hand and reached out with his left. He felt what he thought was the hall wall and not the archway opening of the waiting room. If so, that meant Gracelyn was probably behind him.

He staggered in what he hoped was the right direction to find her, and he'd made it a few steps when he heard a door open. That was followed by a rush of light and the fresh air that his lungs were screaming for. It cleared out some of the gas mist, but his vision was still plenty blurry.

But not his mind.

The thoughts were racing through him. One bad thought in particular. If someone had opened a door to the outside, then it could mean the tear-gas thug was escaping. Not alone, though. He could have Gracelyn with him.

"Gracelyn?" he tried to call out and managed it despite the coughing.

No answer.

He wanted to believe that was because her throat didn't allow her to respond, but his gut told him it was something much worse.

Ruston gathered up every bit of his strength and got to his feet so he could get to that open door. He made it there one staggering step at a time, and he hoped Duncan was doing the same. Someone was moving in his direction, anyway. If it was the killer, then he'd no doubt have a clean shot.

But no gunshots came.

"Where's Gracelyn?" he heard Duncan ask through the strangling coughs.

That gave Ruston another jolt of adrenaline that fueled him to move even faster to the door. He stepped out, the fresh night air engulfing him, and he nearly tripped over something. No, not something.

Someone.

For a horrifying moment, he thought the person on the ground was Gracelyn, but it wasn't. It was Nelda Martin, one of the deputies guarding the doors. She was in a crumpled heap, and there was blood on her head.

Cursing, Ruston stooped down to check for a pulse while he frantically scanned the parking lot that was just on the other side of a grassy area. There were some vehicles, including a Saddle Ridge cruiser that Nelda had likely used to come to the hospital, but there was no sign of Gracelyn.

"Hell," Duncan snarled when he stepped outside. "Is Nelda alive?"

Ruston nodded. "She's got a pulse." He kept looking. Kept listening. And he finally heard something. The sound of an engine being revved. A few seconds later, he saw the black SUV speeding out of the parking lot. He caught a glimpse of the driver.

Someone in a gas mask.

And he saw Gracelyn. Just for a second.

His heart dropped.

Because, like Nelda, she was unconscious and there was blood on her head.

"Gracelyn!" he called out, running into the parking lot.

"She's in that SUV?" Duncan asked.

"Yeah," Ruston managed, and he tried to tamp down the panic that was crawling through him.

"Use the cruiser," Duncan insisted. He rummaged through Nelda's pocket, came up with the keys and tossed them to Ruston. "Go. I'll be right behind you as soon as I get her some help. I can use one of the other cruisers to track you."

Ruston caught the keys and didn't waste a second. He ran

straight to the cruiser, jumped in and started driving. Fast. As if Gracelyn's life depended on it.

Which it did.

He practically flew out of the parking lot, and some of the tightness in his chest eased up just a little when he spotted the SUV. Again, it was just a glimpse before it disappeared around a curve. But at least Ruston knew what direction it was going.

Out of town.

Well, maybe. A sickening thought occurred to him, that maybe there was more than one SUV, that the one he saw was meant to lead him in the wrong direction. That was possible, but since he didn't have a lot of options, he went after it. He had to get to Gracelyn and stop her from being killed.

The image of the blood on her head flashed in his mind, but he had to shove that aside. That would only tear apart his focus, and right now, he needed all the focus he could get. He had to catch up with that SUV.

The plates on the SUV were almost certainly bogus, so Ruston knew he wouldn't be able to rely on that even if he got the license numbers. He had to keep the vehicle in sight and follow it to wherever they were taking Gracelyn.

And that gave him another flood of thoughts.

Gracelyn must have been alive if the driver had taken her. If he'd already killed her, he would have just left her in the hospital. So, this was a kidnapping.

Why?

Again, that brought some bad thoughts. Maybe to use Gracelyn to lure him out? But why not just take him along with her?

Ruston thought back to what had gone on in the hall of the hospital. He'd only seen one person, so it was possible the kidnapper couldn't get both of them out. Even if he'd managed to hold both Gracelyn and him at gunpoint, it would have been difficult to get them out of the hospital and into the SUV. Gracelyn and he would have fought back.

The image of the blood flashed again.

She likely had fought back. And the thug who had her had hurt her. Had probably knocked her unconscious. Or drugged her. Either way, when she came to, she'd try to escape. The kidnapper wouldn't just let that happen, which meant Gracelyn could end up being killed in the fight. That was why Ruston had to keep the SUV in sight. It was the only way he had now of getting to Gracelyn.

The SUV sped out of town, and the driver must have had the accelerator floored, because Ruston wasn't gaining on him. Thankfully, he wasn't losing either. The SUV stayed ahead, tearing across the rural road, and so far there were no other vehicles around. But the road wasn't straight either. There were plenty of curves just ahead. Since the driver might not be familiar with that, Ruston hoped he didn't lose control and crash.

Ruston had to hit his brakes when he got to the first of that series of curves, but once he was through it, he immediately sped up again. Keeping the SUV in sight.

He cursed when his phone rang because it took some effort to get it out of his pocket while keeping the cruiser from going off the road. Duncan's name was on the screen.

"I'm in a cruiser and am tracking your location," Duncan said the moment Ruston answered it on speaker. "You're heading toward the interstate."

"Yeah," Ruston verified. And that wasn't good. It'd be much harder to follow the SUV once it was in traffic.

Ruston didn't add more to that because he had to fight to keep control through another of those curves. Then he cursed when he was through it and saw the SUV. Not on the road but rather turning off onto what appeared to be a ranch trail. That could mean Gracelyn had regained consciousness and was now fighting her captor. Or this could have been the plan all along, for the captor to meet up with someone else.

Ruston followed.

"Keep tracking me," Ruston told Duncan, and he ended the call so he could focus on his driving.

The cruiser bounced over the uneven rock-and-dirt surface. Ahead of him, the SUV did, too. Then it stopped, and Ruston saw the driver bolt from the SUV and break into a run through the woods.

Ruston braked, bolted from the cruiser and began to run, too. Not toward the driver but to check on Gracelyn. Once he was sure she was all right, then he could go in pursuit.

He hurried to the passenger's-side door.

And his heart went straight to the ground.

Because she wasn't there. No one was. The SUV was empty.

He didn't see any blood, and he certainly hadn't seen her with the escaping driver, but he fired glances all around in case the thug had tossed her out of the vehicle.

Still, nothing.

Ruston tried to tamp down his fear and kept searching. His heartbeat was drumming in his ears now. He was breathing way too fast. But he still heard a ringing sound. Not his phone. He followed the sound to the driver's seat of the SUV, where a cheap-looking cell was ringing. A burner, no doubt.

He didn't have any evidence gloves on him, and it was a risk to touch the phone and contaminate any possible evidence. Still, he knew this call had to do with Gracelyn, so he went ahead and answered it.

"You can save her," the mechanical voice immediately said. "No other cops. Just you, Ruston. If you want to save her, you'll come alone."

He had to get his throat unclamped before he could speak. "Where? Where are you taking her?"

"To the baby farm. Get there fast," the voice warned him before the call ended.

GRACELYN FOUGHT HER way out of the dream. A nightmare. With images of blood and the sound of gunfire. The crushing sensation in her chest of not being able to breathe.

She forced her eyes open, slowly. She had no choice about that. Her head was throbbing, the pain pulsing through her, and she didn't want to make any sudden moves. So, she just sat there, glanced around and listened.

She was in a vehicle, belted into the front seat, and her hands were cuffed together at the wrists. That sent a jolt of panic through her, but she tried not to cry out. She didn't want to make a sound until she had figured out where she was and who had taken her.

The images and memories were all tangled up in her head. Everything swirling. And the pain. Mercy, the pain was still there, too. So, that was why it took long moments for her to latch on to anything. Then it all came together.

And she suddenly remembered what had happened.

The tear gas at the hospital. Being dragged out by a man wearing a mask. Once they were outside, she'd seen the injured deputy on the ground, and she'd managed to break away from her attacker. She ran. For only a second or two, though, before he'd grabbed her by the hair and then slammed her onto the ground.

She'd felt the sharp stab of pain in nearly every part of her body. Then she had fallen and hit her head. After that, everything went dark. Until now. Until she'd woken up in this vehicle. But where was she?

That question quickly faded when another, more important one flashed in her mind.

Where was Ruston?

Was he hurt? Or worse? And what about Duncan? Gracelyn was almost certain they'd still been in the hospital when she had been taken.

She moved her wrists a little, testing out the restraints. Flex-cuffs. It was what cops used to restrain perps. But it was also what Devin had used on Allie.

Allie.

Her thoughts went there for a moment. She wasn't sure how much time had passed since she'd been dragged away from the hospital, but Allie had still been in surgery then. Had been critical. Would the killer send someone after her, too?

Maybe.

But Gracelyn had to hope that the medical staff and the deputies would be able to stop that. Even if they couldn't, she couldn't help Allie herself. Not from here. She'd have to escape to do that.

"You awake?" the driver said.

It was a man. She didn't know who he was, but she thought it was the same person who'd barked out that order for her to move at the hospital.

"Who are you?" she asked, and she tried to make that sound like a demand. It didn't.

Her throat was still burning from the effects of the tear gas, and her vision wasn't 100 percent either. Everything was swimming in and out of focus, but she could see that the man was still wearing a gas mask that concealed all of his face. That blurred vision wasn't helping any with her figuring out where they were either. A country road...somewhere.

"My name's not important," he said, his voice a low, rasping growl. "Just consider me a lackey. A well-paid one," he added with a chuckle. The laughter turned her stomach.

"A lackey," she repeated. So, not the killer. Well, maybe not. She didn't think it was either Devin or Tony, anyway, but the killer could turn out to be someone who wasn't even on their radar. "Where are you taking me? And where's Ruston?"

"Ruston's on a wild-goose chase." He chuckled again.

Oh, that didn't help the panic building inside her. If he was telling the truth, Ruston wasn't coming for her. That could be good, she supposed, since she was probably going to become bait. That was the only reason she could think of as to why she was still alive.

"Why didn't you just take Ruston when you took me?" she asked.

"Too risky to have you both together. My orders were to get you, and once I drop you off, then I can wait around for your boyfriend to show up."

Her bait theory was right. She didn't ask why the lackey was so certain Ruston would come for her. No need. Because Ruston *would* come, and she knew there was nothing she could do or say to stop him. That meant she had to try to end this before Ruston walked into a trap.

But what exactly was this?

Gracelyn sat up in the seat and stared out the windshield at the scenery. Oh, God. She knew where he was taking her. Back to a nightmare.

Back to the baby farm.

"Now, don't go hyperventilating on me," the man said as if it was part of his continuing joke. "Before I drop you off, I'm to give you a message. My boss knows the medical examiner found the username and password for an online storage site that Zimmer set up. If you give it to him, he won't gun down Ruston."

So, that was what the killer wanted. Zimmer had hidden away something that could ID the killer.

"I don't know that information," she said.

"Then you'll get it." He pressed the phone function on his dash screen, and she saw Ruston's name and number pop up. "Tell Ruston what you need and ask him to bring it to you."

He didn't give her a chance to respond or even gather her breath. He just pressed the number, and Ruston immediately answered.

"Who is this?" he demanded. "Do you have Gracelyn?"

"I do indeed have your little darlin'," the man verified, "and this is how you'll get her back. Tell him, Gracelyn. Spell it out for him."

"Ruston," she managed to say. She wished she sounded stronger. Because she was. Despite the nightmare bubbling up inside her, she was a heck of a lot stronger than she sounded.

Think, she told herself. Ruston would be just as frantic as she was, so she had to be smart about what she said.

"I'm okay," she told Ruston and hoped he believed that. If he thought she'd been injured, that might cloud his judgment. He might be willing to do anything to get to her.

"Where are you?" he asked, and yes, there was a sharp intensity in his voice.

"Apparently, on the way to the baby farm."

Ruston cursed, and she heard the sound of a vehicle engine. He was coming for her.

"The lackey who took me didn't tell me the name of his boss, but the killer wants the username and password of

Zimmer's accounts," she explained. "The ones he tatted on the inside of his wrist."

Gracelyn had purposely added that last bit of wrong information to confirm to Ruston something he no doubt already knew. That if he showed up at the baby farm, it'd be a trap to kill them both. Once the killer had the username and code, then he'd have no use for Ruston and her.

"Now, here's the deal, Ruston," the lackey said. "You gotta come alone and you gotta bring that username and password. Understand?"

"Yeah," Ruston said, his voice flat and cold. "If you hurt Gracelyn, I'll kill you. Understand?"

The lackey chuckled. "We'll see about that when you get here. Hurry, and if you're not alone, then Gracelyn dies on the spot."

With that, he ended the call and turned onto a familiar road. She had memorized this road and the surrounding area before Ruston and she had gone in undercover. It hadn't changed in a year. The trees that lined the narrow road seemed just as menacing. So did the building that sat just ahead. Not an actual house, but a compound that had once been owned by militia members. It was a mishmash of structures that had been cobbled together. Some parts freight containers, other parts prefab houses, all joined together by what she knew were mazelike halls.

There were no lights on that she could see. No obvious security either. The place looked deserted.

But she was betting it wasn't.

No. There was likely at least one person inside, waiting for her. Waiting for Ruston, too. And she wondered if it was Devin, Charla or Tony.

This would be a way to tie up many loose ends if the killer managed to get access to Zimmer's files and eliminate Ruston and her. But why was the killer so sure that Ruston and she had anything that would incriminate him?

One answer came to mind.

Because the killer knew they wouldn't stop until they got to the truth. They would hunt until they had eliminated the threat to Abigail. Any one of their suspects would know that, too.

The gravel crunched between the tires of the SUV as the driver pulled to a stop. "Man, oh, man, this mask is hot. Sweatin' up a storm underneath."

"You can take it off," she challenged.

He laughed again, that low chuckle that made her want to punch him. This wasn't a joke. This was her life. Hers and Ruston's, and this snake was playing a huge part in putting them in danger.

"Now, now," he scolded. "You don't want to see my face because then I would have to kill you. If you're gonna die, it won't be by my hands."

"No, you'll just turn me over to a killer and pretend the only thing you did wrong was take money to bring me here." This time, she was pleased with her tone. Anger. So much anger. She was channeling every bit of what was churning inside her. "Is that what you plan on telling yourself to help you sleep at night?"

"I sleep just fine," he snarled. He got out and began walking to the passenger's-side door to open it.

Gracelyn got ready. Well, as ready as she could, considering her hands were cuffed. No way to get out of that, and even though she fumbled with the seat belt, she couldn't unlatch it. So, she turned her body and tried to get into a position to do some damage.

The man opened the door, and he leaned in to unbuckle her seat belt. She smelled the sweat on him and could see that the moisture had built up behind the eye coverings of the gas mask. She hoped that meant he also had limited vision.

And that he wouldn't see the attack coming.

The moment he stepped back to pull her out of the SUV, she swung her legs around and kicked him. She aimed for his throat. Missed. But managed to land a kicking blow into his chest.

Cursing, he staggered back, but before he could get out of the way, she kicked him again. This time in the stomach. The air wheezed out of him, and he dropped.

Gracelyn bolted out of the SUV, and she started running as if her life depended on it.

Because it did.

Chapter Sixteen

Everything inside Ruston was a tight tangle of nerves and adrenaline. He'd been in high-stakes situations before, one of those with Gracelyn, but that had been different. She'd been armed then, and they'd been together. Now she was alone, hurt and with a thug who'd kill her in a blink.

And he'd taken her to the baby farm.

Ruston didn't want to think about what kind of mental torture that was for her. He didn't want to think about what her captor might be doing to her either. That would only shatter what little focus he had, and right now, that focus was what he needed to get to her in time.

He used the hands-free system while he sped down the road, and he called Duncan. "Where are you?" Duncan immediately asked.

"I got a call from the man who's got Gracelyn. He's taking her to the baby farm."

Ruston heard Duncan slam on his brakes. He was obviously changing directions as well, and since he didn't ask for the address, it meant he already knew the location. Then again, just about everyone in local law enforcement did.

"Did you recognize the guy's voice?" Duncan asked.

"No, because he was using a voice distorter," Ruston was quick to say. "He wants the username and password that

Zimmer had tatted on him. He says I'm to come alone or Gracelyn will die."

Of course, Ruston knew the plan would be to kill both Gracelyn and him once he had what he wanted. Ruston had to figure out a way, fast, to make sure that didn't happen.

"How the hell did that…?" Duncan started, but he stopped and cursed. "Zimmer might have told someone about the tats, someone who then passed along that info to the killer. Or else the ME's office has a leak," he concluded.

Either was possible, but Zimmer didn't seem as if he trusted anyone enough to share that kind of info. But Ruston immediately rethought that. He could have trusted Tony or Charla. Especially Charla since he'd been her confidential informant.

"I'm guessing the ME filed a report," Ruston said, "and it was either hacked or accessed."

The hacking would point to Devin. The accessing to either Charla or Tony. Which meant they still couldn't use this to confirm the identity of the killer. But Zimmer had likely known that, or had had such strong suspicions, anyway, that he'd then put in that file.

"I can text you the username and password," Duncan said, the hesitation coating his voice. "But we don't know what's in that file yet. Heck, we don't even know where the file's been stored. The techs say it's like looking for a tiny needle in a massive cyber haystack."

"I'm guessing the killer knows that," Ruston concluded. "So, he could have knowledge of where the file is. Maybe he got that from something he found when he killed Zimmer."

Maybe, though, the killer would have to do the same search of that cyber haystack as the tech guys. If so, it'd be a race to see who got there first. If the killer did, then he'd certainly erase everything. But all of that would take time.

Time that Gracelyn didn't have.

"I'm about three miles out from the baby farm," Ruston explained. "Once I'm closer, I'll turn off my headlights. They'll know I'm coming and will be looking for me, but I'm hoping to get close, park and then go on foot."

Duncan cursed again. "I'm at least five miles out. I would ask you to wait for me, but I know you won't. I wouldn't if it were Joelle being held."

"I can't wait," Ruston confirmed. "But when you get here, do a silent approach. I don't want to give the killer any excuse to pull the trigger."

"Will do," Duncan confirmed. "I'll text you the username and password after I hang up. Be careful, Ruston."

"I will." And he would. But that might not be nearly enough. "You, too."

Ruston ended the call and had to slow down to take the final turn toward the baby farm. He drove way too fast on the poor excuse for a road, and as he'd told Duncan, he turned off his headlights when he was about a half mile out. That certainly didn't make driving any easier, but at least there was a moon tonight, and the meager light might stop him from running off the road.

Might.

He rethought that when he hit a deep pothole, and he had to grapple with the steering wheel to stay out of the deep ditches that were on both sides of him.

And that was when he saw it.

The movement from the corner of his eye. Someone running, not on the road but through the grassy area adjacent to it.

His heart crashed against his ribs when he realized it was Gracelyn. Her hands were cuffed in front of her, and she was firing glances behind her. Someone was chasing her.

Since there was no way he could drive to her, Ruston stopped and got out. He couldn't call out to her because he didn't want to alert the killer to their positions. Instead, Ruston jumped over the ditch and started toward her.

He knew the exact moment when she spotted him. Her head whipped up, and she changed directions. She ran to him.

She didn't get far before a shot rang out.

Ruston felt the slam of fear. The fresh adrenaline. The need to get to Gracelyn now, now, now. If the bullet had hit her, she hadn't gone down. She was still running, and he quickly ate up the distance between them. Ruston immediately took hold of her and dragged her to the ground.

Just as another shot slammed into the dirt a few feet from them.

Ruston followed the direction of the shot and saw the gunman. He had his gas mask shoved up on his head, giving Ruston a look at his face. He didn't recognize him, which meant this was a hired gun.

The thug was trying to take aim while he was running. That was probably why he'd missed with the other two shots. That wouldn't last, though. He'd soon stop, and then Gracelyn and he would be way too easy targets.

"Stay down and let's move," Ruston instructed. He wanted to pull her into his arms, wanted to tell her...so many things. But that was going to have to wait. Maybe he'd get the chance to say those things when this was over.

A third shot came. And a fourth. All too close but still thankfully not hitting the intended mark.

The moment Ruston reached the ditch, he dropped down into it with Gracelyn. It was about three feet deep, so they crouched down, but Ruston knew they couldn't stay this way. The gunman would almost certainly be coming for them, and if he managed to approach at the right angle, Gracelyn and he wouldn't be able to see the guy until it was too late.

Ruston quickly took out his small pocketknife so he could cut the cuffs from Gracelyn's wrists. It twisted away at him to see that blood on her forehead, but she didn't seem to be in pain. Like him, she was firing glances at the rim of the ditch, watching for the gunman.

The second he'd removed the cuffs, he took out his backup weapon and handed it to her. Then he peered over the top of the ditch. He braced for a shot to be fired at him. But it didn't come.

And the gunman was nowhere in sight.

Hell.

Where had he gone? There were some wild shrubs, and he could have ducked behind one of those. It was too much to hope that he'd just run off.

He saw some movement from a high patch of grass that was about five yards away, and Ruston turned in that direction so he could take aim. And he waited. Watched. Listened. Knowing that Gracelyn was doing the same thing.

There was a soft clicking sound, and he was pretty sure it came from the same grassy area. Moments later, a cloud of white smoke spewed out into the air.

More tear gas.

It wouldn't have the same potent effect as it had inside the hospital, but it could be just as dangerous, considering it was coming right at Gracelyn and him. Once the gas got to their eyes and throats, they wouldn't be able to defend themselves.

"Stay low and move down the ditch," Ruston whispered.

There was a huge disadvantage to that since the thug would be behind him. He'd no doubt be wearing a mask and could use the cloud of gas to conceal himself until he was right on them.

They moved, not as fast as he wanted, but Gracelyn and he scrambled away from the gas. But even over their movements, he heard another of those clicks. Heard the canister drop into the ditch.

And more tear gas came their way.

The moment the gas hit him, Ruston was right back where he'd been at the hospital. Coughing. Eyes burning. No way to fight back. Gracelyn was ahead of him, and she thankfully kept moving. Ruston tried to do that, too, but he heard another sound. Not the click of a canister being triggered.

The thud of someone dropping down into the ditch behind him.

Before Ruston could even turn, there was more movement. And he felt the barrel of a gun press against the back of his head.

"Cooperate," the man snarled, "or I shoot your woman in the back."

GRACELYN KEPT MOVING. Her eyes were stinging, but she thought she was staying just ahead of the worst of the gas. It wasn't a thick cloud but more of a mist. Added to that, the night breeze was dispersing what there was of it. If Ruston and she could just make it a few more feet, they wouldn't get the worst of it and would be able to defend themselves.

She glanced behind her.

And her heart stopped. It certainly felt like it, anyway.

She saw Ruston, not crouching. He was standing now, and not by choice either. There was a man wearing a gas mask behind him, and he was holding Ruston at gunpoint.

"You both throw down your guns," the guy in the gas mask ordered.

Ruston was coughing, but it wasn't nearly as bad as it had been during the other attack. Gracelyn just wished she could better see Ruston's eyes so she could tell if he'd been hurt. But her own eyes were still stinging, and the moonlight was creating plenty of shadows on his face.

"Guns down now," the thug insisted. "I've got a clear shot of your woman," he added to Ruston.

And he did. All the gunman had to do was aim in her direction and fire. There was nothing she could dart behind for cover, and if she tried to scramble out of the ditch, he'd likely just shoot her.

But why hadn't he just done that already?

And why hadn't he finished off Ruston instead of putting a gun to his head?

Because with both Ruston and her alive, they could be used against each other. Leverage. This snake and his boss had to know that she would cooperate to keep Ruston from being killed and vice versa.

"Last chance," the guy warned them. "Guns down now."

Ruston's Glock slid from his hand and dropped on the ground at his feet. Gracelyn knew what that had cost him, to lose the primary way to defend them. But he'd had no choice.

Neither did she.

Gracelyn dropped her gun as well, but she didn't toss it. She wanted it as close to her as possible. That way, if she got the chance to use it, she wouldn't have to reach that far.

"What now?" Ruston demanded.

"We walk and get the hell away from this gas," he answered right away. "Go to the baby farm. You got somebody there who's anxious to see you."

Gracelyn felt the fresh jolt of adrenaline, and she forced herself not to think of the other attack. Those images weren't going to help her think more clearly, and right now, she had to think. She had to figure a way out of this.

"Out of the ditch," the man ordered. "And remember that part about me shooting one of you? I will, you know. In fact, I'll get paid a bonus, so don't test my patience."

A bonus. She hadn't needed more proof that this was a hired thug, but there it was. Someone—maybe Charla, Tony or Devin—had paid this guy to do the dirty work. That could include murder. In fact, that was no doubt the killer's plan after Ruston spilled the username and password.

The thug shoved Ruston out of the ditch first, following quickly behind him and putting the gun back to Ruston's head. A silent warning for Gracelyn not to try anything. Not yet. But leaving the ditch meant leaving their guns behind, and Ruston wouldn't have a backup weapon on him since he'd given it to her.

But there would be backup.

No way would Duncan let Ruston come here alone. The sheriff was no doubt on his way, but he couldn't just come in with sirens blaring. He'd have to do a silent approach, but hopefully that meant he was making his way to them now.

"You stay ahead of us," the thug told Gracelyn. "And go ahead and put your hands on your head so I can see them."

She did as he said, and they started walking. The air cleared even more as they moved away from the ditch and back on the road. Her eyes were still stinging a little, but she could clearly see the building ahead.

And the shadowy figure that stepped out from it.

Gracelyn couldn't tell who it was, and the person stayed back enough so that she couldn't get a good look at him or her.

"Good," the thug muttered. "The boss is coming out to meet us. Might get home in time to watch the game."

It sickened her that he was being so flippant about this. Then again, she figured the other hired guns had been pretty much the same. Well, maybe not Zimmer. But the one who'd attacked with Zimmer had fired shots at the SUV with Abigail inside, and the two goons in the sheriff's office hadn't seemed to care how many people they killed to get to their targets.

"So, it's just you and the boss," she remarked.

He chuckled. "Honey, I'm the only one the boss needs to finish this."

She thought he was telling the truth. Hoped he was, anyway. She didn't want an army of hired thugs waiting for them.

Gracelyn purposely slowed her steps just a little, not because she wanted to delay facing down the killer. No. She was to the point that she wanted to know the person responsible. But she slowed down so that she could try to get closer to Ruston. If the thug was right, this was a two-on-two situation, and while Ruston and she weren't armed, that didn't mean they were defenseless. If they couldn't stall the killer until backup arrived, then they might have to fight their way out of here.

Again.

"And before either of you think about running again," the gunman went on, "my orders are, I lose you two, then I'm to go after the kid."

Oh, the anger came. Boiling hot. A full rage that Gracelyn had to fight to tamp down before she turned and clawed out this snake's eyes. How dare he threaten that little baby. And he was going to pay for that threat. She wasn't sure how, but he would pay.

So would the piece of slime that was waiting for them.

"Glad you could come," the killer said.

And he stepped out so Gracelyn could finally see his face.

DEVIN WAS SMILING when he walked toward them.

Smiling and gloating.

Ruston intended to make sure Devin didn't have those reactions for long. The goon's threats to Gracelyn and Abigail had been more than enough to fuel Ruston's anger, and it had seethed and soared with each step toward this miserable person in this miserable place.

Devin was armed, of course. He had a SIG Sauer in both hands, which he probably thought made him look like a cool bad guy.

"The Green Eagle," Ruston said like a mock greeting.

Devin shrugged. "I'm not going to come out and admit that," he said. "I mean, since I'd be incriminating myself. Oops." He laughed. "I guess I just did. There goes some of my bargaining power." Using the guns, he put those last two words in air quotes.

"Your plan was to tell me that you'd let Gracelyn live if I gave you what you wanted," Ruston spelled out for him.

"Why, yes." There it was again, that smugness that only fueled Ruston's anger. "But you would have never fallen for that anyway. Gracelyn wouldn't have either. You both know how this has to end."

"Yeah, you eliminate everyone who can put you in a cage," Gracelyn muttered.

"True. And so far, so good," he bragged.

Ruston wished he could have disputed that, but with the exception of this lone gunman, the others were dead. Marty, Simon, Archie and three hired guns. There were likely others who had been silenced in the aftermath of the baby farm.

"So far, so good," Devin repeated. "And that's why I need the info that Zimmer left behind."

"How did you know about it?" Ruston asked, shifting

his weight so he'd be able to either drop down or lunge at Devin. Ahead of him, Ruston could see Gracelyn doing the same thing.

"Computer leaks," Devin admitted. "The ME isn't very careful about what he puts in his reports. He mentioned the tats, but he didn't give specifics." He paused. "I want specifics. Oh, wait. You need a reason to give it to me. How about a quick, easy death for Gracelyn? As opposed to me making it very, very painful."

"Your hired gun said you would go after Abigail," Gracelyn said, and Ruston heard the razor edge in her voice.

Again, Devin shrugged. "Only as a last resort."

Ruston saw the lie on Devin's face. Devin wouldn't come out now and say that he had planned on taking the baby all along because he probably hadn't wanted to give Gracelyn and Ruston a reason to stay alive.

A reason to fight.

But Gracelyn and he already had that reason. They both loved Abigail, and if they literally rolled over and died, it would leave the baby at the mercy of this monster. That wasn't going to happen.

"You were going to kidnap and sell your own daughter," Gracelyn spit out. "Or maybe she isn't yours."

"She is," Devin verified. "Allie brought me a sample of her DNA because she wanted to prove that I was the father. I'm not sure why she thought it was so important to prove, because I didn't give a rat. Still don't."

Ruston was glad Gracelyn was keeping Devin talking. Anything to distract him. Anything to buy them some time.

And right now, he needed a weapon.

"You didn't kill Allie, though," Gracelyn pointed out. "Is she still a loose end?"

He laughed. "Your sister knows nothing, but I figured I could use her in a roundabout way to get the baby. I mean, if Allie ends up in jail, then I get custody. After I prove paternity, that is, and I can prove it. So can you now that the good sheriff took my DNA. He probably did that, hoping to find something to incriminate me, but the only thing that DNA will prove is that I have a legal right to my biological child."

A child he'd end up selling first chance he got.

And that wasn't all the dirty dealings this SOB had done.

"You're the one who blew our covers," Ruston snapped. "How did you even know we were cops?"

Devin shrugged as if that were nothing. No big deal that Gracelyn and he had nearly died. "I make a habit of using a hacker to check out anyone and everyone I do business with. A hacker who breaks many rules to tap into things like police databases and such." He narrowed his eyes at them. "If you two had died then and there, I wouldn't have to be going through this mess right now."

Ruston was already fuming, but that only added to the flames. He glanced around for something, anything, he could use to fight back. There wasn't anything, which meant he was going to have to do this with his bare hands. He was gearing up to ram his elbow into the thug's gut when there was a flash of headlights. They cut through the darkness at the end of the road and then disappeared.

Both Devin and the thug glanced in that direction.

And Ruston made his move.

With the thug's slight shift of his body, Ruston went for a more direct attack. He turned and slammed his fist into the guy's face. He heard the satisfying sound of cartilage breaking. Blood spewed, and the man howled.

From the corner of his eye, Ruston saw Gracelyn dive toward Devin's legs, tackling him and knocking him back against the building. Ruston cursed, though, when he saw that Devin had managed to hang on to both his guns, but the disadvantage of that was it didn't free up his hands to fight back. Then again, he wouldn't need to actually fight if he could get off a shot.

He did.

The blast tore through the air, the sound tearing through Ruston, and he was terrified that Gracelyn had just been shot. He latched on to the still-howling, still-bleeding thug and dragged him in front of him.

Just in time.

Because there was another shot, and Devin had aimed this one at Ruston. But the bullet meant for him slammed into the thug's chest. He dropped like a stone, giving Devin a clear path to shoot Ruston.

But Gracelyn stopped that from happening.

She kicked the gun from Devin's right hand and sent it flying. Devin pulled the trigger of the second gun, but it was a wild shot that didn't come anywhere near Ruston or her. Thank God. However, Devin immediately tried to shift the weapon to his right hand.

And worse.

During the shift, he bashed Gracelyn on the head, knocking her away from him.

Everything seemed to shift to slow motion. Even the sound of Gracelyn's voice yelling to him, "Get down."

Ruston did get down. He dived to the ground, scooping up the thug's gun, and the second he had hold of it, he took aim. Even though she was clearly dazed from the blow, Gracelyn scurried away from Devin, giving Ruston a clear shot.

Which he took.

It seemed as if Devin and he pulled the triggers in that same heartbeat of time. Devin missed.

Ruston didn't.

He double tapped the trigger and sent two shots directly into Devin's chest. Devin froze, the shock registering on his face as his gun slid from his hand. Then he flashed that cocky smile one last time before he took in his dying breath.

Gracelyn's gaze connected with Ruston's. For just a second. And they moved. She toward the thug and Ruston toward Devin. Both of them checked to make sure killer and henchman were truly finished.

"He's dead," Ruston verified after touching his fingers to Devin's neck.

"He is, too," Gracelyn confirmed. She stared down at the goon, and her face tightened. She cursed the dead monster.

"Are you all right?" someone called out.

Ruston automatically took aim a split second before he realized it was Duncan. He was on foot, and he was running up the road toward them.

"We're alive," Ruston settled for saying. "But Devin and his hired gun aren't."

Ruston considered calling that in, but it appeared Duncan was already doing that. Instead, Ruston focused on Gracelyn. In addition to the blood on the side of her head, she had a nasty bruise on her face from where Devin had hit her.

Seeing that made him want to go after Devin all over again, but he pulled her into his arms. And held her.

"They were going after Abigail," she muttered. "They were going to kill us and go after her."

"Yeah," he managed to say through the vised muscles in his throat.

Gracelyn's head whipped up, and she looked him straight

in the eyes. "We need to check on her. We need to make sure Abigail is okay."

Ruston didn't argue. They started running toward Duncan and the cruiser.

Chapter Seventeen

Gracelyn felt both exhausted and pumped up as if every nerve in her body was on high alert. And on the verge of crashing. Her mind was a tangle of thoughts and fears as Ruston sped toward his family's ranch.

It'd been nearly a half hour since the shoot-out with Devin. Time when they'd had to wait for backup to arrive so that Duncan wouldn't be left at the crime scene alone. During those thirty minutes, Gracelyn had spoken with Joelle not once but twice, and Joelle had assured her that all was well, that no one had come for Abigail. Gracelyn believed her, but she wouldn't breathe easier until she saw the baby for herself.

The moment Woodrow and Luca had arrived, Ruston and she had left, and she'd gotten one last glance of the baby farm in the rearview mirror. Despite nearly being killed there tonight, it no longer held that bogeyman fear for her. It was just a place that bad people had used to do bad things.

And now the leader of those bad people was dead.

Gracelyn didn't feel a drop of grief about that. Just the opposite. A monster was dead, and his death made the world a safer place. Devin wouldn't be around to hire any more henchmen. Wouldn't be around to try to kidnap and sell babies.

"I would suggest you go to the hospital for those injuries," Ruston said, "but I'm guessing you'd rather have an EMT come out to the ranch and examine you."

"The EMT," she immediately agreed. "And you should be checked out, too. We both got some heavy hits of tear gas tonight."

Ruston made a sound of agreement and glanced at her. "How are you, really?"

She did a quick assessment. Her head was hurting, but it wasn't a throbbing pain. "I'm okay enough. How about you?"

"Okay enough," he repeated, and he reached over, took her hand and gave it a gentle squeeze. "I thought I was going to lose you."

There was plenty of emotion in his voice, and she thought they were on the same emotional wavelength here. Well, maybe they were. She had been terrified when she'd thought she would lose Ruston. But there had been an extra layer to that terror.

That she might lose him before she even got the chance to tell him how she felt about him.

She was in love with him.

Gracelyn nearly blurted that out now, but Ruston's phone rang, and she saw Slater's name pop up on the dash screen. All her fears about Abigail came rushing back. It must have been the same for Ruston, because he answered it right away on speaker.

"Nothing's wrong here," Slater said right off the bat. "Abigail is fine."

Gracelyn's breath of relief came out like a loud moan. Ruston did his own version of a breath of relief by muttering something she didn't catch.

"How far out are you?" Slater asked.

"About fifteen minutes," Ruston answered. "Thirteen," he amended when he sped up. Good. The sooner they got there, the better.

Slater made a sound to indicate he was pleased about the shorter arrival time as well. "I thought Gracelyn would want to know that Allie came out of surgery, and she's critical but stable."

Gracelyn had to fight through the fatigue to try to process that. Unlike Devin, she didn't wish her sister dead. Yes, Allie had done some horrible things, but she didn't deserve to die.

"When Allie came out of the anesthesia," Slater went on, "she asked the doctor to give Gracelyn a message."

Everything inside Gracelyn went still. And she waited for Slater to finish. Her sister had done so many reckless, dangerous things that Gracelyn wasn't sure what kind of message she'd want to have passed on to her.

"Allie said that Abigail is yours, Gracelyn, that she'll sign over custody to you," Slater spelled out. "She also won't fight going to prison either."

It took a moment for that to sink in. A long moment where her stomach unclenched. Where so many of her nerves settled.

Abigail was hers.

"Why the change of heart for Allie?" Ruston asked.

"I think nearly dying must have given her some clarity," Slater suggested.

Yes, Gracelyn knew all about that. Being near death did have a way of pinpointing everything. Of making you see what was important.

She certainly had.

And Abigail and Ruston were at the very top of her list of important things.

"I alerted SAPD about Allie coming out of surgery," Slater went on a moment later. "Duncan agreed that they'll be the ones charging her. Conspiracy to kidnapping, human trafficking, obstruction of justice, child endangerment and accessory to attempted murder, including the attempted murder of a police officer. The last two are because she was involved in hiring Zimmer and Robert Radley, who attacked you at Gracelyn's place."

Gracelyn mentally repeated all those charges. With Devin dead, Allie wouldn't have any bargaining power for a deal, which meant she would likely spend the rest of her life in prison.

"See you in a few minutes," Slater said, ending the call.

Ruston gave her hand another gentle squeeze and then brought it to his mouth and brushed a kiss on her fingers. "Are you okay?"

She sighed. "Part of me aches for my sister, but this means Allie won't be able to endanger Abigail again."

Ruston nodded, kissed her hand again. She wished the kiss had been on her mouth. While he'd been holding her. She needed that right now.

She needed him.

Soon, she wanted to tell him that, but for now, she sat in silence, mourning the loss of a sister. Yes, Allie had done some unforgivable things, but she'd also given her the greatest gift. Abigail.

Ruston took the final turn to the ranch, and Gracelyn pushed aside her thoughts to prepare herself for what felt like a homecoming.

She was pleased when she spotted the still-armed ranch hands at the end of the road. Standing guard. Keeping Abigail safe. Gracelyn would owe them all a deep gratitude that she'd never be able to repay. The same was true for Duncan, his deputies, Ruston and his family.

Ruston pulled to a stop in front of the house, and Gracelyn hurried out of the cruiser. Slater was already opening the door before she reached it.

"Uh, are you sure you're okay?" Slater asked when he saw her face.

She nodded, though Gracelyn figured she looked pretty bad for him to have that reaction. However, that was yet something else she'd put on the back burner. For now, she raced up the stairs and straight to the guest room. Carmen and Joelle were both there.

And so was Abigail.

She was sleeping, but Gracelyn picked her up anyway and held her close. The tears came. The tears she'd fought so hard to hold back. But there was no holding back now. Abigail was safe. She was also a little riled at being awakened, and she let out a protesting wail that made Gracelyn smile. She hadn't given birth to Abigail, but this child was hers in every sense of the word.

Gracelyn kissed her cheek and looked back at Ruston when he stepped into the room. He went to them, sliding his arm around Gracelyn's waist and delivering his own kiss to the baby's cheek. Abigail immediately stopped her fussing and smiled at him.

"You've already charmed her," Gracelyn muttered.

"One down, one to go," he muttered back.

Their gazes met for a moment, and Gracelyn saw the love. Well, maybe that was what it was. Love for Abigail, anyway, but what had he meant?

His phone rang, and she saw Duncan's name on the screen. Since Gracelyn wanted to hear what he had to say, she eased the baby back in the crib, thanked both Joelle and Carmen and then stepped out into the hall with Ruston.

"You two back at the ranch yet?" Duncan immediately asked.

"We are," Ruston answered. "Just a couple of minutes ago. Slater filled us in on Allie."

Duncan sighed. "Yeah," he muttered like an apology that Gracelyn knew was meant for her. "I have some good news," he added. "The techs located Zimmer's online file."

Gracelyn saw the surprise flash through Ruston's eyes. "How? They said it'd be a needle in a haystack."

"It would have been, but Zimmer had a clue to the storage site in the password, so the techs were able to narrow it down. They not only found the file, but they were also able to access it."

Something Devin would have certainly been able to do had he gotten the username and password.

"The file is huge and filled with photos and details that would have apparently gotten Devin the death penalty," Duncan explained. "Zimmer confirms that Devin was Green Eagle. And there are other names of people involved in the baby farm, people who probably thought they'd escaped justice."

"Are Tony or Charla on the list?" Gracelyn asked.

"No," Duncan was quick to say.

Gracelyn felt nothing but relief about that. Yes, she would apologize to Charla and Tony for believing they were guilty, and she was glad they hadn't been dirty cops.

"Archie, Marty and Simon were on the list," Duncan went on, "and that explains why Devin had them murdered. Devin was basically eliminating anyone who could link him to the baby farm."

Yes, that made sense. It was the reason Devin wanted to

eliminate Ruston and her, too. And Allie. But maybe he'd let her live, with the hopes that she would end up taking the blame for not only the attacks and murders but also for the baby farm itself. Gracelyn could see Devin trying to use Allie as the ultimate scapegoat.

"I'll be tied up here a while longer, but I'm hoping to be home in about two hours," Duncan added. "Is everything and everyone okay there?"

"Yes," Ruston and Gracelyn muttered in unison, and for the first time in nearly a year, Gracelyn could say that was the truth.

She was okay.

The past would always be with her, but it wasn't the past she was looking at now. She was looking at a future.

Gracelyn was looking at Ruston.

And he was looking at her.

He ended the call, slipped his phone into his pocket and immediately pulled her into his arms. He took her mouth in a deep kiss that notched up her "okay" to something much, much more.

But how much more?

What she said in the next few minutes could change everything, but Ruston might not be ready to hear it. Still, she needed to tell him what she'd been holding inside. And she would. As soon as he finished melting her with this kiss.

When he'd left her breathless and on cloud nine, he eased back from her and flashed that incredible smile again.

"I'm in love with you," she said. Gracelyn braced herself for the shock. Maybe for him to back away and tell her that he needed more time.

That didn't happen.

Ruston kissed her again, and this one was so hot that

Gracelyn wasn't sure how she managed to stay on her feet. The man had a way of firing up every inch of her.

"Good." He muttered that single word while his mouth was still against hers.

But he added more words to it.

"Because you and I are of a like mind here," he went on. "Because I'm in love with you, too."

Now she didn't stay on her feet. Or at least she wouldn't have if Ruston hadn't caught her. Her heart filled with so much emotion. Not the bad ones this time either. All the very best ones. Happiness. Need. And love. So much love.

But Ruston added to that, too.

"I say, since we both love Abigail, that we raise her together," he threw out there. "What do you think about that?"

"I think it's perfect," she managed to say.

And it was just that. Perfect. Still, Ruston managed to add to that, too. Because he pulled her back to him for a long, slow kiss.

* * * * *

A COLBY
CHRISTMAS
RESCUE

DEBRA WEBB

Friday, December 21

Four Days Before Christmas

Chapter One

Victoria Colby stood at the window in her office that looked out over the street. This was one of her favorite places in the world and certainly she had traveled broadly. But here, in the Colby Agency offices, this window was her happy place. Watching the snow fall so close to Christmas was just icing on the cake. The winter storm had started two days ago, and the snow hadn't let up since. But, as Lucas reminded her, the storm wouldn't get in the way of their plans this year, so why not celebrate the deepening blanket of white?

It was the season after all.

Her heart felt heavy at the idea of not spending the holidays with her family. It was tradition. But that was impossible this year. Of course, she was literally surrounded by her agency family. Victoria and Lucas couldn't deny having an amazing extended family here at the agency.

And as wonderful as that was, it wasn't really the same.

The whole truth was that celebrating would be a lot more enjoyable if, for one, she didn't feel like her family were scattered so far and wide this holiday. And, secondly, she was worried sick about Tasha, her son Jim's wife. Jim and Tasha were in Sweden and not for a vacation either. Tasha had been diagnosed with a rare type of cancer. Fortunately,

Victoria had been able to get her into a cutting-edge research study that was showing very promising results with its participants. Victoria desperately needed this treatment to work. The idea of her son losing his wife—her precious grandchildren losing their mother—was simply unthinkable.

More unnerving at present: the children hadn't been told about the diagnosis. Tasha and Jim wanted to wait and see how things would go before telling their daughter and son. No point ruining their holidays as well, Jim had insisted. Victoria sighed, her heart heavier still. It wasn't like her grandbabies were actually children. Jamie was twenty-five now. Victoria still couldn't believe her granddaughter was so grown-up. She smiled and traced a melting flake of snow down the glass. Jamie had done everything early. Graduated high school and university years before her peers. Every three-letter government agency on the planet had sought her out well before she had that degree in her hand.

But Jamie had done what Jamie always did—exactly what *she* wanted to do. She had accepted an invitation to be one of only twelve Americans with the brand new International Operations Agency—or the IOA. Practically no one had a handle on exactly what this new multi-country agency was really, but the promise of great things was certainly being bragged about in all the highest places. This agency would extend far and wide, interweaving many allies together in a way never done before.

Victoria was extremely proud of Jamie for choosing a route with global implications, though she had to admit she would have preferred to have Jamie coming on board with the family business. The Colby Agency represented Victoria's life's work. She worried that after Jim there would be no one in the family to carry on the important work they did here.

Her grandson Luke, on the other hand, was just preparing to enter the last semester of his final year at university in Nashville, Tennessee. He was far less in a hurry to get on with his life. Another smile tugged at Victoria's lips. As a child, he had been so like his father. Extremely curious but not quite ready to jump in with both feet. He'd changed his major twice in his freshman year, before finally deciding to go into medicine and transferring to premed at Vanderbilt.

Victoria couldn't wait to see him spread his wings and come into his own.

With all that was going on in their lives, the kids wouldn't be coming home for Christmas either. Everyone—the world it seemed—was too busy. This made her far sadder than perhaps it should have, but this would be the first year that no one in the family had stayed in or come to Chicago to celebrate.

Lucas appeared behind her, and Victoria turned to him. "I fear it's going to be a lonely Christmas."

He touched her cheek with the backs of his fingers. "It's never lonely as long as we are together," he reminded her. "We're alive and well. We'll have plenty to celebrate."

Of course, he was right. She leaned into his strength, and they watched the snowflakes swirl and fall. Whether the family was here or not, it was going to be a beautiful few days. All of Chicago lay under a blanket of perfect, white snow giving the busy and at times troubled city such a peaceful appearance. How could anyone who loved this city not feel the magic of the season? At their ages it was important to enjoy each day all the more.

Victoria should be grateful, and she was. Who could blame her for missing her family?

"Slade mentioned," Lucas said, "that he and Maggie

planned to drop by after dinner at her mother's house. It will be nice to see them and to spend some time with Cody."

Another grandchild who was growing up so very fast.

"That would be lovely." Maggie's mother had no one else and Victoria certainly wouldn't selfishly resent the woman for having at least some family for the holiday even if it meant that Victoria and Lucas were alone. She and Lucas were so very lucky to still have each other.

The reminder that they would indeed have some family dropping by for the holidays brightened her spirits. Although they had not known about Slade until he was a grown man, he was as much a member of this family as anyone else. He had been raised by an evil woman who had done all in her power to turn him against Lucas, his biological father. But time and circumstances had changed that painful connection into a good, solid and loving relationship. One for which Victoria was immensely thankful. Lucas had sacrificed a great deal for his country. He deserved all the happiness that came his way.

"We should send everyone home after lunch," Victoria suggested. It was Friday after all, and the agency would be closed next week. All open cases had been closed by mid-December.

It was something they strove for each year beginning on the first of November. Having the last of the year's cases basically buttoned up by the holidays wasn't always possible, but they worked diligently toward that goal. There were some cases that simply couldn't be wrapped up so neatly in a certain time frame, but all efforts were made. This was good for her investigative team and for the clients they served.

Victoria had to admit that as careers went, she and Lucas had certainly enjoyed unusual ones. She, Lucas and James Colby, her first husband, had begun their young lives together along with their careers working in the government. James and Lucas had been CIA—eventually leading a special black ops group like no other. In time, when Victoria and James had started a family, they had left the more dangerous work serving their government and started a private investigations agency.

But the past had not been ready to let them go and had drawn them deep into a whole other level of danger.

Victoria pushed the painful memories away. They had survived the nightmares and the tragedies and, thankfully, she and Lucas had found their way to each other in time. Although they had tried retirement and moving to a warmer climate, staying away from Chicago and the agency they had built was impossible.

"That is a very good idea, my dear." He kissed her cheek and then nuzzled it with his own. "Do you have something in mind for this evening?"

Victoria smiled. "I suppose we could be like the typical family and spend the weekend watching Christmas movies and baking cookies."

Lucas chuckled. "I don't think anyone would accuse us of being typical."

Victoria thought of the many, many cases they had investigated. The many times they had barely survived with their lives. "Oh yes, sometimes I forget that we're not like other couples."

During their nearly half-century-long careers, they had been kidnapped, shot at, had bombs left for them, had their entire office building burned down and, of course, one or both had been left for dead numerous times. Thankfully, they had always survived. At times by the sheer skin of their teeth.

Funny how even now, looking back at all those horrific

situations, each one had been just another day at the office. And now, their granddaughter was following that same path with the IOA. Luke—not so much. Her grandson had chosen Vanderbilt University in Nashville for his premed work, where a great deal of amazing research was happening. And since Luke was a die-hard country music lover, Nashville was the perfect setting for him.

"I was thinking," Lucas said, "that we might consider a quick trip to Paris. I know how you love that city. A few days there would be a welcome change of pace. We'll be closer and available to rush to Sweden if Jim and Tasha need us. We can have the kids there in a matter of hours if need be."

Victoria held back her first response and mulled over the proposal. "You know, that's actually not a bad idea." Christmas in Paris. Yes. That would be very nice. "I'll run it by Ian and Simon to make sure they haven't made out-of-town plans already."

To her knowledge, none of the primaries at the agency were planning to travel out of town. She turned to her husband. "This was really a great idea, Lucas."

He smiled. "I already have reservations at the Shangri-La. I spoke to Jim yesterday and he was in agreement that he would prefer that we enjoy ourselves for the holidays and not wait around to hear news from Tasha's procedure."

So her husband and her son had been conspiring together. "Do you have flights already as well?" His smile widened to a grin. Why had she even asked? "This really is quite perfect, Lucas. Thank you."

Her cell vibrated against her desk. Victoria started for it and Lucas headed for the door. "I'll inform everyone that I told you about your Christmas present."

She should have known. "So everyone but me knew about this?"

"Not everyone." He grinned, then slipped out of her office.

Victoria shook her head. "Probably everyone but the janitor," she murmured with a laugh.

Luke flashed on the screen of her phone and Victoria's smile spread wider. "Luke," she said in greeting, "how wonderful to hear from you."

Her grandson was always busy, but even still he found a minute here and there to call his grandmother. He had probably heard about Lucas's surprise as well.

"Grandmother."

Victoria's smile faded. The clear and present fear she heard in her grandson's voice had her heart stumbling. "Luke, are you alright?" Had something happened to Tasha and Jim had already called the children? Dear God, she prayed that was not the case.

Had Luke been in an accident? He was speaking to her, which had to mean he was all right...wasn't he?

Or what if something had happened to Jamie?

A fresh wave of fear pounded in her veins.

"Listen to me very carefully, Grandmother," Luke said. "They're only allowing me a few moments to speak with you."

Victoria suddenly calmed. Inside, she went completely still and quiet while her instincts—the ones she had honed over nearly half a century—elevated to the highest state of alert. "I'm listening."

"They want ten million dollars. You have forty-eight hours. But you are not to do anything at all until you receive additional instructions." A pause. "I love you, Grandmother."

The call ended.

"Luke!" Victoria's heart burst into a frantic staccato. "Luke!" She stared at the black screen.

Victoria rushed from her office and paused in the private waiting room just outside the door. She immediately thought of Mildred, her dear assistant of so many years. How she wished she were here now.

Her new assistant gazed up at Victoria with a kind smile. "Is everything all right?"

"Rhea, I need Lucas, Nicole, Ian and Simon in my office *now.*"

Rhea was fairly new, but she recognized there was trouble. Rather than bother with her phone, she ran from the room to personally gather everyone.

Needing to leave her own cell phone free, Victoria reached for the phone on Rhea's desk and called Chelsea Grant. Chelsea was their very best at tracing cell phone calls. "I need you in my office. Now please."

Five minutes later, those closest to Victoria were assembled in her office and she had provided the details of the call from Luke. She struggled to maintain her composure. Memories from when Jim had gone missing at age seven ripped at her insides. *This is not the same. Not the same.*

"The call came from the Nashville area," Chelsea confirmed. "But I'm having a difficult time narrowing down an exact location. The call bounced all over the Volunteer State like a football in a final play free-for-all. If another call originates from that phone, it's possible a drop in signal strength could create a hesitation in the smoke screen they're using. All I need is a call using that phone which lasts a few minutes and a couple of strength hesitations. The signal will automatically go to where it's strongest— where it originates."

"Thank you, Chelsea." Victoria turned to the others. "Thoughts?"

Ian Michaels and Simon Ruhl had been with Victoria

the longest of all her outstanding investigators. Nicole Reed Michaels, Ian's wife, was another of her most trusted. Between the three of them they had a world of experience and knowledge. More important, they were highly skilled in the art of evading danger and recovering assets.

"I'm hearing nothing from Interpol or our friend in the Mossad," Ian said. "My impression so far is that we're dealing with a domestic situation."

"I agree," Nicole confirmed. "My contacts in the CIA, the State Department and the NSA have heard no recent chatter related to our agency or anyone close to it."

Victoria wanted to be relieved at least a little, but she was not. She turned to Lucas. "What are you hearing from Thomas Casey?"

Like Lucas, Thomas Casey had once been a ghost of the highest order. A man who knew all things and who could go in and out of all places—wherever in the world—like smoke undetected. Their contacts and assets were scattered far and wide. But with that level of reach came fierce enemies…fierce competition.

"Ian and Nicole are correct," Lucas said, "this is not an international situation. This is someone closer to home."

"My contacts in the FBI—" Simon went next "—have confirmed rumblings in the southeast but nothing necessarily high level. Yet, they are not willing to take a bigger connection off the table."

Nicole rolled her eyes. "That's just like the Bureau. Always trying to make a situation bigger than it might be."

Simon shrugged. "They have agreed to put out feelers at the university and in the neighborhood where Luke lives."

"In my opinion," Ian said, "we should be heading in that direction even now."

"Luke said I was not to do anything until I received further instructions." The worry and uncertainty had Victoria's heart pounding again. No matter how many times she had faced life and death, knowing that a member of her family was in danger tore her apart inside.

"We should at least call Jamie," Lucas offered. He paced from the conference table to where Victoria sat on the edge of her desk, his trademark limp more visible than usual. He too was worried. These sorts of situations were far harder to tolerate at their ages.

And yet, they would die before backing down. She hoped whoever was behind this understood who they were dealing with.

"I don't want to call her," Victoria said, "until we have something more to share. At this point we know basically nothing."

Lucas leaned against Victoria's desk, putting himself next to her. "You're right, of course, but I feel as if we're doing nothing at all to alleviate the situation."

"The only part that gives me any relief is that Luke sounded somewhat calm despite the fear I heard in his voice," Victoria offered. "His tone was not as frantic as it could have been." Whether the rationale should or not, it gave her some sense of peace.

Nicole looked up from her tablet. "I've moved the requested ten million to a separate account—the one we generally use for ransom demands."

"Very good." Victoria should have already thought of that herself. Perhaps turning seventy-one last year had slowed her cognitively more than she'd realized. No. That wasn't true. There was absolutely nothing wrong with her brain. This was a problem with her heart.

And she was terrified.

"Luke has numerous friends," Simon mentioned, scrolling through the notes on his phone. "I've cued up a list with contact details in the event we need to start tracking them down. His professors. His class schedule. We have everything we need to begin a thorough search for him." His gaze settled on Victoria. "Whenever you say the word."

Her instincts urged her to act, but…the grandmother in her feared not following the directions given.

"We know from our contact at Nashville Metro that his car is at his condo. It hasn't left his parking space," Lucas said.

All their vehicles were tagged with state-of-the-art tracking devices. But having Nashville Metro confirm as much was good news indeed. "Which suggests," Victoria pointed out, "that wherever he is, someone picked him up or that person is at his condo with him." The latter was not likely since they all had panic buttons in their private homes as well. She felt confident Luke would have found a way to trigger that alarm.

The Colbys had suffered more than their share of losses. They did not take chances.

And yet, this ransom situation had happened just the same. Victoria felt powerless.

His cell phone had been turned off and the battery removed as soon as the call had ended, limiting its use as a tracking device. Victoria suspected his phone had only been used to ensure Victoria understood they did indeed have Luke in custody.

Ian said, "Nashville Metro have reported nothing in the way of hostage situations. There have been no new kidnappings in the past seventy-two hours. This appears to be an isolated event."

Nicole looked to Victoria once more. "I've run the enemy list through the steps and found no new activities."

Over the course of the past half century, the Colby name had amassed a good many powerful enemies. The activities of those enemies were closely monitored at all times. It was a necessary evil in the world of high-level investigations. The trouble was that new enemies cropped up and old enemies found fresh ways to hide. It was a never-ending cycle of discovery and catch up.

"Then we wait," Victoria said. There simply was no other choice. Waiting was far more difficult than taking action, but it was, at times, necessary.

Victoria's cell chimed with an incoming call.

Her heart rushed into her throat.

Jim.

"Don't tell him anything," Lucas urged.

As difficult as that would prove, Jim was thousands of miles away and could do nothing about what was happening here. He certainly didn't need the additional stress.

"How is Tasha?" Victoria decided coming straight out with the question was the best way to prevent herself from blurting the truth. Worry twisted inside her, slicing like barbed wire.

"She came through the preparation for the procedure quite well. The doctors are very hopeful."

Her son's voice sounded strained and so very tired. "This is wonderful news," Victoria said, fighting the sting in her eyes. Jim did not deserve this—whatever the hell it was. He had been through enough. Far more than most people were aware. His body bore the scars from the physical torture he had suffered from the moment he went missing as a child. The mental scars had taken years to put behind him. They would never be forgotten, but he had built a wonderful life and Victoria wanted nothing to tear that sweet life apart.

He had paid far more than his share already.

"She'll rest today and then the procedure will go as scheduled tomorrow. If it's successful, we should know by Monday."

This was far sooner than Victoria had expected. If this did not go their way…no, she couldn't think that way.

"Is there anything we can do, Jim?" Victoria offered. "We all have you and Tasha in our prayers, of course."

"That is much appreciated, but we are hanging in there. The staff here is working diligently to make our time as stress free as possible."

"I'm so glad." Thank God. *Thank you, God.*

"I should go and be with Tasha. Please let Luke and Jamie know we're doing fine."

"I will," Victoria promised. "Don't worry about anything here. We have everything under control."

"Thanks, Mom. Love you."

Victoria's chest tightened. "Love you." The call ended and for a bit she stared at the dark screen and struggled to hold back her emotions.

Lucas placed his hand over her free one. "You did what you needed to do."

She nodded. Lowered the phone and looked from one of her dedicated friends to the next. "Whatever else we do, we must—"

Her cell chimed again. She gasped as the name on the screen flashed.

Luke.

"Let it ring once more," Chelsea said.

The phone chimed again, and Victoria answered. "Luke?"

"Grandmother, you will receive a letter of instruction from a special courier in fifteen minutes," he explained. "You are to follow the instructions in this letter very carefully. They have explained the first part of the instructions and I am supposed to pass that part along to you now."

His voice gave the impression of calm, but there was no missing the hum of fear just beneath the surface. The sound of it tore at her soul.

"Whatever we need to do," Victoria said. "Just name it."

"Besides the ten million dollars, there is something he needs and there is only one person who can get it for him."

Him. The person behind this was a man. The information wasn't surprising and wouldn't narrow things down much, but it was something—a small piece of the bigger puzzle. "All right. I'm listening."

There was silence on the line.

"Luke?"

The sound of struggling echoed in Victoria's ear. She held her breath, fear tightening her throat like a snake coiled around it. "Luke, is everything all right?"

"Yes." His answer was strained. "I don't want to tell you but I…" A breath blasted across the line. "I have no choice."

"It's all right, Luke. Tell me what you need, and I will make it happen."

"They want Jamie. She is the only one they will allow to do this. If anyone else tries…they say they will…*kill* me."

Panic rushed into Victoria's chest. "Luke, I—"

"Wait for the courier, Grandmother."

The call ended.

Terror slammed into Victoria, making her jerk with its impact.

"I'm calling Jamie now," Lucas said. "As soon as I know where she is I will send the plane for her."

Dear God. Victoria held tightly to the phone no matter that the connection to Luke was lost, her eyes closing in horror. Now they wanted her other grandchild.

Chapter Two

Jamie Colby watched the guy dressed as Santa stroll down Hollywood Boulevard. It wasn't like there was much of anything open. Just a diner or a coffee shop here and there. A tourist trap or three selling tickets for bus tours to the homes of the stars and other popular sites.

Jamie climbed out of her rented car and stepped to the sidewalk. "Santa has a new follower at three o'clock," she murmured for the microphone disguised as a necklace draped around her throat.

The guy in jeans and a torn T carrying a sign begging for donations had pushed away from the storefront he'd been holding up for about an hour and strolled after Santa. Both looked a little worse for the wear, like they'd slept in their clothes for a few days or a week. Not exactly a top-of-the-line Santa. More a low-rent version. *Who wants their kids sitting on the lap of a guy that sleazy looking?*

But Jamie wasn't complaining. Working an op in LA around Christmas was way better than rambling around her apartment in DC. It was cold and wet in DC. Today in LA—Hollywood actually—it was a pleasant sixty-eight degrees with the sun shining. In a couple more hours the streets would be filled with tourists and life would be buzzing like bees in a honeycomb.

She liked the sunshine and the life beat of this place.

The only downside in her opinion was that after an entire month of hanging around the LA area, Jamie still hadn't stumbled upon any big celebrities. A few unknowns and lots and lots of wannabes. The city was always awash with people who wanted to possess just a little bit of the magic that came from Hollywood. The problem was most would never know what it was like to be a celebrity. Most would work in the service industry or something not exactly legal until they disappeared into obscurity or went back home to Kansas or wherever with their tails tucked between their legs. It was not a journey for the faint of heart.

Jamie had to admit that she'd had the dream once—at fourteen. She'd been in love with the idea of a career on the big screen. What young girl hadn't flirted with the idea? But her grandmother had known exactly how to change her mind. She brought Jamie for a weeklong stay in LA. They'd seen the sights and they'd also seen the parts that no one wanted to talk about—Victoria Colby had made sure of the latter. The reality of life in a big city that was really like a nation of its own with all the issues and ups and downs that went along with a huge population was not such a fairy tale. Bottom line—not everyone could be a star.

Jamie smiled when she thought of her grandmother. Victoria had a way of clarifying all things. She missed her so much. It was snowing in Chicago right now. Jamie wished she was going home for Christmas, but she was on assignment here and her parents had taken a long overdue vacation to Europe. Luke was staying in Nashville to be a part of a special program between semesters. The guy was always looking for ways to gain extra credit. Jamie didn't get it. Anything beyond a 4.0 GPA was totally unnecessary in her view. But good grades had always come easy for her. Luke had to work for his.

"Heads up, Colby."

The words whispered in her earpiece brought her back to full attention. Santa was still making his way along the sidewalk, crossing over Vine. The errant beggar had gained on him to the point of nearly overtaking him.

"It's going down soon," came the voice in her ear.

Jamie picked up her pace and made an agreeable sound for those listening, including her partner.

Every move she made—every move her team made—was under close scrutiny. No one wanted this new agency to fail. But the powers that be weren't interested in throwing money after a new venture that on first look seemed too similar to the ones they already had. In truth there were already far too many government agencies—particularly secretive ones—in the opinion of some. For IOA to survive it had to provide something none of the others did and it had to be better...in every way.

Jamie wanted to be a part of making that happen. Like her grandmother, making a name for herself and a good career just wasn't enough. She wanted to make her special *mark*. A mark no one else had made.

Her friend Kendrick Poe would say she was overthinking it, but he'd already made one hell of a mark for himself so he should totally understand even if he pretended his accomplishments were no big deal.

Besides, just being a Colby set the bar damned high.

For a girl, Luke would say.

Jamie bit back a grin. Her little brother was certain he would go far higher than his big sister.

Not if Jamie could help it.

She was all for her brother going as far as possible as long as she went further. They'd been fiercely competitive—especially with each other—forever.

Up ahead, the beggar guy moved in a little closer on Santa.

Time to move.

Jamie added another click to her pace and walked past the beggar. He glanced at her, but considering her too-tight jeans and cropped sweater he didn't appear to consider her a threat.

Too bad for him.

She had just powered in front of Santa when she turned over her supercool right ankle boot and threw her full body weight into the guy in the red and mostly off-white velvet.

They both went down, landing uncomfortably on the concrete sidewalk.

Beggar guy stared in astonishment for one seemingly endless moment before hurrying away. He'd missed his shot. Too bad. Too sad.

"I'm so sorry!" Jamie cried as she attempted to right herself and Santa. "Are you all right, sir?"

He should be all right, but he smelled way wrong. Inside, she shuddered. Santa needed a serious shower and a freshly laundered suit. He smelled a little like sweat and a lot like alcohol. Jamie really hoped the stain on the front of his jolly jacket wasn't dried vomit.

The man scrambled for his red hat and tugged it back on before allowing Jamie to help him to his feet.

"I'm fine," he insisted, looking around exactly like a criminal would.

When would people learn? If you wanted to do a job

well—even an illegal one—you had to get your act together and leave the booze at home.

"Oh no." Jamie dusted at his coat, noting how the right sleeve had come loose from the body of the jacket at the seam. "You tore your jacket. I hope you weren't on the way to a scheduled Santa visit."

"No." He shook his head, then backed away just enough to look her up and down. "You okay, little girl?"

She smiled and resisted the initial response that shot to the tip of her tongue. She was no little girl. The term was probably just the way he referred to all females younger than him, which would include most of the population in the LA area.

"I think I twisted my ankle." She winced. "I should have been paying better attention to where I was going."

"Probably on your phone," he grumbled, testing his own weight on first his left foot, then his right.

Apparently, he actually had twisted an ankle. Could make her job easier.

"I'm so sorry. Really." She offered her arm. "I insist on seeing you to your destination."

She noted the way he stared beyond her. "Beggar guy is coming back around," the voice whispered in her earpiece. No wonder Santa was staring.

When the collision had occurred the other guy apparently crossed the street and now he was retracing his steps. He had a mission. Good for him. Too bad he'd failed already.

"Well...er..." Santa nodded. "I could use the help."

He was old enough, maybe even close to her grandmother's age. No one would be surprised at him asking for help after a spill at his age. Beggar guy would just have to back off for a bit.

"How long have you been playing Santa?" Jamie asked

as they walked slowly forward. She purposely set the pace slow to buy time and to wear on beggar guy's patience.

"Off and on since I hit sixty-five. The cost of living in LA is difficult on a fixed income."

"I'm sure." LA living wasn't easy on a great income. "So, you're a lifer?"

"Born and raised," he said with a glance over his shoulder.

She chuckled. "I'm surprised you're not an actor or a former one." He actually looked like the type.

"Who says I'm not." He glanced at her this time. "Never judge a book by its cover, little girl."

How ironic. She'd just been thinking the same thing.

"We have a newcomer to the party."

The warning echoed in her earpiece. Time to wrap up the chitchat.

Jamie reached to her left hip pocket as if she were reaching for her cell and slipped out the lightweight handcuffs. She'd slapped the first cuff on Santa's wrist before he realized what she was doing. Simultaneously, she tugged him toward the No Parking sign and snapped the other cuff to the metal post.

Then she whirled and confronted beggar guy who had stopped to stare in shock at what she'd done.

Didn't see that one coming, did you?

There were a few pedestrians on the street. No one wanted to whip out a gun. Well, at least not Jamie. She hoped to do this the old-fashioned way by kicking beggar guy's butt. And then he reached into his jacket and came out with a weapon.

Damn it.

She kicked the beggar's gun out of his hand before he had

it fully leveled on her. Santa was shouting and attempting to tug himself free. *Good luck with that.*

"The newcomer is coming at you," she heard from her earpiece.

"Great," she muttered as beggar guy dove at her. She rolled him into a hold with one arm locked around his throat and her legs locked around his, prying them apart to prevent him from gaining purchase on the ground. Good thing her tight jeans were made of spandex. When he continued to resist, she pounded his head into the concrete a couple of times, and he relaxed.

Newcomer was suddenly on top of her then.

This one was dressed like Batman and wasn't going down quite so easily.

He flipped Jamie onto her back and had both hands around her throat. She clawed at his face. Before she could get in a good dig, his head suddenly jerked to the right and then his body flew off her.

"I thought you might need a hand." A long-fingered hand reached out to her.

She looked from the hand she recognized to the guy in the Wolverine costume.

Poe.

"Really? Wolverine?" Jamie took his hand and allowed him to pull her to her feet. "I had this, you know."

"I'm sure you did," Poe agreed, "but Santa was causing a scene and we don't need that."

The old guy was shouting at the top of his lungs and people were stopping to stare and point. Cell phones were coming out.

Time to go.

"Where's the car?" she asked as she freed Santa.

"Half a block up on the right."

"Let's go, Santa." She secured the newly freed cuff to her wrist. She wasn't letting this guy out of her sight and certainly not out of her reach.

By the time she ushered him forward that half a block or so, Poe had hopped behind the wheel. Jamie opened the rear passenger door and she and Santa climbed into the back seat.

"What's going on here?" Santa demanded.

When Poe had peeled away from the curb, she glanced back to ensure the two followers were still dragging themselves off the ground.

"Not to worry, Santa," she assured him. "We're not sending you back to the North Pole yet."

"Am I under arrest?" Santa demanded. "I need to see a badge. And aren't you supposed to read me my rights?"

"What's wrong with Wolverine?" Poe demanded from the front seat as he took a right on Sunset Boulevard.

Jamie checked behind them to ensure they weren't being followed. "I had you figured for a Deadpool guy."

"Where are we going?" Santa demanded.

"Don't worry," Jamie assured him. "We're going to take very good care of you, Santa."

Poe took Sunset all the way to where it transitioned into West Cesar Estrada Chavez Avenue and then a left on North Main to Our Lady Queen of Angels Catholic Church. This was the drop point. If they were lucky, they would get in and get out without a confrontation.

No one wanted to cause turmoil in a house of God just days before Christmas.

They parked across the street and surveyed the area.

"If they're in the church already..." Poe said without completing the thought.

Jamie understood. If the others were in the church already, they were in trouble. In truth, they had no way of confirming how many of the *others* were on this.

"Let's assume we got here first," Jamie offered.

"Whatever you say." Her partner wasn't so optimistic.

Poe got out and leaned against the closed driver's side door to keep an eye on their destination.

While he got the lay of the land, Jamie needed to convince Santa to cooperate. "Look, I don't know why you needed an exit strategy today, Santa," she began, "but I would prefer to keep breathing so don't give me any trouble. Got it?"

His face wrinkled with confusion. "What in God's name is an exit strategy?"

Clearly the man had not watched enough James Bond. "Someone wants you dead and we're here to make sure that doesn't happen. We extracted you before you reached the location where you were supposed to die, on the corner of Hollywood Boulevard and McFadden Place."

"I was meeting my nephew for lunch."

"I'm sorry to tell you this, but your nephew or someone close to him set you up." She unlocked the handcuffs and tossed them onto the floorboard. "I need you to stay close to me, Santa."

He nodded, the movement unsteady as if the news had knocked him for a loop. Probably had.

The rear driver's side door opened. "We seem to be clear to proceed," Poe said.

Which meant he actually couldn't be certain. Evidently the communication link had dropped. The voices in Jamie's ear had disappeared.

They were on their own without the assist of handy electronics.

Santa eased out and Poe stepped closer, shielding the older man's body with his own.

Jamie emerged on the opposite side and surveyed the sidewalk and the strip mall beyond it on the passenger side, then she crossed around to the other side of the car with Poe and their Christmas package.

"Going in the front door." Poe glanced at her.

Jamie nodded.

They hurried across the street and to the double entry front doors of the church, Santa in tow between them.

The doors were locked.

What the hell?

"Side door," Jamie urged.

They moved around the front right corner of the church, going for the side entrance. Their destination was the door beneath the portico that allowed for dropping off parishioners under the cover of an awning. All they had to do was reach it before they encountered trouble.

Jamie kept a close watch on their surroundings. No one behind them.

No one in front.

No running or shouting.

So far, so good.

Her pulse kept a rapid staccato while they hustled along the side of the building until they reached the secondary entrance. They entered without hesitation.

Inside was dark.

The side door opened into a quiet corridor. Taking a left led to the main sanctuary. Right went toward restrooms and a family room for breastfeeding mothers. Jamie had studied the layout.

"Why are we here?" Santa asked in a too-loud whisper.

"You'll be picked up here," Jamie assured him. At least as long as things went according to plan. She kept that part to herself. No need to get the guy riled up again.

Santa stalled, tugging to free his arm from her grip. "I don't understand."

This was not the time. "As soon as we ensure your pickup detail is here, I'll explain as best I can."

The sound of the door they had entered only moments ago opening had Jamie and Poe parting ways. He went toward the main sanctuary, while she ushered Santa into a coat closet near the restrooms.

The coat closet was actually a room with plenty of hanging space for coats, shelves for hats and hooks for umbrellas. It had once been the only restroom and had housed several stalls, so it was fairly large for the purpose it now served.

"I think there must have been a mistake," Santa whispered.

Jamie pressed a hand to his mouth in hopes of getting the message across without having to say the words out loud.

Under her sweater, in the band that kept her cell pressed against her abdomen, her cell vibrated with an incoming call. Control, the people in charge of this operation, would not contact her via her private cell phone. If the comms link was down, someone would contact her or Poe in person.

The call was more likely a distraction.

She hated the idea that someone might have gotten her private cell number, but it happened. If that proved to be the case, she'd need a new number after this. Always a pain in the butt.

Footsteps in the corridor outside the coat closet had her bracing. She scanned the room and then ushered Santa into the farthest corner from the door. She grabbed the two big coats that someone had left behind and camouflaged him as best she could.

She was about to leave it at that when she noticed the open lid on the built-in wood bench that ran the length of the wall. She tapped Santa on the shoulder and pointed to the big bench. It was at least two feet from front to back. Slightly taller than that and several feet long.

He shrugged and then climbed in. Jamie poked all signs of red velvet into the bench and closed the lid. She placed an umbrella atop it and quickly moved toward the door. She flattened against the wall next to it.

Perfect timing. The door opened. She stepped back, keeping the door between her and whoever was coming in.

As soon as the door started to close, and she spotted the back of the head now swiveling on a pair of broad shoulders, she knew it was not a friend. Definitely a foe.

She reached up, boring the muzzle of her weapon into the back of his skull. "Stop right there."

Surprisingly, he did as she asked.

"Put your weapon on the floor and kick it aside," she ordered.

Rather than bend over to do as she asked, he did what she would have done, he began to lower in the knees.

Oh well, if that was the way he wanted to play it.

Just when he would have twisted to put one between her eyes, she squeezed her own trigger, sending a bullet into his right wrist and sending the weapon he'd been holding flying toward the floor.

He swore. Grabbed for her.

She pressed the muzzle between his eyes. "Don't make me shoot you again. I won't be so nice about it this time."

He glared at her, but his hands went up, blood running down from the right wrist.

The door flew inward again, but this time it was Poe.

"Well, hello," he said to the guy with the bullet wound. "I see you met my partner."

Five minutes later, their pickup crew had arrived, and Santa was on his way to safety.

Jamie had no idea why the man had needed assistance or even who he was. She had no need to know, any more than Poe did. Their mission was to provide him with an exit strategy from his planned engagement and to get him to this church.

They might never know what value he represented, but they had accomplished their mission and that was all that mattered.

Once they were in the rented car, headed away from Our Lady Queen of Angels, Poe said, "You hungry? I'm starving."

Completing a mission was a big rush and it always left her hungry. "How about we get out of LA before we stop."

He hitched his head in acknowledgment. "How about we drive down to the Santa Monica Pier and find something to eat and listen to the ocean roar."

"Somewhere in Malibu will be quieter," she argued. "Too many tourists on the pier."

"Works for me."

Like her, her partner wore jeans and a pullover. His was a UCLA sweatshirt. He was a year older than Jamie and had darker features—brown hair, brown eyes—that sharply contrasted her blond hair. They had been friends for almost two years now. He was a good friend. They teetered on the edge of something more, but work always got in the way. Probably for the best. Who had time for romance?

Her cell started vibrating again, and Jamie reached beneath her sweatshirt and pulled it free of its hiding place.

G flashed on her screen.

She smiled. Her grandmother. "Hey, Grandmother," she said. "Is it still snowing in Chicago?"

"Jamie, we have a problem."

Fear trickled into her blood. "What kind of problem?"

"It's Luke. Someone has taken him, and he needs our help." Victoria's voice trembled on the last word.

There were things she should say. Like how terrible it was to hear this news and why would anyone target Luke? But her throat had closed, and she couldn't seem to make her jaw work.

"Jamie." The male voice she knew as well as her own underscored just how serious the situation was. If her grandmother was so upset...

No jumping to conclusions. Her heart stuttered again, and she managed a breath. She had to listen carefully. "Yes, Grandpa." She swallowed at the lingering tightness in her throat. "What's going on?" Calling Lucas Camp "Grandpa" was like calling a grizzly bear a kitten.

"Colby One will pick you up at the Van Nuys Airport at one. We'll meet you in Nashville."

Poe was splitting his attention between her and the road. He couldn't hear the conversation, but he obviously saw the terror on her face. "What's going on?" he urged.

Jamie made a decision then and there. They had completed their mission. Time off was a given. It was only a matter of how much. "Inform the pilot I'm bringing a friend. I'll see you in Nashville, Grandpa."

She ended the call, and Poe's gaze locked with hers. She explained the situation, the need to scream crawling up her throat. She had to stay calm. Focused. "We have to find him. I...can't..." Big breath. "I can't let him down."

"Don't worry," Poe said softly. "We won't fail… We never have before."

He was right…but this time was different. This was not just another mission… This was her little brother.

Chapter Three

The private airfield near Nashville was off the beaten path, but then Jamie suspected that was why it had been chosen. Whether it was the fear that their calls were being monitored or could potentially be so, there had been radio silence during the four-plus-hour flight from LA to Nashville. She'd contacted their superior at IOA and notified him that she and Poe would be out of reach for a few days. Since they were due time off after an operation it was no problem.

Poe had helped Jamie keep herself together. Not an easy task when she was worried. Luke was not like her. He hadn't embraced this undercover, secret agent life. He was a total pacifist—a man focused on learning how to help others with medicine. Although Victoria had insisted they both learn how to use a handgun, Jamie would bet Luke had not touched one since.

"That's your grandmother?" Poe asked as he watched Victoria emerge from the limo that had arrived.

Jamie smiled. She tried to think how Victoria Colby-Camp appeared to others. A mature woman with silver threads in her dark hair. Tall, trim, well dressed. She looked a good twenty years younger than her age. From all appearances she might be your average attractive, wealthy middle-aged woman.

Except there was nothing average about Victoria.

"That's her." They had used a different airfield. Having two jets arrive from Chicago at the same place would have roused suspicions. Jamie rushed to her grandmother and hugged her as hard as she dared. Even so, she was impressed at the slim, toned body she felt beneath the layers of clothing. Victoria not only kept her mind sharp, but she also kept her body lean as well.

"Jamie." Victoria drew back and looked her up and down. "We don't have a lot of time, so we need to talk fast."

Renewed worry twisted in Jamie's belly. "What can you tell me?"

"Let's talk inside."

Jamie turned to her grandpa, who was watching them across the top of the vehicle. She smiled. "Hey, Grandpa." She hitched her head toward the man waiting behind her. "This is Poe. We work together."

Lucas Camp pointed a gaze at Poe that likely sent a shiver down his spine.

"Sir." Poe gave him a nod.

"Poe," Jamie said, drawing his attention in her direction, "this is my grandmother, Victoria."

Her mission partner nodded. "A pleasure to meet you, ma'am. I've heard a lot about you." He glanced toward Lucas. "Both of you."

Victoria nodded before ducking back into the passenger compartment of the limo. Jamie climbed in behind her. Lucas settled on the seat next to Victoria, and Poe dropped next to Jamie opposite her grandparents.

"What in the world happened?" Worry about her little

brother had torn Jamie apart during the flight here. She wasn't sure how much more of the not knowing she could handle.

"I received a call this morning," Victoria explained. "It was Luke. He said I would receive instructions via a courier and that I should do nothing until I received those instructions. The only thing he could tell me before hanging up was that it had to be you who carried out the instructions."

Jamie and Poe exchanged a look.

"Then, we can safely assume," Poe suggested, "that this someone is aware of your particular skill set."

Jamie nodded. "Agreed."

Lucas said, "We have some idea of what your work entails. What aspects of that work do you believe has put you in someone's crosshairs?"

Jamie thought about the question for a moment. "As you know," she explained, "our agency operates a very diverse team to resolve issues all over the world. Sometimes, like today, our assignments seem sedate."

"Like picking up a Santa-for-hire," Poe clarified, "before he was neutralized and delivering him to a safe location."

Jamie went on. "We have no idea who this Santa was or why someone wanted to terminate him. Frankly, it seemed like the sort of assignment any cop in the LAPD could have handled. But there was a reason we were sent in to do it. We just may never know what that reason was."

"I can shed a little light on that one," Lucas said.

Poe frowned and shared another look with Jamie.

"You have no idea," she said, laughing. "Grandpa isn't who you think he is." This was truer than she would ever be able to convince her friend or anyone else.

Poe gave a nod. "I see."

"Your Santa arrived in LA from a visit to Santiago last

Friday. His wife's mother passed away unexpectedly." Lucas shrugged. "We'll stick with calling him Santa. You may not realize based on his condition today—he has felt a little under the weather the past couple of days—but he was booked solid with many appearances at some very large malls and department stores."

Jamie got it now. "He would have come into contact with a lot of people over the next few days."

Lucas nodded. "By tomorrow, the incubation period will be complete and Santa will be highly contagious with the virus he contracted at the funeral."

"I take it he had no idea," Jamie suggested. No wonder he'd been self-medicating with alcohol. He probably felt like hell and was attempting to cheer himself up.

"None. Eleven other targets were discovered and picked up in the past twenty-four hours. Your Santa was the last."

"Wow." Poe shook his head. "No wonder we had to take all those shots when we received our orders."

"There's no reason to believe you were exposed," Lucas explained. "The date and time your Santa was exposed was known so he wouldn't have been contagious yet, just feeling a little under the weather from all the changes happening in his body."

Victoria shook her head. "I liked it better when we could see the attacks coming." She took a deep breath. "At any rate, based on the instructions delivered by the courier Luke told us about, there is a certain surgeon in Nashville who has perfected a previously basically impossible-to-do brain surgery. The first successful procedure was completed just three months ago. There have been two more each week since and though this is an amazing step, this surgeon is the only one so far who has managed the feat. The hope is that he will be able to train others, but it's not going to be easy, and worse, it's going to take time. For those who have inoperable brain tumors, time is not on their side."

"There is a great deal of fiery rhetoric in the medical field just now," Lucas said, picking up from there, "as to whether this surgeon, Dr. Quinton Case, should be wasting his time trying to teach others to do the surgery or just doing the surgery. He can only do two or three per week because it is incredibly tedious and both physically and mentally exhausting."

Victoria said, "How do you decide which patients will receive the surgery and which won't during any given week? How many lives will be lost while time is taken away from surgery to attempt teaching others?"

"Wow, that's a hard one." Jamie searched her grandmother's face. "But, as horrible as what you're telling me is, what does this have to do with Luke?"

"We can only assume that our kidnapper has someone close to him who needs this surgery since all he wants is the surgeon."

Jamie held up her hands. "Wait. This dude wants me to kidnap this surgeon and deliver him to his location of choice?"

"You have approximately seventy-two hours—or until five o'clock on Monday. At that time, if the surgeon has not been delivered to the drop-off location, Luke will die."

Jamie's heart sank. She turned to Poe. "Though I appreciate your desire to give me a hand with this, I think this is where your participation ends. I can't ask you to do this."

"No way." He shook his head. "I'm not walking away."

"I won't argue with you, Kenny." She wouldn't waste time or energy doing that.

"Then don't because I'm not leaving until you do." He leaned deeper into the seat.

"You should consider what she's trying to tell you," Lucas argued. "There is nothing we can do. In fact, this…right here…is as far as our participation can go. The instructions were explicit. Once we have passed the information along, any involvement on our part or the part of our agency will prompt an immediate termination of the deal. No exceptions."

Jamie turned to her grandfather. Then it was decided—she was on her own. "Under the circumstances, I would suggest you get on with this briefing and go."

Victoria shook her head. "There are steps we can take to prevent you having to do this."

Jamie understood. They could make a preemptive strike. Grab the surgeon and then do the negotiating. "But we both understand how risky that option is. The same with going to the FBI. Anything we do puts us in a situation where we can't guarantee the outcome for Luke."

Victoria shook her head again. "Even following their rules, there are no guarantees of the outcome, Jamie. As you're well aware, things can go wrong either way. People can go back on their word."

"Then there's nothing to talk about." Jamie looked to Lucas. "Let's get this done and the two of you should be on your way. It doesn't take a lot of imagination to figure out they likely know about your arrival, and they'll be watching for your departure."

Lucas passed Jamie a brown envelope. "This tells you everything you need to know about your target. The drop-off location will be given to you nearer the grab time."

Jamie accepted the package. "Thank you."

Lucas shook his head and looked away.

"The limo will drop you at the first transition point where you'll receive the next set of instructions," Victoria said.

"As you said, they know we're here and we have been instructed," Lucas said, his voice tight, "to get back to Chicago."

"I'll take care of this." Jamie looked from her grandfather to her grandmother. "Luke will be fine. I promise." She hesitated a moment. "I'm assuming you haven't told my parents."

"We've been instructed not to tell anyone," Victoria confirmed.

Jamie reached out and took her grandmother's hand. "I will get this done."

They hugged and then Jamie hugged her grandfather. There were so many things she would have liked to say, and she was confident her grandparents felt the same, but there was no time.

Luke needed them to remain calm and to move quickly.

All else would have to wait.

Excalibur Court,
6:30 p.m.

JAMIE HAD WAITED at the airfield until the Colby Agency jets had taken flight. Watching her grandparents leave knowing she had to stay and get this done had been extremely difficult. This was her little brother's life, and her grandparents were the strongest, most capable people she knew. She suddenly felt utterly lost and desolate.

The driver had then brought them to a house in a very high-end neighborhood. The house was apparently unoccupied and sat in a cul-de-sac on a hillside overlooking the home of Dr. Quinton Case. Well, calling the place a home was a bit of an understatement. The Case's estate was a massive property ensconced amid more than a hundred acres of treed serenity.

The house on Excalibur Court had been staged with everything they might need—at least on first look. The supersensitive telescope setup allowed them to see—to a degree—inside the home of Dr. Case. Everything from climbing equipment to serious weapons and one hell of a muscle car getaway vehicle had been provided.

There was food and drink, but Jamie wasn't consuming anything in this house. She'd had the driver stop at a local market where she'd picked up food and water. She and Poe had searched the house for wires and cameras. They'd found numerous devices, though they couldn't be sure they'd found them all.

Whoever had set up this op was good.

Strangely enough, a note for Jamie *and* Poe had been left on the kitchen island. The person who had composed the note claimed to have known she would bring Poe with her and the items he would need had been made available as well. This included clothes and weapons. To Jamie's way of thinking, this was proof whoever was behind this knew both her and Poe.

Poe had spread the map and step-by-step instructions on the dining table. Whoever was funding this op had thought of everything—literally.

"On Sunday night, Case is having a holiday party at his home," Poe said. "And that's when you're supposed to nab him."

"The presumption," Jamie said, "I assume is that this is a time when he will be most vulnerable. Preoccupied. Distracted."

The man was surrounded by security at all times, particularly at his office and at the hospital. Understandable, she supposed. But it was sad that because of his success in creating a lifesaving procedure his life was now in danger.

"No question," Poe agreed. "I'm thinking…" He leaned against the edge of the table. "I find it interesting that they assumed you would want me to come because there was nothing in the instructions about me and no one has showed up to put a bullet in my head or ask me to take a walk. Instead, they left clothes and weapons for me."

"Seems like they know me—us—pretty well," she agreed.

"Makes sense I guess since it doesn't seem like a one-person operation if you ask me," he pointed out.

"Since we haven't been given more detail other than the strike is on Sunday night, I'd say it's too soon to tell. But I tend to agree with you. I'm wondering if we'll be given additional backup when the time comes."

Jamie walked into the living room and up to the telescope. The wall of floor-to-ceiling glass doors opened fully to the balcony outside by sliding away like a movable wall. Not so great this time of year, but amazing for extending the entertaining space to the outdoors in the summer. She peered through the lens and directly into the entrance hall of the grand manor that was Dr. Case's home. "The real question in my mind is getting him out of those woods."

Poe joined her at the wall of windows that looked out over the dark landscape. "Getting him out of the house shouldn't be so difficult. There are numerous egresses. It will only be a matter of evading staff and security. The cameras will be another issue altogether, but they may be providing information on the security system. One would hope."

"It's the woods," she repeated as she surveyed the darkness between this house and the target. "He's not going to come willingly, and we have to be extremely careful with him. Any injury could put him out of commission. That would defeat the whole purpose of nabbing him."

"And therein," Poe said, "lies the answer to why we are here."

Jamie straightened away from the telescope, following his train of thought. "They need him for his ability to do this procedure."

"Which means," Poe picked up where she left off, "our employer either intends to start a school for surgeons who want to be like Case, or, as your grandmother suggested, he has a loved one with an inoperable brain tumor who doesn't have the time left to wait his or her turn for the procedure."

It wasn't necessary to say the rest out loud just in case they were being monitored. Even now, Victoria and her people would likely be running down known patients in need of the potentially lifesaving surgery only Dr. Case could provide. Even if they narrowed the list down to the precise patient and therefore the perpetrator of this plan, would there be time to find Luke wherever they had hidden him?

The risk was entirely too great to take.

The sound of clapping had them both spinning to face the threat. "Bravo."

Poe reached for his weapon.

Jamie was too busy picking her jaw up off the floor. Even if she hadn't seen his face, she would have recognized that hint of a British accent anywhere. "Abi?"

Abidan "Abi" Amar stood near the French doors that led to the living room. He clapped one last time before dropping his hands to his sides. "Jamie." One eyebrow reared up. "Kendrick Poe, I presume," he said to Poe. "A man whose claim to fame is that he purports to be a distant relative of Edgar Allan Poe. How very interesting."

"Actually—" Poe put his weapon away "—my claim to fame is the well-known exit of no less than a dozen Americans from al-Qaeda in Yemen. Everything else I've done in my short career is just icing on that very large cake."

Abi gave a nod. "I may have heard something about that."

"What're you doing here, Abi?" Jamie crossed her arms over her chest and eyed him suspiciously.

To say his appearance was a surprise would be a vast understatement. Abi was not a terrorist, though many might say his reputation suggested otherwise. Be that as it may, her knowledge of him provided some room for error in that assessment.

Abi was a contractor who worked doing whatever he was paid to do—within some vague lines that only he could see. In other words, he wasn't a real bad guy. Just one who did things that were not always legal for money.

He colored outside the lines and he loved every minute of it.

"It is my job to oversee your work," he announced. He surveyed Poe up and down. "Although, I must say my job may have been easier without this complication."

Poe's face darkened. "Excuse me?"

Jamie held up a hand for Poe as she walked toward Abi. "So, you're my backup in this?"

"That is correct."

"Wait a minute, Jamie," Poe argued.

Again, she gave Poe her hand. "First, Abi—" she looked directly at him "—I would not trust you to have my back under any circumstances. Ever. Second, if this…whoever-he-is…that took my brother has you, what does he need with me? I can't fathom why he would *complicate* this situation with additional players. More room for leaks and other issues."

The last was the real question. Abi's skills were equal to Jamie's, maybe greater since he was older and had more experience. He had been offered a position at IOA without even putting his name in the hat or competing in any way, but he'd turned it down. He much preferred being his own boss. He didn't play well with others.

If the person who took Luke—who wanted or needed Dr. Case—had Abi on the payroll, they really didn't need anyone else for a straightforward op like this. In fact, the scenario made no sense at all.

"You see," Abi said, "trust is a very important part of this very delicate situation. I think my reputation for being available to the highest bidder preceded me and the trust level wasn't where it needed to be."

"Good point," Jamie agreed. Abi was just as likely to abduct the doctor and sell his services to someone else as to go with the guy who hired him.

Abi went on, "This is also the reason, I suspect, that they took your brother. A little insurance to keep you focused."

Abi was very handsome by any standards. Tall, muscular, black hair and eyes. Jamie stood no more than three feet from Abi and already the physical draw wanted to overpower her. No way. She had been down that road once. Besides, she could only have one focus right now: rescuing her brother.

The very last thing she intended to do was get involved in any way with this man. He was dangerous on far too many levels.

"What do you know that we don't?" she demanded.

"Really? I'm not sure we have the time to cover everything."

Poe shook his head. "This guy is a real comedian."

Obviously, Poe had picked up on the sparks flying between him and Jamie. She'd have to work harder to smother that connection.

"I know that we only have one shot to achieve our goal because our target is leaving for a holiday on Monday." He shook his head. "Can you imagine? He is the only surgeon who has the ability to do this surgery and he dares to take a vacation." He laughed. "Doesn't say a whole lot for his level of compassion."

"You ever heard of burnout?" Poe tossed back at him.

Both men had a point. "All right," Jamie said, redirecting the conversation. "So we have to get him during the party on Sunday night or risk him getting away before he can do what your employer needs him to do."

"*Our* employer," Abi countered.

"What's the plan to get into the house?" Poe asked.

"You don't need that information yet," Abi said. "You will learn each step as needed. That's the most secure way to move forward."

She and Poe exchanged a frustrated look.

"For now, there are other security issues that need to be addressed. I'll need your cell phones and we'll conduct a little pat down."

"You can't be serious." Jamie shook her head. "No way."

Abi turned his hands up. "It's your choice but you know the consequences."

"Fine." She passed him her cell. There was no option for resisting. "Just do it."

With visible reluctance, Poe held out his cell phone as well.

Abi took the phones to the coffee table, gave them a quick check and then added what was no doubt a tracking device or bug of some sort.

"You are to make no unauthorized calls until this is done." He handed each one their phone back. "You are not to leave this house until the job is finished."

"I take it you're here to stay." Not really a question in Jamie's opinion. He was here for the duration, she suspected.

"I will be here until you complete this mission."

"Look me in the eye," Jamie demanded, "and tell me that you do not have orders to terminate anyone when this is over." Not that she was afraid of him getting the upper hand on her. She wasn't. She was every bit as good as he was one-on-one. But she was worried about what might happen to her brother even if she did get the doctor. And his family. Would Case's family be harmed? As for Poe, like her, he could take care of himself.

"I have no termination orders," Abi said. "Unless, you fail to follow through with your instructions and, I will be honest with you, I declined that part of the deal. If you opt out or fail, your brother's execution will be carried out by someone else, but mark my word, it will be carried out."

She supposed she couldn't ask for more than full disclosure.

"There is just one issue," Abi said.

Here it came. Damn it.

"Your friend here," Abi said with a glance at Poe. "He was not part of the plan."

Poe visibly braced.

"Which means," Abi said, "that I have the less than pleasant duty of informing my employer of the modification."

"Please," Jamie said bluntly, "you have had ample time to do this already. Obviously, you had a clue it was happening because you provided clothes for him."

"Actually, those are mine."

Jamie held up both hands. Oh. She hadn't thought of that. "Whatever. I want Poe here. He's with me—to watch my back. Deal with it."

She held her breath. Hoped to hell he would allow her this one concession.

For a long moment, Abi only stared at her. Finally, he looked away. "You're lucky I'm feeling generous." He shrugged. "Besides, we might need him for a distraction of some sort if we get into trouble."

"I don't plan to get into trouble," Jamie argued. "That's your MO, not mine."

Abi laughed. "Well, let's hope you can keep that record. This is not going to be as easy as it sounds."

The fact that he had inside information compelled her to believe him. "Tell me about the hard parts."

"Dr. Case has a body double."

Dread dragged at her gut. "Are you serious?"

"I am indeed. The most difficult part will be making sure we take the right guy and that we keep his wife and daughter out of the line of fire."

What kind of doctor hired a body double?

"You have some way of proving who the real Dr. Case is?" God, she hoped so. Because all she had was a photo of the man.

"I do and it's foolproof. But that doesn't mean he will make this easy."

Jamie shrugged. "It doesn't have to be easy. It just has to be doable."

She would do whatever necessary to save her brother's life—even give up her own.

"It is doable," Abi said.

"No more issues with or questions about Poe," she pressed.

Abi shook his head. "I will handle the situation."

Poe scoffed. "Somehow I figured that was the answer all along, otherwise you might have to get your hands dirty."

Abi chuckled. "You might be smarter than I anticipated."

The standoff lasted about five seconds. Poe said, "You mentioned a pat down." He gestured to Abi. "Why don't we get that part over with? Jamie and I like to know who we're working with—what he carries, what he's hiding. Things like that. You want to go first?"

Jamie rolled her eyes. *Let the games begin.*

Saturday, December 22

Three Days Before Christmas

Chapter Four

Jamie wiped the steam from the mirror. The shower had cleared her head a bit. She'd barely slept last night. She couldn't stop thinking about Luke and how he must be feeling.

Her little brother was a good guy. His need to help others was so clear in his every decision. The fact that he wanted to be a doctor said so much about him. She had to make sure he came through this safely. No one should be kidnapped and held against his will, but Luke was one of the last people on the planet who deserved such treatment. Jamie wished she could claim credit for even ten percent of his good works. The man was always donating his time and/or ability to one cause or another.

There had been times when Jamie worried that this made him vulnerable. It wasn't that she didn't agree with the work he did, but he had to be more careful to protect himself. He was a Colby. This made him a target far more so than he wanted to admit. She'd warned him time and time again that he had to be careful. He shouldn't just blindly trust anyone.

She scrubbed the towel over her skin. That wasn't fair. Just because he had been targeted and taken hostage did not mean he hadn't been careful.

When she'd dried her body and whipped her hair into a damp ponytail, she put on the jeans and sweatshirt that had been provided. Her host had thought of everything. Clothes. Shoes. Toiletries. The scariest part was that these were toiletries she would have chosen.

She suspected Abi had taken care of those details or at least helped with that part. Or maybe he'd been the one to think of it period. He was quite a diva when it came to personal comfort. No matter. She had carefully checked every single item for tracking devices and anything else that could be used to monitor her movements or subdue her in any way. As she'd done so, her mind had conjured images of her and Abi together...their bodies entwined.

She rolled her eyes and put the thought out of her head. She knew firsthand how he liked things. She and Abi had a thing for a little while late last year. It hadn't been a big deal. She'd run into him after a long and exhausting assignment. She'd had a feeling he'd picked her out of the pack and zeroed in on her. Maybe she was being paranoid, but it had felt that way. There were plenty of others in the agency he could have targeted.

Of course, his decision to go after her had nothing to do with this current mission.

She gave her reflection one last look. There were several items on her to-do list today and she wasn't standing for Abi getting in her way. He might be in charge of babysitting, but this was her op.

When she opened the bedroom door, the smell of coffee had her ready to moan. The house was a large one with five bedrooms—each with its own bath—and a large center great room with its impressive balcony and telescope. Oh, and the infinity pool was inspiring even in the window. The steam rising from it this morning told her it was heated.

"Good morning, sleeping beauty," Abi announced as bread popped out of the toaster.

"Who slept?" she grumbled. She felt confident her grandparents hadn't slept last night either. Like her, they were probably terrified for Luke. She hadn't been able to stop thinking about him.

She stilled, then glanced around the room. "Where's Poe?"

"He's having a look around outside. Checking out the ride that's been provided to you."

Of course he was. *Men*. "I have some things to do."

Abi passed her a plate loaded with toast, each slice smeared with a plop of guacamole. "Great. I'll go with you. Poe can hold down the fort."

"Sorry, but where I go, Poe goes." The toast actually looked quite good. He'd chopped up tomatoes and sprinkled them across the top. She took a bite. This time she did moan.

"You need coffee."

As if it hadn't been fourteen months, two weeks and three days since they'd seen each other, he prepared her a cup of coffee with exactly the right amount of almond milk creamer.

"What is it you want, Abi?" He was up to something. This was another thing that had kept her awake last night. It wasn't like him to be so attentive unless he wanted something more than he'd stated. Then again, she supposed it was his job to keep her focused and content until the job was done. Whatever the case, trust was not something she would be tossing out for him.

"It's my job to ensure you have everything you need and are fully prepared for the op."

She decided the coffee was too good to spoil with a long conversation, so she ate her toast and drank it while it was hot. When she finished her coffee, she asked the burning question. "Why aren't you doing the job? Why kidnap my brother and force me to do something I'm sure you can do yourself?" They had talked about this last night and the trust issue, but she still wasn't convinced he'd been completely forthcoming on the subject.

Abi sipped his coffee and appeared to consider her question. "My employer wants the best and I assured him you are the very best. Think about it—this is not the sort of situation you wish to leave to chance."

"Your employer has a family member who has an inoperable brain tumor." It wasn't a question. They had tiptoed around this issue yesterday too.

"What's on your agenda?" Abi asked, ignoring her question. "You mentioned things you needed to do."

She considered the man and wondered what in his life had formed his decision to go down this murky path. His father had been a high-ranking member of the Mossad and after retirement, his role in Israeli politics became noteworthy. But Abi had been raised by his mother in London and he had not chosen to serve either country in any capacity. He served only himself.

"Initial stop—my brother's condo. I want to have a look around."

"You believe there's something more going on than what you've been told in your briefing?"

She took her cup and plate to the sink. If he was expecting her to do the dishes because he had cooked, he could forget it. "I don't believe or disbelieve anything. I simply wish to have a look at my brother's home."

He gave a nod. "As you wish."

"Later we can go over the plan." She might as well understand how his employer expected this to go down.

"We won't be going over the plan until we are ready to move."

This she found troubling. "You're assuming there's no room for error in your plan. How can you be so sure the plan doesn't need to be tweaked?"

"The plan is perfect."

"There's no such thing as a perfect plan," she argued.

He smiled. "I'll agree to disagree."

The door opened and Poe joined them in the kitchen. "Morning." He looked from her to Abi and back. "Everything okay?"

"We're going to Luke's condo to have a look around."

He nodded, his expression giving nothing of his feelings away. "Can we talk for a minute?"

"Sure."

"Let's take a walk," Poe suggested. "Outside."

"Sure." She flashed a smile for Abi. "We'll be just outside." She wanted a look around out there anyway.

On the way out the door, Jamie grabbed her coat—the one provided with the other items for this op. Poe had nothing but the windbreaker he'd been wearing in LA. Not exactly suitable for December in Tennessee.

Once they were outside and walking around the infinity pool overlooking the wooded valley below, Poe turned to her. "What's the deal between you and this guy?"

With all that was going on, this was what he needed to talk about?

"Nothing." She surveyed the valley and the house that sat in the middle of those woods. The house was their target. Getting in and out of there with the surgeon in tow would never be easy. Whatever Abi thought, the sort of man who had a body double on staff no doubt had serious protection wherever he went. He would not go with Jamie willingly.

On top of the idea that there was a good chance they would end up dead just for trying to get to him, there was the idea of what would happen if they were successful. The authorities wouldn't rest until they solved the case. Beyond that, there was the concern that the surgeon could end up injured or dead.

Luke could end up injured or dead.

So many things could go wrong.

"Come on, Jamie. I can see there's a connection. How do you know this guy?"

"I bumped into him late last year after an assignment for the agency. He attempted to infiltrate my cover. The op was over, so I don't know why he bothered. Maybe just to see if he could. To flirt."

Poe held up his hands. "Maybe I don't want to know." He visibly shook himself. Maybe from the cold. "So I've thought about the layout down there." He looked toward the surgeon's home. "The security protocols he used the last time he hosted a party and his personal security team are detailed in the package Abi provided. The chances of getting in and out of there will be slim. Very slim." He shook his head. "I have a really bad feeling about this."

She smiled sadly. "It's not like I have a choice. I have to try."

"I did some research on Case as well. He's not exactly known as Mr. Personality. I don't think your friend's employer understands that he could very well refuse to do the surgery."

Jamie had considered this could be an issue. "I suppose we'll just have to convince him somehow."

"But we can't make him," Poe argued. "We can put a gun

to his head, but we cannot make him do the surgery. Torturing him or shooting him won't be an option."

"You're saying you don't think the plan is a good one."

He moved his head from side to side. "The doctor will need proper motivation."

Jamie thought of the photos of the doctor and his family she had reviewed. "He has a kid. A little girl."

Poe nodded. "Ten years old. Take the kid for leverage and there won't be any trouble getting him to go along with whatever he's asked to do. I'm guessing that's why Abi isn't sharing more details. He knows you aren't going to like it."

Fury roared through Jamie. "On top of that, it's another reason why he isn't doing this on his own. He'll focus on the kid while you and I whisk away the surgeon."

"That's what I'm thinking. There's a hell of a lot of room for error, especially with a kid in the mix. I don't like this, Jamie."

She swore. She hated when people used kids for leverage. "I don't either."

A quick review of their options was pretty straightforward: do as they were told or do as they were told. "We'll go with the plan as far as we can," she said, feeling suddenly tired. "From there, we'll do what we have to do to ensure everyone survives."

"This friend of yours," Poe said. "Any suspicions he'll double cross us when the job is done?"

"There's always that chance. We just need to be ready for anything that comes our way."

Jamie's attention shifted to the house. Abi was watching them from the other side of the wall of glass. He knew a lot more than he was sharing.

The question was, would it get them killed?

Douglas Avenue,
10:20 a.m.

LUKE'S CONDO WAS a wreck. And as much as Luke despised housecleaning, this was more than just his indifference to chores. The place had been ransacked. She shouldn't be surprised, and she wasn't. Not really. More unsettled. This was Luke's place. His things.

Jamie moved through the condo slowly, taking her time to look at any and all items. The space wasn't that large so with both Poe and Abi prowling around it was on the cramped side.

She tidied the place as she went. Touching Luke's things relieved her somehow. Relaxed her to a degree. He was her little brother. She loved him. She'd always taken care of him.

"There were three of them," Poe said. "Two who pilfered through his things, one who interrogated him."

Jamie hoped the interrogation hadn't included any torture. "I haven't spotted any blood."

Poe shook his head. "Me either."

This was good. She watched as Poe moved around the space, pausing to linger and then tracing his fingers over an item. Poe read crime scenes like no one she had ever met. Just being in the room and touching the victim's things could pull him in deep enough to practically see through the eyes of the victim.

It was an uncanny gift.

Jamie moved on to her brother's bedroom and picked through his things. She tidied what she could and made a pile of what should be in the laundry hamper.

"Finding anything relevant?"

She turned to find Abi propped in the open doorway. "Nothing yet."

"It doesn't appear anything—including your brother—was damaged in the search."

"The question is, why did they need to search? If my brother was simply leverage, what were they looking for?"

"Perhaps—" Abi pushed away from the door and walked deeper into the room "—he refused to cooperate with their questions about you."

"So they were looking through his underwear drawers for information on my whereabouts?"

A smirk twitched Abi's lips. "One never knows about siblings."

"Ha ha." She smiled at the framed photo on the dresser. The fam—their mom and dad and the two of them. If anything had happened to Luke…

No, she couldn't go there.

"I'm sure you knew how to find me," she said as she exited the room.

Abi followed. "I suppose I should have mentioned as much."

"You weren't here when they picked up Luke?"

"I'm afraid not."

That explained the search.

"Did you suggest they use my brother as leverage?" The thought made her furious. She clamped her jaw shut to prevent saying more than she should. Staying on good terms was imperative—at least for now. She could punch him in the face later. When this was done.

He made a big deal of appearing to consider her question. "I may have suggested the concept."

She so wanted to kick his butt.

"Well, at least now I know who ruined my Christmas."

She put the pile of soiled clothes in the hamper and walked to the kitchen. She took her time and had a look around. She didn't really expect to find anything useful here, but she would be remiss if she didn't go through the steps. At the front door, she paused to open the coat closet. She picked through the offerings until she found something suitable for Poe.

"You need this more than the windbreaker." She passed the leather coat to him.

"Thanks."

She turned to Abi. "Where are they keeping him?"

"I'm afraid I have no idea."

Probably a lie. "Why can't I see him? Verify that he's okay."

"You'll see him when the op is complete. You have my word that he is okay."

"Is that supposed to make me feel better?" This man would say whatever he was paid to say. They both knew this to be true.

"I would certainly hope so." He looked from her to Poe and back. "Are we ready to go back to the house?"

Jamie walked to her brother's desk and sat down. She tapped the trackpad to wake the computer. It was up and running and required a password. She didn't attempt to access the system. No need. Her brother was too smart to leave information too readily accessible. She opened the two shallow drawers and picked through them. Nothing of particular interest. Sharpies, pens. She hadn't really expected there to be anything helpful as to his whereabouts, but she wanted to buy time. She was in no hurry to get back to the Excalibur house. But there was one other thing she wanted to find out.

"I'm finished." She stood, pushed in her chair and headed for the door.

They locked up and descended the stairs that led down

to the ground level. Jamie surveyed the street and postage-stamp-size yard that served two condos. The place was like her brother—efficient, well thought out, minimal. He didn't like wasting time. And he didn't like a lot of stuff.

Jamie settled into the passenger seat while Abi slid behind the steering wheel. Poe climbed in the back. She was sure he wasn't very happy about being relegated to the back seat, but someone had to take one for the team.

"We should stop for lunch." She shrugged. "Since we're out, I mean." Mostly, she just didn't want to rush back to the house. And she'd like to see if anyone was following them. She hadn't spotted anyone on the way here. Going back might be a different story.

Nashville was not Abi's home turf. Jamie knew far more about this city than he did—only because her brother lived here. Despite being in charge, out here in the wild, Abi was just one of them.

"Why my brother and why me?" The story he'd given her up to now just didn't fit in her opinion.

"Your reputation precedes you," he said, absorbed in navigating traffic.

"I'm still not buying it."

There was something he was leaving out. Something relevant. And even if there wasn't, it kept him trying to assuage her concerns. She liked making him work for his comfort.

"Perhaps it's best not to dwell on the whys and just do what we must do."

"How did he find you?"

He glanced at her. Now there was a question he hadn't been expecting. "I have a certain reputation."

This was true. "What're you doing? Advertising on the dark web now?"

"I shouldn't answer that question."

Keeping an eye on the exterior mirror on her side, she said, "I'm still not convinced of why they need us both." She and Poe had discussed the idea of Dr. Case's child being a target as well, which would certainly require more than one pair of hands.

But it didn't have to be Jamie or her brother.

"We'll have food delivered to the house," he said as he pointed the car in that direction.

And there it was. This other thing that nagged at her. He wanted to keep her at the house until it was time for the op. Was he concerned something would happen? That she would be injured somehow, making her useless for the purposes of the operation?

As if fate had decided to answer her question, a black sedan appeared in the passenger-side mirror. It was a ways back, but she watched as he made turn after turn and the sedan did the same. Oh yeah. They had a tail.

"Does having me here have something to do with my grandmother?" She hadn't considered the idea until now. The Colby name was internationally known. Mostly she was making conversation while she watched their tail.

"This only has to do with you and your participation in achieving the proper outcome. Trying to read something more into it is a waste of time."

He was sticking to his story, which suggested he could possibly be telling the truth.

But she wasn't ready to let him off the hook just yet.

"Your father was kidnapped as a child."

The question startled her. Jamie glanced back at Poe. He knew about what her father had gone through. They were friends. Good friends. She'd shared more with him than she did with most. She shifted her attention to the driver. But she hadn't shared any of that with this man. Finding this information wouldn't be so difficult, but the question was why did he consider it relevant enough to look into?

"He was. He was taken at seven years old and wasn't found until more than two decades later. My grandparents thought he was dead, so they had stopped looking."

"You know what happened to him during that time?"

"Why are we talking about this?" Poe demanded.

"It's okay," she said to her friend. Then, to Abi, she said, "I do. Why do you ask?" To say this line of questioning was making her tense was an understatement. She did not like the idea of feeling a comparison between her father's and her brother's kidnapping situations. No one who knew those circumstances would.

"No reason. I was just curious."

That was a lie. Until just this minute, she hadn't really considered who his employer was. Now she was more than a little concerned. Was he somehow connected to her family? Or their past?

She suddenly wished she could speak to her dad.

"You ask a lot of questions," Poe said, likely noting her uneasiness.

Abi laughed. "Curiosity killed the cat."

He made a sharp turn and then gunned the accelerator. Oh, she got it now. He wanted to distract them from the fact that they had a tail.

"You got some idea of who our tail is?" She looked to Abi for his answer.

His jaw hardened. He never took failure well. "Not to worry. We will lose him."

"Are you sure?"

He sent her a hard look and then took another treacherous turn.

This was a secret mission with a secret target and a secret benefactor. Who else could know their plan? At first,

Jamie had wondered if it was part of some security detail. It didn't appear to be someone Abi wanted on their tail.

As they drove, seemingly tail-free now, he watched the mirrors closely. Took several more unnecessary turns in Jamie's opinion. She thought of the doctor—their target. He was just a man, but one with very special talents. At this time there was no one else like him in what he could do. He was uniquely necessary to fulfill a need that could be fulfilled no other way.

What was that ability worth? A lot, apparently. Enough to go to great lengths to make this happen.

There was still something—a piece she was missing. Perhaps it was irrelevant in the grand scheme of things, but she couldn't shake the nagging sensation that there was something more she needed to know...to understand.

Poe could feel it too. She saw it in his eyes whenever they grilled Abi this way.

Jamie made a decision. She had to ask this burning question. "Before we move into position for the op, I'll need to know the part you're not telling me."

Abi laughed. "You should let this foolish idea go. You have my word, Jamie. There is nothing else to know."

Funny, that did not make her feel one iota better.

"And that answer," she said, glancing at him, "is why I will never trust you, Abi."

"You can trust me, Jamie. This is a simple matter of monumental importance. That's all. The weight of the concept is misleading on a basic implementation level. Don't overthink it."

The man so loved throwing those opposing adjectives together.

"I hope you're being straight with me, Abi. I don't want either of us to regret this thing you've decided we must do."

He flashed her one of those grins that made breathing difficult. "No regrets."

Then why did she feel as if she regretted it already?

Chapter Five

Excalibur Court,
2:00 p.m.

Abi excused himself and went outside to take a call.

He hadn't stopped for food. But Jamie got why he hadn't.

"I don't like this." Poe stared beyond the wall of glass doors and watched Abi pace back and forth next to the infinity pool.

Jamie braced her hands on her hips and met her friend's gaze. "I'm with you, believe me. If something is going wrong this early in the game, we're in trouble."

"You're thinking of that tail he struggled to lose."

She nodded. "That was my primary reason for wanting to go out today. He's making this all seem so pat—as if everything is in place with no concerns. This—" she looked to the man outside "—is a concern."

Poe turned his back to the outdoor space and fixed his worried gaze on Jamie. "You know when you have this feeling deep in your gut that something is really, really wrong but you can't quite put your finger on the problem?"

Jamie flattened her palm against her belly. "Right here. The same place that lets you know when you need to cut and run."

"Yeah." He glanced over his shoulder at the man outside. "I'm not saying your friend is setting us up, but he knows this is off somehow and he's just going along as if it's all good."

Yeah, she'd picked up on that. "The good news is I didn't get the impression at Luke's place that there was a truly violent struggle or any of the usual issues we should worry about."

Actually, that could be good or bad, but she had decided to see it as a good thing. Victoria had heard Luke's voice. For now, the situation appeared to be running along without any glitches—with the exception of the potential tail they'd had to lose. If the plan played out the way they had been briefed, then hopefully Luke would be released tomorrow night.

She wasn't thinking beyond that. It wasn't like a person or persons could be kidnapped and everyone involved just walked away as if nothing had happened. There would be repercussions. And, frankly, it wasn't like she could pretend she had immunity in the kidnapping of a prestigious doctor—if this went down as planned.

Since Abi appeared in no hurry to get back inside, Jamie decided to use the time wisely. Who knew how much time she and Poe would have alone?

"What do we know about this Dr. Case?" Poe asked. "I mean, really? Beyond the bio on his website and in the file Abi provided?"

"I was just thinking the same thing," Jamie admitted. "The basics are that he graduated from Vanderbilt, then went on to specialize at Johns Hopkins. He spent the next dozen years building his claim to fame in neurosurgery."

Poe glanced outside to ensure Abi remained preoccupied. "Early this year he completed the first successful surgery removing a previously deemed inoperable brain tumor. Since that time, he's completed many more such operations. But he's only one man."

"And patients from all over the country are frantically trying to get on his schedule."

"While he," Poe said, "is talking about cutting back on the number of surgeries he's doing in order to train more surgeons to do the same."

"But the patients are desperate—they're facing death sentences without this surgery." Jamie started to pace. She could only imagine how the patients felt. If the doctor was doing all he could, then this wasn't easy for him either.

"The bottom line is," Poe went on, "what does your friend's employer want with Dr. Case?"

"Ostensibly, this lifesaving surgery for himself or a family member."

"Either way, the man—woman, whoever—has the means to go after what he wants no matter that it's not legal."

"He has the means but he doesn't have the time to wait," Jamie agreed. "So he's buying a place at the front of the line." Certainly not fair but there were those who would do whatever necessary to get what they wanted.

"If he's smart he has created a plan that ensures he will walk away from this without revealing his identity." Poe shrugged. "It's the only possibility that makes sense. Why would he want to live only to go to prison?"

"Which suggests it's a family member, so he doesn't care." Jamie frowned. "The one hitch in that plan is the doctor. How does Abi's employer protect his identity from the surgeon himself?"

"I don't see how he can." Poe considered the idea for a moment. "Unless it's all carefully choreographed in a way that Case does his thing and then he's taken away. The employer's personal physician will take it from there. Which would mean he'd require a private surgery suite."

"Why the Colby Agency?" Jamie shrugged. "I mean, the agency is the best, but there are other players out there who could help with this op. I haven't seen or heard anything as of yet that makes me believe I have a particular skill set that this guy couldn't find in another operative."

"But," Poe said with a look that underscored his words, "it's you this guy—" he hitched a thumb toward Abi "—wanted to play with."

She couldn't deny the possibility. "Maybe, but Abi is smart. He wouldn't allow his personal feelings to get in the way of a successful mission. He's too good for that."

"Then we have to assume there's a personal connection between your family and this mission. Or perhaps that's what he wants us to believe."

That was the part that worried Jamie. Which was true?

"I need to have a closer look around here." She surveyed the large great room. "Can you keep Abi preoccupied when he comes back in while I have a look around?"

"Sure. We'll just pretend to be mates," he teased in a faux British accent.

Jamie shook her head at her friend, glanced toward Abi and then hurried out of the room. She made her way up the stairs and went straight to the bedroom Abi had chosen for himself. He'd made the room assignments. Considering the clothing and toiletry selections he'd prepared for her, he'd had access to this property for at least a day or two before they arrived.

She opened the door and walked into his room. The bed was unmade. The rumpled sheets kept her gaze lingering longer than they should have. She forced her attention to the nightstands next to the bed. She quickly went through the drawers of each. The only personal item she found was a cell phone charger. She moved on to the dresser where she rummaged through his underwear and socks, taking care to feel for any items that might be hidden inside.

She found nothing in the drawers or under them, so the closet was next. Two blazers and three shirts hung on wooden hangers. Jamie checked the pockets and then the extra pair of shoes standing neatly on the carpet.

There was nothing in the room that he wouldn't want anyone to find.

Jamie walked out of his room and closed the door the way she had found it. Abi was too savvy to leave anything lying around that might give away some aspect of his plan. She went through her and Poe's rooms, double-checking for bugs. She found nothing.

Downstairs, Abi had come inside.

"Since we weren't able to stop, I'll order lunch," he announced.

Jamie wasn't sure she could eat, but she kept that to herself. Food was essential to gain energy. "Anything but pizza." She had eaten pizza two nights in a row on the previous mission.

Poe laughed. "Yeah, the only food available near that last motel was pizza."

"No pizza," Abi assured them. "I was thinking Mediterranean."

"Works for me," Poe announced.

"I need to check in with Victoria," Jamie announced. She needed to know what was going on.

Abi looked up from whatever app he'd chosen to use for ordering food. "As long as I can hear the conversation, I don't have a problem with that."

Jamie nodded. "Understood."

Poe caught her gaze. "I think I'll take a nap until the food comes."

Sounded like Poe had some looking around he wanted to do as well. He disappeared upstairs, and Jamie put through the call. Her grandmother answered on the first ring. "It's me," Jamie said, wishing she could be there in person to talk to her. She'd likely been waiting for a call all day.

"Are you okay, Jamie?"

She smiled. She loved the sound of her grandmother's voice. So commanding and yet so caring. "I'm good, yes. We went to Luke's condo today. I didn't find any readily visible cause for alarm."

"Have you spoken to him?"

"No. Maybe I'll get to later." Jamie chewed her lower lip. There was a lot she wanted to say but holding back was the smarter choice. "Any news from Mom and Dad?"

Her mother hadn't been herself lately. Jamie was glad she and Dad were on vacation and not in the middle of this mess.

"I did," Victoria said. "They're doing well. Just missing all of us. I assured them we will all be fine for Christmas. They should enjoy themselves and relax."

"That's exactly what they should do," Jamie agreed. "I hope you gave them my love."

"I certainly did. Jamie…"

She heard the worry in her grandmother's voice. "Really, Grandmother, I'm fine."

"Please be careful. I wish there was more we could do."

"Knowing that you're standing by is enough."

They talked a few minutes more before Jamie was able to say goodbye. She so loved her grandparents. Victoria was the epitome of all that Jamie believed was right in this world. She hoped to be able to accomplish just a fraction of what her grandmother had done with her life. Her grandfather too.

"What's the ETA on the food?" She tucked her cell phone away.

"Should be here any minute." Abi searched her face, her eyes. "I find it difficult to believe your grandparents aren't up to something. But I haven't picked up on any chatter from the Colby Agency."

"They would never do anything that might endanger Luke or me."

"You're lucky to have people who care about you that way."

She felt like that was an opening, but decided not to take it. "I'll find Poe. Let him know the food will be here soon."

Giving Abi her back, she hurried from the room and up the stairs. She found Poe in his room, staring out the window toward the home of Dr. Quentin Case.

"Abi says the food will be here soon."

Poe glanced at her, then waited for her to join him at the window. "I can't figure out what he thinks he's accomplishing by keeping everything a secret until the last minute. You know there's a reason that we're not going to like."

"I know." She leaned one shoulder against the window frame. "The only reason to do that is if he thinks I'll have an issue with the proposed execution of the op."

"The house is right there." He nodded in the direction of the mansion in the valley below. "Why not just spell it out now? It's not like we can't put together a number of scenarios in our heads. We've done this sort of thing too many times."

"Maybe he's worried we'll give him the slip and share the details with the police or with someone else who can stop him." This wasn't the sort of global issue the IOA dealt with, but they would certainly not hesitate to send an extraction team to recover two of their agents. Except contacting anyone at all was a risk she wasn't willing to take. Luke's life hung in the balance.

"Unless," Poe countered, "the employer is Abi himself."

Now this was an avenue she had not considered. "You may be right." Wow. She knew Abi's family. There was his father. His mother. No siblings. No spouse as far as she knew.

"Whatever he's planning," Poe said, drawing her attention back to him, "I don't want you taking the risk too far. You have to protect yourself, Jamie."

She frowned. "Why would I not protect myself? It's the first rule of any op. You can't complete it if you're down for the count."

Poe laughed. "You always do that. Deflect. I just don't want you to throw caution to wind for this guy. He's not worth it, Jamie. He's using you and Luke."

Yeah. She recognized Poe was right on that one. "I'm aware."

He reached up and tucked a strand of hair behind her ear. "You're important to me, Jamie. Our work is sometimes dangerous—maybe not so much when we're plucking Santas from trouble."

She laughed. "Even Santa needs rescuing sometimes."

"True. Just be careful. I don't trust this guy at all."

She hugged him. Closed her eyes and inhaled deeply of his unique scent. "Don't worry. I plan on taking you home for Christmas when this is finished."

She'd made that decision the moment this whole thing started. She wanted her family to know this man. The realization surprised her a little...but in a good way.

10:00 p.m.

JAMIE STOOD ON the patio and stared toward the Case home. The place was lit up like an airfield. If the family had company tonight, it wasn't obvious. No cars parked in the front cobblestoned parking area. Even from here she could see the massive fountain with its flickering lights that sat in the middle of that parking area.

According to Google, the house where Dr. Case lived had only been built two years ago to the tune of several million dollars. He'd built the house even before perfecting the surgical procedure that had put him on the map. He had two children. A son who had started Harvard this past fall. And a daughter who was only ten years old. His wife wrote children's books and spent a lot of time volunteering. Good for her. She was also a nurse, but she donated her time to a clinic in downtown Nashville.

By all accounts, the family was highly respected and more than a little revered in the area.

All the more reason for Jamie to see this through one way or another. Someone had to protect that family during this… Whatever it was. She just hoped she wasn't going to be caught in a situation where she had to choose between her brother and a member of the doctor's family.

So far there had been no mention of weapons, but she wasn't naive enough to believe they were going into this thing unarmed. Particularly considering Case had serious security. There would be weapons, and anytime weapons were involved, trouble was just one tiny mistake away.

That would be the problem. Getting in and out without triggering a gunfight with the doctor's security team.

As if she'd voiced the issue out loud, Abi joined her on the patio. He surveyed the valley below before turning to her.

"It's cold out here," he pointed out.

Her body suddenly realized he was right. She shivered. "I hadn't noticed."

He laughed. "I see that."

She wrapped her arms around herself. "Not that cold. Remember I grew up in Chicago."

He removed the jacket he was wearing and draped it over her shoulders. "I remember."

The warmth from his body immediately seeped into hers. "Thanks." She tugged the coat closer around her.

"Your friend has been pacing the floor for hours."

Poe had paced the floor down here until only a few minutes ago and then he'd called it a night only to pace the floor in his room.

"He's restless."

"He needs to chill." Abi crossed his arms over his chest, the cold night air obviously getting to him since he'd given his jacket to her.

"Maybe he could if you'd give us some insight into how this is going down."

"I'm afraid I can't do that. You will know exactly what to do when it's time to move."

She heaved a frustrated breath. "That's no way to run a railroad," she argued. "Preparation is always key in any operation. Preparation of all players."

He shot her a grin. "Trust me. I have thoroughly prepared for this. For all of us."

"Tell me one thing." She turned to him and fixed her gaze on his.

"One thing," he agreed.

"Does someone in your family need this doctor's help?" If this was personal, the situation was all the more dangerous. Personal was never, ever good.

"No one in my family is involved. This is not personal, Jamie. You have my word."

"Good." She considered what she should ask next. "How did you learn of this mission?"

"So what you really want is two things," he said, eye-brows raised.

"The one thing was just me getting started."

He smiled. "I see that." He exhaled an audible breath. "I was approached by a representative of my employer."

He looked directly at her as he spoke. Gaze open. No blink, no flinch. So far he appeared to be telling her the truth.

"Are you completely comfortable with the plan?" She had worked with Abi before. He was good. Damned good.

"The plan is flawless. You do not need to worry about the plan. I have considered every possibility. There are no weaknesses...no holes."

"Your reputation is impeccable when it comes to plan-ning and executing a mission," Jamie confessed. "I saw firsthand when we worked together how capable you are."

"Capable." He chuckled. "A good word, I suppose."

"No other aspect of anyone's ability is relevant if it's not capable."

He seemed to weigh her words a moment. "We spent a good deal of time together during that mission."

They had spent a considerable amount of time together, and they had shared a *moment*.

The memory had her cheeks heating. She was thankful it was dark to prevent him seeing that she'd blushed at the memory.

"We worked well together," he pointed out.

"We did, but—" Jamie looked directly at him "—it can't be like last time."

Her brother's life was in the balance. She could not allow herself to be distracted.

"The mission hasn't started yet," he argued. "Who knows what we'll find time for before we're finished?"

"Did you drag my brother into this just so you could force me to be involved?"

"How do you know Luke isn't my employer?"

The question startled her. This was something she had not considered. She thought a moment about the possibility. To her knowledge, Luke had no significant other just now. He would have told her. But she couldn't say with complete certainty that there wasn't someone he wanted to help. He was always doing things for other people—especially those in need. This seemed a little over-the-top for his ability. He had a sizable trust fund, but it wasn't like he could withdraw that kind of money without permission.

Unless that was what the ten-million-dollar ransom was about.

The thought had her gritting her teeth for a moment. No, she decided. No way.

"Luke would have come to me if he'd needed help with something like this." Jamie was certain. He wouldn't have gone about it this way. No way.

Abi searched her face, her eyes. "I did not and would not have taken your brother hostage in order to get your attention. It's important that you understand that was not my decision."

"Can you guarantee me he's safe?"

"I can assure you that he is perfectly safe."

"Then you trust your employer enough to take that risk?"

He frowned. "What risk?"

"The risk that if something happens to my brother, I will make you pay."

His frown slid into a grin. "I am very well aware of what would happen to me if I was responsible for trouble with your brother."

"Just so you know, I won't go in without being fully

briefed and feeling confident that all is as it should be. So don't go suggesting it's time to go with the idea of filling me in on the way. I will refuse."

"I'm aware." He tugged the lapels of the jacket a little closer to ensure she stayed warm. "We will go through everything very carefully before we move in."

So they were invading the house.

"I'm assuming we have invitations to the party," she said, mostly just to see what he would say.

"Better to be invited than to have to figure out another way in."

"Your employer is powerful."

"Of course."

That he was rich went without saying. "But he isn't powerful enough to get the one thing he wants more than anything else."

Abi's gaze collided with hers. "There are some things even money cannot buy."

Which told her that Abi's employer had already approached this doctor and been turned away.

"For all those other things," Jamie suggested, "there are people like you."

Abi smiled. "If not me, someone else would do it. At least if I do it, I do it well."

No question. The upside was that what she knew of Abi was as close to good as a mostly bad guy could be.

"I know what you're thinking."

She sort of hoped he did not. "And what's that?"

"You're thinking 'What is a bad guy like me doing trying to help someone do a good thing—like kidnap a doctor to save a life?'"

"The thought occurred to me, yes." It wasn't the usual job Abi was known for.

"You're wondering," he went on, "if I might be growing soft in my old age."

She laughed. She couldn't help herself. Abi was only thirty. "Didn't cross my mind."

"When I was approached about this mission," he explained, "I could not say no. By this time tomorrow you will understand my reasons."

"I'm sure you're aware that no one involved is going to walk away from this legally speaking." It wasn't a threat, merely a statement of fact.

"I have a plan for that as well."

He sounded so certain of himself. "I just hope your plan is as good as you seem to believe it is."

He traced a fingertip down her cheek before dropping his hand. "I have never failed. Never. You are aware of this."

She resisted the need to shiver at his touch. "Just because you've never failed doesn't mean you won't."

That was the part that worried her the most. There was always a first time for failure. And the first time was always the worst.

Chapter Six

10:50 p.m.

Kenny stared out the window at the house below their position. He was more than a little worried about this operation. Not for himself, but for Jamie. And Luke. He didn't trust this guy Abidan Amar. At all.

He was aware of Amar before today. He'd heard Jamie talk about him, but only a couple of times. Now that he'd seen the two of them together, he understood why. They'd shared something when they did that operation together. No question about it. As ridiculous as it sounded, he was working hard not to look and sound as jealous as he felt, but it wasn't easy. If he was completely honest with himself, he would own the fact that he had very deep feelings for Jamie. But first and foremost, they were friends. Best friends. He didn't want to risk damaging that relationship. Not just because they worked together fairly often, but also because she meant a great deal to him. If necessary, he would gladly be just friends forever.

He thought of that one kiss they had shared. A smile tugged at his lips. It had actually been a part of the mission they were working together at the time. But he'd felt the connection as real as breathing. Good God, how he'd felt the connection. He'd been really careful since then. If a move happened between them, it would be because she initiated the action.

Jamie was the real deal, with an amazing family that he respected so much. She'd invited him to family celebrations on a number of occasions and it was during their shared downtime that he really felt the pull. Whatever happened, he was giving her plenty of space and plenty of time to make a move.

The sound of footfalls on the stairs told him she was coming up to the second floor. He moved soundlessly to the door and leaned against it. She hesitated outside his door and his heart bumped hard in his chest. Three seconds, then five elapsed before she went on into her room and closed the door. She'd wanted to say something or…

Give it a rest, Kenny.

Whatever she'd pondered during that brief pause, her sense of professionalism had prevented her from saying or doing whatever had crossed her mind.

For the best. For sure. This wasn't the time to get personal. Too much was unknown, and Luke's life hung in that precarious space of uncertainty.

Whatever this thing was that Abi was up to, Kenny would do everything in his power to protect Jamie and Luke. He almost laughed at the idea of Jamie needing him for protection. Backup, maybe. But she could certainly take care of herself and any jerk who would suggest otherwise did not know her at all.

Still, he worried that she trusted Amar far too much. Kenny didn't trust him one little bit. From that haughty accent of his to the way this whole thing was shaking down, Kenny didn't like it…at all.

He needed to sleep. He climbed into the bed and forced

his eyes closed. He thought of Jamie just across the hall. The way she smiled… The sound of her laugh. She was so beautiful and so smart.

If they got through this…maybe it was time he told her how he felt.

Maybe.

If he didn't lose his courage.

Sunday, December 23

Two Days Before Christmas

Chapter Seven

To her surprise Jamie had managed to sleep. Maybe sheer exhaustion had helped. Whatever the reasons, she was grateful to wake up somewhat refreshed. It was always easier to stay focused with a few hours of sleep under one's belt.

When she was a child, her grandmother had always warned that a lack of sleep stole one's waking life. Stole one's ability to function...to remember. Jamie had always taken sleep very seriously because of those warnings.

For the past hour she had been lying in her bed, mulling over the things Abi had said last night. He had a plan for not only getting the mission completed successfully but also for ensuring no one was arrested. She actually could not see how he planned to make that happen, but she could hope.

What they were about to do was illegal. Not just a little crime either. This was kidnapping. A felony. This wasn't the sort of dance on the edge you walked away so easily from. Though she might be able to argue that in her case she had no choice in the matter since her brother's life was at stake. She was, to a large degree, being forced to participate. Still, the powers that be would wonder why she hadn't called the proper authorities. Fear for her brother's safety was a fairly good defense. Their phones were monitored—

no unauthorized calls. To go against that edict was to risk Luke's life. As for Abi, he was assuredly breaking numerous laws with no mitigating factors to provide relief. He no doubt expected to get away scot-free.

The Colby Agency had the best attorneys in the country but that worry wasn't a priority right now. Jamie wasn't really worried for her future. As long as she avoided shooting anyone, she could potentially see her way clear—legally speaking—of this business. Whatever happened, her endgame was to rescue her brother. Optimally, she would do this without harming anyone else or getting herself shot.

Keeping Poe out of trouble was her top priority next to rescuing Luke. She would not allow Poe to be hurt by this mess. When she'd come to bed last night, she had lingered outside his door. The need to talk to him, to just be with him had been almost overwhelming. But she had made the right decision.

They were good friends. Very good friends. Since that kiss, it had become harder and harder to pretend she didn't feel other things for him. But she didn't want to harm their friendship in any way.

Poe was the reason she'd been so vulnerable to Abi last year. Even before the kiss that she and Poe had shared, she'd been attracted to him. Funny how those things happened when you were least expecting them.

Get your head on straight, Jamie. After a quick shower, she tugged on the wardrobe selection for today. The fact that Abi had known what size jeans she wore wasn't such a big surprise. That he'd done so well selecting items she would feel comfortable in was an added plus. The sweatshirt sported a Chicago Cubs logo. She shook her head. Nice of him to try to make her feel at home. She pulled on a pair of socks and the sneakers she'd worn from LA. She wondered if the Santa she and Poe had rescued fully understood yet that they had saved his life. Sometimes targets were so flustered about being plucked from whatever their circumstances that they never got that they were damned lucky to still be breathing.

She brushed her hair and pulled it into a ponytail. She and Poe needed to discuss a potential exit strategy—for him anyway. This wasn't really his fight and he needed to know she would understand if he ducked out.

But he wouldn't. She knew him too well. She and Poe had been friends for a while now. Good friends. She understood that if he had his way, they would take their relationship to the next level. He had never said as much and was fairly subtle about it, but the signs were unmistakable. Not happening. Jamie didn't want to risk what they had. It sounded cliché, but it was true. Falling in love wasn't on her agenda just now anyway.

She was young. They both were. They had plenty of time to fall in love. Her grandmother would be the first to say Jamie should stay focused on her career for now. All the rest could come later.

She removed her cell from its charger and tucked it into her hip pocket. Since this mission was to go down tonight, maybe Abi would be ready to share the details this morning. No matter that she wouldn't say as much, on some level she understood his hesitance. The sooner he shared the ins and outs of the mission, the sooner she and Poe could consider options for reacting differently than was intended. The sooner a leak could happen. He was just practicing extra careful precautions.

She walked to the door, leaned against it and listened. All quiet. She eased the door open and looked both ways. Hall was clear. The distinct scent of coffee wafted from downstairs and had her leaning in that direction. But before going down, she wanted to see if Poe was still in his room.

Across the hall, she listened at his door. She didn't hear anything so she rapped softly on the door. "Poe," she whispered, "you up?"

Usually, he was up before her. It was possible he was already downstairs, but since she hadn't heard voices, she suspected not. She couldn't see him and Abi standing around in the kitchen staring at each other without exchanging at least a few words.

Then again, maybe she could see them glaring at each other, circling the room like two wrestlers about to tangle.

She knocked again and when no answer came, she opted to give the knob a turn and see if the door was locked. It was not. It opened with little effort. The room was empty. Bed unmade. No surprise there. Poe wasn't exactly the neatest dude on the planet. He would insist he had other assets, and he would be right. She had never met anyone who could read a scene the way he could. He almost had a sixth sense when it came to seeing the details. The FBI had wanted him so badly, but like her, Poe had wanted to do something different…something maybe more relevant.

Certainly, this operation had not been on either of their agendas.

Since the bathroom door stood partially open, she checked in there and found no sign of Poe. A towel hung over the shower door, suggesting he had showered before leaving the room or before bed last night. She wandered back into the hall. Maybe he had gone downstairs, and he and Abi actually were down there staring at each other, waiting to see who broke first.

Listening intently for any sign of life, she descended the

stairs and made her way through the living room and into the kitchen.

No Poe. No Abi.

Then she spotted Abi on the patio, savoring his coffee. Steam rose from the mug he held, matching the steam wafting from the pool. He stared toward the house belonging to the doctor. She wondered if he was suffering second thoughts about what he had agreed to do.

Where the heck was Poe?

She made a full round of the first floor. Checked the powder room and the small library. She even had a look out the front windows. No Poe.

Worry started its slow creep around the edges of her mind. Poe wouldn't just leave without telling her where he was going. Besides, she was fairly confident that Abi wouldn't allow either of them to leave until this was done.

When she still found no sign of Poe, she opened the door onto the patio and joined Abi. "Good morning."

He gave her a nod. "Morning." He frowned. "No coffee?"

"I was looking for Poe. Have you spoken to him this morning?"

Abi's gaze narrowed. "I haven't seen him this morning. Did you check his room?"

"I did. He doesn't appear to be down here either." Now she was getting worried. Her nerves jangled. Poe wouldn't just try to leave without telling her. Her worry turned to suspicion, and she had a bad feeling that Abi knew more than he was telling.

"All right. Let's have a look," he suggested. "We can cover more ground if we split up. I'll go outside. You go through the house again."

She shook her head. "No. You go through the house. I want to look outside." She'd already been through the house.

He started to argue but then decided against it. "Fine. Just keep a low profile. There are neighbors up here."

Jamie walked to the front door, pulled on her coat and headed outside. Excalibur Court was a single, dead end street. There were about a dozen large houses that circled the short street. The ones on their side overlooked the valley below where Dr. Case's house sat nestled amid the thick woods. On the other side of the street, the houses backed up to another cul-de-sac. The area was thickly wooded so there was some amount of privacy despite the number of houses.

Jamie walked to the end of the drive and surveyed the cul-de-sac. There were no vehicles in the driveways. There were probably rules about leaving a vehicle outside the garage. There was one dark sedan at the end of the cul-de-sac parked in the common area. She watched it for a moment. Didn't see anyone inside. The street was quiet. A breeze whipped through the air, reminding Jamie that it was almost Christmas and cold. Lots colder than in LA.

She liked the Los Angeles area, particularly the weather, but she spent most of her time in DC. Went with the territory of her work. She never knew where her next assignment would be. So far in the past year she had been assigned in all directions. Poe had worked with her on three missions.

Worry niggled at her again.

Where the hell was he?

She called his cell. Three rings and it went to voice mail. "Hey, where are you?"

A deeper worry started to gnaw at her. He wouldn't just leave like this. Not possible.

She walked around the yard. Ventured several yards into the woods at the back of the house. No sign of Poe. She called out his name a couple of times with no response. This was wrong. Then she went back in the house.

Abi was on his phone.

Maybe Poe had called him with an explanation? But why wouldn't he call Jamie?

She kept her cool until Abi ended his call. Then she demanded, "Was that him?"

"No. It was not. In fact, that was a colleague who is monitoring the comings and goings on the roads in and out of this development and he says no one has come in or gone out this morning."

She wasn't surprised that he had backup watching the street. He would be a fool not to have support nearby. It would be nice if he shared details like that, but arguing about it right now wasn't an option.

"Something's wrong." Jamie moved to the wall of glass doors that led out onto the patio and looked out over the valley below. "He wouldn't just leave."

Abi joined her. "Are you sure about that?"

She turned on him. "What I'm sure about," she said pointedly, "is that if he isn't here, then something has happened to him and since you're in charge of this operation, it's your job to know what that is."

He moved his head side to side in a somber manner. "I have not seen him this morning."

"Then I suggest you back up the footage on your security cameras and see what happened." If he dared to tell her there were no cameras, she might just have to punch him.

He nodded. "I can do that."

In the living room, he picked up the remote to the television and turned it on. Then he opened a drawer on one of the side tables and withdrew another remote. This one he pointed at the television screen and made a number of selections.

A new app opened, and several views of the house appeared on the screen. He ran the video back and, sure enough, just before daylight, Poe exited a side door in the kitchen.

"You didn't set the alarm?" This was ridiculous. Why would Abi take that sort of risk?

"I did set the alarm before I went to bed. I can only assume he disarmed it. It was armed when I got up this morning, which is why I didn't consider that he'd gone outside."

Poe was good. Figuring out a way around the code to disarm the security system wasn't outside his purview, but why would he do that without telling her?

"The question," Abi went on, "is why would he leave?"

"It would not be because he wanted to," Jamie argued. If Abi was accusing Poe of something he could just back off. Poe would never double-cross her. She gestured to the screen. "Are there exterior cameras?" It was a silly question. Who had such an elaborate security system inside and then nothing outside?

Another click of the remote and they were looking at the yard around the house. The front was clear. So was the back. The view extended to the woods. While she watched, Abi ran the video back until it showed Poe as he walked out that side door.

Jamie held her breath as she watched him walk around the iron fence that separated the pool area from the rest of the yard. He continued past this area and straight toward the woods.

"This is wrong," Jamie said, outright fear rising inside her now.

"We should go out there and have a look," Abi suggested.

He led the way to the same kitchen side door that Poe had used. They exited the house and walked the cobblestone path toward the grassy area between the pool and the woods.

There was no way Poe would leave like this without telling her. *No way.* There had to be something about this that she didn't know. A call from someone who had warned of imminent danger. Something.

Once they were in the woods, the lack of light made seeing any disturbance of the underbrush difficult. Jamie stood still and visually searched the area, looking for any indication that a person had cut through that underbrush.

Then she saw what she was looking for. A bent twig on a limb. She headed in that direction. Abi was right behind her. She inspected the bushes and the ground. Someone had definitely been through here recently.

She turned on the flashlight app of her phone and scanned the ground. The light flashed over something shiny.

Her heart bumped harder against her sternum.

She reached down and sifted through the leaves. Her fingers hit a cool and firm object.

Her gut clenched as her fingers curled around a cell phone.

The screen of Poe's cell instantly lit with the missed call notifications from her attempts to reach him.

She started forward, looking for more indications of where the brush had been parted. Her heart pounded so hard she couldn't catch her breath. Why would he come out here? Why wouldn't he tell her whatever was on his mind?

A thought occurred to her, and she whirled on Abi. "You didn't plant any tracking devices?"

He looked away before answering the question. "Only on you. I wasn't expecting you to have company."

Fury roaring through her, she started to search once more. If Poe was lying out here injured, she needed to find him.

Abi didn't argue or question her actions. He just followed

suit, picking his way through the brush and searching the same as she did.

An hour later it was obvious they weren't going to find him.

The underbrush became spotty as they neared the drop down the hillside. At that point there was no longer any indication Poe had been out there.

They went back in the house and watched the security footage. Poe went into the woods, but he never came out.

This was wrong, wrong, wrong.

Jamie paced the floor. Where would he have gone? She supposed he could have cut left and come out around one of the other houses.

"I need to check with the neighbors." That was the only possible next move.

"You can't do that," Abi argued. "We cannot call attention to ourselves."

"I don't care. I need to find my partner—my friend."

Abi held up his hands. "What you need is coffee."

Had he lost his mind? "I don't need coffee."

He poured a cup and placed it on the island. "Just sit down and drink. We need to think."

She took a breath and then did as he asked. She slid onto a stool and picked up the cup. She hadn't had any coffee this morning and suddenly she needed the caffeine desperately.

"First," Abi suggested, "let's approach this logically."

She drank from the cup rather than taking a bite out of his head.

"Let's consider the reasons Poe would leave." He gestured to her. "You know him better than me. What do you think?"

"Someone may have called him with information he couldn't ignore."

"Do you have the pass code for his phone so we can see who he has spoken to?"

She made a face. "If I did I would have already checked. All I saw were the latest notifications and that was where I called him. To see beyond that I would need the pass code."

"We can assume someone may have called him not only with news he couldn't ignore, but also with something he didn't feel he could share. Does he have family who may have needed his help?"

Jamie shook her head. "No one he's close to."

"What about your employer?"

"Maybe. But I can't imagine why he wouldn't have told me." That was the part that made no sense at all. Poe would not just leave like this…not while leaving her behind.

"Then we have to assume it's someone from this end."

She was surprised that Abi made the statement. "Is there someone who wanted to stop this mission? Maybe someone who feels it's the wrong move?"

"That's always possible, but I was not informed of this if that is the case. I can make some calls. See if there's something I should know. Check with my people to see if he's left the area."

Why the hell didn't he just say that already?

"I would appreciate that." She took a breath, forced her nerves to calm. "He wouldn't leave like this without telling me unless he felt there was no other option."

"Drink your coffee," Abi said again. "I'll make some calls."

He walked outside onto the patio. Jamie watched and finished off her coffee. There was a chance Poe could have decided to take a risk to put protective measures in place. Not that she was going to share this with Abi. Poe didn't trust Abi. He was concerned about how this would shake down and, in Jamie's opinion, there was reason to be concerned. Poe may have believed that the best way to head off trouble was for him to bow out, making it look as if it was not voluntary. Then he would take up a position to watch, to be in place in the event Jamie needed an extraction.

It was an option they always discussed for their joint missions. It wasn't one they'd ever had to use. More important, they had not talked about the option in this situation.

Whatever the case, the fact that he didn't share his decision with her may have been to allow her to look completely uninvolved to Abi.

If that wasn't the case, then something bad had happened to Poe and Jamie was really worried. The possibility that Abi could be involved was all the more troubling.

If he was injured—or worse—and someone wanted answers about what they were doing, Poe was in serious trouble because he had no real answers. Until now, Abi had shared basically nothing with them beyond the name of the target.

Which, she supposed, was the point. You couldn't tell anyone what you didn't know.

For Poe, that could end up being a very bad thing. Not having the answers his abductor wanted wouldn't keep him alive.

Chapter Eight

2:00 p.m.

Kenny struggled to stay put as he watched Jamie take a walk around the cul-de-sac. She was still looking for him. She'd come outside and looked around several times. The worry and despair on her face cut straight through him.

He hated, hated, hated doing this to her, but it was necessary. It was the only way to provide any possible protection for her in the hours to come. He didn't blame Jamie for doing what she had to do. Her brother was being held hostage. She had no choice but to go along with what Amar wanted.

On some level, Jamie considered him a friend and Kenny couldn't say that he was an enemy, but what he could say was that the man was for sale to the highest bidder, which made him something worse than an enemy in Kenny's opinion. At least you knew the ultimate intentions of your enemy. There was no way to know for sure about a man like Amar. Where was he going with this? What did he expect to happen when all was said and done?

This was the trouble for Kenny.

Amar would do whatever necessary to accomplish his mission.

Kenny was not going to give him free rein to do as he

pleased. There had to be options for egress if the mission went to hell. Since Amar refused to share the details, Kenny had no choice but to intervene. Jamie was far too personally involved to fully trust her instincts.

He'd awakened early this morning and made the decision. He had to do something. Couldn't just wait. Waiting too long never proved to be the right strategy.

Jamie had no idea, but Victoria Colby-Camp had given him a burner phone to use for contacting her. He had not used it inside the house because he couldn't be sure what sort of monitoring Amar had going. The man was well prepared. Instead, Kenny had taken a walk around the cul-de-sac, much like Jamie was now, and made the calls. Victoria knew where they were, and she knew the identity of the target.

When he'd shared his concerns with Victoria, she had agreed that he had to make a move. With her blessing, he felt certain his decision had been the right one. Even Victoria felt Jamie wasn't thinking clearly. She was too worried about her brother. She was following orders toward that end. She would not be happy that he had voiced the concern to her grandmother, but he hoped it would prove the right move in the end.

Kenny watched Jamie walk back toward the house. The one he had chosen as his hideout was empty. The only unoccupied one in the cul-de-sac. The owners appeared to be on vacation. Perhaps visiting with family for the holidays.

The burner vibrated and he answered. "Hello."

"Kenny, we have some updated information."

Victoria and her team had been working to put together a list of potential patients suffering with inoperable brain tumors who possessed the means to put together an operation such as this one.

"I'm listening."

"We have a list of five patients in the state of Tennessee who have the means to take on an operation of this scale. We've put an investigator in place near the residence of each. Beyond that, we have another half dozen across the southeast who fit the same profile. I'm leaning toward the patient perpetrator as being local. Someone who would know Dr. Case's reputation well. Someone who had been exposed repeatedly to the headline-making leaps Case had taken in the field of neurosurgery."

"Sounds like you have the situation covered as well as anyone could." Good news in Kenny's opinion. "I've seen Jamie walking the cul-de-sac. She's still looking for me. She appears to be fine. Visibly worried, of course."

"I'm certain she's concerned," Victoria agreed.

"I'm uncomfortable misleading her this way," he admitted, "but it feels necessary. I'm trusting she'll understand that if I'm making a move like this, it's for the best."

He was good on that part, no matter that it felt wrong.

"Thank you for letting me know that you've had eyes on her. I've sent Ian Michaels to your location. He'll take a position the next street over. He has a vehicle for you if you need one." She confirmed the house number where Michaels would be waiting.

"Excellent." Kenny felt some sense of relief at the news. "I plan to try and keep eyes on Jamie, but I have no idea how they plan to get to the house where the party will take place. Amar claims to have invitations for tonight's party, but he could be lying."

"Lucas has done some careful research into Abidan Amar. His reputation is not quite as terrifying as I had feared, but he has a history of playing fast and loose with risk. I don't want him doing this with the lives of my grandchildren."

Kenny could imagine Amar doing exactly that. What he couldn't see was Jamie or Luke as "grandchildren." But he understood and the idea made him smile. "The security system he has in place won't allow me to get close to the house again, but I left the bug you provided in the main living space. Hopefully, I'll hear the plan when he finally reveals the details to Jamie. Otherwise, I won't take my eyes off the place and when they move, I'll move."

"Keep me posted," Victoria urged. "We are prepared to do whatever necessary to help."

Sadly what they could do was limited. Any mistake could cost the life of the youngest Colby. They had no idea where Luke was or who was holding him. Outside interference could set off a deadly chain reaction.

"I will," Kenny assured her. "Thank you, Victoria."

He ended the call and considered that for months he had heard Jamie talk about her grandparents. He had done some deep research and despite how nice and normal they seemed, Jamie hadn't exaggerated one little bit. The Colby Agency was unlike any other agency of its kind. Victoria and her husband, Lucas, were legends, as were most of the investigators. If Kenny were in trouble, he would definitely want the Colby Agency on his team.

Frankly, he hoped to get to know them better in the future. He hoped to get to know Jamie a lot better as well. There were moments between them that made him believe the idea was possible. Either way, their friendship was invaluable, and he would do whatever necessary to protect that relationship.

Amar's voice sounded and Kenny turned to move closer to the speaker of the receiver.

Amar had apparently gotten a phone call.

His responses gave Kenny basically no information.

Hopefully he would relate the update to Jamie when the call ended.

Whatever was going down was scheduled to do so tonight. Kenny needed to be prepared to intervene if necessary. To provide backup for Jamie either way. Listening and watching until there was a move was the only way for him to actually have her back. Had he stayed at the house, Amar would have made all the decisions and Kenny would have had no choice but to follow his orders. Amar would have possessed all the power.

This was the right move—as difficult as it had been to walk away from that house knowing he was leaving Jamie behind. The decision gave him some leeway to move as he saw fit.

The conversation between Amar and his caller appeared to be coming to an end.

Kenny held his breath. He couldn't afford to miss a word.

"Was that your point of contact?" Jamie asked.

"It was."

Kenny hoped the man intended to provide more detail than those two words.

"Do we have some change or addition to the mission?" Jamie prompted.

"Nothing I need to share at this time."

Her sigh was audible. "Really, you're going to stick to that worn-out line? Why even bother to involve me in this if you're going to keep me in the dark?"

"I have my orders, Jamie. When I can tell you more, I will. Every step of this operation is a strictly need-to-know basis only. You're familiar with how this works. I know you are. Let's not get bent out of shape with the rules."

"When you decide to stop playing games, let me know."

The sound of her walking out of the room wasn't what

Kenny had hoped for. Maybe she was bluffing in an attempt to prod him into talking.

Then again, he had to admit that hearing her tell him off like that gave him a little kick of satisfaction.

As satisfying on a personal level as the exchange was, the real question was, how long did the guy intend to keep the details from her?

This was not the proper way to run an operation.

Chapter Nine

2:30 p.m.

"Jamie, wait!"

She hesitated at the bottom of the stairs. She was over his secretiveness. If they were in this together, he needed to tell her what the hell was going on. Good grief, they were only hours from when this thing was supposed to go down.

And Poe, damn it, was nowhere to be found.

She took a breath and turned to face Abi. "This thing is scheduled to go down tonight and you're still keeping me in the dark. Why am I even here?" She braced her hands on her hips. "You apparently intend to do this entirely alone. What am I? Arm candy?"

He laughed softly, then looked away. "You surely could be, but we won't go there." He blew out a breath then. Obviously not looking forward to coming out with it.

She braced her hands on her hips, out of patience. "Are we in this together or not?"

"There's been a slight change," he said. "Nothing to worry about. Originally, we were scheduled to arrive at eight tonight but now we're to be there at seven-thirty. I'm not pleased with the sudden change, but I can only assume some other sort of intelligence became available, prompting this schedule change."

The fact that he was genuinely upset seemed to suggest he was telling the truth. Either way, she was over this whole cloak and dagger game. They were on the same side after all.

"I need you to walk me through what's going to happen tonight. This beating around the bush has gone on long enough."

"All right. Let's sit down and I'll walk you through it."

It was about time. She followed him back to the living room area. He went to the bar and grabbed a couple of bottles of water and passed one to her. If not for that sudden phone call, she would be convinced his decision to share had something to do with Poe's absence. She hoped that was not the case.

"We will arrive at the party like any other guests. I've seen the list of invitees, and none are familiar to me. I'm assuming I will not be familiar to any of them. Same goes for you. Which is part of the beauty of the situation."

"Is there some aspect of his private residence that has been deemed more accessible than, say, the hospital or his clinic?" The private residence of a man such as Dr. Case likely included serious security services and a well-trained security team.

"The hospital where his surgery privileges are has state-of-the-art facial recognition for everyone going in and coming out," Abi explained. "It wouldn't prevent us from coming in, but it would not forget our faces. I'm sure neither of us wants that to happen."

"A good reason to rule out that location," she admitted. A hospital with facial recognition technology. Wow.

"His clinic is not equipped with technology quite so advanced, but the location creates a difficult exit strategy. Too congested…too many cameras on the surrounding buildings."

"I suppose the fact that the clinic operates only during regular business hours, daylight hours, creates a problem of its own."

"The cover of darkness is always an ally," he agreed.

"I'm sure there will be security cameras at the doctor's residence." Really, she was confident this was the case.

"You're right, but we have access to the system so no issues there."

Of course they did. Abi was too good to move forward without that key piece of intelligence.

"There will be some sort of precipitous event," she suggested. "A distraction?"

"A power outage. It's not so unique, but it will work and it's not so unusual this time of year."

"You have the layout of the residence?" Familiarizing herself with the floor plan would be useful. As for the power outage, that was always a workable strategy. Power outages happened—as he said, particularly during extreme temperatures. Living this far outside the city proper was asking for additional issues when it came to utilities.

"I do." He pulled out his cell and opened an image. "We enter via the front as one would expect."

The front door appeared to open into a large entry hall. He moved on to another image that showed a photo of the entry hall.

"Security will be here confirming that all who enter are on the list. From there we'll follow the others into the grand hall."

The grand hall was an area that branched off into a living room, dining room, library and—well beyond all that—a kitchen. Any one of those rooms was larger than the entire first floor of this house. The grand hall worked like a massive hub connecting all the other rooms. It made for the perfect area to linger in groups without interrupting the flow of those filtering into and through the other rooms.

"Once we're in," he went on, "we'll mingle, have hors d'oeuvres and a nonalcoholic drink. Just to blend in."

"Where is our egress?"

He slid the photo left, moving to another image. "Our priority exit is through the kitchen. We have two secondary options. Through the French doors in the library and off the back terrace outside the main living area."

"What's the layout for transportation around the property?" She'd looked at the house and property via the telescope, but some aspects were blocked from view by landscaping and other obstacles.

"We'll have two options for leaving. A helicopter from the doctor's helipad. This would give us a sort of emergency style departure. The hope would be that other guests assume there has been an emergency and the doctor had to go. The other option is via a limo that will be standing by in the front roundabout."

So far she had no complaints.

"What method of inducement do you plan to use to ensure his cooperation?" This was the part that concerned Jamie the most. She hoped he didn't intend to use drugs or physical coercion. Despite her reservations with either of those avenues, the problem was, there weren't that many other options. At least none she liked any better.

"We have that covered," he said as he closed his phone and slipped it into his hip pocket.

"Meaning?" she pressed. "Are we going in armed? Will he be drugged?"

"No drugs. No weapons."

She and Poe had discussed the possibility that the man's child would be used to gain his cooperation. "Then we're using the kid." Dread congealed in her gut. She hated the idea. Hated it even more than the drugs or weapons.

"You have my word," he said, his gaze pressing hers, "if it becomes necessary to use the child, she will not be harmed in any way."

Damn it. She knew it! "You can't make that promise. Things go wrong. Accidents. Mistakes. You can never predict how people will react to these situations."

Abi held up his hands as if to quiet her, which made her all the angrier. "This will happen quickly. In an orderly manner. There will not be time for mistakes or accidents."

People always thought a simple plan would go easy—no glitches. But there was no simple plan when it came to abducting another human. Not unless you rendered them unconscious.

The plan sounded perfect. Well thought out. Concise. Except all of that would go out the window when Dr. Case or his wife understood what was happening. If a guest happened to overhear…it would all go to hell in a heartbeat.

"You can't be sure of anything. Not one single thing that involves another human."

"You can't be sure I'm wrong."

She wasn't going to argue the point with him. Moving on, she said, "You've mentioned that we have a very narrow window of opportunity. Why is that the case? It's a party with guests who will be coming and going. Is there some sort of step or arrival—maybe a departure—that will happen that somehow renders our plans unusable? Is something turning into a pumpkin at a certain time?"

He didn't answer right away. And he didn't laugh.

Mostly he stared at her, obviously attempting to decide how to answer.

He was just as worried as she was, but he would die before he would admit as much.

"It's the kid, isn't it?" Jamie shook her head. He might as well just spit it out. "It has to happen before she's tucked in for the night."

"Something like that," he confessed.

"I'm not good with this." But what could she do? Her brother's life was on the line. "If anything goes wrong—"

"I will not allow the child to be hurt," he insisted. "Really, you have my word on that."

She didn't doubt he meant what he said, but he could not guarantee the child's safety or the doctor's cooperation. He could only deduce the outcome based on common human behavior. The odds might lean slightly in his favor but there were no guarantees.

"What happens if the doctor is injured?" Had his employer thought of that? What they were about to do posed significant risk to all involved. "Then no one will have the benefit of the lifesaving surgery only he can do at this time."

"We can talk about what-ifs all night," Abi said. "But it's our job to make sure the what-ifs don't happen. We get the doc and his daughter out with no hitches. We do what we have to do and everybody's happy when the night is over."

Jamie held up her hands in surrender. Further discussion was pointless. "Moving on, please. At this point, I need some sort of assurance from you that your employer had nothing to do with Poe's disappearance." The facts were troubling. She had not heard from him, and his cell had ended up on the ground in the woods behind the house. If he'd been taken by someone involved in all this, why hadn't they heard anything? If he'd decided some other action was necessary, why hadn't she heard from him by now?

"I have no idea why or how he left other than what we found on the security system." Abi shrugged. "He told me nothing. I saw and heard nothing."

"You don't receive any sort of notification when someone enters or exits the house?"

"This is not my house. I'm a guest here just as you are. I had no reason to want to monitor who went in and out. It was only relevant if we were here and frankly, I wasn't expecting you or Poe to cut out on me."

"He wouldn't cut out without a reason," she said to ensure Abi understood this wasn't Poe just cutting out.

"You want to know what I think?" He braced his hands on the island. "I think he decided he didn't need to be part of this."

Jamie shook her head. "No way. He wouldn't do that. He would never leave me in the lurch."

Abi shrugged. "Maybe I'm wrong. I guess we'll find out tonight. If he shows up and tries to interfere, we'll have our answer. If he doesn't show up, we'll have an answer as well."

Jamie shook her head again. "You'll see." She wasn't standing around here and throwing her friend under the bus. She knew Poe too well. He had either set out on a plan of his own because he knew something was rotten with this one or someone had taken him. End of story.

She thought of his cell phone and worry dug deep beneath her skin. She desperately hoped her allowing Poe to come here with her wasn't going to be the reason he…

No. She wasn't going there.

"Let me know when you're ready to move." Jamie needed a few minutes to herself. Some time to decompress and get her head on straight. Tonight, was far too important to go into it rattled like this. Psyching herself up for a mission was always a smart step.

Abi touched her arm to slow her departure. "I'm counting on you, Jamie. I can't do this without you."

"Yeah."

Jamie had never felt so torn. This was not like her usual missions. It was wrong. More wrong than anything she'd ever been asked to do. But it was also the only way to save her brother.

She couldn't say no…couldn't walk away.

And because of that she had no choice but to do all within her power to ensure that Dr. Case and his daughter cooperated—but also that they survived this thing unscathed.

For the first time since she was a little girl, she wished her grandmother were here beside her to give her an assist. She could use some of Victoria's wisdom and strength right now.

Lionheart Court,
7:30 p.m.

JAMIE EMERGED FROM the limo that had picked up her and Abi. He waited for her outside the car, looking too handsome in his black suit and black bow tie against the white shirt. His dark skin and black hair gave him the sophisticated look of a foreign diplomat. In his jacket pocket was a red handkerchief.

Her floor length sheath was the exact shade of red as the handkerchief. So were her very sleek high heeled shoes. None of which was made for running or for tackling an enemy.

After seeing the formfitting dress, she'd decided to wear her hair up in a French twist. Seemed appropriate. Whatever others thought of them being at this party, they certainly made a handsome couple. Jamie felt as if she'd arrived at senior prom with the most popular boy in school, but couldn't remember why she'd decided to come when none of her friends would be here. Only this boy who was so handsome and far too charming.

There were always strangers involved with her missions, but these were not simply strangers. These were civilians who had no idea that this party had been targeted by someone who had so much money at his disposal that he could choose to disrupt this gala and the life of the man hosting it to get what he wanted.

Jamie took a breath and cleared her head. She knew what she had to do. Fretting over the details wouldn't get the job done.

Abi took her hand and draped it over his arm. "In case I haven't already told you, you look amazing."

She smiled at the man who held the door open as they entered the home of their target. "You look quite fetching yourself, Mr. Amar."

He flashed her a smile.

Once they were deep into the entry hall, he leaned close and whispered, "Do you think we look so nice that they'll never suspect we're here for nefarious purposes?"

"As long as they don't look too closely."

He smiled. "Touché."

Apparently, the doctor had many friends. The crowd was larger than Jamie had expected for a family holiday gathering.

They entered the grand hall, and it was like entering a Christmas wonderland. Beautifully decorated trees…garlands and ribbons…so tastefully done. The scent of cedar hung in the air. Holiday music played softly from speakers hidden somehow in the architecture. The ceiling towered two stories above, looking exactly like something from a

European castle. The floor was marble and the furnishings were museum quality. Servers strolled about with their trays. But Jamie wasn't the slightest bit hungry or even thirsty.

"Recognize anyone?"

She had seen photos of Case and his family on the internet and on Abi's phone. Jamie spotted Dr. Case near the massive stone fireplace almost immediately. He was surrounded by what she presumed were colleagues. Maybe close friends. This didn't feel like a family holiday gathering. This was almost certainly a business function accented with holiday decor.

"Several other surgeons," he said, leaning close enough for her to feel his lips brush her forehead. "A number of local politicians."

Interesting. Abi had certainly familiarized himself with those in the doctor's orbit. Not surprising really, she decided. This was exactly what she did when prepping for a mission.

She spotted Case's wife. She too wore a red dress. Jamie glanced at Abi. "Am I wearing red because she is?"

He smiled. "It's a very good color on you. Far better than on her. And your blond hair is natural, unlike hers."

Hovering near Mrs. Case was her daughter. Ten-year-old Lillian Case. And of course, she wore a red dress to match her mommy. Oh, dear God. Jamie felt sick at what could go wrong.

"Do you have any assets here or nearby?" She gazed around at the lavish crowd. Some part of her hoped to spot Poe. Damn it. Where was he? "Someone to call upon for backup in case we need it?"

"No assets inside. Just the two of us."

At least he wasn't ruling out the possibility of backup somewhere on the property.

Better than nothing.

Jamie considered the most likely tactic for making this happen in a crowd of this size, in a house of this size.

"I'm guessing the family has a routine for their daughter. A certain time to go to bed. Mommy tucks her in, and Daddy pops by for a good-night kiss. Where's the nanny? Have you made arrangements for disabling her?"

"The nanny tucks her in. Then Mommy and Daddy go to the room for a quick good-night. It's all very affable and everyone disappears quickly. The nanny goes home after. But tonight the nanny is not an issue. She's on vacation for the next ten days."

One less potential liability.

"You know—" Jamie glanced around in search of a server "—I think I might need a real drink after all."

"Allow me," Abi said before making a slight bow and then hurrying to the nearest server.

Jamie watched Mrs. Case for a moment and then her husband, the doctor. She wondered if either could possibly comprehend how their lives were about to change. The ability to breathe suddenly felt unnatural, difficult.

This was wrong.

And yet she was helpless to stop it.

Abi reappeared with two flutes of bubbling liquid. Jamie accepted hers and took the smallest sip. "Thank you."

"Case's wife writes children's books."

Jamie nodded. "You mentioned that, and I spotted it on her Wikipedia page."

"Her latest is *The Fish in My Dreams*. It's about a little girl who dreams of swimming deep into the ocean with fish on her feet instead of shoes."

Jamie laughed. "Sounds like something her daughter dreamed and told her about."

Abi nodded. "That's what she says in the dedication to her daughter."

Jamie slipped her arm around his. "I'm guessing we should tell her how much we loved the book."

"The daughter will remember you talking to her mother," he agreed.

The whole point.

Jamie led the way across the room. Mrs. Case looked up as they approached.

"Mrs. Case," Jamie said, her smile broadening, "I'm Jasmine Colter. I just wanted to say how very much my little niece enjoyed your new book."

Lillian leaned closer to her mom, her cheeks pink.

"It's Lillian's story really." She beamed down at her daughter. "She has very vivid dreams."

Jamie nodded to Lillian. "Such a great story, Lillian. I hope you'll be telling more stories with your mom."

Lillian smiled finally. "Ducks are coming next."

"Oh my. You're writing a story about ducks?"

Lillian nodded. "For next year."

"How wonderful. We'll be sure to get it."

They chatted for a moment more until another guest arrived to share her praise for the book. Jamie and Abi wandered to the other side of the room.

"We are twenty minutes out," he told her.

Jamie left her barely touched glass on a tray. "I think I'll drop by the powder room."

"I'll be right here." His position allowed him to see the wife, daughter and the doctor.

Jamie nodded and headed through the lingering crowd.

Taking a bathroom break while wearing a dress like this was never fun. But she might as well take advantage of the opportunity. No way to know when she'd have another chance. Ducking behind a bush wearing this wouldn't be so easy.

She made quick work of the necessary business. After a swift wash of her hands and check of her hair and makeup, she smoothed her dress. It was almost showtime. Maybe they would all get through this without a glitch, and she would be on her way home tomorrow with her little brother in tow.

"Hang in there, Luke." She hoped she would be seeing him soon.

She exited the ornate powder room and went in search of her date. Well, *date* wasn't really the right term. *Partner in crime*. No sign of the mother and daughter. She surveyed the room again. She spotted them by the larger Christmas tree. It was then that she noticed their dresses fit particularly well with the holiday decor. Every last thing was meticulously coordinated.

"They'll be going up soon," Abi told her. "When the doctor goes up, that will be our cue."

"Have you heard from your getaway driver? You've confirmed that all is as it should be?" Her nerves were jangling.

"I have. All is exactly as it should be."

"When and how will your employer release Luke?"

His gaze collided with hers. "Once Dr. Case is at the designated location, you will be taken to Luke's condo, and he will be there waiting for you."

"And when will the doctor be returned to his home?"

"By noon tomorrow I'm told."

She wondered if he would be considered missing or kidnapped during that time. If so the police and the FBI would launch into action. Or would he simply be made to call his wife and assure her that he'd had an emergency at the hospital?

"Until then," Abi said, drawing her back to the conversation, "he'll be caring for an emergency situation. It happens all the time. His wife and daughter will think nothing of it."

Jamie searched his face. He'd just lied to her, or he'd made the sort of mistake he shouldn't and he'd glossed right over it.

"Does he usually take his daughter with him to emergencies?"

Abi stared at her for a long moment. "Before the mother realizes she is missing, little Lillian will be back in her room."

"What will she tell her mother? Another dream for a book?"

Suddenly all the holes in his elaborate plan were far too visible and Jamie had a bad, bad feeling swelling in her gut.

He smiled. "Sounds like a bestseller."

As long as no one died or was gravely injured, she reminded herself. Jamie settled her gaze on the doctor. How did a man like him—who possessed a skill like no one else—get through each day knowing he could only save a few? How did he decide who he would save and who he would let go?

Did he have the typical god complex associated with some in the profession?

Even as she asked herself this question, his shoulders seem to visibly slump beneath the weight of his success.

Or maybe she wanted to believe he cared that much. After all, imagine the dedication and work required to reach the sort of skill level he possessed. To achieve what no one else had.

She would soon know how he saw himself. More important, how he saw the patients in need of his help.

She hoped for the sake of all involved that he would be reasonable…not that there was anything reasonable about what was coming.

Chapter Ten

Mrs. Case motioned for her daughter who was admiring the many decadent looking desserts spread across silver trays. Or perhaps it was the chocolate fountain in the middle of that table that had her mesmerized.

Either way, Lillian turned away empty-handed and skipped toward her mother. Almost bedtime. Sweet treats were apparently off the menu.

Jamie wondered if it was Abi's appearance at the dessert table that had alerted the child's mother. He'd insisted on finding something chocolate.

If his sudden need for chocolate hadn't made Jamie suspicious, seeing Dr. Case withdraw his cell phone from his jacket pocket for the first time since their arrival certainly did. The doctor turned from the trio to whom he'd been engaged in conversation. The three continued with whatever discussion they'd been having but the doctor's posture changed dramatically as he listened to the more personal conversation.

Abi appeared next to her with a delicious looking offering. She shook her head. "Something's happening."

She'd no sooner said the words than Dr. Case ended his

call and moved back toward the trio he'd abandoned. She didn't need a listening device to get the gist of what he was saying. His body language spoke loudly and clearly as he patted one man's shoulder and gave nods to the others. He was excusing himself.

Next to her, Abi suddenly reached for his cell phone.

Jamie ignored his subdued murmuring. She was far more interested in what was happening with the doctor. He crossed to his wife and daughter, said a few words, then dropped a kiss on each of their cheeks.

He was leaving.

He hurried from the room. Jamie drifted toward the front of the great hall, then on to the entry hall just in time to watch him disappear through the front double doors with no less than four men dressed in black accompanying him. Members of his security team, no doubt.

When she turned back to find Abi, he was moving in her direction. He put his arm around her shoulder and leaned close to her temple. "There's an emergency at the hospital."

"Are we staying here to await his return or going to the hospital?" She smiled up at him as if they were sharing secret love messages.

"We go with the doctor."

A final glance at the wife and daughter showed the wife smiling with friends and the daughter having wrangled a dessert without her mother noticing. The other guests appeared unconcerned about the doctor's abrupt departure. The servers continued offering drinks and finger foods and the music played on.

Jamie followed Abi from the house. The night was colder than when they'd arrived or perhaps it was only because the anticipation-fueled adrenaline related to what could happen had worn off, reminding her she'd opted not to wear a coat.

Abi said nothing until they were in the car traveling away from the house. "You'll find a change of clothes in the back seat."

She'd expected there would be a change of clothes for them at their next destination, but she hadn't anticipated it being in the car. Turned out to be a good decision.

She tucked up her dress and slid somewhat awkwardly over the console into the back seat. A pair of jeans, a sweater and sneakers were folded neatly on the seat. When had he done this? She supposed he had not. More likely someone had prepared everything to his specifications.

Unzipping the dress wasn't exactly the easiest feat, but she managed. She eased the luxurious fabric down her hips and over her legs.

"You have everything under control back there?" He glanced in the rearview mirror.

"I do." She pulled the sweater over her head and tugged it into place. She kicked off the heels and slipped into the jeans. This was a relief. She'd always felt more at home in jeans than in anything else.

She folded the dress and placed it on the seat, then set the shoes atop it. A quick search of the floorboard using the flashlight app on her cell helped her find a pair of socks. When the socks and sneakers were on, she was set, except for her hair. Making quick work of the task, she removed the pins, shook her hair free and then did a quick braid. It was best if she didn't look anything like the blonde in the red dress from the party.

"Any idea on how this changes our plans?"

"We'll wait until—"

Jamie's gaze swung to the rearview mirror. She didn't have to ask why he'd suddenly stopped talking. The bright lights filling the mirror provided the answer.

They had a tail.

"Brace yourself." Abi's fingers visibly tightened on the steering wheel.

Rather than risk looking back, Jamie braced her feet against the back of the passenger seat and eased down low in her seat.

The crash of metal was followed by a hard lurch forward as the other car rammed them. A new wave of adrenaline rose inside her.

Abi righted their forward momentum. "There's a weapon under my seat if you can get to it."

Jamie eased down into the floorboard and felt around under the driver's seat. The weapon sat snugly in a holster that had been secured to the bottom of the seat. A bit of creativity was required to remove the weapon from behind since it had been installed with the driver in mind.

"Got it."

She eased up into the seat, keeping her head low.

"He's coming again," Abi warned.

Jamie got onto her knees facing the rear window and watched as the vehicle neared. It was impossible to determine if there were more occupants than the driver. She powered the window down and leaned out as far as she dared.

"He's coming," Abi warned.

Jamie closed one eye and focused on the front passenger side wheel barreling toward her. She took the shot.

Tires squealed as the car seemed to spin sideways and rush backward. In fact, it was only because they were going forward that the distance stretched out between them.

"Bravo!" Abi shouted.

The car rocketed forward as he pushed the accelerator for all it had to offer.

Jamie powered the window back up but kept her focus on the disabled car. It was dark, black maybe, and it wasn't moving.

Once it was out of view, she climbed over the console and settled back into the front passenger seat. She placed the weapon on the console and secured her seat belt.

"Who could have known about your plan?"

He slowed for an upcoming traffic signal. "I don't think this was someone who had advance knowledge of our plan. I'm thinking this was more like security picking up on our interest in the doctor's departure from the party."

"You're suggesting they monitored the guests who left when or soon after the doctor did."

"I am." He made a left turn.

"Maybe."

"Either that or your friend Poe tried taking us out of the game."

Of course he would come up with that scenario. "No. Poe would have followed us and then confronted us at our destination."

"At least one of us has faith in his motives."

"Whoever that guy was, if he works for the doctor, he's going to notify security at the hospital. They'll be watching for us."

"No problem." He glanced at her. "I have a plan."

Two more turns and he pulled into a slot in a parking area between two other vehicles. When he'd shut off the lights and the engine, he shifted in his seat to face her. "There's a sweater back there for me and a pair of sneakers. It might be easier for you to reach them."

The two items were in the floorboard after the erratic driving. She released her seat belt, got on her knees in the seat and reached into the rear floorboard. She passed the sweater and then the sneakers to him. His grin told her he'd enjoyed seeing her in that awkward position. She rolled her eyes.

His jacket, shirt and bow tie flew over the seat. He tugged the sweater over his head and rolled it into place. He powered the seat back to facilitate changing his shoes.

His cell vibrated and he took the call. "Yes."

Jamie surveyed the area. A multistory building sported a Nashville Eye Center logo. The hospital that was their destination, Saint Thomas, stood across the street. On that side of the street there were steps leading up to the parking area, making their current position well camouflaged from anyone who might be watching for their arrival. *Good move.*

He put the phone away and turned to her. "A patient he operated on early this morning developed an issue, which is why he's been called back here. We're going to hang around and then follow him back to the house." He sent her a pointed look. "At a safe distance and in a different car, of course."

"Of course."

They exited the car and headed across the street. The wind whipped across her face, making her flinch. Despite knowing that Poe wasn't the one who had followed them, she couldn't help looking around. Where the hell was he? She glanced at Abi. If he was responsible for whatever had happened to Poe...

She wasn't prepared to go there just yet. There had to be another explanation. Poe would not abandon her under any circumstances. However, as she'd already considered, he very well might take a different tactic to help with whatever he feared was coming.

She had every intention of giving him the benefit of the doubt either way...until there was no longer room for doubt.

They didn't enter the hospital through the lobby. Instead,

they used the garage entrance. It was open twenty-four hours a day and since they had not arrived at the garage in a vehicle, the chances that security had spotted them via the cameras was unlikely. The cameras were only at the entrance and exit. Crossing over a short concrete wall in an area well camouflaged by shrubs near the entrance had protected them from view. Then they took the stairs to the level where the sky bridge crossed over to the hospital. Too easy.

"You have some idea of where we're going?" Jamie asked as they moved along the corridor. So far no one had paid attention to their arrival.

"Surgery, I presume." He flashed a smile.

Maybe it was that hint of a British accent, but his answer grated on her nerves. Of course the doctor was here for a possible return to surgery but that didn't mean she and Abi would be hanging out there. The goal was not to be spotted by the doctor's security team.

Careful to avoid eye contact with anyone they passed, they wound through the hospital until they reached the entrance to the surgery center. From there it was necessary to fly under the radar. Visiting hours were over and the usual excuses for their presence were no longer available.

Three people were seated in the surgery center's waiting room. Jamie assumed they had friends or family who'd had to undergo emergency surgery. Then again, for all she knew, surgeries were scheduled all hours of the day and night.

"You wait here," Abi said. "I'll have a look around. See if there's a need for anything beyond just hanging around."

If this was a true emergency with a patient, they had nothing to worry about.

"Whatever you say." She walked into the waiting room and took a seat where she could watch the corridor through the glass wall. If any dudes in all black showed up, she was following.

Abi watched her for a moment before going on his way. She pulled out her cell and then put it back. She couldn't call Poe. His cell was back at the house, disabled. Damn it. She thought of the car that had followed them on the way here. Case's personal security couldn't have known they were at the house on Excalibur…could they?

Why would they? The doctor's personal security team wouldn't likely have gotten a heads-up on a potential kidnapping plan.

Would they?

Only if Abi's employer was very, very bad at keeping secrets.

Then again, it could be as Abi suggested and the follower had been a member of Case's team who'd followed them from the house to ensure they weren't trouble…except she wasn't buying the idea that they would go so far as ramming a guest's car. Following it, she could see. After some time to mull it over, she was confident Abi had gotten that one wrong. Or simply gave her the story to cover the fact that he had no idea where the car had come from.

A man in scrubs and a surgical gown entered the waiting room and one of the two women who had already been present when Jamie arrived rushed toward him.

They spoke, heads together, for a moment, then the man patted her on the shoulder and left.

Standing in the middle of that waiting room, the woman lapsed into tears, her hands covering her face.

Since no one else moved to go to her, Jamie did. She grabbed the box of tissues on the table next to her chair and walked over to where the woman stood crying. "Are you all right?" Not exactly the most original conversation starter, but there it was.

The woman looked at her, eyes red and filled with tears. Jamie offered her the box of tissues.

She tugged a couple free. "Thank you."

"Would you like to sit down?" Jamie asked.

The woman blew her nose, dabbed at her eyes and then shook her head. "I'm fine. Really. I'm only crying because I'm so grateful."

She glanced around the room. The television was set to a news channel with the sound muted. The two anchors' words scrolled across the bottom of the screen.

"Do you mind if we step into the corridor?" She shivered. "It's really cold in here."

She was right. It was cold as hell in here. "Of course." Jamie followed her into the corridor. "You were saying you were grateful."

She sagged against the glass wall as if she could no longer hold her weight. "It was all just a mistake."

Since they were at a hospital—the surgery area of the hospital—a mistake wasn't necessarily something for which to be thankful.

"My husband had surgery this morning." Her face furrowed into a frown. "A brain tumor. We were so incredibly thankful when the surgery was a success. But then tonight the nurse insisted on calling the doctor back. She said my husband was having a possible bleed—a brain bleed."

Jamie made a horrified face. "Oh, that sounds terrifying."

"It was. The strangest thing was that he seemed fine. But after she told us this and gave him something in preparation for a second surgery, he had a seizure." She clasped her hands together against her chest as if in prayer. "I was certain I was losing him." Her lips trembled.

"But he's all right now?"

"It's the craziest thing. Dr. Case's assistant—" she made a face "—not assistant but resident or whatever he is. A doctor," she said, frustrated at herself, "who works with Dr. Case said that everything was fine. It was some sort of error."

So this was why Dr. Case had been called back to the hospital. A mistake. Jamie wondered how often something like that happened. "Do you recall the nurse's name?"

The other woman made a face and shook her head. "The resident or doctor asked me that as well. I believe it was Johnson. Brenda or Beverly Johnson." She flattened her hands to her chest. "My Lord, I have to call our daughter and my husband's sister. They're all waiting to hear. Fearing the worst, I'm sure."

"I'm certainly glad all is well, Mrs...? I'm sorry, I didn't get your name."

"Teresa Mason. My husband is Johnny." She smiled, her lips trembling. "And he's going to be fine. The doctor said so."

"That's wonderful. My name is Jamie, by the way. Can I walk you back to his room?" She mentally crossed her fingers. If this woman's husband was Dr. Case's patient, then Jamie was sticking close to her for as long as she could.

"That would be so kind of you. They said he would be back in the room very shortly. I want to be there when he arrives."

Jamie walked alongside the lady who rambled on and on about the two of them, she and her husband, having recently shared their fortieth anniversary.

"How did you hear about Dr. Case?" Jamie asked. "I understand it's tough to get on his schedule."

"Oh my, yes, it is. We were so very lucky in that he was

on call when Johnny lost consciousness. We had no idea anything was wrong. Dr. Case is the only reason he survived that brain tumor. We had no idea it was even there."

Jamie was surprised that surgeons like Case were ever "on call." Then again, she wasn't that familiar with the way physicians' schedules worked and certainly she had no idea how much of their time was owed to or pledged to a particular hospital.

"The other doctor said Dr. Case would pop into the room once Johnny was settled."

Jamie would try her best to hang around until Case arrived. No reason to believe he would recognize her. Once they were in the room she should shoot a text to Abi. He might not be aware of the ruse that brought Case to the hospital.

In Jamie's opinion the whole thing screamed of a setup for when the doctor left the hospital. He would have only a few security guards with him. Far less backup than he had at his home.

She and Mrs. Mason had just entered the room when Mr. Mason was rolled through the door on a gurney that looked more like a bed. Since there wasn't a bed in the room, Jamie assumed it was not just a gurney.

"He'll be groggy for a while," a nurse explained as she and a colleague moved his bed in place. "And he may sleep off and on. But don't worry. We'll be watching him closely."

Mrs. Mason parked herself next to his bed and took her husband's hand in hers. "Thank you so much," she told the nurses. "I appreciate all you do."

Jamie wondered how many people bothered to express their gratitude in this way.

The nurses made their way out and another figure entered. Dr. Case.

Jamie stayed put in the corner by the visitor's chair. She avoided direct eye contact. She felt confident he wouldn't recognize her, but why take the chance.

"Mrs. Mason, thankfully we did not have to go back in. As my associate told you, we determined that all was well. We'll take another CT scan in a couple of hours just to be sure. Once that's completed, I'll let you know those results as soon as we have them. But I'm confident you have nothing to worry about."

"Thank you so much, Dr. Case."

He gave her a nod, then looked to Jamie. "May I speak with you in the corridor?"

Holy cow. Was he speaking to her? Since he stared directly at her, she assumed so. Mrs. Mason was whispering softly to her husband.

Jamie mustered up a vague smile. "Sure."

Maybe he had recognized her.

Oh hell.

Once they were outside the room and the door closed, he set his attention on Jamie. "Were you here in the room when the nurse told Mrs. Mason I needed to be called?"

Aha. They were attempting to nail down the reason this happened. "No. I'm sorry. I wasn't here." At his frustrated look, she shrugged and offered, "I went for coffee."

"Anyway," Case said. "I'm here now and I'll be hanging around for a while. Just as a precaution."

Obviously, he was worried this Nurse Johnson had done something more than make a fake call. Damn.

"If you or Mrs. Mason notice anything unusual, don't hesitate to call for assistance."

"We will. Thank you."

Case walked away. By the weary set of his shoulders, he

seemed exhausted. His day had begun very early and certainly had not ended the way he had anticipated.

She decided to call Abi rather than bother with a text.

"Where are you? I'm in the waiting room."

She gave him the abridged version of what had occurred. "Doesn't sound like Case is going home anytime soon."

"I'll make some calls about this fake nurse."

"Dr. Case feels overly safe here at the hospital," she said, thinking about how he'd come to the room alone. "He didn't have any of his security personnel with him when he visited the patient's room. Considering what just went down with the nurse, I'm not so sure that's a good thing."

"That is a very astute observation, Colby," Abi said. "I'll have to ensure he's made aware of this oversight."

Jamie had no idea how he intended to make that happen.

"You want me to hang around here? Case said he would be stopping back by?"

"Yes, please do. I have something else to look into."

"I'll let you know when I see him again." She ended the call and put her phone away.

At the Mason's door, Jamie knocked softly and pushed the door inward far enough to step inside. "Mrs. Mason, Dr. Case will be back after the next CT is taken. Do you need anything for now? My friend is still in surgery, so I have some time if you need anything."

"You are so kind. I'm good for now though."

"Great." Jamie frowned. "They seem a bit concerned about this Nurse Johnson."

Mason made a distressed face. "It's so strange. It makes me wonder if she was even a nurse or if she was high or something."

Jamie wondered the same thing. "What did she look like?"

"Brown hair. Short and spiky." She scrunched her face

in thought. "Kind of tall." She shrugged. "I always think anyone taller than me is tall. But a couple or three inches taller than me for sure. Thin. Kind of willowy."

"I'm sure they'll get to the bottom of it," Jamie assured her. "They have cameras everywhere here. Maybe she was from one of those temp agencies." Jamie shrugged. "There are so many staffing shortages these days."

If the point of this nurse's lie about Mr. Mason was to get Dr. Case back to the hospital, why would she just disappear without completing the rest of her mission? Had her backup failed to step up? Or had the plan not been executed as of yet?

Which meant Dr. Case could be in danger right now.

"I think I'll take a walk," Jamie said. "You sure I can't get you anything?"

Mason shook her head. "No, thank you." She exhaled a big breath. "I really appreciate your help tonight. You were so very kind."

"You're very welcome, but it was nothing. Just being a good human."

As soon as she was in the corridor, she called Abi again. "I think we might still have a problem."

"I was thinking the same thing," he said, sounding breathless. "Case is in the doctor's lounge. I'm close by. Two members of his security team are stationed at the door. So far no word on who this nurse is or who is behind whatever went down or is going down."

"Then we're not going anywhere until he does."

"You got it. We need to know where he is every moment until we make *our* move."

Hopefully someone else wasn't going to beat them to the next move.

Chapter Eleven

Chicago
Colby Residence,
11:00 p.m.

Victoria opened a box of ornaments she'd had for at least thirty years, maybe forty. How time flew. There were dozens of boxes of decorations and here she was trying to pull this all together at nearly midnight. But she certainly couldn't sleep.

She stared at the tree. On the way home last evening she'd insisted that Lucas stop at the pop-up Christmas store on the corner and pick out something lovely. They'd thought they wouldn't bother with a tree this year since no one would be home for the holidays anyway and the two of them were set to go to Paris.

But she wasn't sure she could go. Not until she knew for certain that Jamie and Luke were safe. She suspected Lucas had picked up on her hesitation, which was why he didn't question her request for a tree.

She picked up a glossy green ornament. How could she leave with all this uncertainty hanging around them like a dark cloud? Tasha's situation remained unknown. Luke was missing. Jamie had been forced to throw in with a man Victoria did not trust to find her brother.

"You should come to bed, dear."

She looked up as Lucas entered the room. He wore those favorite pajamas of his. She smiled. The blue ones that made his gray eyes look so bright. She loved those pajamas too. She loved him. So very much.

"I thought I'd hang a few ornaments." She draped the green ornament on a branch. The smell of cedar had filled the house and she so loved it. How foolish she had been to even consider not putting up a tree.

It was a tradition. She and Lucas always had a tree.

Lucas joined her and picked out a blue ornament from the box. "I love these ornaments."

They were plain. No glitter or painted flowers or other symbols of Christmas. But there were literally hundreds of them. Red ones, pink ones. Silver, gold, blue and green. Even a few white ones. By the time the branches were loaded with ornaments, they would be beautiful.

"Wait. Wait." Lucas held up a hand. "We have to put the lights on first."

How had she forgotten the lights? "That was always your job," she said, not wanting anything to do with that chore. "I'll make hot chocolate if you string the lights."

He gave her a look that suggested he wasn't quite sure that was a fair trade, then he smiled. "Hot chocolate sounds lovely. Perhaps you'll add a little rum to mine."

"Mine too," she agreed.

Victoria padded into the kitchen. She set a pan on the stove and added the milk, then turned on the flame. While the milk heated, she combined the chocolate and sugar and added it to mugs. Hot chocolate was a winter favorite around here. If it snowed, they had hot chocolate. She glanced out the window over the sink. The snow was still coming down. The weather forecast predicted it would snow all night.

It was beautiful and a little heartbreaking. It would be the perfect time to have everyone together. But that wasn't going to happen.

This would be the first time they'd been spread so far and wide at Christmas. Victoria couldn't help feeling a little nostalgic and a lot sad.

Her cell vibrated in the pocket of her robe. Her heart rate sped up as she pulled it free of the silk. It was Kenny. "Kenny, do you have news?"

"I'm at the Saint Thomas Hospital in Nashville."

Victoria's heart dropped into her stomach. "Is everyone all right?" Please, please let her grandchildren be safe.

"Yes. Jamie is here. I've seen her. She and Amar followed the doctor from his house to the hospital. But I was careful that neither she nor Amar saw me."

"Was going to the hospital part of the plan?"

"No, ma'am. Whatever happened, it was some sort of emergency. The doctor left the party and Jamie and Amar followed not far behind. There was a small incident en route with someone who was following them. I've sent the license plate information to Michaels in hopes we might learn who it was."

More thumping in her chest. "What sort of incident?"

"The unidentified driver attempted to run them off the road. He might be someone who works for the doctor and who thought their following him from the party was suspicious, but I'm leaning more in the direction of another outside source."

Dread congealed in Victoria's belly. "Someone else who wants to, perhaps, kidnap the doctor."

"I fear so," he said. "I'm also concerned as to how this stacks up based on what you've learned about Dr. Case."

The additional intelligence her people had collected certainly shed a bad light on Dr. Case, but there were always two sides to every story. At this point it was best to reserve judgment.

"Very well," Victoria said, the next step clearing in her mind. "Given what we know, I believe it's time for you to return to the team."

"I agree. At this point I feel too removed from what's happening to be useful."

"Call me as soon as you've made contact with Jamie again."

"Will do. Good night, Victoria."

The call ended and she said a quick prayer for Jamie and Luke as well as Kenny and Amar. The smell of scorching milk shook her from the worrisome thoughts.

"You need some help in there?"

She shook off the troubling thoughts and emptied the milk, then started over. "Just giving you plenty of time to string those lights."

"Ha ha!" he called back to her.

She looked out the window and this time she couldn't help smiling. Why was she so worried about Jamie and Luke? They were Colbys. They would get through this and complete the mission too.

It was the Colby way.

Monday, December 24

One Day Before Christmas

Chapter Twelve

4:00 a.m.

"Your people have no idea who set this event in motion?" Jamie was having a difficult time getting past the notion that Abi and his backers had no idea how this *mistake* went down.

He kept his focus on the dark highway as they drove back toward the Case home. The doctor and his entourage were half a mile ahead. Abi had carefully kept his distance since leaving the parking area at the hospital.

"If my people have intel on last night, they're not sharing the information with me." He glanced at her through the darkness. "Frankly, unless there's a reason for me to know, I actually do not care to hear about it."

Now that was a cop-out. "Please. Do not try to spin this for me. Remember who you're talking to, friend. This is not my first rodeo."

The entourage up ahead took the turn to Lionheart Court.

Abi slowed, giving them ample time to move farther along the private drive leading to the doctor's home before they reached the intersection.

He blew out a long, low whistle as they passed that exit. "At least we know he made it home without being whisked away by a competitor."

Jamie waited until Abi had blown past the turn the doctor and his team had taken and then took the next right on Lady of the Lake Lane, which would take them to Excalibur. Following the doctor hadn't been an option. They had been at the hospital keeping an eye on the situation for hours. Case hadn't wanted to leave until he was certain all was good with Mr. Mason.

Jamie hoped the patient's continued stability meant he was out of the woods for good. Mason and his family would certainly have a lot to celebrate this Christmas. To find yourself on death's door and then suddenly pulled back by the skill of a surgeon was the very definition of a miracle.

Abi pulled into the garage of the Excalibur house, and she wondered again where Poe was and what in the world he was doing. If he had come here to help her and he'd ended up in trouble, she would never forgive herself.

She should call her grandmother to see if she had heard from him. Though she couldn't see Poe calling Victoria and not calling her, there could be a reason she didn't understand. She got out of the car and reached back inside for the dress and shoes she had worn to the party. Abi tucked his weapon in his waistband and grabbed his discarded clothes as well. There were things she wanted to say, but right now, she wanted a long, hot shower and a couple hours of sleep.

She wasn't sure either would happen, but she could hope.

Abi reached for the door of the house and stalled. He instantly reached to his waistband and the weapon he had tucked there not ten seconds ago as he got out of the vehicle.

He jerked his head toward her and she stepped to the side of the door. Abi held the weapon ready and eased in through the door that Jamie could now see stood ajar.

She gave him five seconds and then she followed.

They moved through the main room and had just entered the kitchen when the overhead light came on.

Jamie blinked.

Poe leaned against the sink, an apple in his hand. "Took you guys long enough to get back."

Abi growled and lowered his weapon. "I could have shot you," he warned.

"Good thing you didn't," Poe shot back.

Jamie skirted around Abi and the island to stand toe-to-toe with Poe. "What the hell, man? Where have you been?"

He smiled. "Good to see you too."

Now she was just steamed. "You disappear—leaving your phone as if you've been attacked and dragged away. What was I supposed to think?"

He had better have a good explanation. Right now her temper was pushing toward the out-of-control mark. This was not in any way shape or form the slightest bit comical.

"Your doctor's body double was on the move."

Abi made a face that said he wasn't buying it. "What exactly does that mean?"

"I took a walk. Early. I took those very nice binoculars you had in the kitchen down by the cliff and had myself a look around. While I was watching I saw someone run out of the house. He seemed in a panic." Poe shrugged. "Like the devil was after him."

"That happened this morning?" Jamie shook her head. "Yesterday morning, I mean?"

"That's right. When I zoomed in, I thought it was Case— Dr. Case. Two men—security, I presume—rushed out and tackled him."

"How do you know it wasn't Dr. Case?" Jamie glanced at Abi. The man she spoke with at the hospital had to have been the real Dr. Case…right? He hadn't actually done any surgery. He only met with the patient and viewed a CT scan.

Uncertainty swelled inside her. What if it wasn't him?

"I can't be certain, of course," Poe admitted. "But amid all the yelling—not that I could hear any of it well enough to understand what was being said—another figure appeared at the front door. I zoomed in and he, I think, was the real Dr. Case. He started pointing and barking orders, which would seem to confirm my initial conclusion. The two security thugs dragged the other *Dr. Case* into the house."

"How does this explain why you disappeared?" Abi asked, his distrust showing.

"Apparently, while I was watching this go down, there was another member of the security team watching me. I took off in a direction away from the house so he would hopefully believe I had come from a different location. I dropped my phone and didn't want to risk going back for it."

"So where have you been?" Jamie demanded.

"Well, I thought I was in the clear, but I ran right into the guy. He took me down to the house and that's where they kept me until about two hours ago."

Jamie had known Poe for a while now. She trusted him completely, but there was something wrong with this story. No, what was wrong was with the way he was telling it. "You're saying you've been held hostage all day and night?"

"In the basement. I could hear the music when the party was going on."

"How did you get away?" A cold hard knot formed in Jamie's gut. So maybe he was telling the truth.

"About nine o'clock last night, a guy walked in and told me I was free to go. I walked back up here, but the two of you were gone."

"I'm finding this a little difficult to believe," Abi said. He looked to Jamie. "Are you buying this?"

"Are you okay?" Jamie searched her friend's face. "I mean, really okay?"

He nodded. "I don't think they intended to shoot me or anything. They just wanted me out of the way for a while."

Jamie turned to Abi. "Can we be certain the man at the hospital was the real Dr. Case?" Damn, this was not good. Luke's life depended on them delivering the surgeon—the real, miracle producing one.

A single moment of hesitation elapsed and in that fleeting second, Jamie knew Abi was about to lie to her.

"I can't be certain."

Now Jamie was furious. "You said you could tell the difference."

"Wait, wait, wait," Abi argued, stepping forward, bellying up to the island, "I would need to be close to him to confirm it's really him. He has a birthmark."

"Oh. My. God. Birthmarks are like tattoos—they can be recreated. Faked!"

"Not this birthmark. It wouldn't be so easily faked. It's a deep scar beneath his ribcage. He could certainly have had it repaired at some point in his life if he'd chosen, but creating the same look wouldn't be an easy task—particularly if you only wanted it to be temporary."

Jamie told herself to remain calm. Arguing with him would accomplish nothing. "As long as you're certain."

"I'm certain."

"What're we doing now?" Poe asked. "I got the impression they thought I was the trouble they'd maybe heard a rumor about. Then they let me go. I figured whatever was supposed to happen had happened, but then you two came back. So apparently, it didn't."

"We were at the party prepared to carry out the mission and there was an emergency at the hospital and Case had to go there," Jamie explained. "He just got back home. We followed him there, then came here."

"Whatever happened over there this morning," Poe said, "and tonight, it feels like something totally unrelated to what we're here to do."

"Did you hear anything while you were there?" Abi asked, his own concern visibly growing.

"I was in the basement, so not much. Except there was a lot of moving around. Big sounds like furniture."

Jamie considered what she had seen at the doctor's home. "Everything appeared to be in place. It didn't feel like there were items missing."

Abi turned his hands up. "Maybe it was just the cleaning and prep for the gala."

Poe shrugged. "I guess so. I'm just saying that's about all I heard while I was down there."

"Were you provided with food and water?" Jamie could see them sending someone down with water at least.

"A guy brought a tray at lunchtime and then later in the evening—before the party started."

"You didn't see anyone else the entire time?" Abi pressed.

"No one."

"I need to think about this." Abi glanced at Jamie, then left the room.

The sound of the glass doors opening and then closing told Jamie he'd gone onto the patio, probably to watch the house below.

Poe looked at Jamie then. "There's something off with this. He's not telling us everything."

Jamie nodded. "At this point I don't think I can even pretend he's being completely up front." She looked directly at Poe then. "I was really, really worried about you. I walked the cul-de-sac." She exhaled a big breath. "I was scared that you were in real trouble."

Poe took her by the arm and ushered her toward the stairs.

He looked to see that Abi was still on the patio. "Come with me."

They hurried up the stairs and into the en suite of the room Poe had been using. He closed the door and turned on the shower.

"That story I gave downstairs was for Abi."

Her anger flared again. She had suspected he was not telling the truth. "Poe, what does that mean?"

"It means I am worried about what's happening here. I do not trust this guy. He is lying about too many things."

Jamie waffled between thinking he could be right and lashing out. "What things exactly?"

"I talked to your grandmother."

His words stunned her. "What?"

"I told her my concerns and she did some digging. This guy Case didn't start out being the good savior surgeon that everyone thinks. He purposely only performed certain surgeries. The patients he chose paid him huge bonuses under the table. That's why he has a body double. He fears for his life. But that seems to be shifting so I don't know exactly what's happening. This is just part of the talk about him."

This was not what Jamie wanted to hear. It didn't represent the way Case had presented himself at the hospital.

"His body double is actually his identical twin brother. All of this—" he glanced at the door, then lowered his voice "—all of this is wrong. Whatever Abi is doing it's not what he says he's doing. If some rich guy wanted the surgery, all he would have to do is pay the bonus price."

Jamie thought of the Mason family. How could they have paid a bonus for surgery? Why wouldn't someone—anyone—file a complaint about this?

"Your grandmother gave me this information," he said. "I couldn't have known otherwise. Her investigator, Ian Michaels, is here in case we need backup." He pulled a weapon from his waistband at the small of his back. "That's how I got this."

Jamie felt sick. "I'm not saying you or my grandmother is wrong, but there has to be an explanation. Abi wouldn't do this." There was bad and then there was *bad*. "And what you're saying about Case just doesn't fit with the man I met last night."

"I'm with you, Jamie. Whatever you decide. I swear I am. I just need you to think long and hard and decide if there's a chance you might be wrong."

"I get it." She did. She really did. "You have my word that I'm taking all that he says with a grain of salt."

"Good."

A knock on the door made them both jump.

"Is this a private party or am I invited?"

Jamie and Poe shared a look. Poe shut off the shower and opened the door. Abi walked in, making the bathroom seem far smaller than it had been moments ago.

"Who wants to tell me what's going on?" He folded his arms over his chest and leaned against the door frame.

"We've learned some information that seems to counter the intelligence you have," Jamie admitted.

Abi looked to Poe before meeting her gaze. "And where did you get this intelligence?"

"My grandmother." She squared her shoulders and crossed her arms over her chest. "I trust my grandmother implicitly."

"What is this intelligence?" He looked between the two of them again.

"Dr. Case is charging bonuses from the patients he chooses to help. His so-called body double is actually his identical twin brother."

Abi nodded. "Well, your grandmother's intelligence is not without merit."

Fury blasted Jamie. "You didn't think I needed to know any of this?"

"Well, there are mitigating circumstances that prevented me from telling you these things."

Jamie held up her hand. "Start from the beginning and tell me those things now. Right now."

"Shall we retire to the living room where it isn't quite so stuffy and humid?"

Jamie sidled past him. She had not been this furious in recent history. These two men were people she trusted. Well, Poe more so than Abi, but she trusted them both on some level. And one or both were yanking her chain in a very dangerous game.

If not for needing to stay in complete control for her brother's sake, she could definitely use a drink right now. This was beyond nuts. When she reached the great room, she couldn't sit down. Instead, she leaned against the bar and waited. Poe took a position next to her. Abi sat on the sofa with an I-see-how-it-is face.

"Dr. Case has an identical twin brother who was used as his body double when the need arose. And, for a while, it did appear that he was choosing patients who paid a bonus for his services. But then, about two months ago he learned that his twin brother was scamming his patients. He was pretending to be the surgeon and, in a way, filtering the patients. Only those who were prepared to pay a huge extra fee under the table were put on the surgeon's schedule. When he found out, Dr. Case chose not to press charges since the man was his brother. Instead, he warned that if his brother ever showed his face around him again, he would see that he paid for what he had done."

Jamie could see where this was going. "So the scam was discovered and remediated before your employer was in need of surgery. Since Dr. Case never chose patients in this way, he would cut off his hands before agreeing to such a thing."

"Exactly. Which leaves us with the plan as I've lain out to you already."

Jamie turned to Poe. "Sound plausible to you?"

Abi rolled his eyes. "Really?"

"I can see that scenario happening," Poe said, ignoring Abi. "Nothing the Colby Agency found opposes the possibility of that scenario."

"Knowing all that, what do we do now?" Jamie asked. "My brother is still caught in all this."

"While we were at the party," Abi explained, "I left a couple of bugs in the house. Popped a couple of tracking devices on cars. We're just waiting to hear there's movement."

"Is the Case's vacation still on?" Jamie asked. How long were they going to be in a waiting stance? She needed to find her brother and get him out of this mess.

"The vacation is still on. At some point this morning, the family is supposed to prepare to leave. The time is being withheld for reasons that are obvious."

"If the family loads up to go on vacation," Poe said, "there will be all manner of security involved. Are we going to end up in a shootout?"

"We are not. We will step in before they get into the family limo to make their escape," Abi explained.

"Have you spoken with your employer since the emergency fiasco? Any update on who this fake nurse was?" That still bugged Jamie.

"We have reason to believe someone else has decided to make an attempt on the doctor."

Having one desperate individual ready to cross so many lines to make something happen was one thing but to have two—at least—competing to achieve the same goal was more than a little disturbing.

"How do we know there won't be additional attempts?" Jamie started to pace. She couldn't help herself. The situation was not contained at all. There were far too many variables.

"We have no control over what others do," Abi argued. "We can only move forward with our own plan until some sort of roadblock pops up in our path and then we go around it." He looked directly at Jamie. "That's why I told my employer we needed the best."

This conversation was feeling repetitive. "I appreciate the vote of confidence, but this is far too risky for comfort."

Poe added, "My gut says that we should move on our own count and not based on the movements of others."

"Waiting could be a mistake," Jamie agreed. She turned to Abi. "It gives the other team more opportunity to try a second strike."

"We are not moving prematurely," Abi argued. "There is nothing to be gained by jumping the gun, so to speak."

"Let's talk about this," Jamie pushed back. "We just spent six hours at the hospital because someone posing as a nurse called in a fake emergency. Now, we're tired—the security supporting Dr. Case are no doubt tired as well. And we're standing around here as if we have all the time in the world and no one else is even thinking about this sort of thing."

"All right." Abi pushed to his feet. "I will call my employer and see if he will agree to our moving forward now."

He walked outside and closed the glass doors behind him.

Poe turned to Jamie. "We need to be prepared. Luke is

depending on us to ensure this goes down right and, frankly, I'm losing any and all confidence in what he's doing."

"I'm with you and ready to go," Jamie assured him.

"I should call Victoria and let her know what's happening."

Jamie shook her head. "I should call her."

"Sure. She'll be happy to hear from you."

Jamie took out the cell and put through a call to her grandmother. It was even earlier in Chicago, but she wouldn't mind.

"Jamie, are you all right?"

She sounded so worried, and Jamie's chest ached at the idea. "I'm fine, Grandmother. We're on standby for the moment. We had a false alarm and the mission had to be delayed but we should be moving out soon."

"Poe is there with you now?"

"Yes, he is. He's updated me on everything."

"Good. I'm not sure Abi's employer is on the up-and-up, Jamie."

"I know. I'm worried about that too. Hopefully we'll know something soon. I'm ready to move."

"Just be careful. You have a guardian angel."

Jamie smiled. "I will, Grandmother. Don't worry, I know."

They said their goodbyes, and Jamie ended the call just as Abi returned from his private call.

"We will be moving out shortly," Abi announced. "We have a very short time for any final preparations."

"Thank God." Jamie took a breath. "I just need one last assurance from you, Abi, that this man—your employer— is properly prepared for the intentions he has laid out. This is a very delicate situation. If I note even the slightest hint that some untoward situation is going down, I will not help make that happen."

"No one," Abi insisted, "wants to keep Dr. Case alive more than my employer. You can rest assured that every precaution will be taken to protect him and his family."

Jamie turned to Poe. "Are you still prepared to do this? I will understand if you want to walk away. If any part of this goes wrong…"

There was no need to explain. Everyone in the room understood exactly what she was saying.

"I'm in," Poe said. "We do this together." He turned to Abi. "The three of us."

Abi nodded. "Thank you."

"Let's do it," Jamie announced.

Abi gave her a nod as well. "It is the right thing to do."

As long as no one died…she could live with doing whatever she had to do to save Luke.

She hoped that guardian angel her grandmother had sent was ready as well.

Chapter Thirteen

Lionheart Court,
7:00 a.m.

Jamie scanned the area around the house as the sun peeked above the trees.

It was almost time.

She, Poe and Abi hovered in a group of trees at the edge of the wooded area. Beyond their position was the landscaped yard that surrounded the home of Dr. Case.

Half an hour ago they had received word that they should move into place. The three of them had come down the hillside, which surprised Jamie. She'd expected to go in a vehicle, but Abi assured there would be a vehicle waiting for them when the time came. He had better be right.

"You're going in through the front," Abi said to Jamie. "Poe and I will approach from the rear."

Sounded easy enough. *Not.* "Do I have a cover?" Going in via the front door surprised her. Security was inside and around the house. Not just one or two either. They had already established that there were a lot of security personnel. Whoever answered the door was not going to let her in without one hell of a good explanation.

Abi smiled. "You talked to him at the hospital, did you not?"

The memory of the woman who'd started to cry in the waiting room pinged her, followed immediately by the flash of recall with Jamie and the doctor chatting in the room belonging to the woman's husband. Jamie had walked right into that one.

"I guess I did," she admitted.

Abi glanced at his watch.

When had he started wearing a watch? Apparently, he'd added it for the final step. She didn't recall him wearing one to the party. Change always set her on edge.

"You should go now." Abi turned to Jamie. "A car is coming up the driveway now. You're trading places with the driver."

Jamie spotted the headlights at the farthest end of the drive just before the two round orbs went out. "See you inside," she said to Poe before disappearing into the trees.

Sprinting through the trees wasn't so easy, but she managed. There was just enough daylight to prevent any head-on collisions with the flora or face-plants after tripping over roots. The car stopped as the driver somehow realized she was near. Probably a tracking device in the clothes she was wearing. Abi wasn't one to take chances. A good thing, she supposed.

The driver's-side door opened and the man behind the wheel emerged. He walked right past Jamie and into the woods without a glance or a word. Weird.

She watched until he'd disappeared and then she climbed into the car. Maybe she was accustomed to working with team members she knew and liked. This was strange territory.

After putting the car into Drive once more, she rolled slowly toward the house. When she reached the fountain that sat in the middle of the parking area, she slowed to a stop. By the time she put the car into Park and shut off the engine, a member of the security team was at her door.

She opened the door and started to get out, but he held up a hand. The weapon still sheathed on his hip warned that he was dead serious about her staying in the vehicle. "Let's see some ID."

"My name is… Jamie *Mason*. I'm here to speak with Dr. Case about his patient, my uncle, and what happened at the hospital last night."

He passed along a summary of what she'd said to whoever was on the other end of his hidden communication device. A few seconds later he evidently received a response because he stepped aside and said, "You're cleared to come inside."

Jamie wondered again how Abi had set her up for this. How could he have known that she would approach the woman in the waiting room? Calculated guess? The idea also made her wonder if the whole thing had been a setup. Clearly, the incident with the patient had been… But the wife in the waiting room? Had the fake nurse sent her to the waiting room rather than allow her to stay in the room? Made sense if the supposedly accidental meeting between her and Jamie was the plan.

She followed the guard to the front door. He led her into the entry hall and then disappeared back through the door they'd entered.

Eight, no ten suitcases of varying sizes were lined up in the entry hall ready to be loaded into a vehicle. The family was ready to head off to some ski slope loaded with fresh white snow or some city glittering with ritzy shops. Maybe she should take a vacation. Her parents were in Europe. She couldn't remember the last time she'd actually taken a vacation. Or a holiday for that matter.

She traveled extensively with her work but that wasn't the same.

At all.

Work usually involved being stuck in some location where the target could be monitored 24/7. Once she'd spent days in a jail cell with a target for a cellmate. It was almost Christmas, and she had no idea if she would even be spending it with family, maybe her grandparents, or completely alone.

If you can't save your brother...what difference does the holiday make?

She blinked away the thought and focused on what she had to do. Dr. Case was the key to rescuing Luke. She had to keep that in mind above all else.

Movement at the far end of the larger hall snagged her attention. She focused on the man striding her way. *Dr. Case.* At least she hoped it was the real Dr. Case. What if it was his twin brother?

She steeled herself against the worries and readied to spin a tale that would keep her in the house until Abi and Poe showed up. At least she assumed that was the point.

"Ms. Mason." Case studied her a moment, a frown working its way across his forehead. "I checked on your uncle a little while ago and he was doing fine."

"He is," Jamie agreed. "One of the nurses said you and your family were leaving for an extended vacation and I really felt it was important that I speak with you before you go."

"I wouldn't call this an extended vacation," he offered. "We'll be gone the rest of this week and through the weekend, but I'll be back at the hospital on Monday." He studied her another moment. "What is it you need to speak with me about?"

Damn it, Abi. Come on.

"The nurse," she said. "The one who triggered the false alarm. Johnson, I believe her name was."

He nodded. "The hospital is working with the police in conducting an investigation. To my knowledge she hasn't been found as of yet."

"I think I saw her back at the hospital this morning and I didn't know who to tell." This obviously was a lie, but she was winging it. If she had to buy much more time, she wasn't sure how that was going to go down. The doctor was clearly already suspicious, and she was basically holding her breath.

He reached into his pocket and withdrew his cell phone. "Did you inform security?" He tapped the screen and pressed the phone to his ear.

"I told the nurse on duty at the desk—the one near my uncle's room."

For a few seconds, Case was preoccupied discussing her assertion with whomever he had called. Then he thanked the person and ended the call.

"Security is keeping an eye on everyone who enters the building. There has been no sign of her coming through any of the entrances."

Jamie made a face. Damn. Of course they were monitoring the comings and goings after the incident. "Well then, maybe she never left."

This appeared to give him pause. He withdrew his phone and made a second call. He passed along this suggestion, then hung up.

"Thank you," she said before he could start asking her questions. "I was just really worried about my uncle's safety, and I wasn't sure anyone would actually listen to me. You seemed so kind and so concerned. I felt the need to come straight to you. I'm so sorry for the intrusion."

"Daddy! Daddy!"

Lillian rushed into the room. Her pink sweatshirt sported a popular cartoon character. The pockets of her jeans were trimmed in pink and then there were the furry pink boots. The kid liked pink for sure. She glanced at Jamie, then smiled.

If the kid recognized her...

"This must be your daughter," Jamie said before the child could say a word.

Case smiled. "This is Lillian. She's very excited about the trip."

Jamie smiled. "Well, anyway, thank you, Dr. Case, for hearing me out and making sure my concerns are taken seriously."

This was it. She was out of time and options.

"Have a nice holiday, Ms. Mason."

"I thought your name was Jasmine."

Jamie's pulse reacted to the girl's statement, but she kept her smile in place. "That's right. Jasmine Mason. Most people call me Jamie."

The child frowned as if she wasn't sure that was correct.

"Have a lovely vacation," Jamie offered before turning to the door.

"How do you know Ms. Mason?"

Jamie cringed at the question he'd asked his daughter. The doctor realized something was off.

"We talked about the books," Jamie said, turning back to them and using a last-ditch effort to control the narrative.

Come on, Abi. Damn it.

"I told her about the ducks," Lillian said, her cheeks turning pink again. "I think she liked the idea."

"I absolutely did," Jamie said.

The front door suddenly burst open, and Jamie almost sighed with relief.

But the man who barreled over the threshold wielding a weapon was not Abi or Poe. Not unless they had found ski masks to don after parting ways with her.

"On the floor," he shouted.

Lillian threw herself against her father.

"What's going on?" Case demanded. "Rodgers!"

"Rodgers is not coming," the man in the mask said. "And neither is anyone else on your security team. Now get on the floor. Face down!"

He pointed the weapon at Lillian. "Now!"

Case lowered to his knees, taking his daughter with him. "Let's do as he says, Lilly."

Jamie was sinking to her knees when the guy pointed a look in her direction. "You," he ordered, "take the kid and wait outside."

"What?" Jamie pretended not to understand. Where the hell were Poe and Abi?

"Do it!" The masked man nudged the kid with his foot.

Lillian cried out. Her father tried to pull her into the protection of his body.

"It's okay, Lillian," Jamie said as she moved in the girl's direction. Jamie kept her attention fixed on the guy with the gun. "We'll just step outside for a minute."

More bodies flooded the entry hall. Two, no, three more wearing the same masks. All armed. What the hell was going on?

"Take the kid outside," the first man repeated.

"Come on, Lillian." Jamie offered her hand.

Dr. Case stared up at her, his grip firm around his daughter's arm. "What're you doing?"

Jamie looked directly into his eyes and tried her best to show him with her own that he could trust her. "Whatever it takes to stay alive." Lillian took Jamie's hand. "I'm not going to let anything happen to you," Jamie promised. She shifted her attention to the man with the gun. "We're going outside like you said."

He jerked his head toward the door. "Now!"

Jamie held on tight to the girl's hand. She hovered close to Jamie, her slim body shaking with fear. Outside, two more cars had arrived. They sat askew as if they'd skidded to stops and were left where they landed.

Since the guy in the mask hadn't given any specific instructions about what they were to do once they were outside, Jamie hurried around the far left corner of the house and disappeared into the landscape, using mature shrubs and miniature trees as cover.

The girl was sobbing now. "Where are we going?"

Jamie drew her down into a squat behind a clump of large shrubs. "Be as quiet as you can," she whispered. "We don't want them finding us out here."

"What about Mommy and Daddy?"

Jamie hadn't seen Mrs. Case. "Was your mommy upstairs?"

Lillian nodded. "She told Daddy she had one more bag to pack."

"Okay. Let's stay calm and see what we can find out." Which really meant stay put until Jamie could figure out what the hell was going on.

So far she'd heard no gunshots—always a good thing. But where the hell were Abi and Poe and whatever backup Abi had put in place or ordered or whatever? Everything had fallen apart and she had no clear idea of what to do from here…except protect the child.

Jamie gauged the distance to the car she'd arrived in. It was still parked near the fountain. If she could reach that car, she could take the child out of here, tuck her away in the Excalibur house and then come back to see what she could do with the unexpected takeover in the doctor's house.

None of what was happening made sense.

She leaned closer to Lillian and explained, "I need to get you someplace safe."

"We can't leave Mommy and Daddy," she whimpercd.

"Listen to me, Lillian," Jamie whispered with all the urgency she could muster. "I can't help your mom and dad while I'm taking care of you. I need to settle you someplace safe so I can help them. That's what they would want. Trust me."

"I can't leave them," the girl insisted.

Shouts echoed from the front of the house. The door was open again. Someone was coming out or going in. Judging by the furiously raised voice, the coming or going—whichever it was—was not voluntary. Jamie listened intently to make out the words. Someone was not happy with how something had been done.

"Find her!"

She heard those words clearly.

"Now!"

They were looking for Lillian. A new wave of tension poured through Jamie. She considered the distance from their hiding places to the woods. It wasn't the direction she'd wanted to go, but she was out of options and quickly running out of time.

Jamie pressed a finger to the little girl's lips. Hoped she understood that it was imperative that she didn't make a sound.

If they could make the tree line, Jamie would find the way

to the house. She would call Victoria, then Ian Michaels. Poe had said he was close by. He could help.

Jamie clasped Lillian's hand in hers and gave it a squeeze. She leaned closer once more and whispered, "We're going to try and make it up the hill through the woods. Just be careful where you step and stay close to me and try not to make a sound."

Lillian nodded her understanding.

Holding tight to her hand, Jamie headed for the tree line. She wanted to go faster, but she wasn't sure how Lillian would do, so she set her pace to match the girl's.

The beam of a flashlight suddenly obstructed their view.

"Hold on there," a voice commanded.

Not Poe. Not Abi.

Damn it.

Jamie froze. Lillian did the same, gluing herself to Jamie's side.

"You were supposed to wait by the cars."

"No one told me where to wait."

"Well, I'm telling you now. Let's go?"

The beam of the flashlight shifted and in the moments it took her vision to adjust, she spotted the weapon in his hand.

"Fine," Jamie said, feigning frustration. She wasn't really sure what her part was supposed to be in this. Did they think she was someone else? Maybe the nanny who was on vacation. Who knew if their intel was up to par. Either way, it was best to play along until she had a better grip on what was going down.

The man with the gun ushered them back to where the two poorly parked cars waited. Another of the team opened the back passenger door.

"Get in," their guide ordered.

Jamie ushered Lillian into the car and slid in next to her.

"What about Mommy and Daddy?" Lillian cried softly.

"I'm sure they'll be fine," Jamie lied. What else could she do? No doubt these thugs were here for Dr. Case. He was far more valuable than anything else they might find in that house.

Jamie just couldn't say what the intent was.

For now, the only choice was to ride this out and see where they landed.

8:15 a.m.

THE DRIVER HAD stopped at the end of the long driveway leading away from the Case home and forced Jamie to put a sack over her head as well as one over Lillian's. Then they'd driven away. Upon arrival at their destination, an older house and certainly nothing in any of the subdivisions near the Case home, they'd been allowed to remove the sacks. A quick glimpse at the digital screen on the car's dash showed they had driven nearly twenty minutes and approximately twelve miles. The new location had to be something off a different road. Jamie had tried to keep up with the turns. There had been about four. A couple of lefts and a right, possibly a second right or at the very least a slight fork to the right.

The driver had then sequestered Jamie and Lillian to a bedroom inside the new location. Evidently the house was unoccupied since there was no bed, just an old futon. The place appeared to have been empty for a while considering the dust and cobwebs. Not to mention it smelled musty.

"I'm scared." Lillian hugged herself. "I need to go home."

Jamie pulled her into her arms and held her close. "I will get you home, Lillian. Don't worry about that."

Jamie had seen only one guy. But he had a weapon. Still, he couldn't be everywhere all the time. All Jamie needed was an opportunity to make a move. She was banking on the idea that Abi would have planted a tracking device on her somewhere. He was too careful—too determined to cover all the bases—not to do so. At least she could hope.

One way or another, Jamie intended to get this child out of danger.

The sound of the guy's voice drew her to the wall between the bedroom and whatever lay beyond it. She cupped a hand, pressed it to her ear and then to the wall.

"We're here. Yes."

He was checking in. If Jamie was lucky, he would give away something about the plan. There had to be a plan.

Another issue she tried not to dwell on was what this situation would do to their timeline. Luke's face flashed in her mind. How long would it be before whoever had taken Luke would lose patience? Or maybe decide to cut his losses? Her gut clenched at the idea.

Not going there. Not yet.

"We'll be ready," their captor said. "Yes. Half an hour. Good."

Something was happening in half an hour.

Were they moving to a different location?

Jamie couldn't wait around to see what that would entail. Not to mention there was a strong possibility help would be coming to assist with the move. She needed to get the kid out of harm's way before any sort of backup arrived. She could not just wait around, assuming Abi would have her location and he or Poe would come to their rescue.

Her odds were far better right now, in this one-on-one situation.

She glanced at the girl. Keeping Lillian safe complicated everything. But if Luke were here, he would tell her to protect the kid at all costs.

Jamie drew in a deep breath and walked to the door and banged on it. "I need the bathroom."

A cliché request, but if it worked, she could live with it.

After the sound of something metal being handled—a lock maybe—the door opened. The man still wore his mask. That was a good thing. It meant he didn't want them to be able to identify him. To some degree, this suggested there was a perception that the hostages would at some point be released. Otherwise, what would revealing his face matter?

"Down the hall." He jerked his head left.

Jamie reached for the girl's hand.

"No. She stays here."

Jamie shook her head. "She's scared. She needs to stay with me. We're only going into the bathroom."

"If you give me any trouble," he warned, "I will kill you both."

"Don't worry. We're not going to give you any trouble."

Lillian clung to Jamie as they made their way to the end of the hall. Jamie took in all the details she could of their location as they made the short journey. Typical ranch house with a narrow hall. The doors along the hall opened into the three bedrooms—all basically empty like the one they'd been locked in. The final door, at the end of the hall, was a bathroom that sported generic beige tile along with harvest gold fixtures.

"Don't close the door all the way," he ordered.

"Got it."

In the bathroom, she left the door ajar. "Why don't you go first?" Jamie suggested.

While Lillian did her business, Jamie studied the small room. There was a window, but it looked painted shut. Getting out the window wouldn't likely be easy. She checked behind the shower curtain and under the sink, careful not to alert their keeper.

When Lillian was done, Jamie relieved herself, using that time to continue her study of the small room.

Once they had washed their hands and exited the room, she asked, "Any bottled water around here?"

"You couldn't get a drink from the sink?" He gestured to the bathroom.

Jamie shrugged. "No cup or glass."

He swore and stamped back down the hall. Jamie took Lillian's hand and followed him. The hall opened into a small living room that fronted a kitchen-dining combination. The rest of the house was unfurnished other than a couple of plastic chairs. Definitely vacant. Probably a rental.

In the kitchen there was a six-pack of bottled water on the counter. No dust, which told her it had been provided for this operation.

"You can each have one but don't ask for anything else."

Jamie passed a bottle of water to Lillian and then took one for herself. "Thank you."

"When are my mom and mad coming?" Lillian asked.

The man looked at her for a long moment. He grabbed a bottle of water for himself, twisted off the top and took a long swig. Then he said, "Don't worry, kid. As soon as we get what we need, you'll be back with your family and on the way to your fancy vacation."

Wouldn't it be great if it were that simple? The trouble was that Jamie couldn't assume he was telling the truth.

"Let's go," he said with a gesture toward the end of the house where the bedrooms were.

Holding Lillian's hand, Jamie led her back to the bedroom. She'd been right. A padlock had been added to the door. Once they were inside, he locked it.

Jamie slowly walked the perimeter of the room. This bedroom was on the back side of the house. She peeled back the dusty paper that had been taped to the window. She squinted to see beyond the dirty glass. The overgrown grass in the small backyard led right up to the woods. Definitely an advantage.

Next, she checked the lock on the window. It moved. She set it to the unlock position. The window was an old one—wood, not vinyl or aluminum. The screening was long gone. The issue with wood windows was if they had been painted without being moved up and down afterward, then often, they were glued shut. Not so terrible if one had a utility knife with which to cut them loose.

She turned to Lillian and leaned close to whisper in her ear. "Talk to me about the vacation. Try to sound natural."

Lillian nodded and started talking. "We're going to New York."

"Wow, that sounds exciting." Jamie braced herself, her hands on the wood sash. She pushed. The sash didn't budge.

She took a breath and tried again. Pushing upward with all her strength. The sash moved the tiniest bit, giving her hope.

"I hope it snows," Lillian was saying. "We almost never get snow here."

"That would be nice," Jamie said. She readied herself and tried again. This time the sash moved about three inches.

While Lillian went on about all the sites in New York she wanted to see, Jamie braced her hands on the bottom of the sash this time and shoved upward.

The window went up another four or five inches.

Jamie glanced toward the door and nodded to Lillian to keep going. Then she shoved one last time with all her might.

The sash went up as far as it would go. Jamie shook her arms to release the throbbing tension.

Now all they had to do was climb out.

Jamie went first. She surveyed the backyard but saw nothing of concern. She motioned for Lillian to climb out.

"I'm sure your mom will take you shopping." Jamie talked while she helped her make the drop onto the other side.

"I hope so," Lillian said, her eyes wide with worry.

Jamie glanced left. Not that way because they would have to pass the kitchen window and the back door.

She pointed right and to the woods. Then she leaned close. "Keep as quiet as possible, but move as fast as you can."

Lillian nodded.

Jamie took her hand and started moving away from the house that was to have been their prison…or maybe their grave.

Chapter Fourteen

Kenny struggled to control his anger until they had the doctor and his wife settled in the great room of Amar's employer. Another rich guy, apparently, who had decided his life was more important than the doctor's, the Case family's or any-damned-one else's.

But that wasn't really the reason Kenny felt so furious. He was mad as hell because Amar had seen trouble coming and he had hesitated long enough that Jamie and the doctor's kid had been taken by the other team—the other set of bad guys.

Kenny walked out onto the terrace where he could properly pace and mutter the swear words burning inside his throat.

Like the doctor's home, there was a pool and all the usual trappings of überwealth. The home was older than the one on Lionheart Court, but the location was likely the draw. Kenny shook his head. What the hell was he doing here?

They had kidnapped a surgeon and brought him to this place.

He told himself he'd made the right decision. Jamie's

brother was being held hostage. It wasn't like he could ignore the situation and he sure as hell didn't trust Abidan Amar to straighten this out. So he'd come along. He'd dove in and done what he could to help. For Luke. For Jamie.

Now Jamie was missing too.

The French doors opened, and Amar joined him on the terrace. Kenny looked away, not trusting himself to look the guy in the eye.

"We have a problem," Amar announced.

Kenny wheeled on him. "You think? Like who the hell took Jamie and the kid? Do you have a handle on that situation?"

"Unfortunately, I can't say who took them. A competitor it seems who isn't looking to save a life, but is positioning himself for a ransom demand."

Kenny took a breath and told himself not to punch the guy. Doing so would not fix the situation and right now they needed to figure out how to help Jamie and that little girl. This was not the time to allow emotions to reign.

Of course Amar couldn't say who had taken Jamie and the kid. He'd totally missed whatever happened this morning. He and his people should have picked up on the trouble in the air.

"Your people were already on the ground when the other guys showed up—and there was only three of them. Three! They came in right under the noses of your people and walked away with Jamie and the girl."

If there was ever a situation that screamed of incompetence, this was it. Kenny struggled to regain his composure. Amar was not incompetent. Kenny knew this. He was just angry. Even the best plan could go awry. He also knew this firsthand. Rather than focus on pointing to how badly

Amar had failed, they both needed to focus on how to rescue Jamie and the child.

"You are correct," Amar agreed. "There is no excuse for what happened except to admit that someone on my team failed. However, I've just been told that we have some security footage that may help us nail down who these people were and hopefully find them."

Kenny was over simply talking about this. They needed to act. To do that, he had to focus and to focus he had to find calm. "What is the problem you mentioned?"

"Dr. Case will not move forward with the surgery here until his daughter is found."

Well, Kenny didn't blame him. He'd been kidnapped. His family had been dragged from their home and his daughter had ended up God only knew where. Why would he cooperate? Only a fool would do so.

"What's your plan?" Surely the man had a strategy for straightening out this screwed up mess.

"I'm glad you asked." Amar's sly smile was more of a smirk, and it seriously rubbed against Kenny's last nerve. "We have someone waiting to see us downstairs in the game room."

Kenny followed him back into the house, beyond the great room and down the stairs to the walkout basement. It was like another house, the floor space no doubt as spacious as the layout upstairs.

Amar turned down a hallway to the left, which led into another large room with doors leading to the outside. A man wearing black, as they all had been this morning, was secured to a chair in the center of the room. He glanced at Kenny, then Amar, before looking away. His own smirk suggested he was not worried about whatever they had come to do.

Never a good sign.

"Mr. Reicher."

He turned to Amar as he approached, but said nothing.

Kenny stayed back a few steps and watched. This was Amar's show. He'd give him some time to see if he could pull this debacle together. Jamie liked the guy. Respected him. He must be better at this than he'd shown so far.

"Your girlfriend—Darla, I believe, is her name—and her baby are on the way here. Is there anything you'd like to share with us before they arrive?"

Reicher's face paled a little. "I have nothing to say."

Amar smiled. "Really. Darla says her baby is your son, Paul junior. She's very excited to bring him to see the Christmas surprise I told her you had arranged."

His face tightened. "She doesn't know anything about all this."

"That's too bad, Mr. Reicher. I think she may be very disappointed about what she finds here today."

He looked away a moment.

Kenny was out of patience. "That little girl your friends took better be safe," he warned, stepping closer. "If something happens to her…"

Reicher glared at Kenny. "She's fine. Nothing will happen to her if Dr. Case is delivered as requested."

Amar shrugged. "You see, Mr. Reicher, that is not going to happen. We have the doctor, and he is the important one. I'm sure you realize this. And as much as we want his daughter to be safe, she really is not our top concern."

Kenny bit his tongue to prevent calling him a liar. But he understood the tactic. He didn't like it, but he understood it.

"I don't think the doctor will see it that way," Reicher argued, the fear in his eyes impossible to conceal.

"I have a onetime offer for you, Mr. Reicher," Amar said.

"You tell me where my friend Jamie and the girl are and— assuming they are unharmed—I will allow you to leave with your girlfriend and your son when they arrive." He laughed. "Hell, I'll even throw in a little bonus for that Christmas surprise. But, if you waste this opportunity, there is nothing I can do for you."

Kenny shook his head. "He doesn't deserve a deal. I say we just beat it out of him."

"But I've already called Darla and she's on her way." Amar checked his watch. "We have maybe ten minutes before she arrives."

"Okay," Reicher said. "Just don't hurt her or tell her about any of this."

That was easier than Kenny expected. Maybe too easy. "Tell us where the girl and my friend are being held."

"They're in a house on Trinity Road. I can give you directions."

"How about you take my friend there," Amar suggested. "That way there are no miscommunications."

"But what about Darla and the baby?"

"I'll let them know to go home and wait. You'll be there soon."

Reicher looked from Amar to Kenny. "How do I know I can trust either of you?"

Amar withdrew a knife, opened the blade and sliced it through the bonds holding Reicher to the chair. "I suppose you're just going to have to take a chance. If you're not willing to take a chance, then you're in the wrong line of work."

Kenny grabbed the guy by the collar. "Let's go." He shoved him toward the door.

Amar leaned in closer to Kenny. "Once you have Jamie and the girl, just leave him at the house and get back here. We're running out of time."

Kenny nodded. "I just hope Jamie doesn't regret trusting you because I sure as hell do."

In the corridor before they reached the stairs, one of the men working on Amar's team approached Kenny and Reicher. "This way, gentlemen."

They were led to a door that opened into a six-car garage. Outside the garage, one of the black sedans Amar's people had used waited as if everyone had known this was the way things would work out.

"I'll be your driver," the man said as he opened the rear passenger-side door.

Kenny waited for Reicher to get in, then he dropped into the seat next to him. He removed his weapon and held it ready. "Don't waste my time," he warned Reicher.

Reicher gave the driver the street address.

The drive took longer than Kenny had hoped, but he didn't know a lot about the area. Trinity Road was closer to where they had been in the Excalibur house than where they'd ended up today. Staying in the same general vicinity as the home invasion for hostage containment made a sort of sense, he supposed.

Trinity Road led away from the more heavily populated areas and had older houses set back off the road. It was heavily wooded in some areas.

"Up ahead on the left," Reicher said.

When they turned onto the long drive, a man with a weapon emerged from the woods.

Kenny poked the muzzle of his weapon into Reicher's side. "Unless you want to die now, I would suggest you think carefully before you speak to this guy."

Reicher nodded, then, hand shaking, powered his window down. "I'm here to pick up the girl."

"Good luck with that," his comrade said. "That lady with

her opened a window and they took off. I've been looking for them for the past hour."

Kenny's pulse thumped with the news. He barely resisted the urge to grin.

"We'll help you look for them," Reicher said. "Get in the car." He slid toward Kenny.

The other guy got in. As he closed the door, he looked at Kenny. "Who the hell are you?"

Kenny pressed the muzzle of his weapon to the man's forehead. "Toss your gun into the front seat."

He hesitated.

"Do it," Reicher said. "We're not going to win this one."

The new guy reluctantly did as ordered.

"Anyone else here?" Kenny asked.

The new guy shook his head. "Just me."

"Drive up to the house," Kenny said to the driver.

The car rolled forward, stopping at the small ranch house. Kenny and the driver emerged and ushered the two men into the house. Kenny walked through. Spotted the raised window in the bedroom and smiled.

"Go Jamie." He crossed to the window and surveyed the area into which the two had taken off.

Back in the living room, the driver had the two standing with their backs against the wall. Kenny looked to the driver. "You have anything we can use to secure these two so we don't have to shoot them?"

The driver nodded and hurried out of the house.

Kenny looked to the guy who had been guarding Jamie. "How long ago did they escape?"

"Maybe an hour."

Damn. They could be anywhere by now. Maybe even back at the Excalibur house. "If I don't find them, I'll be back."

When the two were secured, Kenny and the driver headed outside.

"Let's make sure they have to walk out of here if they somehow manage to get loose."

"Good idea," the driver agreed.

"What's your name?" Kenny asked while he slashed the tires.

"Landon."

"Well, Landon," Kenny said as he got back to his feet, "maybe we need the car's fob to ensure it's no use to anyone."

Landon nodded and went back into the house. Half a minute later, he returned with the car's fob. He popped the hood and did something under there. Kenny wasn't much of a mechanic so he had no clue what. He could change a tire and check the oil. That was about the extent of his vehicle maintenance skills.

When Landon closed the hood, he said, "They won't be going anywhere in this vehicle." Then he dropped the fob on the ground and used the heel of his boot to disable it as well.

"Take the car," Kenny decided, "drive slowly along the road. I'll walk and have a look around in the woods."

"You got it," Landon said.

Kenny scanned the overgrown grass and quickly spotted the signs of recent movement. He followed that path into the woods.

"Jamie!" If they were still in these woods, maybe they would hear him calling.

Once he was deeper in the woods, the path wasn't as easy to follow. He trudged through the underbrush and called Jamie's name over and over.

The sound of a car horn blowing had him stalling in

his tracks. He listened. Coming from Trinity Road. Maybe Landon had found them.

Kenny started to run through the woods. When he emerged, he was in the yard of another property. He kept close to the tree line along the yard's border since he had no desire to get shot. Then he saw Landon's car on the road. Kenny broke into a hard run.

As he reached the road and the car, the rear passenger window powered down. "Looking for me?"

Jamie. His knees almost gave out on him. "You and Lillian okay?"

She nodded. "We're good. Get in."

Kenny opened the front door and dropped into the seat. To Landon, he said, "Let Amar know we're headed back with what we came for." He turned to Jamie then. "Where were you?" He glanced at Landon. "How did he find you?"

"We were hiding in the church a mile or so up the road. The guy who'd been holding us had come through looking for us, but he didn't think to look under the altar."

Kenny laughed. "But you thought to hide there."

Landon ended his call. "Smart move," he said to Jamie. "I spotted the church as we drove in. When we were told you had escaped on foot, I figured you went to the church. That's where I would have gone."

Kenny had to admit he would probably have done the same. He looked to Lillian then. "Your parents are going to be very happy to see you."

She nodded. "Jamie saved me."

Jamie smiled. "We did it together."

Kenny was just thankful they were safe. He was pretty sure he'd never been so relieved in his life.

"I don't think that guy was very good at his job," Lillian suggested.

"We're just lucky he wasn't," Jamie pointed out. She looked to Kenny. "And we're very lucky that my friend is really, really good at his job."

Chapter Fifteen

Lillian wanted food so they had to stop. Thankfully, she recognized where they were pretty quickly once they were on the main road and directed the driver to her favorite drive-through. Jamie wasn't really hungry, but she understood the necessity of eating. She hadn't gotten any sleep, so forgoing food was not a good idea. She needed her head clear and her body energized.

"So this is the place." Jamie assessed the mansion where the doctor and his wife had been taken.

"This is it," Poe said, surveying the estate as the car parked in front of the house.

It wasn't as new as the doctor's mansion, but it was every bit as ostentatious in its own right. The whole situation was over the line. One rich guy kidnapping another to get what he wanted. How screwed up was that? Maybe growing up a Colby made her understand at a fairly young age how completely upside down the world could be, but there were still times, like this one, when she just couldn't get past the reality of how bad it really was. More than just upside down.

What was wrong with these people?

The part that bothered her the most in all this was that she actually got it. These people were desperate. Desperate people, no matter how wealthy, did desperate things, creating desperate situations.

Jamie got out of the car and held the door for Lillian. The girl was still shoving fries in her mouth when she got out. Poor thing, she really had been starving. Kids were like that. She remembered when she and Luke were that age. They were always clamoring for food—especially fast food.

The double front doors opened, and Abi stood in the doorway. "Welcome back."

Jamie's first thought was to punch him, but what kind of example would that set for Lillian? It was better if she behaved herself until the two of them had a minute alone to talk in privacy.

"Let's get this show on the road," Jamie shot back. "I'd like to see my brother."

Abi stepped aside and gestured for her to enter. "The doctor and Mrs. Case are waiting in the great room."

Lillian stuck close to Jamie as they walked through the entry hall and on to the great room. Like the Case home, the whole place was decked out for Christmas with a massive tree and tons of garlands. Under the tree, dozens of wrapped presents waited.

Mrs. Case gasped and rushed to her daughter. She paid no attention to Jamie, which was good. Dr. Case did the same.

Poe gave her a nod from the other side of the room. Jamie responded in kind. This was the best part of what they did—reuniting families or couples after a situation had pulled them apart. They didn't always get this moment.

After a good deal of hugging and weeping, Dr. Case stepped back from his family and walked toward Abi. "Let's get this done."

"Very well." Abi gestured to the door. "You know the way."

Jamie glanced at Poe. "I'm going with them."

Poe nodded. "I'll hang around here."

Jamie hesitated. There were many things she wanted to say to him—things she probably should have said before now—but all of that would have to wait. Jamie needed to know what was happening with the doctor. This was the part that her brother's life depended upon. Poe would look after the daughter and the wife.

She wasn't allowing Abi or the doctor out of her sight until Luke was free. Whatever else happened, she intended to see that her brother was brought home safely.

Abi led the way down to the walkout basement area. There they walked through a massive game room and into a short corridor with no windows. At the end of that corridor was a door like one found on a bank vault. Jamie wasn't sure whether to be startled or impressed. Abi entered the code as if he'd been here many times before. Jamie decided she could safely assume the owner of this place was Abi's employer.

The door opened and they walked into a small curtained off area. The sort of space found in a mobile hospital setup. There was a sink, a temporary shower and a smaller curtained off dressing area. This, she surmised, was the prep area for the space beyond. No doubt a state-of-the-art surgical setup. Now she was totally impressed.

Case glanced back at Jamie and Abi and then started to strip off his clothes. He didn't need a block of instructions on what came next. Jamie turned her back and gave him some privacy. When the water in the small shower started running, she faced Abi once more.

"This guy has a surgical suite in his basement?" Was this for real?

"When he made the decision to go this route, he went all out."

Jamie shook her head. "This is way over-the-top, Abi."

The water in the shower stopped, preventing the need for Abi to respond. Jamie kept her back to Case as he dressed in what she presumed would be his surgical scrubs and gown. A sense of dread that would not be tamped down climbed into her throat. What if the patient died? Case was unquestionably a skilled and highly sought after surgeon who hadn't lost a single patient so far—according to his bio. But that didn't mean it couldn't happen. No matter that she and Abi had done what they were expected to do, would Luke still be released if the patient didn't make it?

Focus on the now, Jamie. Don't borrow trouble.

Case opened the curtained door and entered the surgery suite. The glimpse Jamie got of the room beyond this prep area was stunning. She couldn't imagine the money spent to prepare for this…but then, what was the value of a loved one's life? Most likely it was whatever a person possessed.

Abi gestured to the rack of scrubs. "If you're planning on going inside, you need to scrub down and dress for the occasion."

"We don't have to shower the way the doc did?" Jamie would be the first to admit that she could use a shower, but she didn't want to miss a moment of what was happening.

"Not unless you're planning to help with the surgery. But since he already has a nurse, another surgeon and an anesthetist, our assistance is not required."

Jamie gave a slow nod. "I'd like to see what's going on in there, considering I have a great deal to lose."

"Understandable." Abi peeled off his sweater, grabbed the bottle of Hibiclens soap and started the necessary process. Jamie did the same. They scrubbed down and pulled on surgical gowns.

When they stepped beyond the larger curtain, Jamie was almost startled. The lights. The equipment. It was incredible. The real thing—maybe even more state of the art than the average surgery suite found in hospitals. Right in the center of it all was a surgical table complete with the patient and surrounded by all the necessary equipment and, apparently, personnel. A clear enclosure separated that center area from the rest of the room. It was like a room with invisible walls inside a bigger room.

She watched as they prepared the patient—not an adult… a child. Her chest constricted.

As Abi had said, there were three people besides the surgeon, all suited in surgical gowns. Two working closely with the doctor, the other standing at the patient's head. The anesthetist.

The setup really was incredible. She shouldn't be surprised. If this was going to be done right, they needed not only the proper equipment, but also the proper personnel as well. No expense appeared to have been spared.

Another man, middle aged, stood well beyond the activity on the other side of the smaller surgical room. Was this the child's father?

Jamie leaned closer to Abi so she could whisper. "Is that him?" The doctor and those working around the patient were talking among themselves. She didn't want to distract or disturb them.

"Yes." Abi followed her lead, speaking in a whisper. "The father—my employer."

"Did you know the patient was a child?" Jamie understood that the patient's age didn't make what they had done right…but it somehow made it more palatable.

"I did. That's the only reason I agreed to the job."

Jamie's attention shifted to the ongoing procedure. The conversation between the doctor and those helping was so soft that she couldn't make out their words through those clear walls. It was the sounds of the machines that made her feel oddly discombobulated. Or maybe it was the whole situation that created such a sense of being overwhelmed.

"Should we go now?" She suddenly felt out of place even watching.

"I'm staying. You don't need to."

She nodded. "Okay. Going upstairs then."

Jamie exited the sterile environment, peeled off the surgical gown and pulled on her sweater. She tossed the gown into the provided hamper and opened the door. As she walked out, the door closed behind her, locking her out. She flinched at the sound or maybe it was the idea of what was happening in there.

Forcing her mind away from this thing they had done, she considered that she should call her grandmother and let her know she was okay and that the procedure was happening. Hopefully, Luke would be released soon. She shook herself. Good grief, it was Christmas Eve. She needed to see if anyone had heard from her parents.

One thing was certain—this was the most bizarre holiday of her life.

The trudge up the stairs was harder than she'd thought. She supposed she was more exhausted than she had realized or maybe all the emotions were just catching up with her. She had necessarily restrained her feelings related to Luke being held hostage. Now they were working overtime to bubble up.

Upstairs, Lillian and her mother were on the sofa in the great room, watching television. Mrs. Case looked as exhausted as Jamie. There was no shortage of guards. All dressed in black and stationed at every door and at the larger windows. Not just to keep the doctor in either. To keep new intruders out, she supposed.

Worry tugged at Jamie's brow. Where was Poe? She walked to the front door and had a look outside. No Poe out there. Then she walked back through the great room and on to the kitchen before she found him.

He stood at the island, a host of vegetables piled around him. He glanced up as she neared. "I decided to make a salad. Fast food never fills me up."

She went for a smile, but didn't quite feel it happen. "Sounds smart. Can I help?"

"You interested in cucumbers?"

"Sure. A salad isn't a salad without cucumbers."

She washed the long English cucumber and selected a knife. "Thick or thin slices?"

"Prepper's choice."

She thought about bringing up the morning's event and then the identity of the patient downstairs, but decided she needed to think on it for a while. There was a lot wrong with how those hours went down, but she couldn't be certain it had been what she now suspected.

Poe grabbed a couple of carrots and started to chop. He was very skilled.

"You've had lessons," she suggested.

"A class in Paris." He shrugged. "Another in Rome. I love to cook."

How had she not known that?

When they had prepped all the veggies and tossed them into a larger bowl, they cleaned up. The mundane work helped with the questions and emotions nudging at her. A little more *mundane* would be most welcome.

Poe tossed the hand towel on the counter by the sink. "I'll see if anyone is hungry."

"Do you have a cell phone? The guy who drove us to the other location took mine."

"Sure. Amar gave me another." Poe passed his cell to her. "I'm glad you're back, Jamie."

"Me too."

"I was worried. Really worried."

She nodded. "I've worried a lot during this thing."

He held her gaze for a moment longer as if he had more to say, then turned and headed for the great room.

Jamie had a feeling they both had things they needed to say.

She walked to the sink and stared out the window as she entered Victoria's number. As always, her grandmother answered on the first ring. "It's me," Jamie said since the number would not be familiar.

"I'm so grateful to hear your voice. Are you all right, Jamie?"

"I'm fine. Tired, but fine. The surgery is taking place now. Hopefully, Luke will be released soon."

How was it that saying the words almost made this thing feel like it was a normal mission? This was not normal. It was not even close to normal. They had broken a good number of laws, not to mention they had kidnapped a man and his family from the other thugs who had attempted to kidnap them. Add to that how someone on the opposing team had kidnapped her and the girl and they'd had to escape.

How crazy was that? Worse, she still couldn't even begin to fathom what the coming ramifications would be.

Mrs. Case and Lillian came into the kitchen with Poe. He served them both as if he'd trained at a five-star restaurant. Even when Lillian insisted there should be meat on a salad, he managed to rummage in the refrigerator and find deli slices of turkey, chopped it and added it to Lillian's salad.

The man was good. He was kind. Jamie smiled. And handsome.

"I can send the jet for you and Luke when you're ready," Victoria insisted, drawing Jamie's attention back to the call. "I'm anxious to have you both home."

That was the thing. No matter where Jamie lived and worked, Chicago would always be home.

"Sure." Whatever Victoria wanted to do would be fine by Jamie. At this point any sort of vacation from her everyday life would be great. "Have you spoken to Mom and Dad today?"

"I did and I'm so happy to say they'll be coming home tomorrow. They've decided that as much as they've enjoyed their little getaway, that Christmas is about being at home with family. I didn't tell them what was happening with Luke. I'm hoping the two of you will be here by the time they arrive and that this whole nightmare will be behind us."

Jamie hoped so as well. "I'll call you as soon as I lay eyes on Luke."

They exchanged goodbyes and Jamie took Poe's phone back to him. "Thank you."

"Everything all right with your grandparents?" He heaped salad onto a plate.

"Yes, and she just told me that my parents are coming home tomorrow so it'll be a good day." As long as she got Luke back home safely.

He passed her the plate. "Eat."

Jamie thanked him and joined the Case family at the island.

Mrs. Case set her fork aside and turned to Jamie.

Jamie braced for her fury. Not that she could blame the

woman. Look what they had done to her family...to their holiday plans. The thought sickened her. She couldn't tell the family that she'd only taken part in this because her brother's life was at stake. They certainly didn't need any added stress after all they'd been through. Besides, what kind of excuse was that? Who was to say whose family was the more important one?

No one...because that was not true any way you looked at it.

"Lillian told me about how you helped her escape that man. How you helped her run to safety and to hide."

Jamie managed a smile that felt like an imitation at best. "It was a team effort." She and Poe shared a look. She suspected he didn't feel heroic any more than she did.

Lillian blushed. "You're a superhero. Like in the movies."

"You were pretty heroic yourself, Lillian. You were strong and brave. You should be very proud of what you did too. Like I said—a team effort."

Mrs. Case smiled a weary expression as she turned back to her salad. Jamie felt sick at the idea of what she must be thinking. Though the woman was obviously grateful that Jamie had helped her daughter, she likely recognized as well that Jamie was part of the original kidnapping crew. That reality couldn't be ignored.

Lillian picked at her salad, eating mostly the turkey, before skipping back into the great room to resume the movie she'd been streaming.

Poe took his salad and followed her.

Jamie forked the greens and took another bite. She generally liked salad, but it all tasted bland today. She suddenly wished she had gone with Lillian and Poe. Sitting here with Mrs. Case and feeling what was no doubt the weight of her mounting accusations was not exactly sparking her appetite.

After an entire minute of silence, the older woman said, "My husband is very upset. He feels this entire event is a travesty."

It was actually, and Jamie wasn't going to try to excuse her actions. She had done what she had to do to keep her brother safe. She wouldn't do things any differently if she had to do it over and over again.

"He has," Mrs. Case went on, "tried very hard not to think of all the patients he can't save. He is only one man. But it has been very difficult. The burden of all those other lives has weighed heavily on him. Particularly in light of what his brother did for months before we realized what he was up to."

She didn't explain further, and Jamie didn't ask. She was already aware of the twin brother's deceit.

Mrs. Case went on, "The past few hours have driven that point home. It's one thing to know what's happening, but another altogether to be faced with the reality."

Jamie could only imagine how horrifying the ordeal had been and the number of emotional levels that horror had hit. As Mrs. Case had already said, the weight of having to turn patients away was awful enough, but to be forced to look at a child who desperately needed that help, and whose father was willing to do anything to make it happen, was immeasurably painful.

Working hard to keep her voice steady, Jamie confessed, "I will tell you I am not proud of the part I played in this. But—"

"If you hadn't," Mrs. Case argued, "my daughter might be dead. My husband might even be as well. Or me. You and your people kept us safe."

Jamie opted not to correct her. Yes, she, Poe and Abi may have provided a buffer between the Case family and the bad guys from the other team, but the truth was they weren't that different. They'd all been here for the same goal ultimately—to get Dr. Case to do what they wanted.

"They wanted twenty million dollars," Mrs. Case said. "For our daughter."

"There was a ransom demand?" Jamie wasn't aware that had happened, but she wasn't entirely surprised.

"Oh yes. Once you and Lillian were taken away, another man informed us of what they expected. We had twelve hours to pull the money together—which was absolutely ludicrous—before they were going to kill Lillian."

"Wow…that's terrible." Jamie replayed those minutes over in her head. The men had operated on a reasonably professional level. They had appeared prepared for what they had come to do…mostly. "They told me nothing. I had no idea."

"Your people saved us—*you* saved our daughter."

As much as Jamie appreciated being called a hero, there were some things that didn't add up for her. First, a twenty-million-dollar ransom demand should have come with a bigger team. What kidnapper who believed an asset was worth twenty million dollars only sent along one guard with that asset?

This was wrong somehow. Frankly, everything that had gone down felt wrong on some level.

There had been just three in the other crew in the first place. Three. With a twenty-mil ransom demand. Oh yeah, there was something very wrong with this situation.

Poe came to the door. "Jamie." He hitched his head toward the great room.

Jamie produced a smile, one slightly more real this time, for Mrs. Case. "Excuse me." She slid off her stool and went to the door. "What's up?"

"We need to talk."

She followed him beyond the great room to the entry hall. The guard there seemed to sense their need for privacy and stepped outside to monitor the door from there.

Poe glanced around. "Something is off with what happened this morning."

"I couldn't agree more." She hitched a thumb toward the kitchen. "The wife just told me there was a ransom demand for Lillian. Twenty million dollars."

Poe shook his head. "That's crazy. One of those guys—from the two left behind when the one took you and Lillian—basically split after you two were gone. Abi called in a backup crew to clean up the mess, but let's face facts, we already had more than three—besides us—here in the first place, which begs the question, how were we overtaken by three thugs?"

Jamie had an idea about that. "I think it was a setup to make the Cases believe we're the good guys."

"You mean we're not," Poe said with a shake of his head. "Don't answer that. I already know what we've been in this op." He blew out a big breath.

This was just another aspect of this whole business that weighed on Jamie. "I shouldn't have let you get involved with this."

He harrumphed. "Like you could have stopped me."

"We just have to make sure the rest of this goes off without a hitch. The family gets taken back home and no one dies."

Her chest tightened as she thought of Luke.

Keep him safe.

3:00 p.m.

BY THE TIME the doctor and Abi surfaced, Lillian had fallen asleep, and her mother was pacing the floor.

Jamie wasn't sure what would happen next, but if they were all lucky, it wouldn't involve the police. Or worse, the FBI, considering they had kidnapped the doctor and his family.

"How did it go?" Mrs. Case asked, looking tattered around the edges.

Dr. Case gave her a nod. "Very well. I'll be seeing him when we return from our vacation for a follow up. Until then, the doctor who assisted me will keep an eye on him. But I'm not anticipating any issues."

Jamie shared a look with Poe. That was certainly not the announcement she'd anticipated.

"A car will be here for you and your family in ten minutes," Abi explained.

Wait. Wait. Was this it? No accusations. No cops. No nothing?

Dr. Case turned to Abi. He looked from him to Poe, then to Jamie. "I realize what has happened today. Don't doubt that I am fully aware." His gaze lit the longest on Jamie.

This was the part she had been expecting...dreading.

"But in reality, all the three of you took from my family were a few hours of our time." He glanced at his daughter. "I wonder if you—" he looked from Jamie to Poe and then Abi again "—had not made the decision to help the child downstairs, what would have happened to our family? Those other men were clearly unconcerned for the safety of my family. Their only desire was money." He shook his head, regret clear on his face. "The idea that my work has come to this tears me apart. Anyone who needs the help I can provide should be able to have it without such theatrics. This has opened my eyes to what I know I must do next. It wasn't bad enough what happened before..." He heaved a heavy breath. "The only answer is that more surgeons must be trained in this procedure. It's the only way to see that we meet the need of all…not just that of certain patients." He exhaled a weary breath. "Thank you for helping me to see this more clearly."

Abi nodded, but said nothing. He turned to Jamie and motioned for her and Poe to follow him to the kitchen. They gathered around the island.

"A car will be arriving shortly." He set his gaze on Jamie's. "The driver will take you to your brother's condo. Luke will be delivered there at approximately the same time." He turned to Poe then. "If you need a different car, just say the word."

"I'm going with Jamie." Poe looked to Jamie. "We have a mission report to complete."

Abi nodded. "Very well." He smiled. "We make a good team."

Jamie laughed. "Except for the fact that you were keeping all sorts of details from us." She leaned in closer and spoke more quietly. "Like the three guys from this morning. Give me a break. After the doctor's monologue in there, you really expect me to believe that was a coincidence? And where did you find them? Thugs-R-Us?"

Abi didn't smile, but the twinkle of amusement in his eyes was unmistakable. "No one is calling the police," he said. "In my humble opinion, that implies it was a brilliant strategy."

"You couldn't have warned us?" Poe argued, sounding more than a little ticked off.

Abi bumped him on the shoulder with the side of his fist. "The goal was authenticity. It's hard to fake, wouldn't you say?"

Poe held up a hand. "Whatever."

"In any case," Abi said, "thank you for your help. Your

car will be here any moment." He smiled at Jamie. "You'll be pleased to find Ian Michaels behind the wheel."

Whoa. Now wait a minute. "How did you get in touch with Ian?" Poe had told her that Victoria had sent Ian to provide any necessary backup, but that was the last she'd heard about him being here. Too much had gone down for her to even think about Ian. She decided it might be best not to mention this to her grandmother's long time loyal investigator.

"I called your grandmother," Abi explained. "I told her you would be ready to depart within the hour and she said Michaels would pick you and Poe up for transport back to Chicago." He chuckled. "She also invited me to your Christmas party. Unfortunately, I'm unavailable. I'm sure you understand."

"Of course. You're a busy man." Jamie barely resisted the urge to roll her eyes.

"One more thing," Abi said. "For the record, the ransom demand for Luke…" He shrugged. "Just a little something for more of that authenticity."

Jamie did roll her eyes that time. "Good to know." She extended her hand. "Until we meet again, Abi."

He gave her hand a shake. "I am certain we will." He turned to Poe next and extended his hand.

"I, for one," Poe said, "hope to never see you again."

Abi laughed. "I'm confident that can be arranged."

When the first car arrived, Jamie, Poe and even Abi stood on the portico and waved goodbye to the Case family. As the car drove away, Lillian turned around in her seat and waved some more. Jamie kept waving until the car was out of sight.

"This must be the enigmatic Mr. Michaels," Abi said as a second car rolled up to the house.

Jamie turned to face her old friend. "Take care of yourself, Abi."

He hugged her. She didn't resist. Given their occupations, it could easily be the last time they saw each other.

Poe only allowed the other man a nod before walking away.

Ian emerged from behind the wheel and gave Jamie a hug. "I am so glad to see you," she admitted.

"Always." Ian drew back. "Let's go pick up your brother."

Jamie and Poe relaxed in the back seat as Ian drove away, though it was impossible to relax completely until she laid eyes on her brother.

The drive to his condo felt like a lifetime and when they arrived, Luke was sitting on the front steps. Jamie rushed out of the car and into his arms.

"I didn't have a key to get inside," Luke said.

Jamie laughed. "Oh my God, it is so good to see you. I've been worried to death."

He shrugged. "It wasn't so bad. I played video games the whole time."

Jamie resisted the urge to kick him. "Don't tell Poe," she warned. "I'm not sure he would take it as well as me."

Luke made a zipping gesture across his lips. "I won't say a word."

"Come on." Jamie ushered him toward the door. "There's a key under the mat."

"Who put a key under my welcome mat?" Luke frowned. "That's like the first place a burglar looks."

Jamie decided not to tell him that she'd put the key Abi had used under there in case she needed to come back. To her way of thinking, if Luke was missing, there was nothing else in the condo worth worrying about.

Inside, he looked around and groaned. "I need to water my plants."

"Pack your bag," Jamie told him. "I'll water your plants. We have a jet waiting for us."

They were going home. Together. For the first time in far too long.

Chicago
Tuesday, December 25

Christmas Day

Chapter Sixteen

Colby Residence,
7:00 p.m.

Victoria surveyed the buffet and the table in her dining room. Pride welled in her chest. She was so very grateful that her favorite caterer had been able to pull this off on such short notice.

Everything was perfect. The food, the desserts, the lovely drink venues. There was Wine Avenue in one corner, Champagne Falls—a fountain—in another and Everything Else Lane—with nonalcoholic choices—in yet another. The whole setup was so creative.

"It all looks lovely," Lucas said as he moved to her side.

She smiled up at him. "The decorations too." Lucas had been the one to oversee that part of the preparations. How he'd gotten holiday decorators on Christmas morning was a mystery. But then, Lucas was a man of many talents.

He'd never failed to accomplish a mission.

"I think we should share a private toast before the guests start to arrive," he suggested.

"Good idea."

They wandered to the champagne fountain and allowed the flowing bubbly to fill their glasses.

"To family," Lucas said as he tapped his glass against hers.

"Family," Victoria echoed. She closed her eyes and drank deeply. She was so very thankful that her family was home.

Jamie and Luke had arrived just before midnight last night. Victoria and Lucas had been up until two this morning just looking at those beautiful kids and pinching themselves. And listening to the story of all that happened in Nashville. The best part was that their grandchildren were safe, and they were home.

Jim and Tasha had arrived home this afternoon. The kids had gone to have some private time with them. Jim said they planned to tell them about the cancer and how fortunate they were that the treatment appeared to be doing its job. If all continued on this course, by spring Tasha would be cancer free.

It was all they could have hoped for.

"I think Poe is a very nice young man," Lucas said, drawing Victoria from her deep thoughts.

She smiled. "He is, and I'm quite certain he's madly in love with our Jamie."

"Well, of course he is," Lucas boasted. "She's brilliant, beautiful and…he doesn't deserve her."

Laughter bubbled from Victoria's throat. "You would say the same thing about anyone who showed an interest in her."

"I would. And I would be correct in my deduction."

Victoria nodded. "You would."

"She and I talked for a bit this morning," Lucas said before drinking more of his champagne.

"Really?" Victoria had seen the two of them having another cup of coffee after everyone else had left the kitchen this morning. "What did you talk about?"

"I asked her to come to work for the agency."

Victoria's heart skipped a beat. So many times she had wanted to ask Jamie that question, but she'd always satisfied her desperate hopes with simply letting Jamie know that she was welcome at the agency if she ever wanted to be there. Not once had Victoria come right out and asked.

"How did she react?"

Lucas inclined his head and considered the question for a moment. "She seemed surprised but not offended in any way. She asked me if the suggestion was only coming on the heels of the fright we had with Luke's kidnapping."

"What did you tell her?" Victoria couldn't wait to hear this.

"I told her that of course any and all things of that nature impacts our feelings, but this latest event wasn't the reason I asked."

Victoria's eyebrows went up. "I'm sure she was surprised by that claim."

Lucas shrugged one shoulder. "Perhaps, but it was true. I asked because I think we need her. The agency needs her. I've stayed on top of what she's doing for IOA. Like all these suitors, they don't deserve our granddaughter. She belongs at the Colby Agency."

Victoria struggled not to allow the sting in her eyes to become evident. "She is the one who should fill my shoes one day." Her voice wobbled a little, but it was the best she could do.

"Just a few weeks ago," Lucas went on, "Jim said the same thing."

Victoria felt taken aback by the news. "I wasn't suggesting Jim shouldn't run this agency. He has every right."

"He is aware of how you feel. You've asked him to do this before, but he always defers to your choices regarding agency matters."

This was true. She'd tried to retire, to turn the reins over to Jim, but he'd always come up with a reason that she should return.

"Do you think he feels as if I don't trust him or that anyone here doesn't trust his ability?" The notion twisted inside her like barbed wire. She loved her son. She wanted him to have what she and his father and Lucas had built. Jamie should be working with him and one day she absolutely should step into Victoria's shoes. But first, Jim would have his time.

"I think he doesn't trust himself to sit at the top. He loves this agency, and he loves being a part of it, but he does not want to be *the one*."

Victoria nodded. "I see. I'm sorry I didn't realize how he felt."

Lucas touched her cheek with a fingertip. "Jim doesn't make that easy."

This was true. She moistened her lips and asked, "What did Jamie say?"

"She wanted to think about it for a bit, but she promised to give us an answer soon."

At least it wasn't an immediate no. Victoria finished off her champagne. "That's all we can ask for."

"Indeed," Lucas agreed.

The doorbell rang and they put their glasses on a nearby tray and hurried to answer. Forget Paris. There was nothing like family and friends at Christmas.

Ian and Nicole were the first to arrive. In the next half hour, everyone from the agency who was available had arrived. It was a houseful for sure.

Victoria was so very thankful to see Tasha and Jim. Luke arrived with his parents, looking very handsome in a white suit, shirt and tie. Before she could grab Luke in a hug, he kissed her on the cheek.

"You look ravishing, Grandmother."

Victoria grinned. "Thank you, Luke. You look pretty amazing yourself." She hugged him and he kissed her temple and whispered, "I love you." She peered up at him. "Love you too." Then he hurried off to say hello to Lucas.

"Luke is right. You look great." Jim hugged her. "Merry Christmas, Mom."

Victoria hugged him fiercely. How she loved this man. "Merry Christmas to you and Tasha." She drew back, reached for her daughter-in-law and hugged her a bit more gently. "You two look incredible." How very strong this woman was. Victoria was so proud that she was the mother of her grandchildren.

"Thank you, Victoria." Tasha smiled. "And thank you for having this beautiful party."

Victoria barely restrained her tears, but she refused to cry considering all the blessings they had received in the past forty-eight hours. Lucas rescued her by coming for hugs of his own.

Lastly, Jamie and Kenny arrived. Victoria lost her breath when she saw the two of them. Jamie wore a pale blue sheath, and she looked stunning. She and her mother were nearly the same size and Victoria suspected the dress was Tasha's. Kenny looked quite dapper himself in a black form-fitting suit, crisp white shirt and black tie. As a couple they were quite spectacular. The perfect power couple with their whole futures ahead of them. She hoped their relationship worked out.

The food tasted as wonderful as it looked. Lucas had set the Christmas music to a soft whisper and the smiles and laughter that filled their home was the perfect finishing touch. This Christmas was all that Victoria could ask for.

"Grandmother."

Victoria looked around to find Jamie standing beside her. To her gorgeous granddaughter she said, "I hope you're enjoying yourself."

Jamie smiled, the expression so big and beautiful it filled Victoria's heart with renewed pride. "I'm having a wonderful time." She hesitated a moment, then continued, "I spent some time this afternoon talking with Dad and then with Poe."

Victoria was afraid to breathe. Of all the things she had faced in her life, this might very well be one of the scariest.

"I've decided to put in my resignation at IOA and come to work with you and Grandpa."

As much as Victoria wanted to shout and jump for joy, she held it back and remained cool and calm. "That is wonderful to hear. And you're certain about this?"

Jamie laughed. "I am certain. I've been thinking about it for a long time. I'd like to be closer to my family. Running around all over the world has lost a bit of its mystique."

"If you change your mind..." Victoria offered.

"I will not," Jamie said resolutely. She looked across the room to Kenny. "You should know that Poe is coming as well, but I'll let him tell you."

Victoria beamed. "I am so pleased. I'm certain your father and mother are pleased as well."

Jamie's eyes turned a little watery then. "They're very happy about it."

Victoria hugged her granddaughter. "Merry Christmas, sweetheart."

Jamie drew back. "Merry Christmas to you, Grandmother."

"I hope I'm not too late."

The deep male voice with just a hint of a British accent drew everyone's attention to the man who'd entered the room.

"Abi," Jamie said. "I thought you couldn't come."

Looking very handsome in a black suit, shirt and tie, Abi crossed the room and pressed his cheek to Jamie's. "I re-arranged a few things." He looked to Victoria then. "How often does one get invited to a Colby Agency party?" He gave Victoria the same treatment. "Thank you for inviting me."

Victoria gave him a nod. "Glad you could make it."

"Well, just look who the cat dragged in." Kenny appeared next to Jamie. He thrust out a hand. "Merry Christmas, Amar."

He shook the offered hand. "Merry Christmas, Poe."

Victoria decided that maybe this party had needed a little jolt of excitement and intrigue.

It was the perfect Colby Agency Christmas, as well as a celebration of the next generation.

* * * * *

COMING SOON!

We really hope you enjoyed reading this book.
If you're looking for more romance
be sure to head to the shops when
new books are available on

Thursday 19th December

To see which titles are coming soon, please visit
millsandboon.co.uk/nextmonth

MILLS & BOON

LET'S TALK
Romance

For exclusive extracts, competitions and special offers, find us online:

- **f** MillsandBoon
- **X** @MillsandBoon
- **⬡** @MillsandBoonUK
- **♪** @MillsandBoonUK

Get in touch on 01413 063 232